# AN UNEXPECTED SURPRISE

Grady motioned with his head toward the bag sitting beside him on the floor. It was a big plastic bag, tied shut at the handles. "I got something for you, too."

"You did?" Annie's eyes lit up as if it were Christmas morning and she'd just spied the new two-wheeler she'd asked Santa to bring her. "You didn't have to—what is it?"

Grady grinned. "Why don't you open it and see. There was this shop out in the mall. They didn't have any pink ones left, only had one left at all, as a matter of fact. I had to tell this big sob story about my little sister being sick with the chicken pox before the clerk would sell me the display one, and . . . hey! What are you doing?" He felt his heart stop, skip a beat, then start up again. "Oh, Annie, don't do that. Come on, honey, don't do that. Please."

But she was doing that. Annie Kendall was standing smack in the middle of the main aisle in Macy's, right next to a girl spraying perfume on everyone who passed by, hugging a three-foot-high blue plush bunny rabbit to her and crying like a baby.

Grady stood there for a few moments, feeling helpless, then dragged girl and bunny into his arms, holding Annie tightly, kissing the top of her head and trying to comfort her with words that made no sense, especially to him.

What he didn't say was, "I think I might just be falling in love with you, Annie Kendall." But he

just the same, inside his

Books by Kasey Michaels

CAN'T TAKE MY EYES OFF OF YOU

TOO GOOD TO BE TRUE

Published by Zebra Books

# TOO GOOD
# TO BE TRUE

## Kasey Michaels

ZEBRA BOOKS
Kensington Publishing Corp.
http://www.zebrabooks.com

ZEBRA BOOKS are published by

Kensington Publishing Corp.
850 Third Avenue
New York, NY 10022

All Kensington titles, imprints, and distributed lines are available at special quantity discounts for bulk purchases for sales promotions, premiums, fund raising, educational, or institutional use.

Special book excerpts or customized printings can also be created to fit specific needs. For details, write or phone the office of the Kensington special sales manager: Kensington Publishing Corp., 850 Third Avenue, New York, NY 10022, attn: Special Sales Department, Phone: 1-800-221-2647.

First Printing: February, 2001
10 9 8 7 6 5 4 3 2

Printed in the United States of America

*For Adam Charles Csencsits: all the blessings wrapped up in one very special boy.*

*If you want to know what the Lord God thinks of money, you have only to look at those to whom he gives it.*

—Maurice Baring

# One

*"Will you walk into my parlor?"*
*said the spider to the fly.*
　　　　　　　　　—Mary Howitt

Archie Peevers had the lined, time-ravaged face of a man who might be wearing a nightcap as he stared in horror at the Ghost of Christmas Past just then floating menacingly at the foot of his bed.

Banishing the thought as unprofessional, if accurate, Grady Sullivan stood just inside the double doors of the cavernous bedroom on the second floor of the Peevers Mansion and stared at the man who'd made a fortune in toilet paper and who'd probably just figured out he couldn't take it with him. The fortune, that is, he corrected mentally, not the toilet paper.

Grady remained in the foyer of the bedchamber—yes, the place was big enough to have a foyer, and velvet draperies in the archway as well. Entering Peevers Mansion had been like turning his wristwatch back several dozen years.

Agatha Christie could have planned an entire murder-mystery novel to take place in this one room of the old mansion, and never run out of descriptive phrases. Somber. Bloodred-velvet drapes. Dark, heavily carved furniture from another age, one best forgotten. The overall musky smell of old age.

The victim's body laid out for viewing.

"It looks like I'm already too late. He is dead, right?" Grady asked the butler, Dickens (now *there* was a coincidence Grady could hang his hat on).

"No, sir. Mr. Peevers most certainly is not deceased. I'd know, sir," Dickens intoned severely, his expression a reprimand—directed toward him or Peevers, Grady wasn't sure. The old guy, nearly as ancient as Archie Peevers, Grady decided—who dated, figuring conservatively, from the last ice age—was really into this butler thing. Dickens actually wore a black tuxedo complete with starched, white, collared shirt and tails.

Tall, nearly as tall as the six-foot-two-inch Grady, the butler had the build and posture of a Marine drill sergeant and a voice so deep Grady was tempted to call him "Lurch." If it hadn't been for the man's mop of silver hair, and the fact that Grady believed the old guy could probably slam-dunk him without raising a sweat, he might even have said so out loud.

"He's not dead? Well, I'll give him this, he does a damn good impression of dead," Grady responded instead, still coolly looking at Archie Peevers, who still hadn't moved. He just lay there, jackknifed against about a dozen pillows, his long, bony fingers crossed over his chest, his nearly colorless grey eyes staring unblinkingly in the general direction of the foyer, his skeletal body barely visible beneath the covers.

"I don't want to sound like a bad comedian—but how can you tell? Do you have a mirror you can hold up to his mouth, to see if he's still breathing?"

At Grady's last question, the corpse blinked. Then it grinned, which was worse, as the fine set of dazzling white dentures had been made for a much younger and fuller face. "Gets 'em every time, don't it, Dickens?" Archie Peevers cackled as he sat up. Not laughed, cackled. Grady knew the difference. In fact, if the old fart laid an egg, it wouldn't surprise Grady even a little bit.

"We were playing possum, were we? How very naughty of you, sir," Grady said, his own tone caught halfway between sarcasm and deliberate condescension toward the batty old man in the bed. Oh, okay. So it was all sarcasm. Grady hadn't been happy to be dragged all the way from Philadelphia to Peevers Mansion just outside Bethlehem, Pennsylvania, on such short notice.

It was Wednesday, for one thing, six days earlier than he thought he was supposed to have reported for the job. Grady's day on the golf course. It was September, and hot as hell, for another. But here he was, and here he'd be staying for about a month, if the contract sent to him by the Peevers's lawyer, someone named Jefferson Banning, couldn't be broken.

"No, smart-ass, we were checking you out," Archie snapped back at him. "Don't want me a bodyguard who pisses his pants the first time he's tossed a small shock, ain't that right, Dickens? Now come here, come here, or do you expect me to keep shouting at you?"

"No, I don't think so," Grady said, shaking his head. "Sorry, but you jolly boys are just going to have to find yourself another straight man." He turned to Dickens, who looked ready to grab him in a half nelson. "I'll find my own way out, okay?"

"Oh, shit on it!" Archie shouted, and Grady watched as the supposedly dying old man threw back the covers and aimed his bare, skinny, blue-veined legs and feet toward the floor. "Who told me you could take a joke? Quinn-somebody. Can see how wrong he was. What's your idea of funny, boy? Milton Berle in a dress?"

At the mention of his partner's name, Grady stopped in the process of turning his back on the eccentric millionaire and turned back, to watch the walking cadaver all but skip across the room. Archie Peevers was suddenly the vision of good health, if not the sort any sane editor would advertise on the cover of a "better health" magazine.

Grady did a quick inventory of his recollections concerning the Peevers job. He was to come to the Peevers Mansion, camp out there for a few weeks, assure some nutty old bird that his nearest and dearest weren't trying to kill him for his money. Simple job. Almost kindergarten level, plus moving him out of the city during the hottest days of late summer. Piece of cake. Walk in the park.

Except that he now knew Quinn had been a part of it. Quinn, who he'd pretty much trapped into an assignment a few months ago. Quinn, who should be over the moon about how well that assignment worked out—considering he was now happily married to the object of that assignment.

But that was just like Quinn. He'd promised to get even with Grady, and Quinn always kept his promises. Grady could see it now. Jefferson Banning had contacted

D&S, talked with Quinn, and Quinn had sicced him on his unsuspecting partner and good friend, telling the lawyer not to mention his name.

No wonder Maisie, their receptionist, and the person who really ran D&S, had asked if she could please, please come along for the ride, even offering to make the job part of her vacation time. She probably had a video camera tucked up in her luggage, already planning the entertainment at the office's annual Christmas party.

Okay, so he'd wring Quinn's neck once this was over. And maybe Maisie's, too, as it was her job to screen the nutcase jobs at the door.

Still, he asked. Just to be sure.

"You talked to my partner in D&S Securities? You talked to Quinn Delaney? I thought your representative had come straight to me with his proposition."

Archie raised one extremely long, gnarled index finger, poking it in the air above his head. "*Exactly* my point, sonny! Who can't you trust? The ones closest to you, that's who. Your loving family, and all that crap. You shouldn't trust your own partner. I know I can't trust that brood of vultures I call my family. Which is why you're here, remember?"

"Because you think your relatives are out to kill you. Gee, I can't imagine why, you're such a sweet old fart," Grady said, walking past the toilet-paper king and sitting down in one of the bloodred-velvet high-backed chairs in front of the cold fireplace. "And you want me to watch your back while I also sort through those same relatives, figuring out which one of them has the guts to really sneak in here and slit your throat, or whatever."

"Ha! None of them has the guts to do that, sonny.

Poison. That's what I think. Poison, pills, a midnight toss down the stairs. Something low and sneaky. Which is why I have a plan of my own. You may be good, sonny, but I'm better, and it's my life we're trying to save, remember. Dickens, show him my plan," Archie said as he skipped across the room in his knee-length nightshirt and hopped back into bed.

"Yes, sir, Mr. Peevers," Dickens said, bowing from the waist like a character in an old English movie. He crossed the room to a huge chest of drawers, put one liver-spotted hand on each ornate brass pull, and slid open a drawer, reaching inside to take out a thin manila envelope.

Grady took the envelope from the man's outstretched hand, one eloquent eyebrow raised as the butler backed away, taking up his position against one wall, his hands now folded in front of him as he stared into the middle distance. Grady made a mental note to check under the guy's tails, just to see if he could find the spot where Peevers inserted the windup key.

He turned the envelope over a few times, still debating whether or not he really wanted to be here, then opened it, dumping its contents on his lap.

"Who's this?" he asked, picking up all that spilled out, a single photograph of a young woman. A smiling young woman caught somewhere between the ages of twenty and twenty-five. A woman with a curly mop of coal black hair and grey eyes. Nearly colorless grey eyes. Wiseass eyes. A wiseass smile. Nobody's fool, this woman, and yet he doubted anyone else would see that. All they'd see was a beautiful woman. Grady saw a smart, beautiful woman. Not his type at all. He liked his women beautiful, sure, but dumb. They were less trouble that way.

This little lady had Trouble written all over her.

Grady looked at Archie, looked at Archie's eyes, saw the same nearly colorless grey. "Another relative crawling out of the woodwork, Mr. Peevers? I thought I already had been made aware of all of them. Attorney Banning forwarded me quite a large file, complete with pictures."

"Banning?" Archie snorted. "Do you think I'd trust an attorney with every little secret? Especially Jefferson Banning, who stands to make a bundle as executor of my will now that his daddy's dead and he's inherited me. No, this little girl is extra. A sort of surprise I'm springing on my dear relatives now that you're here to watch the fun."

Grady might have felt he'd been caught in a time warp, was playing a part in an Agatha Christie novel, or had found himself on one of the less successful Disney World rides, but he was still pretty quick to pick up on Archie's game.

He held up the photograph again, looking at the photographer's mark on the back. *Liisa of Baltimore.* Out of state. "Ah, yes, the obligatory missing Peevers heir," he intoned seriously, wishing he could get away with a Charlie Chan accent without having Dickens wake from his trance and stomp on him. "How very . . . *predictable.*"

"Ain't it just, sonny? But what works, works. Right?" Archie said, rolling back onto the pillows as he laughed out loud. Not a pretty sound, or a pretty sight, but Grady refused to look away.

"Who is she, really?" he asked, once Archie had

laughed himself out in appreciation of his own joke. That took a while, especially as his hilarity was followed hard by a coughing fit that reminded Grady of a cat choking on a hairball.

"Who is she? Damned if I know, sonny. Calls herself Annie Kendall. Says she's my long-lost granddaughter. Her mommy being a bastard birth, of course." His grin faded suddenly, and he motioned to Dickens to finish the story.

"Mr. Peevers did indeed have a romantic interlude some fifty years ago with a young lady by the name of Sally Beckman, a maid here at Peevers Mansion. Miss Kendall asserts, without proof, that she is Miss Beckman's granddaughter and, as follows, Mr. Peevers's granddaughter as well. The mother, Mr. Peevers's daughter, and the grandmother, Sally, are both deceased."

"Sally, dead," Archie said, leaning back against the pillows once more. "Sally, Sally, Sally. Love of my life, she was, Sullivan, and no lie. Dead now, of course, and my child, too. Only the granddaughter left. I'd give her every penny, if she's really my flesh and blood. Better than those buzzards circling, waiting for me to croak. Not that they're circling. They're too busy milling around downstairs, eating like elephants and drinking up all my best booze. Oh, Sally, Sally. You're the only one who really loved me."

"Yeah, right. I think I'm getting misty." Grady looked at Archie, who was looking and sounding like a ferret with dyspepsia, then at the stoic Dickens.

And Grady knew. In that instant, watching Archie's bad acting, seeing the slight tick in the butler's cheek, he knew.

Archie Peevers didn't still pine for Sally Beckman, if there ever even *had been* a Sally Beckman. This guy didn't like anybody, yet alone love anyone. It was an act, all an act. And he, good old Grady, had been cast in the role of helpful dupe—with no honorable way out.

Damn, damn, *damn.*

Grady wanted out of the room at least, and he wanted out now. He needed to think. "Speaking of booze, old man, do you have anything to drink in this mausoleum? Because I sure could use a belt."

"Then you'll be taking the position of bodyguard, sir?" Dickens asked.

Grady looked at the photograph once more. Nice face, nice eyes. Killer smile. An air of confidence that was nearly palpable. And, smart as she thought herself to be, probably without a clue as to how much trouble she could be in, coming to Peevers Mansion, trying to take a slice of the old man's money. Although she didn't look like a con artist. Then again, how many successful con artists *look* like con artists?

"Yeah, I'm taking the job, especially since I already signed the contract that says I'm to be here for a month at two thousand a day. I'll assume you've already arranged to have my assistant's and my luggage transferred to our rooms? I'd like to meet with my assistant now, if you don't mind, go over the packet of information from Attorney Banning one more time, and then meet with Mr. Peevers again after lunch."

"Yes, sir," Dickens said, also ignoring the overacting Archie, who was now hugging one of his pillows, stroking it, still repeating, "Sally, Sally." He walked to the nightstand beside the bed, the one holding about two dozen prescriptions bottles, poured a glass of water, and tapped two small blue pills into his palm. "Here, sir. These will help calm your jangled nerves."

"Dickens, how good you are to me. And how grandly I'm going to handsomely reward your many years of service when I'm finally called to my reward."

"Yes, sir, just as you say, sir," Dickens said, bowing before he took the empty glass and replaced it on the table. "I'll bring your lunch in one hour, sir."

"He's really dying?" Grady asked, as the two of them left the bedroom, closing the double doors behind them. "And why don't I think he is?"

"Probably, sir, because Mr. Peevers has been dying for the past ten years, which is when he took to his bed and began playing with his offspring and the rest of us."

"Playing, Dickens?"

"Yes, sir. You'll become quite used to seeing Attorney Banning climbing the front stairs, to make changes in Mr. Peevers's will. It's at least a weekly occurrence these past few months, and certainly does serve to keep us all hopping."

"Except maybe one of you is getting a little tired of the game?" Grady suggested, beginning to understand why Archie Peevers thought he needed a live-in bodyguard and general snoop.

"Hopping, sir, is quite exhausting. There is a small refrigerator in your room, stocked with most anything you need, including liquor, sir," Dickens said, then left Grady standing in front of a closed door in the west wing of the mansion. "The bell for lunch will ring in one and one-quarter hours. Promptness is always appreciated, sir."

"Sure, sure," Grady said to the butler's retreating back. "Catch you Lurch . . . er, *later.*" Then he opened the door to his bedroom and saw Maisie sitting on the edge of the bed, her stubby legs swinging back and forth a good two feet off the floor as she grinned at him.

"Don't make yourself at home, you traitor," Grady growled, slamming the door behind him.

"And don't you think we're bunking together, honey, not that I couldn't get the hots for you and your pretty green eyes if I gave it half a try, which I won't," she said, standing up. "We've got connecting rooms. I just unpacked your stuff, like a good little assistant." She cocked her head to one side. "Tell me, honey, don't those skimpy little underpants ride up?"

"I'll thank you to stay out of my underpants, Maisie," Grady said with a straight face, walking past his "assistant" and flinging the manila envelope on the bed before collapsing in a chair. "I owe you one, you know. You and Quinn both."

"You owe me more than one, honey," Maisie quipped, taking a long silver file out of her skirt pocket and running it over a nail as she leaned against one of the tall bedposts. "We can start with a raise in my salary, once we're finished here. Be a good boy, honey, and make sure that doesn't take too long. I think I saw this dump in a horror movie once."

"Why, Maisie, I thought you'd love it here," Grady said, and she stuck out her tongue at him. He looked around the high-ceilinged room full of dark wood furniture and heavy draperies. "You know, this place would make a hell of a funeral home."

"Not if you do your job right, honey." Maisie laid

down the nail file and picked up the envelope, slid the photo of Annie Kendall onto the bed. She frowned, looked at Grady, picked up the photograph, then frowned again.

Maisie had a blatantly dyed, artificially curled mop of red curls around her full, round face, a face Charles Schulz might have drawn. Right now the fairly impressive brain under those rioting curls had her looking like the comic version of *perplexed*. She tossed the photo back onto the bed. "Who's the girl? Pretty thing. Almost beautiful. Should I be jealous, honey?"

"She's a last-minute addition to our cast of characters," Grady told her, unable to sit still. He got up, went over to the desk he'd seen in front of the large double windows, and opened the top file on the pile Maisie had laid out for him. "An illegitimate granddaughter, supposedly, who Archie may give all his millions to, or at least that's what he hopes his relatives will think. Damn."

"I don't get it, honey. If he gives all his money to her, our job is over. You're home again, home again, honey, and no more weeping and gnashing of teeth from all the eligible and ineligible ladies in Philadelphia. Why are you so upset?"

"Why am I so upset?" Grady raked his fingers through his shaggy sandy hair. "I'll tell you why, Maisie. I don't believe old Archie's in any danger. According to his lawyer, there have been no attempts on his life, nothing. I believe we're wasting our time. But if I'm *wrong* about that—and it's a big *if*—and if Archie is right? Well, then, don't you see what he's doing, why we're here?"

"Not a clue, honey," Maisie admitted. "But run your ideas by me, and maybe I'll catch on."

"If someone is really trying to kill the toilet-paper king, Maisie, then the smartest thing he could do is to give them someone else to kill. Another target, Maisie. Play it up big, say how this is his long-lost granddaughter, he's sure of it, and he's going to give her all his money just as soon as I can check her credentials—not that he mentioned that part of the job, but it figures."

Maisie shook her head. "Nope, sorry. Still don't get it, honey. But don't stop trying."

"I said, Maisie, he wanted a *new target,* if one of his relatives really is trying to kill him. Me, I guard Archie. Meanwhile, bang, bang, the granddaughter's dead, the killer is locked up, everyone else is scared back into submission, and Archie goes on cackling and playing his game for another ten years—at which time he'll be ten years older than dirt. His kind never die young, or so Grandfather Sullivan always said. Got it now?"

"Ah, yes, now I understand. A sort of deep, twisted Machiavellian plot, or whatever that is, right, honey?" Maisie sat down on the bed, picked up the photograph of Annie Kendall once more. "She does have those same grey eyes I've seen on a lot of the other photos. Very distinctive shade of almost nothing. Is she really a Peevers?"

Grady shook his head. "No way. It's too pat, too B-movie, too bad novel. He's hired her, I'd bet on it. He hasn't left the house in ten years, so she probably came to see him, trying to run a con, and he either called her on it and they've gone into business together, or he decided to pretend to go along with her. Either way, he's using her. And he's put me smack in the middle of the whole damn, twisted thing. I wouldn't be surprised if someone took a potshot at me, just because I'm going to be the one who's been hired to prove she's legit. Archie didn't get around to that part yet, but I think I'm safe in assuming at least that much."

"Wow, and I thought I was going to get to work on my tan on company time. Honey, this isn't the sort of assignment I had in mind when I volunteered."

"So you're leaving?" Grady asked.

Maisie grinned. "Leaving? What? And give up show-biz? Honey, don't be ridiculous. Now, when does this Annie Kendall get here?"

# Two

*If I am not for myself,*
*who is for me?*
　　　　　—Hillel "The Elder"

Supertramp's vintage "Good-bye Stranger" blew out through the eight speakers of the low-slung red convertible sports car: "I was up before the dawn . . ."

"Yadda-yadda-yadda . . . I must be moving on," Annie Kendall sang out with enthusiasm, the wind catching the words as the car whizzed past the uninspiring scenery bordering Route 22. Rounded, pink-tipped nails pounded out the beat on the steering wheel. Slim shoulders moved to the melody. Annie's head, wrapped in a bright pink scarf, bumped and jived to the point that the trucker who'd been pacing her in the passing lane, just to watch her, grinned in delight and blew his horn.

Annie laughed, and waved, then floored it, leaving the truck to follow after her as she whipped into the left lane in front of him, the speedometer edging toward eighty.

The huge pink plush bunny strapped into the passenger seat was thrown back, its long ears trailing in the wind.

Annie loved to drive. She loved to drive fast. She loved the sun on her face, her compact disc player cranked to the max. And why shouldn't she? She was young, heart-free. She still found the world to be a delicious place.

And she was Granddaddy Peevers's little ace in the hole, and that wasn't so bad, either!

Peering through her round-lensed, massive, black-tinted sunglasses, she spied the exit for Route 512 approaching and eased up on the gas in order to get back into the right lane. Ten more minutes, and she'd be there. Annie, her brand-new car, her small mountain of luggage in the trunk and backseat, the bunny, along with her written invitation from Archie Peevers to "come visit and plan to stay for at least a month."

Oh, yeah. She had it all. And she'd probably need it all, if her first short "appointment" at Peevers Mansion could be used to measure what this "visit" would be like. Filthy old man. First he'd tried to scare her, then he'd tried to pinch her bottom. She'd been just about to deck him when he announced to that zombie butler of his that she was "perfect, just perfect."

If he only knew, the rat bastard.

Annie slowed the car around yet another turn in the narrow macadam road she'd been driving on for the past few minutes, and then watched as Peevers Mansion appeared to her right. "Dracula's summer home," she told the rabbit, wincing a little, then took a deep breath, reminding herself that nobody was going to lock her in the joint—she could leave at any time.

One pinch, as a matter of fact, and she was outta there. No matter what Poppy said.

She pulled the sports car into the circular driveway in front of the massive grey-stone building and cut the motor in front of the main doors. Twisting the rearview mirror for a better look, she removed her scarf, fluffed up her mop of ebony curls, and shoved her sunglasses up on her head.

*The better for you to see me, my dears,* she thought as she reached for her knapsack-sized purse and rummaged in it for her lipstick even as she stashed away the concealing sunglasses. Her eyes were the clincher, Archie had said and, after looking at his eyes, she'd agreed.

She took another deep breath, shook off the lingering Supertramp tune that kept running in her head, "Take the Long Way Home," and opened the door, stepping out onto the drive in her three-inch taupe pumps. She brushed down her taupe-cotton skirt, flicked a bit of lint from her pink, sleeveless sweater, and reached into the backseat for her suit jacket.

She was "designer," from head to toe. Never look like you need the money, Poppy had said. Poppy had said a lot of things, but it wasn't Poppy who was going to be staring down a wild-eyed bunch of Peeverses for the next month.

So she'd bought the bunny. An impulse purchase, certainly, and the thing wouldn't make much of a bodyguard. Still, as she reached inside the passenger side and undid the seat belt, at least she had something to talk to now. Okay, so the bunny didn't talk back. Annie had considered that to be just one more selling point. "Come on, bunny, it's you and me against the world," she said, tucking the huge stuffed animal under her arm.

Dickens answered the door personally when she banged on the knocker, and quickly, as if he'd been standing on the other side, watching out the peephole for her arrival.

"Miss Kendall," he said in that deep rumble Annie remembered from her first visit. He was like a stereo with the bass cranked up full. "And friend," he added, eyeing the bunny as if it might bite.

"Dickens," she answered as breezily as she could manage, then lifted her chin, trying to look as imperious as her slim five-foot-four frame could manage. "My luggage is in the car. See to it, please."

Dickens bowed from the waist. "Certainly, Miss Kendall. Will there be anything else? Spit shine your shoes? Wipe the gravy off your chin at dinner? Burp you, you insolent little twit?"

"Now, now, Dickens, play nice," Annie said, smiling her first genuine smile inside the Peevers Mansion. "Or else I'll just have to have Granddaddy Peevers toss you out on your pointy posterior. Now, do I head upstairs to my rooms to wait for the dinner gong, or is there anyone here for me to shock?"

In answer, Dickens took her by the elbow and all but pushed her into a small room to the right of the foyer, a room designed to accommodate meetings with those not exalted enough to enter the drawing room. "There's been a development."

Annie raised one expressive eyebrow, felt a tightening in her stomach. "Archie kicked the bucket? Man, that *would* put a crimp in things, wouldn't it?"

"Mr. Peevers enjoys his usual nauseatingly good health," Dickens shot back. "But he has, very much against my wishes, enjoined the services of a bodyguard, a Mr. Grady Sullivan, of D&S Securities, out of Philadelphia."

"A bodyguard?" Annie shook her head, then looked down at the rabbit. Had Archie been reading her mind? Not that she wanted anyone to think she was bright enough even to dream anyone at Peevers Mansion could cause trouble that would necessitate bringing in paid muscle. "Nope, I don't get it," she said, blinking her eyes, hoping she looked less than brilliant. "Why a bodyguard?"

"Who can explain Mr. Peevers? Perhaps he feels he is in danger. Perhaps he feels *you* will be in danger."

"Me? Danger? Not Archie, but *me?* Damn, I hadn't thought of that one . . . ," Annie said, her words trailing off as she bit on her knuckle, a habit she'd been trying to break for ten years. Now she'd better react, right? "Yeah, well, Dickens old sport, can't say it's been grand knowing you," she added, turning toward the door.

Dickens clamped a hand around her elbow, drawing Annie "and friend" back into the room. "Or perhaps," he said slowly, "Mr. Peevers has hired Mr. Sullivan to investigate your background, to prove to his family that he hasn't entirely lost his mind, that he isn't just accepting you as his granddaughter."

"Investigate me? Sure, like that's really going to happen. Still, it is a pretty good idea, I suppose." Annie rolled her eyes, even as she shook off Dickens's grip. "In other words, this Sullivan guy is a dupe, a fool, and probably—hopefully—a lousy detective who'll say anything Archie scripts for him. Okay, that works. But why didn't you just say so? Never mind, I can answer my own question. You get your jollies playing the big, bad butler."

Dickens shot his cuffs, rolled his head on his shoulders. "One takes one's pleasures where one finds them. I was also following orders, as Mr. Peevers wished for you to know that there'd been an addition to our small gathering. Speaking of which, Mr. A.W. and his wife are in the drawing room. Would you like me to announce you?"

"A.W? Oh, okay, that's Archie's oldest son, right? Arthur William, known to Archie most affectionately as Asswipe, if memory serves? Charming. And his wife would be—Mildred? No, Mitzi. Mildred was too lower class, so she changed it. She's the social climber who tells everyone Archie made his money in personal-care products rather than admitting that he's the toilet-paper king. How am I doing so far?"

"You recite well enough," Dickens said, sniffing. "Now let's see if you're worth everything Mr. Peevers is paying you."

"Gee, thanks for the pep talk." Annie tried to hide the flinch she felt at Dickens's words, but failed. This was the part she hated; coming off as a moneygrubbing con artist. She was, in some ways, but she didn't like to feel like one, damn it. "Lead on, Macduff, it's show time," she said, waving a hand so that the butler could precede her out of the room.

As they passed through the foyer, Annie fought down the sudden urge to open the door, run down the marble steps, fling herself into her convertible, and roar off for parts unknown, parts unknown being where she had come from in the first place.

Instead, she took a moment to look around the foyer, which would be pretty impressive if this were 1900 instead of the new millennium. As it was, the walls were dark, the furniture darker, and a chandelier that must have weighed a half ton could barely bring light into the massive, high-ceilinged vault of a place.

"Bet there's a great echo in here," Annie quipped, following after Dickens. "What do you say I give it a try?"

"Of course," Dickens agreed loftily. "Cement your low background to everyone right from the get-go. That should help matters enormously. May I suggest a *yodel?*"

Chastened, Annie shut her mouth with a snap and eased her tension by doing her imitation of Dickens's poker-backed walk, muttering under her breath in best Igor-fashion as she hunched up one shoulder, "Valk this vay, valk this vay . . ."

They valked . . . er, *walked* this way until Dickens stopped in front of a double set of closed doors, then flung them open before stepping inside the drawing room to announce: "Miss Annie Kendall to see her aunt and uncle Peevers."

"Well, *that* should get their attention. I'll bet you've been practicing the line for a week," Annie complimented under her breath as she stepped from behind the tall butler and peeked into the room. "Here, put this with my luggage, will you?" she asked, then thrust the bunny into Dickens's chest so that he had no option but to take hold of it.

"Disabuse yourself of any notion that you and I are coconspirators, Miss Kendall. Mr. Peevers is expecting you upstairs when you're done here," Dickens replied stiffly, and just as stiffly wheeled about on his heels, the bunny tucked under his arm, and left the room.

A small, terrified part of her would miss him. Not as much as she'd miss the bunny, but she'd miss him.

The drawing room was enormous, dwarfing the huge foyer, and quadrupling it for pure ugly. During her first visit, and coming in through the servants' entrance, she hadn't been privileged to see more of the mansion than Archie's apartment, which had been pretty bad; but this was worse. Ugly quadrupled *had* to be worse.

Archie must have made a killing fifty years on a sell-out of red velvet, because this room was as full of it as his apartments. Dark, clotted-blood red velvet. It hung from the floor-to-ceiling windows. It wrapped around Victorian chairs and hard-as-a-board Victorian sofas. It covered tables, draped over the grand piano, banded with foot-long fringe.

There were deep red carpets spread all over the dark parquet floors. Red shades on the lamps. Bloodred over white-flocked wallpaper on the walls.

Walking into this room was rather like being reduced to an infinitesimal dot, then inserted inside a vein while a voice announced: Hello, I am Joe's corpuscle; would you like a tour?

She wasn't alone in this gargantuan Blood Bank Bordello. There were two people deeper in the room, just now rising from a pair of velvet couches and staring at her as if she were some virulent virus just injected into their midst.

A.W. looked a lot like Archie, only younger and heavier and a lot less jolly. He wore gold-rimmed glasses, had the bulbous nose of the dedicated drinker, and as the sun lit him from the back, Annie could see that his ears had gone hairy. His belly preceded him as he took his wife's hand and walked toward her, and his wing-tip shoes squeaked with each step.

Mitzi Peevers had been caught in a time warp. She wore her hair in a blond bubble that probably wouldn't lose its shape in a Force 5 hurricane, and she seemed to have a deep commitment to blue eye shadow and Barbara Bush pearls. Tall, she looked nearly anorexic, obviously a proponent of the "nobody can be too rich or too thin" school. What had Archie said about Mitzi? Oh, yeah, Annie remembered now: "Mitzi's all right. She's got balls. I think she ripped them right off the asswipe on their wedding night."

Trying to dislodge Archie's words from her mind so that she could concentrate on the moment, Annie held out her hand, smiled, and said, "Hi. I'm Annie Kendall. I guess maybe you weren't expecting me?" She could have said, "Hello, I'm Annie Kendall, your worst nightmare." She congratulated herself for fighting down the impulse. Much better to play dumb than flip. After all, they were going to hate her anyway. Why give them encouragement?

A.W. said nothing, just looked to his wife, which seemed to be a reaction born of long habit.

"Dickens said we're your aunt and uncle?" Mitzi said, her voice very much at odds with her tall, thin body, as it was deep, and seemed to come from her toes. "I doubt that highly."

"Well, okay. So you're my *great*-aunt and -uncle? Or maybe something like aunt and uncle once removed? I never could figure out this stuff, could you? Especially as Mom was a bastard. Do you think Miss Manners covers bastard children anywhere?"

Annie was playing for time, speaking just to fill the silence as A.W. and Mitzi glared at her, looked down their noses at her.

When in doubt, Annie had decided, babble.

"So, I guess you're wondering why I'm here, and I'm being about as clear as mud, right?" she said quickly. "Truth is, I'm kind of confused myself, as Mom never spoke of it, but it looks like I'm one of you. Archie boinked my grandmother when she worked here a zillion years ago, and Mom was the result. They're both dead now, Mom and Grandma, and I really thought I was alone in the world. But I'm not, I'm a Peevers, and you're my family. Isn't that the coolest thing? Archie's over the moon about it."

"A.W.," Mitzi rasped, listing slightly to one side, "lead me to a chair. I feel faint."

When A.W. didn't move, Annie stepped forward, ready to take the woman's arm. Mitzi's reaction was swift. She threw up her hands, screeched, "Don't you *dare* touch me!" then grabbed A.W. by the shoulder and whipped him around, shoving him toward the facing sofas.

A.W. looked back over his shoulder as he was dragged along, and Annie took that as meaning she should follow them, join them on the sofas. After all, if she waited for an invitation, she could grow roots through the carpet.

By the time Mitzi had extracted a short, gold cigarette holder from one pocket and a cigarette from the other, lit the cigarette with a solid silver lighter on the coffee table, she seemed to have regained her poise.

"So, you've come here claiming to be my father-in-law's illegitimate granddaughter. Is that right?"

"Yes, ma'am, except I'm not really a bastard; just my mom, and I'd rather we didn't mention that again, okay," Annie said, smoothing her hem that fell two inches above her knees when she was sitting down. Shocking the Peevers was fun, but now she had to step back, measure every word she said. "When my mom died I went though her things, and found her birth certificate. Oh, the father was listed as unknown, in case you're wondering, so I guess you could say I have no *real* proof. But, with the birth certificate was a letter, addressed to me. Mom wrote that if I was ever in trouble I was to contact my grandfather, Archie Peevers, for assistance. Otherwise, Mom said, I was to stay as far as I could from the man, because he wasn't very nice. She sure had that one right, as I found out when I contacted Archie a few weeks ago. Although I've decided he's just cranky because he's old and ill, poor man."

"I don't believe a word of this. First that private investigator, and now this . . . this . . . *person,*" A.W. said, hopping up from his seat and heading for a sideboard littered with cut-glass decanters and an ice bucket. It was only three in the afternoon, but Annie imagined A.W. was in need of a little liquid refreshment.

Mitzi was still staring at Annie, her eyelids narrowed to slits. "Your grandmother. What was her name?"

"Sally," Annie answered easily, for she was well rehearsed. "Sally Beckman. I believed she worked here at Peevers Mansion as a maid of some sort. Archie seduced her when she was only sixteen, and she ran away rather than stay and face her shame. Archie didn't even know she'd been pregnant until I showed up. Man, I have to tell you," she said, leaning forward in her seat, "I thought he was going to *croak* when he saw my eyes for the first time! You've got them too, don't you, Uncle—that is, Mr. Peevers? No, that's too formal. I guess I'll just call you A.W. and Mitzi, and you can call me Annie."

Mr. Peevers couldn't speak at the moment. He was otherwise occupied, downing three fingers of neat scotch, so Mitzi answered for him. She usually did anyway.

"You can't really sit here and tell us that Archie *believes* this ridiculous claim?"

Annie wriggled in her chair once more, the sweet, not too bright young thing confiding in those older and wiser than herself. "Now, here's the thing," she said, spreading her hands. "I don't know what to believe, and I don't think Archie does, either. That's why he invited me here, asked me to come for a whole month, which is really nice, because I'm . . . well, let's just say I'm between jobs at the moment."

Mitzi ground out her cigarette in a crystal ashtray and lit another. "Did you hear this, A.W.?" she asked, as her husband sat down beside her once more. "Archie's known about this girl, even invited her here. To wag her under our noses. God, but I hate that miserable man!"

It was time for Annie's exit, she was sure of it, so she stood up, smoothed down her skirt once more. "I know what you're saying, you know," she said, making her bottom lip tremble. "And I know you're thinking that I'm only here because I want Archie's money."

"And we're wrong?" Mitzi asked, one overplucked eyebrow climbing her brow.

Annie grinned, clearly letting her small audience know

she was about to pull their legs. "Yes, ma'am, you are. I'm here because I have no family, and now I've found out that isn't true, that I do have a family. I've already told Archie that I don't want a single penny of his fortune. I only want to be a comfort to him in his old age and infirmity."

"Oh, God," A.W. groaned, sinking back on the cushions. "She's a con artist. Isn't she, Mitzi?"

"Say *that* to the old man, and you'll be cut out of the will. You know how he likes to think he's the smart one around here," Mitzi warned tightly, then glared up at Annie. "You seem like an intelligent girl, Miss Kendall. How much? How much to get you out of our lives?"

"Why, thank you, Mitzi, for the offer, but I think I'll decline. Although, if you play your cards right, I might be inclined to give you and A.W. here an allowance."

And with that, Annie turned and left the room, collapsing against the wall outside the door to catch her breath, talk her knees into holding her up until she could get to Archie's apartments.

And these were only the first two! She still had so many Peeverses to meet, all of them forewarned, she was sure, by A.W. and Mitzi as to who and what she was.

This sure had been a lot easier when she had listened to Poppy tell her how it was going to go.

# Three

*The king was in his countinghouse*
*counting out his money . . .*
— Anonymous

His first night spent under Archie Peevers's roof hadn't done anything to improve Grady's mood, and his mood hadn't been all that great in the first place.

Now, having been summoned by his client, he leaned against the mantelpiece in Archie's apartments and glowered at the old man, who was sitting cross-legged in his bed, preening himself before a hand mirror held by Dickens.

"Do I look sick enough?" Archie asked. "Sullivan? Dickens? Maybe some pale powder on my cheeks? I don't want to look too robust tonight when Asswipe and the rest of them come barreling in here for their after-dinner visit to tell me they're going to have me certified and locked up. I held them off yesterday, saying I was too sick, but that trick won't work twice."

Grady studied Archie for a few moments. There was

no question the man was old. Skinny and wrinkled and old. But there also was no mistaking the man's good health, not after seeing the man in action ten minutes earlier when Grady had come into the room, to see Archie, nightshirt tails flying, chasing some young woman around the chairs in front of the fireplace.

The maid, young and blond and unbelievably stacked, had giggled, straightened her tight blouse, and run past Grady, looking him up and down as if she might be interested and hoped he was, too. Which he wasn't. After all, a man had to have some standards.

"You see them all every day after dinner?" Grady asked, pushing himself away from the mantel. "Then why am I here now? It's hours until dinner. Or are you having second thoughts about this whole thing? If so, I can be packed and out of here in ten minutes."

Archie pushed the mirror away and looked at Grady. "Your heart's not in this yet, is it, boy? All right, we'll make it five thousand a day, and not a penny more. So, you ate dinner with the fruit of my loins last night. What did you think of them?"

In answer, Grady pulled a small notebook out of the back pocket of his khaki slacks and began thumbing through it. "A.W.," he read. "Oldest son and totally whipped by wife Mitzi, who spent the entire first course telling me of all the people she knows on the Main Line."

"Quite the social butterfly, our Mildred," Archie said, nodding. "Surprising what money can buy these days. Shame you missed Asswipe Junior, who's busy flunking out of his third college. In Switzerland, thank God, practicing his snowboarding. I gave him twenty thousand dollars after he promised not to come back here until Christmas. Who knows, maybe I'll be lucky, and he'll fall off a mountain."

Grady couldn't be sure, but he thought he actually heard Dickens mutter, "Amen."

"Let me tell you something about Asswipe," Archie continued, "give you some idea of how he thinks. I don't go in to the office anymore, you know. Haven't for twenty years, have been locked up here for the past ten. But that doesn't mean I don't run the place, even if I had to give Asswipe a title. Anyway," he went on, grinning around his too-large dentures, "we have a board meeting once a week, and I use one of those squawk boxes or whatever they're called now, to talk to everyone, listen to them yes-sir me like the spineless twits they are, Asswipe included. Big square box, stuck right in the center of the conference table. Asswipe painted it pink, and supposedly he throws spitballs at it when I'm talking."

"Charming," Grady said, trying not to look at Archie. He wanted to talk about Annie Kendall, who had taken dinner in her room last night. If he hadn't been told she was in residence, he'd believe she was a figment of Archie's overactive imagination. But today he would demand to meet her. No question.

"Yeah, well, I'm just trying to tell you. If anyone's going to try to kill me, boy, it won't be Asswipe. He's got all the spine of a jellyfish. Mildred will have to hire a hit man, and don't think she hasn't thought about it! Now, go on."

Grady flipped over the page after scribbling "watch

Mitzi" in the margin. "Muriel Peevers, spinster daughter of Archie Peevers—"

"Ah, Muriel," Archie interrupted yet again, batting away Dickens's hands, as that man tried to secure a nightcap to Archie's head. "Let me tell you about Muriel. Her mother was a Barton. Barton's Cigar Tobacco? Ring a bell? Not that I wasn't doing all right, mind you, but marrying money never hurt anyone. Thing was, I had to take the woman along with the money. Couldn't go near a Corona until she was dead two years. She kept going to the office, you understand, to be with her dear daddy. Then came home smelling like tobacco. Came to bed, smelling like tobacco. They're not kidding, you know—tobacco can kill you. Damn near killed me, just smelling it."

Grady closed his eyes, pinched the bridge of his nose with his thumb and forefinger. "If we could get on with this? Now, about Miss Kendall . . ."

"When I'm ready," Archie said, then went on with his story as if Grady hadn't interrupted. "Anyway, we named Asswipe after her daddy, which got me another bucket of money. When Muriel was born, I just couldn't pass up another chance for a bundle. Muriel . . . cigars. Get it? Don't just stand there like a stump, boy! Do you get it?"

"Got it," Grady answered, beginning to feel sorry for Muriel, for all of the Peevers children. He'd had a small talk with Muriel after dinner last night, and rather liked the woman. She looked like her father, which pretty much explained her marital status, to Grady's mind. Fifty if she was a day, and looking older, Muriel was devoted to her "Daddy." Try as she might to impress Grady with the depth of that devotion, he'd come away with the idea that she'd much rather be devoted from a distance, but didn't have what it took to make the break.

"Archie, Junior," Grady said, pushing on, wanting to get this over with so they could move on to other things. Like Annie Kendall, for one.

"Junior? Ah, now there's a waste of good seed," Archie said, sitting up so that Dickens could plump his pillows for him. "There wouldn't have been a Junior, you know—the wife had been sleeping alone for ten years, thank God. But I could see by then that Asswipe wasn't going to amount to a hill of crap, so I had to do something. What is it they used to say? Close your eyes and think of England? All cats are grey in the dark? All that stuff? Doesn't work, let me tell you. Trick was to get drunk, but not too drunk, you know what I mean? Too drunk and the little soldier won't be able to stand up and salute."

Grady coughed into his fist, trying not to laugh. There was no getting around it; he was working for a true Original. An original *what,* he still wasn't quite sure. And he silently agreed with Archie about his youngest son. Junior surely was a waste. He must look like his deceased mother, which wasn't much of an endorsement, and his blatantly dyed black hair and too-tight silk shirts gave him all the appeal of a racetrack tout. And then there was Daisy . . .

"You're thinking about the woman, aren't you? You'd have to be, with that sort of deer-in-headlights look you've got right now. Not Junior—who nobody thinks about if they can help it—but the woman, right?" Archie asked. "She was there, wasn't she? Of course she was.

She's always there, hoping to be wife number four. What did you think of her?"

There were two ways Grady could go on this one, and neither of them appealed. "She seems to be fond of Junior," he said at last, trying his best to take the high road after watching Daisy and Junior groping each other at dinner.

"Ha! Good one, son. You could go into politics with an answer like that. Daisy. Hah! Empty-headed as a Daisy, maybe, but there's a well-oiled Venus flytrap between her legs, I'm thinking, because Junior seems to spend most of his time there. You should see what I've seen from this window, with the two of them out there in the gazebo. Sent Dickens outside with a bucket of water to throw on them one time, didn't I, Dickens?"

"Yes, sir, you did," Dickens said, having completed his "arranging" of Archie, stepping back to admire his work. "She's been waiting for ten minutes now, sir. Shall I fetch her?"

Grady flipped the notebook closed and slid it back into his pocket. Finally! "She? You mean Annie Kendall?"

"No," Archie snapped. "I mean Eleanor fricking Roosevelt and her all-girl band. Are you always this dim, boy?"

"I took this course, a few years ago," Grady remarked calmly, seating himself in one of the chairs in front of the fireplace. "Twenty ways to kill a man without leaving a mark. Maybe, in my spare time, I'll show a few of them to your kids. God knows they need all the help they can get."

"Ah, touchy, isn't he, Dickens?" Archie said, pretending to shrink against the pillows. "Oh, very well. I'll be nice."

"Sure you will," Grady said, crossing one long leg over the other. "And I'll take that five thousand a day. If I'm supposed to keep you alive, I need some pretty hefty incentive, and, believe me, your sunny disposition just isn't cutting it. Now, before Dickens lets Miss Kendall in here, I think we need to lay down some ground rules."

"Ground rules? Like what?" Archie asked, looking—finally—just a little bit ashamed of himself. Nobody dared to talk to him the way Grady Sullivan had just talked to him. He liked it. He liked having a new audience. Hell, if he weren't so old, and probably dying, he'd be having the time of his life.

"Well, I could start by telling you that I didn't know she was here until this morning, and I should have been informed. That's one, although it's a minor inconvenience. Secondly, I want to know if she's aware of what she's getting herself into."

Archie looked to Dickens, who began examining the tips of his shoes. "Into? What are you talking about, boy? She's my Sally's granddaughter. *My* granddaughter. She came here telling me she is, and I believe her."

"Right," Grady said, standing up one more time and heading for the door. "Forget the five thousand, forget you ever heard my name. I'd suggest you call Fritz and Barani, on South Street in Philly. Fritz is a certified moron who calls himself a private dick because he thinks it wows the chicks, and Barani was a beat cop who got busted for taking a bribe. They should be dumb enough for you."

"If you'll recall, sir," Dickens said, "I *did* tell you I didn't think Mr. Sullivan was suitably money-hungry. Our investigation did provide us with the information that he is independently wealthy and therefore might not be bought as easily as you'd hoped. And then there was that distressing *summa cum laude* degree. Perhaps this is just as well."

Grady stopped, his hand on the doorknob, and turned around. "You investigated me?" He let go of the doorknob and walked back into the room. "Why, you . . . you *miserable* sonofabitch. *You*"—he jabbed his index finger under Archie's nose, then his own chest—"investigated *me?*"

Archie pushed back the covers and got out of bed, showing more of his hairy, skinny legs than anyone could like. "Now, boy—son—don't get your knickers in a twist. Of course I had you investigated. And you passed, with flying colors. Use your head, boy. I'm worth over a billion dollars these days—even more, dead. Do you think I'd let just anyone into this house?"

Archie had a point, much as Grady didn't want to admit it. He took in a deep breath, let it out with a rush. "All right, all right, I'll accept that explanation. But it doesn't change anything. Either you're straight with me, or I'm out of here. Starting with this girl, this Annie Kendall."

"Ah, let me guess. This is the private eye? Not all that private, though, as I could hear him bellowing clear out in the hallway. I hope you don't mind that I decided to join you, as I heard my own name mentioned?"

At the sound of the woman's voice, Grady had turned around to see Annie Kendall, better-looking than the head shot he had in his room, standing ten feet away from him.

"Hi," she said, her smile bright as she came forward, right hand outstretched, definitely in an attempt to put herself in charge of the situation. "I'm Annie Kendall, and you must be Grady Sullivan. Do you carry a gun? May I see it? I've never seen a gun, not up close and personal."

Grady ignored the question as he took her hand, felt her firm grip, the smoothness of her palm. She looked good. She smelled better. Before he found himself thinking in Philip Marlowe, P.I., sentences like, "She was an accidental seduction that screamed danger inside my head," he released her hand and stepped back. "Ms. Kendall," he said.

"Annie, please, Grady. I'll call you Grady. After all, if you can't be on a first-name basis with the man who obviously thinks you're either an unscrupulous, gold-digging impostor or a hired red herring, what good is there left in this world? Oh, don't frown. I talked with Archie yesterday, and he told me what he'd decided you think of me."

"I didn't say you were a gold digger," Grady said, wondering how she'd gotten her eyes to look that same strange, near-colorless grey as Archie's. Contacts couldn't do that, could they? The color had to be real. "For all I know, you're as much the victim here as you are anything else. Or haven't you figured that out yet?"

Annie looked to Archie, who had crawled back into his high, wide bed and was watching the two of them. "Archie? I think the ball's in your court?"

"All right, all right," Archie said, clearly depressed that

he was going to have to give up at least some of his game. "Annie here came to me a few weeks ago, telling me she's Sally's granddaughter. *My* granddaughter. Now, I figured she was blowing smoke, except that I did have this . . . this *thing* with Sally for a while. Not that it matters. Girl doesn't have any evidence but an old letter. I was going to send her away, and then it hit me. If I said she *might* be my granddaughter, even moved her in here, I could have some pretty spectacular fun watching Asswipe and the others going crazy, wondering if I was going to cut them out of the will and put Annie here in it."

"Some pretty spectacular fun," Grady repeated, shaking his head as he looked at Archie, then at Annie. "I wouldn't believe that, except I've had the dubious pleasure of listening to you yesterday and today, and such a stupid, selfish stunt sounds like something right up your alley. But *I'm* here, or so you told me, because you're afraid one of your nearest and dearest is going to try to kill you. Was that a lie?"

"Dickens?" Archie said, waving toward the nightstand on the other side of the bed. "Show him."

"Yes, sir." Dickens withdrew a pair of thin rubber gloves from his pocket and took his time putting them on, one finger at a time. He then walked around the bed, bent his rigid back as he pulled open the top drawer with both hands, reached in, and pulled out a small glass filled with what looked to be orange juice. A thin plastic wrap had been spread across the opening.

"Orange juice?" Grady said, taking the glass when Dickens offered it, then peeling back the plastic wrap and sniffing the liquid. "What's so unusual about—

damn. I smell almonds. Somebody put *arsenic* in your juice?"

"Correction, boy. Somebody has been *putting* arsenic in my juice. Every morning, for at least a month. That's this morning's glass. Not enough to kill, obviously, as I think I drank some that first day, before I noticed the bad taste—what is it? We get old, we lose our hair, our teeth. Do those idiots think we lose our senses of smell and taste, too? So, do you believe me now? One of my nearest and dearest as you call them is out to snuff me slowly, wipe me out, cancel my check, punch my ticket, shut out my lights. Damn straight I hired you!"

"Why didn't you just go to the police?" Grady asked, pretty sure he already knew the answer.

Archie sat up in the bed, the tassel hanging from the end of his nightcap slapping against his cheek. "This is my *family*, you idiot. You don't call the police on your family, your blood, your seed." He settled himself against the pillows once more. "Not until you have rock-solid proof, anyway."

"The orange juice is proof," Annie pointed out, walking over to sit on the edge of the bed and take hold of Archie's hand.

"I could have put the arsenic in there myself," Archie told her. "That's just what those circling buzzards downstairs would say, just to prove that I've lost my marbles and need to be locked up in a rubber room. I can't take the chance. No, I've got to catch whoever it is red-handed. It's the only way."

"Red-handed, huh?" Grady said, watching Annie stroke the back of Archie's hand, almost as if she had some feelings for the old goat. "Would that be while that someone is trying to kill you—or your newly discovered granddaughter?"

"He *is* smart," Annie said, leaning over to kiss Archie's cheek before she stood, turned to face Grady. "Archie really doesn't believe I am his granddaughter," she told him. "He does, however, see the possibilities in letting his children *think* he believes I'm his granddaughter, which is why I was hired. I believe he also has had some more time to consider what he's doing before I got here yesterday, and has hired you, not just to protect him, but to protect me as well, as I *could* be his granddaughter. At least that's what he told me yesterday. That's rather sweet, don't you think?"

"I think I can't tell the players without a scorecard, that's what I think," Grady said, stabbing his fingers through his too-long sandy hair. "Let me get this straight, okay? You came here, out of the blue, to tell Archie you're his granddaughter, and then he decided to—"

"No, not quite right. Archie was fibbing on that one, and I thought I could keep up that story, but I can see you won't settle for less than the whole truth," Annie said, holding up a hand as she interrupted him. "You see, it didn't happen quite that way. I saw an advertisement in a magazine in the doctor's office—I read the personal ads from time to time—asking if there might be anyone out there believing they could be related to a family named Peevers."

"You placed an ad in the *personal* column?" Grady asked Archie, shaking his head. "How many people answered it?"

"They wrote to a postal box, Mr. Sullivan," Dickens explained. "It was all most discreet. We got no more than three hundred replies, and they were all easily sorted out."

"Sandy helped," Archie said, nodding. "He's my doctor. Dr. Milton Sandborn. He's been my doctor forever. Good man, his vitamin shots are what's keeping me alive, I'm sure of it. Anyway, we read the letters together, looked at the color photographs they all had to send, and we picked Annie Kendall. I liked the name, you understand. Once had a good time with a girl named Annie, but that's neither here nor there, is it? It was the eyes that sold us. I'd been hoping for a boy—hell, I've been hoping for a boy for fifty years, and look what *that's* gotten me! But, in the end, we settled for Annie."

Grady began to pace, believing he was finally, *finally,* hearing the truth. A bizarre truth, granted, but it had the ring of misguided sincerity to it. "Okay, I think I'm with you so far. You placed an ad, you hired Ms. Kendall— Annie. You know she's not real, she knows she's not real, and I now know she's not real. You're only doing this to scare your children, and to hope someone takes a potshot at Annie instead of you."

He wheeled around, glared at Annie. "Are you *getting* any of this, or was the money just too good to turn down? You're setting yourself up like a sitting duck. For *money?*"

"The money is one reason," Annie told him, smiling. She had the most infuriating smile. Kind of like she was saying, without words: "You stupid schmuck." She stood next to Archie's bed, held his hand. "I like Archie. I want to help him. And, hey, a job's a job. This one has great fringe benefits."

"You like him." Grady said the words as if he was

carefully pronouncing them in an unfamiliar language. "Yeah. Right. Sure you do. And Pamela Anderson Lee just got lucky with Mother Nature in the boobs department. Cut me a break here, Annie. Just how *much* do you like Archie?"

"About fifty thousand dollars' worth for one month's work," she said with an honesty that made him want to choke her. "Although I will now admit to being a little bit worried. The orange juice, you understand. I was having some second thoughts on my drive here. But, as I was driving here in my brand-new convertible, I fought them down. And now you're here—wasn't that brilliant of Archie?—and I'm not worried at all."

Dickens, who had been quiet for some minutes, approached, holding a large manila envelope. "We've taken the liberty of preparing some background information for Miss Kendall, sir. The old birth certificate with her grandfather father listed as Unknown. The letter, on carefully aged paper, from her mother, telling her she's Mr. Peevers's granddaughter. Information you might share with any of the Peevers children anytime you see fit. You are here, sir, as far as the children know, to investigate Miss Kendall's claim."

Grady took the envelope, slapped it against his thigh a time or two. "You're all nuts. You do know that, don't you? This isn't a game we're playing here. First I'm hired to protect Archie, which is a bunch of crap, Archie, because you're about as helpless as a barracuda. Now you tell me I'm here to pretend to investigate Annie's supposed claim, which is more crap. And you're all running around inciting a possible murderer just because Archie thinks it would be fun. If I can believe you, somebody could get very dead before this is over. Hell, if this keeps up, I could end up the prime suspect."

"Are you always such a party pooper, Grady?" Annie asked. "What a pity. Well, if you'll all excuse me now, I want to take a shower before dinner. I just can't wait to meet the rest of my new relatives."

As she brushed past him, Grady all but growled, "If you think I'm going to become your official taster, you've got another guess coming." She laughed, and left the room.

"You go, too, boy," Archie said, popping a handful of pills into his mouth as Dickens handed him a glass of water. "My lawyer's due any minute, to begin work on a new will. My fifth this year, I think, although I don't keep track. Dickens tells me he has to replace the scotch in the drawing room twice as often after one of Banning's visits. Ah, yes," he said, snuggling under the covers. "We've going to have a great month, boy, a real hell-raising, ball-busting month!"

# Four

*He spoke with a certain what-is-it
in his voice, and I could see that,
if not actually disgruntled,
he was far from being gruntled.*
—P. G. Wodehouse

Grady Sullivan was sitting on the bed when she came out of the bathroom, a huge white towel wrapped, sarong-style, around her body, another small towel turban on her head.

Annie liked the way he looked at her. She also liked the way she'd quickly recovered from her shock, hopefully in time not to let him know she'd been rattled by his unexpected appearance. And she was particularly glad the Peevers household had sprung for very large bath sheets, and that she had actually used one of them instead of walking out of the bathroom stark naked.

If you looked hard enough, Annie had always thought, there was always some sort of silver lining. But now to get Grady Sullivan out of her room, before she started thinking *he* was it!

"I'm sorry," she said as she loosened the towel around her head, turned her back to him so that she could see him in the mirror above the dresser, and began rubbing at her wet hair. "We only receive visitors on Tuesdays. But please do leave your card, and thank you so much for calling."

"Not funny. You didn't lock your door," Grady said. Growled, actually. "I could have been anyone."

"Yes, you could have, couldn't you? But, instead of *anyone,* it was you. So sad," Annie said, now combing through her hair, then pushing at it so that the natural curl asserted itself. "Next time, could you try to be Harrison Ford? Now *that* could prove interesting."

She watched his reflection in the mirror; watched as he clenched his jaw, narrowed his eyelids. She suddenly wanted to know how far she could push him, and how he'd push back. It was probably an irrational thought, but then, when had she started being rational? Certainly not today.

"Did you sneak in here to show me your . . . *gun?*" Annie asked him, doing her best to make her voice low, give her question the air of a double entendre. She didn't think her femme fatale act would actually have him running, screaming, from the room. But she certainly was interested in how he'd respond.

He didn't disappoint. The man was a gentleman. He probably hated that about himself, but he *was* a gentleman. She was safe with him.

In some ways, that was a damned pity.

A slight, embarrassed flush had already become visible under Grady's tan. He was a knockout. If he ever smiled at her, she'd probably melt into a whimpering puddle at his feet. Not that there was any great chance of *that* happening.

Grady stood up, glared at her. "Miss Kendall—Annie," he began, clearly trying to control his temper. "We have to talk."

She shook her head, her three-day-old very good cut arranging her hair around her face. "No, we don't have to talk. Why? Because I know what you're going to say."

"Then say it for me, so that I know you know," Grady prodded, leaning his long frame up against one of the posts of the four-poster bed. He was definitely the kind of guy who liked to *lounge.* An easy, laid-back kind of guy. A slow mover, but with sharp, intelligent eyes. And a sarcastic mouth.

"You're going to say that Archie's bonkers, his idea is bonkers, and *I'm* bonkers for being here. Right?"

"Close. Actually, I was first going to ask you if you think it was one of the heirs, or Archie himself, who doctored the orange juice."

Annie had gathered up fresh underclothes and was about to step into the walk-in closet, to get dressed. But Grady's words stopped her. "Archie? You think he's been poisoning himself? Why would he do that?"

"Because I have a deep and twisted mind? Because I remember reading about tricks like that in my handy-dandy private-investigator handbook? Maybe, but no. Actually, Archie did suggest it himself, remember," Grady said, still leaning against the bedpost, his arms now crossed, looking as if he was prepared to watch as she dropped the towel and stepped into her undies.

She didn't think so.

"No," Annie corrected, but not with as much conviction as she would have liked. "He said his heirs might try to say he poisoned the orange juice himself."

Grady finally pushed himself away from the bedpost, so now he was even taller as he stood there in the suddenly small room, looking down at her. She put up a hand, covered her cleavage. "I know what he said. And, to tell you the truth, that's what gave me the idea. I think he just made up the orange-juice story this morning, just in case I tried to quit again, which I did. Besides," he added, and now he did smile, and now Annie did feel her knees begin to liquefy, "nobody would take the time to slowly kill Archie over time. Much more likely they'd blow him up, and this mausoleum with him. *Bang!*"

Annie blinked, feeling herself becoming mesmerized by Grady's smile, Grady's eyes, Grady's overwhelming presence. And then, shaking her head once more, it hit her. "That old bastard! He *did* fake it, didn't he? Trying to hold on to you, trying for my pity. I have half a mind to . . . to . . ."

"The word you're searching for is *leave*, I believe," Grady supplied when she came to a fuming halt.

"No! That's the *last* thing I'd do! But you might want to add my name to the list of suspects if Archie's found with his neck in a knot anytime soon."

She hadn't had time to wonder what Grady's eyes would look like if he ever got angry, but now she was seeing it firsthand. His eyes sparkled, his lips thinned, and he seemed to grow another six inches right in front of her. "You *idiot!* Don't you understand what's going on here?"

Annie forced herself not to back up a step, or to remember that she was naked under the towel. It was so much easier to feel intimidated, she suddenly realized, when one wasn't dressed. "I know *exactly* what's going on here, Grady Sullivan. And don't you call me an idiot! Now, stand right there—right there!—while I get dressed."

He opened his mouth, probably to yell at her again, but she didn't give him the chance. She just hugged her new silk underwear to her, pulled open the door to the walk-in closet, and then slammed it behind her.

The stuffed plush rabbit was sitting on the floor inside the closet, and Annie swore it was frowning at her. "Oh, sure. Everyone's a critic. But believe me, I *do* know what I'm doing. Sort of," she whispered, picking up the thing and placing it facing the corner.

Three minutes later, after misbuttoning her blouse in her anger, she stepped out of the closet to see that now the man was sitting on the side of her bed. Almost lying on the bed, actually, on his side, one elbow bent beneath his head.

"Just make yourself comfortable, why don't you," she said through gritted teeth, and suddenly wished she hadn't given up smoking three months earlier. She really could use a smoke. She probably could even chew one if she didn't have a match.

"I thought I would, thank you, as I believe you're about to tell me a fairy tale," Grady said, and nearly purred like a contented tomcat.

Annie had a sudden flash, thinking how nice it would be to neuter the bastard. But, even angry, she knew that would be a terrible waste.

Besides, she had been about to tell him a fairy tale, another great big fib to go with the rest. But that could get confusing, so she stuck to as much of the truth as she could. "Look, I saw the ad, I went on the interview, and I took the job. One month, driving Archie's kids up the walls for fun and profit. Archie's fun, my profit. There's nothing dishonest about it, because I most certainly am not going to be written into his will, or anything like that. And it is not, repeat, *not* going to be dangerous. Archie's blowing smoke on that, and we both know it. We're both here for Archie's fun, only you're probably getting paid better."

She watched as Grady obviously did some quick mental calculations. "With overhead, paying my assistant, who's here with me—her name's Maisie; you'll meet her later, I'm sure—and figuring in the taxes I'm betting you aren't planning on paying . . . yeah, I think I'm still getting the better end of the deal. Sorry about that."

"I insisted on a 1099," Annie grumbled under her breath, pretty sure that the best con artists didn't concern themselves with paying Uncle Sam, but curiously unwilling to have Grady Sullivan believe her dishonest.

"What? What was that?" Grady asked, sitting up. "I had one hand on my ear. I couldn't have heard that right. You're going to report the fifty thousand as *income?*"

Annie slipped her feet into the heels she'd had on earlier, then picked up her brush and began pulling it through her hair once more. It was far from dry, but if she didn't try to tame it while it was damp, she always ended up looking like a startled poodle. The only people who thought naturally curly hair was nifty didn't have naturally curly hair.

"Of course I'm going to report the money. I'm a . . . I think Archie called it some kind of contract worker, or something like that. All perfectly legal."

Grady was behind her again, standing right behind her. Because he was so much taller, she couldn't see his face in the mirror, but she had a pretty good idea that he was smiling. He put his hands on her shoulders. "Pack your bags, Annie Kendall, and get the hell out of here. You don't belong with these sharks. A 1099 form? Damn, just when you think you've heard it all . . ."

She bent her knees and slipped out from under his hands, not stopping until she was standing on the opposite side of the room. "I could really learn to despise you," she told him, not at all honestly, but hopefully he didn't know that.

"That's fine with me, as long as you despise me from, say, Bermuda," Grady said, stabbing his fingers through his hair in a pretty good imitation of near-total distraction. "Because, in case you haven't thought about it, maybe Archie's orange juice *was* spiked. Maybe he's not kidding, and he really believes, for good reason, that one of his nearest and dearest is crossing the line, to become one of his nearest and *deadliest*. Hell, I've only known the guy for two days, and I've already been tempted to smother him with his own pillows. He's not exactly a warm, fuzzy, grandfatherly type, now is he?"

"I like him," Annie said honestly. "No, really," she added when Grady snorted, "I really like him. You know, at the bottom of it, he's just a scared old man waiting to die. That can't be fun."

Grady shot out one arm toward her, as if introducing her to some invisible audience. "And there she is, ladies and gentlemen," he announced, "this year's Miss Gullibility. Let's give her a big hand, everybody. It takes a lot of work to be this naive."

"Oh, put a sock in it, will you?" Annie returned to the mirror and picked up her lipstick, then put it down again without using it because her hands were trembling and she'd probably end up looking like Bozo the Clown. "You know," she said, turning to look at Grady, "you're reacting just the way Archie wants you to react. You *believe* he's in some sort of danger."

"No, I don't believe that. I believe, Miss Kendall," he said coldly, "that if anyone is in danger around here, it's *you.* Archie's going to wave you under his kids' noses like a red flag, just to see what happens. Not just to get his jollies, Miss Kendall. If he really believes he's in danger, and if he really is in danger, he wants to see if anyone makes an attempt on your life. Why don't you chew on that one for a few minutes, Miss Kendall, before you tell me how much you like the old bastard. Or do the words sacrificial lamb mean nothing to you?"

"Name's Annie," she mumbled, averting his gaze. "Do you really think one of his children would try to hurt me?"

"No, I think they'd try to *kill* you, if Archie convinces them he's thinking of rewriting his will, giving his one billion plus to you, and cutting them out. The question you should be asking yourself, *Annie,* is very simple. *Do you feel lucky?"*

"That's from an old Clint Eastwood movie. Couldn't you at least be original?" Annie said, trying to dismiss the sudden fluttering in her stomach. She wanted to talk to Poppy. She needed to talk to Poppy.

Grady rubbed a hand across his mouth, probably to keep from swearing in her presence. "Okay," he said after a moment, "how about this for original? And hare-brained, but I have to work with what I've got. Let's become partners."

Annie looked at him; goggled at him. "I'm sorry," she said, playing for time, "I don't think I heard you correctly. Would you please repeat that?"

Another hand rub, this time over his jaw. Another split-finger stab through his hair. "Don't push, Annie, this is bad enough. But if you insist on staying, and I can't leave—which I can't, thanks to that damned orange juice—then we're going to have to start cooperating with each other."

"Meaning?" she asked, silently conceding that, okay, maybe the man had a point. Wasn't there supposed to be safety in numbers?

"Meaning," he said, pointing a finger toward her chest, "that you tell me anything suspicious, anything that happens that you don't think is quite right. Meaning that you do what I say, when I say, and don't ask questions. *Meaning,* if at any time, in my judgment, you'd be safer somewhere else, you'll go."

"That's not partners," Annie pointed out. "I already have one boss, remember? I don't need two."

"Right! And I'm not going to be your boss. You need a keeper, Annie Kendall, and that's what you're going to get. You and me, stuck together like glue for the next month. I protect you, you listen to me, and, together, we watch Archie and all the little Peeverses. Understand now?"

It was a good idea. It had been *his* idea, which was probably why she felt this need to object, but Annie knew it was also the best idea. "Okay," she said, nodding. "You and me, together. But only if you let me see your gun."

The bedroom door in the adjoining room slammed so hard it shook the lamp on Maisie's bedside table. She popped another butter cream into her mouth, then slid off the bed and opened the connecting doors. Clearly the boss was back.

"It went well?" she asked, watching Grady storm around the bedroom, probably looking for something relatively inexpensive to smash.

"She's impossible!" He picked up a figurine of a shepherdess with a small lamb at her feet, hefted it, then put it down. "Stupid, ignorant . . . *infuriating* woman!"

"Let me rephrase that. It didn't go well?" Maisie prodded, enjoying herself very much.

Grady unbuttoned his shirt, sending one of the buttons sailing halfway across the room as he ripped out of the sleeves, mashed the expensive shirt into a ball, then slammed it into a corner. He had to get dressed for dinner. He had to go make nice-nice with the Peeverses again. He had to sit across the table from Annie Kendall and not give in to the impulse to bean her with a dinner roll.

"*Yes,* it went badly," he said, plopping himself down on the side of the bed. "And the hell of it is that I don't know if I'm overreacting or if she really could be in danger. I just know I have to stick to her like glue for the next month. I think I'd rather sky-dive without a parachute. Come to think of it, that's probably what I'm doing. Damn her!"

Maisie crawled up on the opposite side of the bed and walked, on her knees, across the mattress. "Now, honey, you just sit here a minute and let me rub those shoulders," she said, putting her hands on either side of his neck. "Oooh, feeling a little tense, are we?"

Grady closed his eyes, leaned back against her soft bosom, and let Maisie rub his shoulders, her red-tipped fingers digging into his muscles, easing some of his tenseness. "Damn, Maisie, what would I do without you?"

There was a knock on the door, swiftly followed by the opening of that same door. Annie Kendall stepped inside, looked toward the bed, stopped short. "Oh."

"Hiya, honey," Maisie said, still rubbing Grady's shoulders. "You must be the newest nutcase. I'm Maisie, and Grady here was just saying he couldn't live without me. Isn't that sweet? Now, what can we do for you, honey?"

Annie looked at Grady. "You said . . . you said you'd show me your gun . . ."

"I said *later on* I'd show you my gun," Grady reminded her, very much aware he was stripped bare to his waist, very much aware of what Annie must be thinking. "And did anyone ever tell you that it's knock, then wait for an answer? Not knock and walk in?"

Annie's face looked small and pinched, her grey eyes bruised, hurt. "I . . . I'll try to remember that," she said, then looked at Maisie. "So nice to meet you, Miss, um . . . Maisie," she mumbled, then quickly left, closing the door behind her.

"Well, that went well, don't you think, honey?" Maisie asked just a moment before shepherdess and lamb shattered against the wall. "Oh, okay, honey," Maisie added. "Maybe not."

# Five

*Let me tell you about the very rich.*
*They are different from you and me.*
— F. Scott Fitzgerald

If there was ever any doubt about who was in charge of the Peevers household, the person making the inquiry had obviously never been a guest at dinnertime.

Even before dinner, during the obligatory cocktail hour, Dickens was busy herding the family and guests into the drawing room, reminding them that they were expected to stay where he put them until dinner was served.

"However, Mr. Junior, we will excuse you for a moment while you go upstairs and locate the necktie I took the liberty of laying out for you on your bed," the butler said, holding a half-full glass of scotch in front of the youngest Peevers heir, then leading him toward the foyer before putting it within reach. "There's an obedient little idiot," Dickens then muttered under his breath, although Grady heard him as he walked by, entering the room.

"Evening, Dickens," Grady said happily, giving the man a small salute. "How goes the war?"

Obviously not believing the question worthy of an answer, Dickens turned his back and headed toward the center of the room once more, this time to neatly remove a glass from A.W.'s reach, tip its contents in a nearby plant, then replace the now empty glass on the table, all without missing a step.

From there, he walked over to Mitzi, bowed to her slightly, and inquired if she would care for a glass of sherry.

Before Mitzi could answer, Daisy, who had been picking at the wide pink ruffle around her daringly low-cut bodice, piped up, "What about me, Dickens-poo? Aren't you going to ask me what I want?"

"You are an open book, madam," Dickens said, now bowing in Daisy's direction. "I am already well aware of your desires."

Daisy giggled, Dickens's sarcasm sailing straight over her fairly vacant blond head, but Grady coughed into his fist rather than laugh.

A.W. picked up his glass, frowned when he saw that it was empty. "Dickens? Oh, never mind, I'll get it myself," he said, and followed the butler to the sideboard and its inventory of light, heavy, and downright dangerous booze.

Which left Grady to stand there, still very pointedly not being acknowledged by anyone in the room, to decide between approaching Mitzi or Daisy. No question. Daisy won, hands down.

"Ms. Goodenough," he said, still secretly amused by her surname, "would you mind if I joined you?"

Daisy looked up at him, giggled, pulled at her ruffles some more, to the point where Grady was pretty sure he was seeing something he probably shouldn't be seeing. "Oh, Mr. Sullivan, of course you may join me," she simpered, patting the sofa cushion next to her. "But only until Junie gets back. He's *so* jealous, you know."

"And with good reason," Grady answered, automatically polite. "His fiancée is a beautiful woman."

He wasn't stretching the truth all that far, either. Daisy Goodenough was a beautiful woman. She had the hair, the teeth, the boobs, the body. The only problem was, if there was a bright light in her big blue eyes, it only served to show how empty the rest of her head was.

No more than twenty-two or twenty-three, she was years younger than "Junie," which is probably how the man liked his women. Young, stacked, almost too dumb. And wearing a rock on her third finger, left hand a person could serve dinner on.

Dickens returned, handed Daisy a tall frosted glass with a straw, some bits of fruit, and a paper umbrella topping it. "Next time, if you're good, I'll even put some liquor in it," he said, and Daisy laughed again.

"Isn't he *wonderful?*" she said, as Dickens looked at Grady levelly for a moment, then walked away, his spine stiff as a poker. "He thinks I'm too young to"—her voice lowered to a whisper—"imbibe strong spirits. That's what he said—imbibe. That means taste, I'm pretty sure. Personally, I think he's got a crush on me."

Junior returned to the drawing room, just in time to save Grady from having to answer, and he got up quickly, taking up a new position in front of the fireplace.

Junior, now wearing a tie of rigidly striped maroon

and navy with his yellow-silk shirt and baggy brown slacks, called out a drink order to Dickens, then sat down next to Daisy. Within two seconds, he was nibbling her ear, and Daisy was giggling again.

Once more, Grady did a mental inventory. Archie, Junior was about thirty-eight or forty. He dyed his thinning hair boot black, all the better to see the bare patches of white-white scalp. His body was long, and too lean, but with the beginnings of a belly hanging over his belt. His eyes were the same near-colorless grey of his father's. He appeared to have the libido of a dozen rabbits. And, if his IQ could be raised a few points, he probably would have all the native intelligence of a pork roast.

Neither Junior nor Daisy looked particularly dangerous, Grady decided, longing to cross them both off his list of possible suspects. But he couldn't. Nobody could be dismissed, nothing could be overlooked.

After all, no two people could look dumber, or more innocent, than Daisy and Junior. That alone told Grady he had to keep watching them. He just wished Junior would take his damn tongue out of Daisy's damn ear.

"You will excuse me for being rude, Mr. Sullivan," Mitzi said, interrupting his thoughts (and not a moment too soon). "I would very much like to continue to ignore your presence, but I am well aware that this would be impolite. This does not, however, mean that we are less than totally disgusted with Archie for bringing you here, stuffing you under our noses."

"And the other one," A.W. added, first looking to Mitzi, as if for permission to speak. "This Kendall woman, who claims to be one of us."

"Bastard grandchild," Mitzi reminded her husband. "Totally of no consequence."

"But, darling—didn't you say that Dad could be up to something? First the detective here, and now—"

"Oh, do shut up, A.W.," Mitzi said without much heat, but in much the same tone as if she had just asked him to pass the salt.

"Allow me to refresh that for you, sir," Dickens said, taking A.W.'s glass from him, and Grady believed he saw a moment's pity in the butler's eyes.

The small interruption was enough for Mitzi, who all but pushed Dickens aside, the better to see Grady. "You're here to prove the girl's case, aren't you? To investigate her background, judge whether or not her claim is valid? I wasn't born yesterday, Mr. Sullivan. I can see what Archie is up to, so you might as well admit it."

Grady didn't like Mitzi Peevers. He didn't like her even a little bit. But he had to say one thing for her, she was right up front with her thoughts. He decided to give her something else to think about.

"As we discussed at dinner last night, Mrs. Peevers," he said in a slow, easy drawl meant to madden the crisp, fast-talking woman, "I am here to serve Mr. Peevers. That may include checking on the background of Miss Kendall, and it may not. It probably does. But I must tell you now, that's not the only reason I'm here. Mr. Peevers has informed me he feels his life may be in danger."

A.W. sprayed very expensive scotch into the air and all over his expensive blue suit. "What? Dad said . . . but why would . . . where would he get the idea that . . . his *life* in danger? That's ridiculous!"

A.W. was saying all the right words. He showed a mix of disbelief and outrage. Portrayed an air of shock, and innocence. But he ruined it all by looking, not at Grady, but at his wife as he said all those right words.

"We must have him committed," Mitzi pronounced coldly, slicing a look at Grady, her eyelids narrowed, assessing him, trying to read his mind, gauge his reaction to her husband's outburst. "There's no longer any question, A.W. The man is totally insane."

"Sandy says—" A.W. began, but his wife cut him off. "Milton Sandborn is as crazy as Archie. Doctor Sandborn? Hah! Some doctor, A.W. He's a drunk and a druggie. Half of the prescriptions he writes for your father go down his own throat, into his own arm. And you know why, don't you? It's because he wants—" Mitzi stopped talking, her mouth snapping shut like the jaws of a vise.

*Wants a piece of the action, of Archie's money? Is that what you almost said, Mitzi?* Those questions flashed through Grady's head, and he made a mental note to do some checking on one Doctor Milton Sandborn. That shouldn't be too difficult; Maisie could handle it.

Especially if the good doctor made house calls. Maisie was very good at talking people into saying things they'd had no intention of sharing with the world. Talking to him, measuring him, Maisie could then also get on the Internet and do some more investigating. And still have time left to lounge around at the pool and work on her tan.

The list of suspects, already large and fairly unwieldy, kept getting longer. Being as unlovable as he was, and as rich as he was, and with relatives who hated him and a friend who fed him drugs—no wonder Archie wanted someone watching his back.

There was movement at the doorway, and Grady watched as Muriel entered the drawing room, hanging on to the arm of a man about Grady's age. A tall man, with broad shoulders, blond "surfer" hair, a great tan, and a wide white smile. A man wearing an Armani suit very easily, probably because he always wore Armani or some other top designer. A handsome man. A man Muriel clearly liked. A man who smiled down at this woman at least twenty years older than himself, smiled at her as if she were the only woman in the world.

Grady was instantly suspicious. He didn't like to think that Muriel was unlovable, because he had seen nothing in her that would make him dislike her. But muddy-faced Muriel and this blond god, this boy-toy with the shrewd, actually intelligent look in his deep brown eyes?

Hardly.

"Hello, everyone," Muriel said as Grady pushed himself away from the mantel he'd been leaning against, idly wondering what the lucky people in the world were doing tonight. "Isn't this wonderful? I've convinced Jefferson to join us for dinner. Dickens," she added, a sudden tremor in her voice. "Would it be too terrible of me to ask you to set another place at the table?"

Dickens's expression said "I'd rather poke myself in the eye with a sharp stick," but he then bowed and answered, "It would be my pleasure. Attorney Banning? Your usual vegetarian dish, I presume?"

"If it wouldn't be too much trouble, Dickens, thank you," Attorney Jefferson Banning said, smiling around those even white teeth that looked capable of ripping open a still-warm gazelle and munching on its innards. "And how nice of you to remember."

"Eats here three times a week," Junior stage-whispered to Daisy, who giggled. "Isn't like any of us could forget."

"Jefferson?" Mitzi said, as the attorney approached and shook her hand, having been finally turned loose by Muriel, who was actually blushing as she took her seat. "Have you been upstairs again with Archie? Don't tell me he's changing his will *again*."

"Now, Mitzi," Jefferson said, his tone kind yet faintly condescending, as if he'd already fielded this question too many times, "you know I can't tell you that." Then he looked at Grady. "Hello. I'm Jefferson Banning. And you must be Grady Sullivan? We spoke on the phone, but I've yet to have the pleasure. Archie has already informed me that you were here."

Grady stepped forward, held out his hand, returned the lawyer's firm grip with one that should have brought the guy to his knees, and didn't. Clearly Banning was setting up the battle lines, and Grady's grip told him he knew it.

Grady instinctively didn't trust Banning, and the lawyer probably detested the private investigator, just on general principles. Rather, Grady thought, like a shark saying the barracuda's teeth were sharper. Theirs was definitely not going to be a great friendship.

"You wouldn't be one of the Philadelphia Sullivans, would you? Of Harford-Sullivan?" Banning asked, his expression saying that, if Grady were from the well-known banking family, it would greatly surprise him.

"Guilty as charged," Grady answered, making his

smile as big and dumb as possible. It was true; Grady had been born to wealthy parents, and wasn't the sort to rebel and be ashamed of that fact. He liked being rich, he enjoyed moving in Society. But he also liked what he did for a living. Loved what he did for a living. At least until a couple of days ago; now the jury was out.

He'd started his life after college as a beat cop, along with his now partner in D&S, Quinn Delaney. His maternal grandfather liked to tell people D&S Securities was some sort of investment firm, but his grandfather Sullivan, once a Philadelphia cop himself, had been delighted with Grady's career choices. As for his parents, his dad, Patrick Sullivan, and his mother, the former Miss Leticia Harford—well, Grady figured there was still time, they'd get used to the idea, someday.

Jefferson Banning tilted his head to one side, examining Grady closely through narrowed eyes. "Won the Governor's Cup last year in a three-hole playoff with Bert Tilson? I heard that was one hell of a battle. Three extra sudden-death holes, until you eagled that par five. Damn long hole, as I recall. You must have an amazing drive."

"I got lucky. And Bert gave me a good fight," Grady said, trying not to look too pleased with the lawyer's comment on his golf game. Okay, so maybe he liked the man a little. It wouldn't be right to prejudge the guy on the basis of his white teeth and the way he'd been looking at Muriel. Maybe he was just a friendly sort, who didn't like private investigators. Golfers, he seemed to like well enough.

"Fascinating!" Jefferson said, giving Grady's hand one last squeeze. "I'd love the chance to take you to my club for a round. Did you bring your clubs?" When Grady nodded, because he went nowhere without his golf clubs if he could help it, Jefferson reached into his pocket, pulled out an ivory-colored business card. "Give me a call, okay?"

"Junie plays golf," Daisy piped up happily. "Don't you, Junie. Maybe you could join them for a quadruple?"

"That's *foursome,* sweetums," Junior answered, having at last taken his tongue out of his fiancée's ear. "And it would only be three of us. Banning, Sullivan, and me. Three, Daisy." He grinned up at Grady and the lawyer. "Isn't she adorable? Pity A.W. here never took up the game. It might be nice, an outing at the club with Dad's hack lawyer and his bodyguard."

*Mental note to self,* Grady thought: *Junie isn't as dumb as he looks. Or acts.*

"Junior," Mitzi said in the tones of one speaking to a particularly backward child, "you know that A.W., being the eldest, has had to devote himself to the company. Not everyone can spend his life like a grasshopper, just singing and playing through the days, marrying and copulating where he will."

Junior didn't miss a beat before answering heatedly, "At least I get some, which is more than Asswipe here can say. Hell, he probably thanks God every night that he doesn't get any. Come on, sweetums. We don't have to take this, we're outta here."

Jefferson leaned closer to Grady as Junior and Daisy made their exit, Daisy asking him what "cop-u-what-she-said" was. "Not exactly the Brady Bunch, are they? Or even David and little Ricky, come to think of it. But they can be fun."

While Jefferson seemed so friendly and mellow, Grady asked, "Have you met Annie Kendall?"

The lawyer shook his head. "Not yet, which is why I let Muriel talk me into staying for dinner when I have a nice thick porterhouse waiting in my fridge."

"Porterhouse?" Grady repeated, raising one eyebrow. "You're kidding, right?"

"It drives Dickens nuts when I unexpectedly stay for dinner and shoot his menu plans straight to hell. Archie's idea, actually, but I went along with it. God knows I have to do something to keep my humor, and my sanity, running out here several times a week, playing Archie's games. As it is, right now Dickens is cursing us all as he rearranges the table yet again, removing two place settings after adding one for me."

Okay, so now Grady didn't just think Jefferson Banning was all right. Now he really liked him. He wished he didn't, as everyone who came under Archie Peevers's roof had to be considered a potential murderer. He decided to introduce him to Maisie, if she ever showed up in the drawing room, she and the absent Annie Kendall. Maisie could see through a fake in ten seconds, five if she was really on her game.

Just as if the thought had conjured them up, Annie and Maisie entered the drawing room together, laughing at some shared joke.

He excused himself and walked across the room, to meet them more than halfway.

"Grady and me?" he could hear Maisie saying. "Honey, when pigs fly! I work with him, remember? That means I know all his faults. If I told you the number of 'it's been nice knowing you' bouquets of roses I've sent for that man—oh, hello, Grady. Don't you look nice tonight, honey, all buffed and polished. Annie and I were just getting to know each other better. Weren't we, Annie?"

"Remember that raise, Maisie?" Grady growled, and Maisie looked up at him, batting her heavily mascaraed eyes. "Then ask yourself if, with all my faults, I'm to be trusted to keep my promise."

"Aw, honey," Maisie said, stepping up to him, running one manicured finger down his necktie, giving the end of it a small flip that pulled it out from his suit jacket, "you don't really think I'm scared, do you? You sweet, silly man."

Then, as Grady watched Maisie's eyes widen, undoubtably at the sight of the blond god Jefferson Banning, she mumbled, "Excuse me, honey, I think I've found me a live one. Be patient, gorgeous, Maisie's on her way," and she left Annie and Grady to look at each other, then burst out laughing.

"Is she always so . . . well, so like that?" Annie asked.

"Actually, she's pretty much on her best behavior tonight," Grady admitted as he opened his suit coat, tucked his tie back inside. "You're lucky, you know. Three more minutes, and you'd have been late. I think Dickens would probably then order you out into the gardens, where he'd chop off your head with a petrified flamingo."

Annie laughed again, and Grady decided he liked the throaty sound of that laughter very much. He liked the way her dark curls bounced around her head with a life of their own. He liked her smile, and the way she smelled, sort of like honey and cream.

He offered her his arm just as a slightly frazzled-looking Dickens appeared in the far doorway to announce that dinner was now being served in the small dining room.

*Maybe,* Grady thought, *I'll just relax tonight, take the evening off, and get to know Annie Kendall a little better.*

After all, all work and no play had never been one of his favorite plans. . . .

ing Detective appeared in the set doorway, to announce
that dinner was now being served in the small dining
room.
    Fine, Annie thought. I'd sit next to Nicole Peevers, if
it would get me to know Jeffson Banning a little better.
After all, work and play and might make me sane and
his drawing room.

# Six

*Here comes a candle to light you to bed,*
*Here comes a chopper to chop off your head.*
                      —Anonymous

    Annie sat beside Jefferson Banning back in the draw-
ing room after dinner, listening to him tell her yet another
story. He'd had her laughing almost to the point of tears
all through dinner, telling story after story, many with
the punch line showing himself as the butt of the joke.
She'd been enjoying herself so much that when the
Peevers family said their chilly good-nights right after
dessert, she could smile at them and sincerely wish them
a good evening.
    ". . . so there I was," Jefferson was saying now,
"knee-deep in bubbles, reading the directions again, and
finally figuring out that I'd used dishwashing detergent
instead of dish*washer* detergent before I left the apartment to pick up a pizza for dinner. Big difference between the two products, if you've never tried it, believe
me."

"It was really that bad?" Annie asked, still chuckling over Jefferson's description of the wall of suds that had nearly met him at the door when he got back from the shop with his pepperoni and double cheese pizza.

"Remember, I wanted to do it right, so I filled both cups inside the dishwasher to the brim with the stuff. Annie, honey, Vesuvius was a smaller eruption. I was still shoveling mountains of suds out of the kitchen an hour later, when my mother phoned to ask how I was doing my first night alone in my new bachelor pad. I swear the woman had this *radar* that alerted her every time her little darling screwed up."

"What did you tell her?" Annie asked, holding her coffee cup just below her mouth and taking a quick look at Grady, who didn't seem to think the story funny at all.

"I told her everything was just great, of course," Jefferson said, then winced comically. "That's when she told me she was calling from the car phone and she and Dad would be knocking on my door in five minutes, bringing me a housewarming gift."

"Busted!" Annie said, shaking her head.

"Not really," Jefferson said. "They were bringing me Mrs. Bateson, the family housekeeper, along with a huge picnic basket holding dinner for four. Mrs. B had the floor mopped up in no time—she'd brought a mop and bucket along with some other stuff, which I'd neglected to buy. Remember, I was fresh out of college. To me, having my own place meant I should have the world's coolest stereo, a couch, a bed, a lava light, and that's about all. So I was trying to clear the mess with bath towels. *Lots* of bath towels. And, since the pizza was already cold, besides having fallen out of my hands in my shock when I'd walked into the kitchen, the roasted chicken was pretty neat, too."

"Do you always land on your feet?" Annie asked, as Grady got to his feet and walked over to pour himself a drink. He'd been drinking water all night, said no to coffee or an after-dinner drink, but now he was pouring himself a neat scotch. For some reason she didn't want to investigate, this made her mood even brighter.

"Most times, I do," Jefferson admitted. "Except, when Dad retired from the practice to sit on the federal bench, and my brother and I split up the practice between us, I drew the short straw and got Archie. Personally, I think Grey cheated, but I've never been able to prove it, and he refuses to testify under oath."

Maisie came back into the room after having excused herself to repair her makeup, and Jefferson stood up quickly, saying he had to leave, as he was taking depositions in a civil case the next morning.

Looking to Maisie, who was making a beeline for the lawyer, and then to Jefferson, a big strong man who just now looked a little *hunted,* Annie also rose, saying, "Of course."

She'd stretched out her leg at one point during dinner, only to come into contact with Maisie's panty-hose-clad foot as the secretary reached out under the table to play footsie with Jefferson. Annie knew it had to be the lawyer, because he had the strangest expression on his face, as if he wanted to say something but couldn't figure out exactly what. Maisie, who had been just about sitting on her spine across the table, straightened up for a moment, smiled knowingly at Annie. But by the time the second course was being served, she was sliding down again, obviously ready for another round of her little game.

Annie put out her hand, and Jefferson took it. "I can't thank you enough for such a wonderful evening. I had been worried how it would go, being with the family for the first time, but you made it all so easy. Even enjoyable."

Grady grumbled something under his breath, crossed one leg over the other, and sipped his scotch.

"Grady?" Jefferson said, turning to him, so that Grady stood up, took the lawyer's hand. "I guess we'll be seeing a lot of each other these next few weeks, if Archie has anything to say about it. It can be a real bitch—excuse me, Annie—playing pawn to his king, but it pays the bills."

"I'm pretty sure it does more than pay the bills, Jefferson," Grady said, his smile wide, his tone friendly. "What do you guys get an hour? Six, seven hundred?"

"Higher," the lawyer said, "and, sometimes, the odd free vegetarian meal as a bonus. Call me, and we'll set up a golf date, all right? Maisie? It's been . . . an experience."

"Of course it has, honey," Maisie chirped, preening. "It always is."

Then Jefferson took his leave, and Annie didn't think he'd noticed that Grady was still a little white around his mouth, and that there had been a small tic in his left temple as the two shook hands.

"You don't like him," Annie said, the moment Jefferson had gone. "Why?"

"I don't know Banning well enough either to like or dislike him, although Maisie might want that job, right,

Maisie? Now, Miss Kendall, what do you say we get us some air? Not you, Maisie," he added quickly, as the secretary looked as if she wanted to join them. "You go on upstairs and get on the Internet, get me that information I asked for."

"Oh, honey, I'm impressed. You're so sexy when you slave-drive. You'll get your information when I get to it, as usual," the secretary said, looking down, frowning at the sight of the fingertips of one hand as she held it out in front of her. "I must do my hair, and give myself a manicure. Definitely." She looked at Grady once more. "Priorities. It's how I make your world go around so smoothly, honey."

"Maisie," Grady said, as Annie laughed, shaking his head in defeat. "Just once, won't you humor me, let me think I'm your boss and you're my employee?"

"Ha! Yeah, right. I'll think about it, honey," Maisie answered, then turned and walked out of the room, her backside twitching as she navigated in her high-heeled shoes.

"She can't even make a decent cup of coffee, but we'd fall apart without her. Now, let's get that air, all right?" Grady said, taking Annie's elbow in preparation for walking her toward the French doors that led out onto a patio and the gardens beyond. Maybe he thought she wouldn't go with him otherwise, or maybe he thought she couldn't find the French doors on her own. Not that it mattered, because Annie rather liked the feel of his hand on her bare flesh.

She decided not to push Grady any more about Jefferson, even if it could be fun, and instead turned the conversation to her new "relatives" and what he might think about them.

"Your *relatives?*" Grady asked after she'd asked her question. "Jumping the gun, aren't you? According to the game plan of this ridiculous house of cards Archie's building, isn't that still to be proved?"

"You know I can't prove it," Annie said, keeping her voice low even as they walked across the patio and down the steps to the garden. "But this is method acting, immersing myself in the role, living the part twenty-four-seven. All the best actors do it."

"Probably all the best con artists, too," Grady remarked, stopping to break off a white rose, strip it free of thorns, then hand it to her. Surprised, and rather touched, she took it, held it under her nose to sniff the fragrance. "Because *normal* people don't answer personal ads where someone is asking you to audition to be their long-lost heir."

Annie tipped up her chin, tossed the rose into the shrubbery. "And how do you know that? There could be dozens of us out there, finding our way home through the personal ads." Then she let her chin drop. "Okay, okay, so that's a stretch. It isn't like us long-lost heirs have a club or anything, attend regular meetings, pay dues, even plan bus trips to the casinos in Atlantic City. But it *could* happen. Just because it isn't happening in this case doesn't mean it never does. Now, tell me what you think so far about the family. Remember, you did say we'd be working together."

"I said that? Oh, I don't think so," Grady answered as they walked along, out of the garden, and out onto the wide sweep of lawn that stretched acres in front of them in three directions. The huge grounds had been well landscaped with a small boxwood maze, with small stands of trees here and there, with several seating groups, and not one but two gazebos. The whole place looked like something out of a planned English country estate. Not that Annie was paying much attention to the dusk-dim scenery at the moment.

Grady Sullivan was maddening! An extremely maddening man. Smart mouth, smart smile, too-smart twinkle in his gorgeous green eyes. The funny thing—not ha-ha funny, but *weird* funny—was that, handsome as Grady was, Jefferson Banning was even more handsome. Bordering on the gorgeous, when you got right down to it.

And yet she already knew she could only ever look at the handsome lawyer as a friend, someday maybe even a good friend. Whereas—to think "lawyerly"—she couldn't look at Grady and his too-long sandy hair, the laugh lines around his eyes, the fullness of his smile, without wanting—now using Maisie's terminology—to jump his bones.

She really hated that about Grady Sullivan.

Annie kicked at a stone that had dared to mar the plush green grass. "No, you didn't say that. What you said was that I'm to stick to you like glue so you can baby-sit me, save me from my own idiocy."

"I don't think I used quite those words, but that sounds good. Which means, by the way, that I don't want you dashing off to some love nest with our friendly lawyer."

"Oh yeah? For the month, or ever?" Annie asked, because she couldn't help herself.

Grady stopped walking, turned to her, took both of

her hands in his. He was so much taller, and the sun had nearly disappeared, so that she had to look carefully to try to read the expression on his face.

*"What?"* she all but exploded after he just stood there, staring at her for long, uncomfortable moments. He just stood there, looking at her as if she were some new species of crawling insect or something, and rubbed his thumbs over the back of her hands, which sure wasn't helping matters.

"I don't know," he said at last, shaking his head. She could hear the confusion in his voice, see it in his eyes. Along with another emotion that once again had her knees daring to do an impossible bend-over-backwards routine. "I make it a rule never to mix business with pleasure. I sure don't get romantically involved with nutcases."

"Meaning you'll never kiss Archie? That . . . that seems reasonable," Annie said, her voice coming out a little squeakily, much to her disgust.

"Damn, but you're a pain in my backside," Grady said, and the next thing Annie knew he was kissing her, and she was kissing him back for all she was worth.

There hadn't been a cloud in the sky when they'd come outside, but suddenly Annie thought she heard thunder. She certainly could see the flash of white-hot lightning behind her closed eyes and feel the hot wind of an impending storm rush over her body, heating it inside and out.

He slanted his lips first one way, then the other, teasing her with his mouth, his tongue. His arms held her tightly, closely, but gently enough that she could free her own arms and wrap them around his neck as she pushed her body closer, closer.

The thunder crashed again, the sound sharp, like the breaking of glass.

Grady lifted his head, looked back toward the house, his muscles even more tense than they had been. "What was that?"

Annie, realizing what she had been about to say yes to, even before he'd asked, stepped back, ran a hand through her curls. "What was what? I didn't hear anything." Only the mental boom and blast of thunder, and the too-fast beating of her heart. That's all.

Grady pointed, even as he took her hand and started back toward the house at a trot that, thanks to his long legs, had her running to keep up. "There, on the second floor," he said. "See it? Third window from the left corner. It's broken."

Annie, still trying to catch her breath after Grady's stirring kisses, and not at her best in three-inch heels, dared to take a quick peep upward as she ran. "Where? Oh, there. Ohmigod! *There!* That's Archie's rooms!"

She stopped, shocked, and Grady left her where she stood, running ahead, seemingly trying to set a new world record for the hundred-yard dash. Annie took two deep breaths, bent to take off her shoes, and set off after him.

Everyone in the house must have hit the second-floor hallway at the same time, some coming from their rooms, Annie and Grady having run up the front stairs.

"I heard a crash," A.W. said, tightening the sash on what had to be the ugliest smoking jacket this side of any of the tuxedos worn at last year's Grammy awards.

"He must have fallen, broken a hip," Mitzi declared,

still holding the book she'd been reading when she heard the crash, her index finger marking the page on the closed book. Annie could see the title: *How to Be Your Own Financial Advisor.* Interesting.

Junior and Daisy ran down the hallway, Junior's mouth smeared with Killer Red lipstick, Daisy's hot pink fur-trimmed peignoir looking as if she'd put it on backwards.

"Any special reason you're just standing here?" Grady asked, as the four all but hugged either side of the hall-way to let him past.

"Well, Dickens isn't here, and . . ." A.W. shut his mouth and shrugged. "He locks his door, all right? Dad locks his door to keep us out at night. Dickens has the only key."

Grady spat out a word that made Annie flinch, al-though it was sort of suitable, considering that Archie was, after all, the toilet-paper king. He then added, "Did anyone check the door? Are you sure it's locked?"

"Dad wouldn't like it if . . . ," A.W. began, then shut up once more. Annie began to wonder if the man ever completed a sentence.

"I knocked one night," Junior supplied helpfully, "and he sent me a note the next morning telling me one more stupid mistake like that and he'd have me neutered, then mount what he'd sliced off and hang it in the foyer of the plant. We don't disturb Dad at night, Mr. Sullivan. Believe me."

"I phoned Dickens's room a few moments ago," Mitzi said, in a voice that made this sort of lunacy sound almost reasonable. "I'm sure he'll be here in his own good time. It's not as if we can hear Archie crying out in pain."

"Figures. The butler has his own telephone. I'm only

surprised the bastard doesn't have an unlisted number," Grady said, and Annie nearly laughed out loud. But this was too serious for laughter. Archie's window was broken, and it was terribly quiet in his rooms.

"Maybe he can't call for help!" Daisy exclaimed as if reading Annie's mind (now there was a frightening thought!). The blonde grabbed on to Junior, nearly climbing him as if he were a tree. "We only got back from dinner about a half hour ago, and we didn't hear anything then. But then we heard a crash, didn't we, Junie? A *big* crash! Maybe he's fallen into a mirror and sliced his head off. Oh, Junie, maybe he's *dead!*"

There was that swear word again, muttered under Grady's breath, but Annie was sure she was the only one who'd heard it either time. "Look, we're wasting time here," she said, stepping past Grady, who appeared to be prepared to launch himself against the door, breaking it down. "How about I try the knob, okay? It could be open."

It wasn't, and Grady stepped as far back as he could, turned to one side, and prepared to run across the hallway, knock the door down. Annie privately thought he'd break his shoulder on the first try, as this was an old house, and it was a thick, solid door, but the look in Grady's eyes didn't lend itself to her wanting to point that out to him.

Grady was saved from possible physical harm by the arrival of Dickens, who was dressed in knife-pleated black slacks and a black turtleneck sweater that hugged his flat midsection. Although, at first glance, he looked immaculate, Annie noticed small colored stains on his cuff, and the smell of oil paint hung around him. Clearly the man was off duty at this hour, and just as clearly he appeared to be less than happy he'd been disturbed.

"I was concentrating on my latest painting," he announced, looking at Annie, seemingly aware of her scrutiny. "Everyone should have a hobby. Now, if you'll all just stand back?" He looked at the small crowd in the hallway, then extracted a key from his pocket and inserted it in the keyhole.

Grady waited only until the key turned in the lock, then pushed Dickens out of the way and stepped up to the door, a pistol Annie had somehow missed as she'd run her hands up and down his back appearing in his right hand. "Nobody comes in until I give the all clear, understand?"

Considering the fact that A.W. had stepped behind his wife at the sight of Grady's weapon, and that Daisy had fainted dead away in Junior's arms, Annie didn't think Grady had much to worry about if he was afraid a hysterical gaggle of loving children might try to trample him to get to their dearest, darling daddy.

Grady pushed the door back slowly and carefully, then stepped inside more quickly than Annie could imagine. The weapon was now held in both hands as he stretched his arms out in front of him, fanning them back and forth with each sharp turn of his body, just like in the movies.

Then the door closed, softly, and Annie and the Peeverses and Dickens were left in the hallway. They all seemed to have mutually agreed to have a moment of silence, just in case Archie had gone to his final reward. The silence was deafening, and then unexpectedly shattered.

"What's going on? Why are you all standing out here?"

Mitzi shrieked, Annie flinched, and the imperturbable Dickens turned and bowed to Muriel Peevers. "Your father may have met with a misadventure," he said, then added, "or Mr. Sullivan is in the process of making a total ass of himself and getting himself fired. We are awaiting his reappearance to be sure."

Muriel pulled the edges of her wilting-lilac-dyed chenille robe close against her thin breast even as she attempted to shield everyone's view of her inexpertly rolled pink curlers with her other hand. She suddenly looked small and lost and very afraid. "Daddy could be hurt?"

"A window broke," Annie said, putting an arm around the shaking woman, trying to comfort her. "We really don't know if anything's wrong. Mr. Sullivan is just being careful, doing his job." She said those last words while glaring at Dickens, who only shrugged and began picking at a bit of dried paint on his sleeve.

The door opened and all conversation stopped as Grady reappeared. "He's all right," he said first, looking at Annie. "Shaken up, but all right. You can go in, but don't touch anything. Dickens?" The butler came to attention. "He wants you to call Dr. Sandborn."

"He needs Sandy? Oh, God—*Daddy!*" Muriel cried out, rushing forward so quickly that Annie couldn't stop her. The rest of the Peevers clan followed her, leaving Annie and Grady alone in the hallway. She watched as he replaced his weapon in the shoulder holster beneath his suit jacket. He rubbed a hand over his face, almost as if he was scrubbing it clean.

"So?" she asked at last. "Are you going to tell me what happened? Did he fall? Is he all right?"

"That would depend," Grady answered. "He was on the floor next to the bed, his face as white as a sheet. Just cowering there, his hands over his head, his knees drawn up, his backside stuck in the air. Not a pretty sight, I can tell you. He was shaking so badly I knew he was breathing, so I quickly checked the dressing room and bath, but he's the only one in there. I put him in a chair because he won't get back into bed. Not that I can blame him. Poor old Archie. He's had quite a shock."

"Why?" Annie tried to look past Grady, but the anteroom was so large, and the the bedroom itself even larger, and darker, that she couldn't see anything but the glowing white-blond of Daisy's hair in the light of the single lamp that had been lit.

"Take a look," Grady said, "but like I said to the others, don't touch anything."

Still looking at Grady, Annie slowly walked into the antechamber, then passed by the deep red velvet curtains and fully into the bedchamber.

There was Archie, slumped in a chair beside the fire, Muriel kneeling at his feet, holding his hands.

There was Junior, his arm tucked protectively around Daisy, his hand low enough to squeeze her bottom, which he was doing.

There was A.W., looking at Mitzi.

There was Mitzi, her mouth pursed and twisted to one side, looking at Archie's bed.

Annie looked at Archie's bed, too.

And saw the short, deadly crossbow arrow stuck into the headboard, just above the pillows.

Annie, her stomach turning over inside her as all the little hairs on her arms and legs prickled and stood up straight, borrowed Grady's swear word and used it herself.

# Seven

*The quarrel is a very pretty quarrel
as it stands; we should only spoil it
by trying to explain it.*
                —Richard Brinsley Sheridan

Doctor Milton "Sandy" Sandborn arrived within twenty minutes, fully pushing wide the front door Dickens had only cracked open, using his offensive-lineman-wide shoulders to advantage as he then barreled through the foyer and disappeared up the stairs without saying a word to anyone.

Grady had gotten only a cursory look at the man, but the doctor certainly did make an impression. Six-foot-five if he was an inch, and with the aforementioned NFL lineman's heft and breadth, remarkably only slightly gone to seed now that he was in his early seventies, Sandy Sandborn was about as easy to overlook as a pissed-off elephant in an elevator.

A thick shock of silver hair. A drinker's red, bulbous

nose. Fat, droopy jowls you could hang on and use for a swing.

He dressed well, for a mountain. A thin mauve-silk mock turtleneck that molded to his body, seemed to choke him into his red-faced look that said he either had high blood pressure or had recently been gagging on something. Designer jeans, with a label that looked no larger than a postage stamp when slapped to his back pocket. Prada slip-ons with no socks. And a black bag large enough to hold two bedpans, a nurse, or half a pharmacy.

Grady, after hearing the Peeverses talk about the doctor, was betting on the half a pharmacy.

He was still looking up the staircase when Annie came out of the drawing room. "That was the doctor, wasn't it? Shouldn't the police have been here by now, too?"

"They should have been," he answered tightly, "if they'd been called, which they haven't. Archie wants to keep this in the family."

"But—but that's ridiculous. Somebody took a *shot* at him with that arrow! I'll go talk to him . . ."

Grady grabbed her arm, wheeled her around, signaled with a dip of his head that Dickens should open the door, and took Annie outside. He slipped off his suit jacket and draped it over her shoulders in the cool night air, pretending not to notice as she goggled at the shoulder holster strapped to him.

"Look, *you* know we should call the police. *I* know we should call the police. It's logical. But we're talking Peevers here, Annie. We're also talking one suddenly turned-up possible long-lost granddaughter, a bunch of nitwit heirs who could flunk a sobriety test at ten in the morning, and a fortune worth more than a billion dollars. Would you really want the local cops nosing around here—nosing around in your background?"

Annie, her mouth closed, pushed her tongue against her bottom lip, running it back and forth a time or two, as if trying to taste her answer before she voiced it. "Okay. No. No, I don't think I want the local police asking me questions. The only way I stay credible, because I agree with Archie on this one, is for you to know the truth and then not tell it while you pretend to investigate my claim."

"Right. Maybe more convoluted than I would have put it, but right. You can't stand the heat, Annie, not if Archie wants to go on with this stupid game he's playing, and he's already assured me that he does. He also told me he trusts me to find out who tried to turn him into the meat portion of a Peevers shish kebab."

"Are you thinking he planned this? I mean, like the orange juice? Is that another reason you agreed not to call in the police?"

Grady shook his head, remembering the look on Archie's face when he found him, the way the man was shaking, nearly drooling with fright. "No, Archie didn't have a hand in this one. That's the one thing I'm sure of, in the midst of all this idiocy. Now, come on, I want to take a look around, and we're back to that stick to me like glue idea, okay?"

"We're going looking for clues? Oh, neat!" Annie said, allowing him to take her hand, lead her around to the back of the mansion and a view of Archie's broken window. "What clues are we looking for?"

"A sign with 'I stood here,' and a big red arrow pointing to the spot would be good," Grady said, "but I don't think we're going to be that lucky."

"There's no need to be sarcastic," Annie said.

"No need? I'm out here in the dark, armed only with my big bad gun—which means nothing, as I'm sure nobody's hanging around, hoping to be caught—and the flashlight Dickens handed me, without even a plastic bag to put any evidence in if we find any, investigating a crime scene with a woman who thinks having her supposed grandfather nearly impaled by a crossbow arrow is *neat*. All we really need now is your Junior Detective Kit and maybe a secret decoder ring."

"Oh, don't be so touchy." Annie pulled free of his grip. "I really don't like you, you know. And you used the word *impaled* incorrectly. It's much nastier than just having an arrow shot through you, believe me. I read this novel once, all about some ancient land where these terrible rulers used to impale their enemies. They stripped them naked and tied them to stakes so that they were sort of standing on tiptoe over another really, really sharp stake stuck into the ground. As they got tired and couldn't stand up straight anymore, they'd start to slide down, and—*what?* Why are you looking at me like that?"

Grady had stopped dead, was looking at her, knowing his eyes were nearly popping out of his head. "You're weird," he said at last, shaking his head. "Who reads books like that?"

"I did, back in high school. I loved books about the pirates of the Mediterranean and stuff like that. Swashbuckling and righting wrongs and winning the fair lady. And stop looking at me that way. I'll bet you read crime thrillers, and nothing can get gorier than those books, unless you really like reading a blow-by-blow of an autopsy."

"No thanks, I've seen those firsthand," Grady said, wishing he didn't still remember his first autopsy. He'd been a green rookie, and thought he'd been doing well. Right up until the moment the Y cut was made. That had been the last thing he'd remembered until he woke up on the floor, listening to the sound of the saw as the medical examiner sliced open the guy's skull. He'd gotten better at observing, but he'd never numbered it among his most favorite things.

He turned the subject back to Annie's reading habits. "Aren't you supposed to be reading those Oprah books, or something? Isn't that what women read?"

"Right. Sure. If you like a lot of boo-hoo and *uplifting messages* and unhappy endings. I read stuff where the guy gets the girl and the bad guys get what's coming to them. And I'm not weird," she added sulkily.

"Yes, you are. You're here, aren't you?"

Annie gave him a push in the stomach. "Oh, sure, bring *that* up again. Grady-one-note. Pass the salt— you're brain-dead because you took this crazy job. Let's take a walk—you actually asked for a 1099? It's a lovely evening, isn't it—you've stupidly put yourself in possible danger, you know. Is that it? Have you covered it all now? Told me everything that's wrong with me, how *dumb* I am? Because, you know, if this is going to be a running gag—and not a very funny one—I'm probably going to have to hurt you."

Grady looked at her for long moments, trying very hard not to laugh. She was adorable. Nuts, but adorable.

"Are you through?" he asked at last. "Because, if you are, I've got a job to do. Coming?"

He walked out past the patio, onto the grass, far enough away from the house to be able to stand and look up at Archie's window. Annie stood right beside him, also looking up.

"The trajectory would be all wrong, if the shooter stood on the ground," she said after a moment. "The arrow would have hit the ceiling, right?"

"The *trajectory?*" Grady repeated. "I thought you didn't read crime novels."

"I have very eclectic tastes," Annie answered, still looking up, and not at him. "So sue me."

"Nah," Grady answered, taking her hand and walking away from the house, toward the nearest stand of trees. "I'll let the Peevers heirs do that. Unless just putting you in jail is enough for them."

"Here we go again," Annie said, sighing. "Wind him up, folks, and he'll tell you all about Annie Kendall and how she's screwing up her life. Now, why do I think you don't care about that, Grady? Why do I think that I'm just in your way, another problem you hadn't counted on? Which doesn't explain that kiss, earlier, but I'm sure it was a pity kiss because poor dumb, weird Annie Kendall might just feel better if big wonderful Grady Sullivan tosses her a cookie. There, there, little girl. Just take this, then go sit in a corner and behave yourself."

Grady stopped walking yet again. At this rate, it would be dawn soon, and he wouldn't need the damn flashlight. He bent his head, scratched behind his ear, tried not to look at Annie. That wasn't hard, because it was now fully dark, and with very little moon.

"About . . . earlier. About the kiss . . . ," he began, then wondered just when he'd reverted to awkward schoolboy status. "Look, Annie," he said, taking her arms, "what happened earlier out here? Well, it was physical attraction, that's all."

Even in the dark, he could see her rolling her eyes. "Well, of course it was. *I* knew that. Physical attraction, plain and simple. And proximity. And probably the fact that I'm the only eligible woman here except for Muriel, and I really don't think you're her type. You didn't really think I was hearing wedding bells or something, did you? It was a kiss, Grady, no big deal."

"Yeah, okay," he said, wondering why her easy agreement bothered him. Hadn't she felt anything at all? Damn. He'd reacted straight down to his toes. "Just so we understand each other. So we're clear on this, right?"

"As a bell," Annie agreed, then motioned with her head. "That clump of trees over there. Do you think the arrow came from that spot?"

Arrow? Spot? Still looking at Annie's mouth, remembering the taste of it, it took Grady a second or two to remember why he was out there, why they both were out there.

"Could be, although it's not quite in line with the window. If the shot came from there, the perp was no amateur."

"So? Dickens was pretty late coming upstairs," Annie pointed out. "And he says everyone should have a hobby. Maybe he has more than one. I only say this because I don't really like the guy all that much. And remember. It's almost always the butler that's done it."

"Dickens paints, Annie," Grady reminded her, then

saw her chin thrust out once more. "Okay, okay, I'll take a look around in his rooms tomorrow. You can keep him busy somewhere else while I do my B&E."

"Perp, B&E. Boy, you can take the boy away from the cop, but you just can't take the cop out of the boy. You were a cop, right? I mean, the way you handled that gun upstairs earlier? And I don't think private eyes get invited to autopsies."

"Security professional, please, not private eye," Grady said with a small smile, then moved the flashlight so that the beam searched higher into the trees. "That one looks like a possible hiding place. Nice low limbs, easy to climb. Sturdy trunk, and definitely high enough. Now, you stay here. I'm going to take a look."

"Yes sir, Officer sir," Annie said, saluting smartly.

Grady grumbled under his breath and lowered the beam to the ground, watching every step he took, looking for other footsteps, anything that would tell him he was on the right track.

There hadn't been time for dew to form on the grass, but since it hadn't been mowed too recently, and the grass was at least five inches long, each time Grady took a step there was a slight depression from his weight. If he made marks, so had the hopeful killer.

Still twenty feet from the stand of trees, he caught his first break. Definite footprints leading off the brick path that meandered through the grass. Large prints. Male. But not deep. The guy had to be a lightweight. *Or maybe he was walking with a stake tickling his backside,* Grady thought, then shook his head, shivered. It was going to take a while before he got that particular image out of his brain, thanks to Annie.

"Why are you stopping?" Annie asked, still standing on the brick path. "Do you see something? What do you see?"

He shook his head, waved her over. "Come on, just step where I'm stepping, okay? It's not like we're trying to preserve a crime scene or anything." When she had joined him, standing directly behind him, her hands on his waist, trying to lean around him to see what the flashlight revealed, he said, "Footprints. See?"

"The perp's?" she asked, her tone hushed, awed. "Cool!"

"You know, Annie, I've seen the old Nick and Nora Charles detective movies. I watched *Hart To Hart* reruns on television, the ones with Robert Wagner and— Stephanie Powers, wasn't it? I'll admit to never missing an episode of *Murder, She Wrote*. I love television, especially the older shows. *The Honeymooners, I Love Lucy.* But not once, not once, mind you, can I recall ever seeing Gracie Allen and George Burns working together to solve a crime. And yet, tonight, I can almost imagine what that episode might be like. So, yes, Gracie, to answer your question—this is pretty cool."

"You know, even when you're nice you're a pain," Annie said, giving him a push in the back. "Now, come on. Aren't we going to follow the footprints?"

That had been the plan, but now Grady altered it, just because Annie had thought it to be the logical next step. He fanned the flashlight to the right, then to the left, looking to see the returning tracks as the perp walked back to the path, if that's what the guy had done.

He fanned the flashlight again, then held it on one

spot. "Damn. That's interesting," he said, talking to himself.

"What? What's interesting? Is it a clue?"

"You tell me, Annie," he said. "Look at these footprints." He moved the light to illuminate the first set he'd found. "See them?"

"Yes, yes, I see them. So?"

"Now look at these, and tell me what's wrong with them."

He moved the flashlight to the left, illuminating the second set of footprints. Then he waited. Knowing Annie, even as little as he did at this point, he didn't think he'd have long to wait.

"Okay, same footprints. Same size and all, right?" Annie said, squinting at the ground. "And going the other way, like as if he was walking back to the path. That makes sense—*oh!* Wait a minute!"

She stepped out from behind him, carefully picking her way over to the second set of prints, then hunkered down to get a closer look. "That's impossible!"

Grady joined her. "Not really. Now, give me your thoughts. What happened here?"

Annie traced a finger over the edge of one of the imprints. "The shoes are on the wrong feet," she said unnecessarily. "Either that or the guy was walking with his legs crossed, and I don't think that's possible."

"Right. Now your thoughts?"

Annie stood up, nearly knocking Grady in the chin with her head. He hadn't realized he'd been standing so close to her. "They weren't the guy's shoes? He wore them, took them off to climb the tree then, in the dark, and because he was in a hurry to get away, he slipped his feet into the wrong shoes when he got down out of the tree. How am I doing?"

"Quite well," Grady said, pretty impressed with her deductive reasoning. "You might also notice, if you look at the footprints I'm leaving as I walk, then at yours, that these prints aren't as deep as mine."

"Meaning? No, wait, I think I've got it! Maybe it wasn't a man. Maybe it was a woman?" She frowned. "Or a really skinny man?"

"Yeah, that's what I'm thinking," Grady admitted. "It gets curiouser and curiouser, doesn't it? Let's go look at the trees, figure out which one the guy—person—used."

"You'll ruin your slacks," Annie pointed out a minute later as Grady grabbed on to a low-hanging branch, ready to pull himself up into the first crook of a tall maple tree.

"I've got a hefty expense account," he answered, testing the limb's strength, then starting his climb.

He hadn't climbed a tree since he was a kid, but some skills weren't forgotten. In less than a minute, he'd climbed about as high as he thought it was safe to climb. Then, leaning out onto the branch facing the house, he split the leaves and looked toward the broken window.

"No, definitely not an amateur," he said, mostly to himself. "But it could be done."

Then he noticed a small half-broken branch just ahead of him. A second one to his left. Just small branches, barely branches yet at all, but almost twigs, with just a few leaves on them. If that wasn't enough, when he ran the beam of the flashlight up and down the limb he was half-lying on, he saw where some bark had been scratched.

And then the kicker. A small piece of black knit cloth, stuck to the end of a short, thick, dead stub of a branch.

Dickens had been wearing black. It looked like Grady was going to have to do as he said and take a small tour of the butler's private quarters.

He eased the piece of cloth off the branch, shoved it into his pocket, then retraced his steps to the ground. "This is it," he told Annie. "This is where the arrow came from."

"The guy didn't happen to carve his initials in the tree for posterity while he was waiting up there, did he?"

"No, sorry about that," Grady told her, smiling. He did not, however, tell her about the scrap of black material. After all, he wasn't nuts. She was already too involved in his investigation.

So he threw her a bone. "We weren't more than fifty yards from this spot when we heard the glass break. That means, to my mind, that the guy was already in the tree before we came out here."

"About a half hour after dinner," Annie said, biting on her knuckle until he took her hand in his and aimed her toward the path and the house. "We were in the drawing room with Jefferson, and Maisie was upstairs fixing her makeup. Not that she's a suspect, because she works for you. But Dickens left right after he put out the coffee tray, and everyone else excused themselves right after dessert. It could have been any of them."

"Or none of them," Grady told her quickly, visions of Annie assembling all the Peeverses, and Dickens, and then grilling them like something out of a Charlie Chan movie floating through his mind. That's all he needed.

"The person could have been hired. There's enough money floating around here for that to be possible."

They were on the patio by then. "A hit man?" Annie's face was visible in the lights over the patio, and Grady didn't much care for the excitement shining in her eyes.

"It's only a possibility. Now come on, it's time for all good little Junior Detectives to go to bed."

She stopped just outside the French doors. "Bed? Are you serious? Aren't you going to question everyone? I mean, now, while the crime is . . . *fresh,* and all of that?"

"One, Annie," Grady told her, his hand at the small of her back as he gently pushed her forward, into the house, "Archie is probably drugged and sound asleep, so there's no use trying to talk to him. As for the others, they're either in bed, drunk, or screwing like rabbits— you divide that up among the various Peeverses any way you want to. Tomorrow morning will be soon enough."

Clearly Annie didn't agree with him. "Sure, time enough for all of them to make up good alibis."

They were at the stairs, and he took her hand, leading her up to the second floor. "True, or time enough to think too much, end up by tying their tongues in knots. It's a toss-up."

But she wasn't done yet, not that he'd expected her to give up so easily. "What about the doctor? Dickens?"

He stopped in front of her door, fighting down the memory of having seen her earlier in nothing but that skimpy towel, the memory of their kisses in the gardens. "Sandborn could be gone by now, but I've seen him, remember? No way did he make those small dents in the grass; he's too big."

"And Dickens? I'll bet he shines everyone's shoes, or

has access to them, at the very least. And he's tall, but thin, not nearly as heavy as the doctor. He could be our man, right?"

He bent down, kissed the tip of her nose. "Say good night, Gracie."

"But—"

"I said, say good night, Gracie," Grady repeated, turning the handle and opening the door to her room. Without really looking, he reached just inside the door and flipped on the overhead light

She looked at him, then looked into her room. "Um . . . Grady?"

"What now, Annie? It's late, I'm tired . . ."

"Well, so am I, but I don't think I'm going to sleep in here tonight. Look!"

Grady looked. "Sonofabitch. Five thousand a day isn't enough, not at this rate."

# Eight

*It has been said that the love of money
is the root of all evil.
The want of money is so quite as truly.*

—Samuel Butler

"This is bad," Grady remarked as he surveyed the wreckage that had been Annie's bedroom.

The man was a master of understatement.

Bombs had done less damage. Tornadoes could be more merciful. Rampaging rhinos picked their way more carefully through china shops. In her worst teenage years, her room had never looked like this.

Annie blinked back tears as she picked up her new ivory-silk teddy, that had been sliced nearly in twelve. Not in two, or even in three. Twelve.

She looked around the room. Shreds. Every piece of her clothing was in shreds. "I didn't know they made this heavy-duty a Cuisinart," she mumbled, dropping the teddy, picking up a pale yellow cashmere sweater that deserved better than it had gotten. She hadn't even worn it yet, damn it.

Grady was standing in the middle of the room now, looking about as useless as a mime's megaphone. And just as speechless. Until, that is, he opened his mouth and said something really coplike, and really stupid. "Is anything missing?"

Annie exploded. "Missing? Is anything *missing?* Don't you mean—did he *miss anything?"* She bent down, scooped up an armful of ruined clothing, tossed it at him. "Here. Put Humpty Dumpty back together again, and then maybe I can tell you if anything's missing."

"You're upset," Grady said, then winced. "Sorry. Did it again, didn't I? I've never been good with this stuff, comforting the victim. There's just not many things to say that sound even remotely right."

"Tell me about it," Annie said, one hand on her hip, the other pressing against her forehead as she made her way through the wreckage and into the bathroom. "Damn!" she called out a second later, and Grady followed after her.

"Here, too?" he asked, sticking his head around the corner. "Oh, well, that's not nice. Step back, Annie. Maybe we can preserve some of this, even take fingerprints."

Annie nodded dumbly, still looking at the message smeared on the huge mirror with her new Mauve Magic lipstick: *Get out now OR DIE,* followed by three exclamation points.

"Short, not too sweet, and definitely to the point, huh?" Annie said, carefully backing out of the room. She had to be careful, because all of her makeup and other toiletries were scattered all over the floor. "And yet so B-movie, don't you think?"

She was doing okay. Not great, but okay. She had looked into her room, seen every stitch of the expensive new clothing she'd just bought with the advance Archie had given her, and she wasn't lying on the floor, screaming and kicking her feet.

But she was close. So she did what she could do to keep from screaming. She began to babble. "You know, I saw this movie once, where the girl got a message like this one. Except it was written in the blood from the body lying on the floor."

"What did she do?" Grady asked, turning her away from the sight of the mirror and guiding her over to the bed. He sat down beside her, not touching her, giving her some space, allowing her to make the next move . . . if there was going to be a next move.

"She stuck it out," Annie told him, closing her eyes, shivering. "Nobody was going to scare *her* away. It was probably only as the bad guy in the devil mask was slicing her throat that she realized she hadn't been cast in the lead, and was expendable. Let's clean this up, okay? Is it all right if we clean this up? Because I don't think I can look at this much longer without getting really, really *mad*."

Grady looked at the mess, and agreed. "We'll fold it all up and put it back into your suitcase. Where is it? In the closet?"

"Yeah, over there," Annie said, pointing vaguely in the direction of the walk-in closet. Then she came to attention and ran ahead of him intending to throw open the door. Maybe, just maybe, there was still something left on the hangers. Just a skirt, or a suit. Hell, she'd settle for a blouse.

She'd almost made it when Grady stopped her, holding out his arm and motioning for her to step back. His other hand was already extracting his gun from its holster.

"There could be somebody *in* there?" Annie asked, whispering her question. Which was silly. They'd been talking normally ever since they'd entered the room. If there was anybody in the closet, he certainly knew he was trapped.

"Rather too neat to make this mess, then close the closet door, don't you think?" Grady said, also whispering, so maybe she'd been right to lower her voice. "We might have interrupted whoever it is before he could clear out. Now, go into the bathroom, okay? I'll let you know when to come out again."

"Okay, I—wait a minute!" she said, her whisper doing a pretty good imitation of an angry shout, just at a lower volume. She grabbed his arm and pulled him away from the closet door, pulled him all the way across the room. "I'm not going into that bathroom. You saw what was written there. A person could get the creeps in that room. Besides, what if the guy shoots you, huh? Then where am I? I'll tell you where I am, I'm stuck in the bathroom with no way out, that's where I am. You should have thought of that, you know. And don't look at me that way. You know I'm right. You just don't want to admit it."

"I'd admit to being Elvis's long-lost twin, if it would shut you up and get you the hell out of here," Grady gritted out, shaking off her hand. "So all right. Go over to the door, ready to run away if the big bad wolf jumps out and shoots me. Oh, and very nice, that was, talking about me being shot. Really beefs up the old self-confidence."

"Don't mention it. Now, are you going to open that door anytime soon, or should I ring for someone to bring us tea and cakes while we wait for the guy to come out on his own?"

Grady motioned with the weapon. "Over there. Now."

Once she'd stepped over bits and pieces of her new wardrobe and had her hand on the door handle, she nodded, giving Grady the go-ahead to open the closet door.

He gave her such a dirty look! She was being helpful, wasn't she? What was wrong with the man? Still, he then nodded back at her and crossed the room, his weapon in his right hand as he flattened himself against the wall, then reached over for the knob.

The door flew back on its hinges, banging against the wall, and Grady stepped, crouching, into the opening, doing that two-handed sweep deal again.

Annie held her breath, waiting.

Finally, Grady bowed his head, dropped his arms, replaced the weapon in his holster. "Now I know why the door was closed. Somebody's got a nasty sense of humor," he said as she joined him, pointing inside the closet. "Is it yours?"

The walk-in closet was large, and empty of her clothes, so that it was easy to see that no one was hiding there. Not that the closet was completely empty.

In the middle of the closet, perched on the vanity chair from the bathroom, was a huge water-filled pot, the sort people cook spaghetti noodles in, or maybe clams. Inside that pot was a huge, very soggy pink plush rabbit. It was the scene from *Fatal Attraction,* done on a cheaper budget and without the stove.

"A boiled bunny?" Annie said, hugging herself as she shivered. "Poor bunny."

"Is it yours?" Grady asked.

Annie walked inside the closet, picked up one huge, droopy pink ear. The bunny, which had seemed such a good idea at the time, was something Annie somehow didn't want to admit to owning right now, at least not in front of Grady Sullivan. Later, when he was gone, she could give the thing a decent burial. "I never saw this rabbit before in my life, Officer. You don't really think I travel with a *bunny,* do you?"

"No, I suppose not," Grady said, looking at her strangely, as if he might press her. But then he didn't. "Stupid question. Stupid trick. And yet curiously effective, plus telling us that whoever did this planned it, and took their time with it. How long were we outside after dinner?"

"And again later, looking for clues, remember?" Annie pointed out, dropping the bunny's ear and wishing she'd never seen that damn movie where Glenn Close boiled a *real* bunny. A fake one was bad enough, when it was in your own closet. "I didn't come to my room at all after I'd gone down to dinner, so this could have happened almost anytime all night."

"Still, Junior and Daisy left before dinner," Grady said, taking her hand and leading her out of the closet, then closing the door, cutting off her view of the potted rabbit.

Annie rubbed her palms together, trying to hold on to

her composure. "Junior and Daisy? Do you really think—?"

"I would, except that I saw their car pull out of the drive before we went in to dinner. Not that they couldn't have made a show of leaving, then come back to do this. Daisy did seem to make a point out of letting us know they'd been out to dinner and just got back shortly before the window was broken."

"So you're going to question them?" Annie asked, finding it difficult to believe Junior and Daisy could be capable of planning their own escape from a wet paper bag, let alone something like this.

"I told you, Annie, I'm going to question everyone. For now, let's finish cleaning up this mess. Because you're right. I don't want anyone to come in here and see this. Maids, anybody. For now, only whoever did this and the two of us know. I want to see everyone's faces when I tell them, not have them coming to me with the news."

They worked in silence until every bit of ruined clothing was packed up inside Annie's brand-new designer suitcases, and then Annie asked, "Remember that B-movie I told you about? How the girl was expendable?"

"I remember. It's the Hollywood way," Grady said carefully, obviously trying to keep things light. "The young blond soldier with the gal back home in Iowa always bites it, you can bet your buttered popcorn the cowboy wearing the black hat or the Indian named Broken Nose is the bad guy, and the major stars all live, because A-list stars aren't expendable."

"You're right." Annie touched Grady's arm, so that he

looked at her. "So what part am I playing? Am I expendable, Grady?"

He reached out, touched her cheek. "No, Annie, you're not expendable, and I'm going to make sure nobody else thinks you are."

"How?"

"Look, you've got every reason to get out of here. I could send you to Philadelphia. Quinn—that's my partner—could find a safe place to stash you until I figure out what's going on here. Because, honey, either Archie is playing one hell of a scary game, or there really is a possible murderer in this house. We can leave first thing in the morning."

How surprising. All Annie had wanted to do was to run. Run as far and as fast as her shaky legs could carry her. Yet the moment Grady gave her the out, she didn't want it.

"No," she said, shaking her head as she bent down, picked up a pair of slacks that now had their own built-in air-conditioning, then stood up, facing him. "I don't think so." Then she smiled, dredging up any courage that might still be hiding behind her fright and bringing it out to try on. She even smiled. "Besides, I can't go to Philadelphia, Grady. As you can see, I have nothing to wear."

And then she cried. Her bottom lip began to tremble, her eyes squeezed shut, a sob hitched in her throat. Still holding the ruined slacks, still seeing her dearest bunny in her mind's eye, she reached out both her arms so that Grady dragged her close, and she cried.

\* \* \*

"She won't leave." Grady selected three more M&Ms from the china dish, a red one, a blue one, and a yellow one, and popped them into his mouth as Quinn Delaney then yelled at him through the phone lines. "My thoughts exactly," he said when Quinn stopped to take a breath. "Now, if you have any idea how to boost her out of here, I'm all ears."

"You appealed to her intelligence?" Quinn asked. "Explained the situation, pointed out that you had enough to do guarding Peevers without having to watch her as well?"

"Did it," Grady said, poking through the candy for more blue ones.

"Offered to get Peevers to reimburse her for the clothing that was destroyed?"

"Even told her I'd pay her for them out of my own pocket. Come on, Quinn, be inventive. All the usual stuff didn't work. I need help here."

"Where is she now?" Quinn asked, and Grady could hear faint rustling through the lines, as if Quinn was getting out of bed, trying to think better on his feet. "Obviously she can't stay in that room. Didn't you say there was about a gallon of water poured on the mattress?"

Grady flinched in remembrance. He'd held Annie for a few minutes, while she'd gotten her emotions back under control, then sort of *eased* her onto the bed. He hadn't been quite sure what he'd do when he got her there, but a pretty good idea had been forming in his mind. Right up until he'd felt the cold wet mattress against his back. At least now he knew what had been used to get the mattress that wet, not that he thought the bunny boiler had done it all with his trusty little paper cup taken from the bathroom. "I've got her bunking in with Maisie for the night."

"Maisie? Good God, I forgot. She's there with you, isn't she? Well, then that's okay, she's not alone." There was a short silence while Grady waited for Quinn to re- alize what he'd just said. After all, it was past midnight now, and the guy could be excused for being a little groggy.

"Wait a minute!" Quinn said, and Grady smiled; the first real smile he'd smiled in some hours. "That can't be good. I mean—*Maisie?*"

"Yeah, right. She gave up her usual two-week vacation teaching Wacka-wacka Woman 101 to the up-and-coming sisterhood of ditsy dames to act as my assistant here. I figure that by tomorrow, noon at the latest, Annie will be walking with a wiggle, cracking her gum, and calling everyone honey. I need help here, Quinn."

"You always need help, Grady. What else is—*ow!* Damn it! Sorry, Grady, I just nailed the door with my big toe. That'll teach me to try to walk and talk in the dark at the same time. Hang on, Grady—sorry, sweetie, I didn't mean to wake you. No, no, go back to sleep. It's just Grady. I'll go in the next room, okay?"

"How's Shelby?" Grady asked. "You know, I hesitated before I called you, considering that you two are still newlyweds."

"Don't worry about it, and she's great," Quinn told him. "She's great, we're great, and I can't imagine why the whole world doesn't want to be married. Which makes me ask—what's this Annie Kendall like? You're sounding pretty protective, buddy. Can I tell Shelby to stop poring over her address book, looking for blind dates for you?"

"Yes—*no.*" Grady sat down on the edge of his bed. "Look, I mean, yes, Annie Kendall is interesting. No, don't let Shelby try to fix me up. And a great big *no* to your next question, which is bound to be what am I doing about the fact that Annie Kendall is so damn interesting. I'm doing nothing, that's what I'm doing. I'm on the job, remember?"

"I remember that I was on the job, too," Quinn told him, laughing. "Look where that got me."

Holding the portable phone in one hand, Grady reached up to rub the back of his neck. He didn't remember ever lying to his partner before tonight. Just another reason to keep his distance from Annie Kendall.

"Quinn, Shelby was an heiress pretending to be just an everyday woman. That I can understand, Shelby needed to get away from it all for a while. Annie, on the other hand, is an everyday woman pretending to be an heiress. And that smacks of the illegal, the kind of thing that could get her sent away for a while. She answered a personal ad, hired on to help Peevers drive his heirs nuts. Not exactly my kind of woman, you know? Hell, Quinn, I don't even know if Annie Kendall is her right name."

"You're crazy about her," Quinn said evenly, and Grady fought the urge to throw the phone against the wall. "She's unusual, not at all the kind of woman you usually hook up with, she's tying you in knots, and you're crazy about her."

Grady didn't answer. It would only lead to a juvenile

exchange of "Am not!" and "Are too!" so he just waited for Quinn to finish.

"Grady? Are you sure you can't talk her into coming down here? Shelby would get a kick out of meeting Annie. So would I. I haven't heard you this flustered and unsure of yourself since the day we first interviewed Maisie. Remember? You asked her if she could type and she asked if you were good in bed. You know, I never gave it much thought before, but strong women scare you, don't they, pal? You date brainless models, brainless socialites, brainless *anythings* with long legs and a great pair of—stop me here, Grady. I'm a married man."

"I'm going to hang up now, Quinn," Grady said through thinned lips. "Not that you haven't been a great help . . ."

"Hey! Don't go away mad, Grady," Quinn said, chuckling. "I'll be good. But I have to tell you, if the girl won't leave, I don't think you can make her go. Bottom line, I think you're going to have to move her in with Maisie at night, keep her close to you all day, and hope for the best. Besides, this could all be for show, and she's in no real danger. Just how much do you believe this Peevers guy? He seemed like a bit of a weirdo when I spoke to him."

"Which is why you sicced him on me," Grady reminded him. "Don't think I forgot that, *pal.*"

"Such an ungrateful friend," Quinn said. "I get you an all-expenses-paid and otherwise monetarily rewarding month-long vacation in beautiful suburban Bethlehem, Pennsylvania, home of . . . well, it has to be the home of something, right? Anyway, so there's somebody running around with a crossbow, somebody else running with scissors—that's bad, nobody is supposed to run with scissors, right? What did you expect, Grady—perfection?"

"I hate people who can be happy at someone else's expense," Grady grumbled, knowing Quinn was only turning the tables on him for his own reaction when Quinn had asked his help while guarding Shelby. "Look, just have someone drive up here tomorrow with the kit, okay?"

"All right," Quinn said, "but we both know you should be reporting all of this to the local cops. Besides, what are you going to do with the fingerprints if you do get them?"

"Let me worry about that, okay? Just send the kit. The big one, because who knows what the hell else I'm going to need before this is over. Maisie's already burning up the Internet, running everyone who lives here at the house, although I doubt she'll find anything. We all know how the rich can cover their tracks, and I'm pretty damn sure neither of the Peevers boys served in the military or otherwise had their fingerprints taken. I'll just have to muddle through."

"What about the butler? Dickens, is it? I can get into places Maisie can't. Give me his full name, and I'll run him."

Grady thought for a moment, then shook his head. "I don't have a first name on the guy. But I'll have it by tomorrow night, and if Maisie can't find anything, I'll send it down to you."

"How are you going to learn his first name? You're going to play twenty questions with the guy? Try Rumplestiltskin first, it might save a lot of time," Quinn joked, then turned serious. "Look, if this isn't all some elaborate setup by Peevers, you could be dealing with some pretty desperate people. Make sure you call me tomorrow night, and every night. Otherwise, pal, I'm going to be up there wanting to know why."

"It's so comforting to know you care," Grady said. He pushed the button ending the call and threw the phone on the bed. He began taking off his shirt.

"I heard what you said, honey, but what did Quinn say?" Maisie asked from the doorway as she shut the connecting door behind her.

He turned to look at her, then wished he hadn't. She was wearing some sort of silk nightshirt that skimmed the dimples on her knees and had two painted hands on it, seemingly grabbing her breasts from behind. She struck a pose, did a good imitation of playfully devouring him with her eyes. Like Dickens had said, everyone should have a hobby. The butler painted. Maisie vamped.

"Go back to bed, Maisie," he said tiredly.

"Not until you talk. I'm telling you, honey, they can say all they want about putting a glass against the wall and hearing what's happening on the other side, but it doesn't work. Now come on, talk to me, honey. Otherwise, I'll just have to bug the room when the kit gets here, and you know how I hate exerting myself. I might even have to ask for another raise. Looking good tonight, by the way, honey. I'm liking that five o'clock shadow."

"Is Annie asleep?" Grady asked, rebuttoning his shirt and ignoring Maisie's last statements because he had no idea in hell what he *could* say. Besides, although he knew her heart wasn't in it, Maisie just seemed to have this need to keep running her gaze up and down any male she saw, pretty much reducing him, at least, to feeling like a choice piece of raw meat.

"Long gone to slumber land, and wearing my best nightie," Maisie said, hopping onto the bed, her almost ever-present nail file at the ready. She frowned at the fingers of her left hand, then set to work on one red-tipped fingernail. "First we found something for her to wear tomorrow—undies and such. You don't need to hear about that, except to say that, well, if you think she isn't going to have to stuff her bra, honey, then you don't have eyes in your head."

"Can't she just wear her own—never mind, forget I asked. You're right, I don't want to know. Just get her out of here tomorrow morning, take her shopping. Use the company credit card, I know you have one."

"Me?" Maisie patted her red curls. "Why, honey, I don't think so. I'm not *authorized,* am I?"

"Then who charged that new desk chair you've been sitting on the past three months?"

"Oh, that," Maisie said, holding up her spread fingers and blowing on her nails. "I did that over the phone, honey. Anybody can do that. But," she said, slipping to her feet and running her hands down each side of her body, "there's no way anybody is going to see *this* and think I'm Grady Sullivan. Nope, you'll have to do it. Besides, Muriel and I are going to her day spa tomorrow, for the works. Her treat, too. I think I'm going to talk her into doing something with that hair of hers. I mean, did you *see* it? Honey, I mean, even the *cat* wouldn't drag *that* in!"

Grady pinched the bridge of his nose between thumb

and index finger. "It's late, Maisie," he said, hoping she'd take the hint. "Can we discuss this tomorrow?"

"We can," she said brightly, breezing past him in her concealing yet revealing nightshirt, so that now he saw another pair of painted hands "grabbing" her bottom. Where did the woman *find* these things? "But I'm warning you, if that little girl snores, she's bunking with you tomorrow night. Now, *that* ought to give you sweet dreams, right, honey?"

Grady looked at the closed door for long moments, then went into the bathroom and threw back two aspirin. At least he could get rid of one headache. . . .

# Nine

*"Don't give yourself airs. Do you think*
*I can listen all day to such stuff?*
*Be off, or I'll kick you downstairs!"*
                              —Lewis Carroll

Annie was in the first-floor library shortly after six the next morning, showered, dressed in the same clothes she'd worn the previous evening, and waiting for Dickens to tell her breakfast was served.

There was no such thing as "serve yourself" in the Peevers Mansion, which was a pity, because Annie was starved. She always ate when she was upset, and if the rest of this month was going to go the way her visit had started, she'd be a blimp before it was over.

To take her mind off food, and not wanting to go back upstairs to listen to Sickeningly Happy Morning Person Maisie expound on the many glories of makeup and why Annie, who was much too pale, really should consider foundation and blush to keep people from thinking she was a cadaver, Annie had come to the library.

She figured it was the one place she had little chance of running into a Peevers.

The Peeverses seemed to have purchased their books according to the color of the covers, and limited themselves to pricey first editions and nonfiction guaranteed to put their reader in a coma after the first five pages.

She walked around the perimeter of the large room, skimming a finger along the spines of the books in the built-in shelves, finally stopping when she saw a bright spot of color in the otherwise dull-looking inventory.

There were five of them, all the same book, all the spines a bright red print on white. She pulled one from the shelf, and her eyes nearly popped out of her head.

*The History of Toilet Paper,* by Archie Peevers, Sr.

The title was huge, and in gold foil. Archie's name was in red. In between the two, was the drawing of a toilet. With the seat up.

Fascinated in the way people are when passing by a wreck on the highway, Annie headed for the nearest chair, already opening the book. It only took her a few seconds to realize that no recognizable publisher had printed the book, so Archie had probably paid to see his name in print.

She hoped it hadn't cost him too much, because this was pitiful. Just pitiful. On the inside cover, History had been spelled History. This didn't bode well for any notion of having just discovered The Great American Nonfiction Experience.

Sitting down, her legs curled up under her, Annie scanned the table of contents, then began to read. Worse than pitiful. The first chapter wasn't about toilet paper at all, but about Archie. Archie and his childhood. Archie and his genius. Archie and his company. Archie, Archie, Archie.

An autobiography with a toilet on the cover.

Somehow it just . . . fit.

Closing the book, Annie looked at the table next to her, and the telephone on that table. Did she dare? It still wasn't quite seven, too early for most of the Peevers household to be up, and even Grady had to be either asleep or not looking for her in the library.

She decided to chance it.

Lifting the handpiece of the huge old black telephone with its rotary dial, she kept one eye on the door while she dialed the number she'd committed to memory. By the time she'd finished dialing the now mandatory area code and number, even though this was a local call, she'd decided that rotary phone use could be easily classified as an Olympic sport. She dialed the last number, the third zero in the string of ten numbers, then stuck her index finger in her mouth because it was beginning to throb.

Two rings, and then: "What? Who died?"

"Poppy?" Annie said, whispering even though he'd yelled. "Is that you?"

"Annie, is that you? I thought I told you not to contact me unless—what's wrong?"

"Did you take a shot at Archie last night?" she interrupted, still whispering, one hand cupped around the large round mouthpiece.

"Some questions, most especially insulting questions, don't require answers, Annie," he answered tightly.

"And some answers need questions, like on *Jeopardy*," Annie shot right back at him. Honestly, the man acted as if she should just blindly trust him. She didn't blindly trust anyone. "For instance, the answer is, her room was broken into and all her clothes were cut up, and someone left a message on her mirror telling her to get out of Dodge or die. Don't you think that answer needs a question, Poppy?"

There was a long pause, then he said, "Get out of there. Now. Today."

Annie felt herself bristling. She really did have a thing about not liking people to order her around. She'd been ordered around enough in her life, and she was tired of it. "Why?"

"Why?" He was shouting again, so that Annie had to hold the phone away from her ear. "Because . . . wait a minute. Do you think Archie did it? We both figured he has more up his sleeve than just you. Do you think it's part of his plan?"

"If it is, nobody let me in on it. And, according to his bodyguard, nobody let Archie in on the arrow that came through his window last night. The old guy was scared spitless, even if he tried to act like he wasn't."

"Yeah. Still, I'll say it again. Get out of there. I thought Archie would be behind any so-called attempts on his life. Shake up the troops, have them all at each other's throats while he sat back and cackled. I didn't think you'd be a target for anything. I had no intention of putting you in danger."

"I know, Poppy. But I can't leave now. It would look too suspicious. People could even think *I* tried to kill Archie. After all, I am the new kid on the block, remember?"

There was another pause, this one even longer. "Now give me the real reason, Annie," he said. "And don't tell me you've fallen in love with Archie, because nobody falls in love with Archie. I don't think his own mother liked him much."

Annie closed her eyes, remembered the way her room had looked last night. Remembered the bunny. Her poor, sweet, innocent bunny. Remembered Grady, remembered their kiss. "I won't run away, Poppy. I won't be scared away. You know why I'm here."

"I know I'm an idiot for even suggesting this whole thing to you in the first place," Poppy said. "All right, we'll talk later. Just be careful, okay?"

"Okay," Annie said, then eased the heavy handpiece back onto the receiver.

She sat quietly for a few moments before deciding the call to Poppy had been a waste. She'd been pretty sure he hadn't had anything to do with the arrow, although she wished he'd felt more sure the whole incident had been Archie's idea.

What she'd really wanted was to tell Poppy about her room, but mostly about how violated she'd felt when she saw it, how scared. But she didn't want him to tell her to leave, throw in the towel, call it a day, without playing out their little game to the end.

She just wasn't used to people caring about her, worrying about her, any more than she trusted people, even Poppy. Even Grady Sullivan.

Although she'd really like to trust Grady Sullivan. . . .


It was to be a command performance. Archie had commanded everyone to be lined up outside his rooms at ten o'clock, and he very definitely wanted them to perform.

Grady knew this because Archie had all but handed him a script, telling him what he wanted Grady to ask everyone, even providing scribbled follow-up questions.

"You think you can handle this, sonny?" Archie asked from his bed. "You start off by asking each one of them where they were last night at precisely 8:47 in the P and M. Then you tell them they're all full of shit, and to tell you the truth or you're calling in the fuzz. I'll say no, don't do that, but you'll yell at me, tell me you'll do it, and I'll just cower here in my bed and then plead, beg, for my beloved family to please, please cooperate with you. Now, you got that?"

Grady looked at him levelly. "You've watched too many good-cop bad-cop interrogations on television," he told him. "Besides, I work alone."

"You work for me," Archie pointed out, glaring at Dickens, who was trying to coax him into taking his small mountain of morning medications. "And so do you, you miserable old fart," he reminded the butler. "Now, both of you. Let's see some happy smiling faces and hear some 'Yes, sirs, no sirs, anything you say, sirs.' "

"Yes, sir, I'd like to catch the guy and throw him in jail just because he missed, sir," Grady shot right back, smiling most obediently.

Archie threw back his head and cackled. "Oh, you're a live one!" He looked down at the small clear-plastic cup holding his pills, then grabbed the cup from Dickens, threw back the pills, and swallowed them with a half glass of orange juice. "We keep some up here in my own fridge," he then said, gesturing with the empty glass. "Not that you asked."

"I think you're a nasty, possibly perverted sonofabitch,

Archie," Grady told him, "but I never said you're stupid. Now, if we can get started? I still have to take Annie to the nearest mall to replenish her wardrobe. That was going a little too far, Archie, even for you."

Archie looked at Grady, and Grady kept looking straight back at him. "I told you, sonny, I didn't do that. Wasn't a bad idea, granted, and I even might have done it if I'd thought of it, but I didn't do it." He reached up to his mouth with both hands, took out his upper plate, inspected it, licked a bit of leftover breakfast off it with his tongue.

Grady looked away from the unappealing sight, figuring that's exactly what Archie wanted him to do: stop staring. Archie obviously didn't like anyone beating him at anything, even a staring contest.

"Besides," Archie went on, now with his teeth back in his mouth, "come to think of it, I wouldn't have done it. Might have scared little Annie away, and that's the last thing I want. It could take me months to find another one who suits as well as she does, and if I keep parading long-lost granddaughters around here, maybe they will be able to lock me up."

Grady shifted to one side so that he could pull a small flip pad from his back pocket. He was also buying himself some time, because he had to admit to himself that Archie was right. The old guy wouldn't have tried to scare Annie off, not unless he'd let her in on the joke beforehand, so that she wouldn't turn tail and run.

Not that he believed Annie Kendall turned tail and ran very often, if ever. She was more the sort of brave heroine who went down that dark passage, opened that closed door, or agreed to meet the suspected murderer at midnight in a deserted alley. He was still trying to figure out if he admired her courage or wanted to shake her until her teeth rattled, then buy her a bus ticket to Philadelphia and Quinn.

Paging through the flip pad, Grady mentally reviewed his list of suspects, his gaze at last alighting on the page reserved for Dickens. "How about we start with you," he said, looking at the butler, who was standing at attention beside the head of the bed, his hands folded in front of him. "Where were you last night, Dickens?"

"Well, of all the stupid, lamebrained—don't answer him, Dickens," Archie said, throwing back the covers the butler had just arranged and hopping out of bed.

*Note to self,* Grady thought meanly. *Listed under the heading Things That Disgust Me. Can't look at Archie when he's taking out his teeth or when he's upright, with those damn bandy legs sticking out of his nightshirt.*

"Archie," Grady said, snapping shut his flip pad, "I have to suspect everyone. Even you. After that really bad trick with the orange juice, especially you. Ah, and I thank you for not trying to tell me you didn't do it. Except I saw you last night, remember, and you were scared out of your gourd. You might think you're a good actor, but nobody could fake that puddle I found on your floor last night, or the way you were shaking, trying to dig your way through the carpet."

"I'm old, I have a weak bladder. So sue me!" Archie blustered, but he wouldn't meet Grady's eyes. "Now, tell me why I should have you waste time by interrogating Dickens, my loyal retainer?"

"Because you're unlovable, Arch," Grady said reasonably. "Eminently unlovable. Surely you've figured that one out?"

Again, Archie cackled, then climbed back into his bed, which made Grady a happy man. "You're a pisser, sonny," the old man declared. "Dickens, you're officially a suspect. Now answer the boy's questions."

The butler drew himself up to full Lurch height and tipped up his chin. "I served coffee in the drawing room, sir, oversaw the clearing of dishes, supervised in the kitchen, then retired to my first-floor rooms, where I changed from my daytime attire and worked on my painting—sir."

"Anybody with you, see you?" Grady asked, trying very hard not to pull up a mental image of one of the Peevers maids serving as the butler's nude model.

"No, sir," Dickens answered. "Does this truly make me a suspect?"

"That depends, Dickens. Do you have any other hobbies besides your painting? Needlework? Stamp collecting? Scuba diving? *Archery?*"

"No, sir, I most certainly do not," Dickens responded with a slight inclination of his head, and totally without expression. "Now, if we're through here, I do believe I hear the herd gathering without. Shall I bring them in, sir? And would you like them served up Peevers *en masse,* or one at a time, like *hors-d'œuvres?*"

"Much as I'd like to say something brilliant like, we'll do it two by two, the way Noah did," Grady said, admiring the butler's sangfroid more than he'd like, "I think we'd better take them one at a time. For one, I have a fascination to learn whether or not A.W. can finish a sentence on his own. No offense, sir," he ended, looking at Archie.

"None taken, sonny," Archie said, grinning around his too-large teeth. "But don't bother asking Asswipe if he can shoot a bow and arrow, because that would be a waste of time. My spies tell me he can't even hit the squawk box with a spitball from more than ten feet. Or Junior, either, for that matter. Only boy I know who flunked out of Cub Scouts. Only thing that boy ever could tie a knot in is his tongue, although I wish it was his dick. Dickens—let's start with my firstborn, for my sins."

"Yes, sir," Dickens said, walking past the now standing Grady, giving him a piercing look that could just possibly give the butler a good view of Grady's liver. "With your permission, sir."

"By all means, Dickens," Grady said, happy that he hadn't flinched. Talk about the guy you wouldn't want to meet up with in that dark alley Annie Kendall would have walked down without a second thought!

Moments later, A.W. burst into the room, stepping past Dickens and totally ignoring Grady as he rushed to the bed, his arms outstretched in front of him. "Dad! Are you all right this morning? I couldn't sleep all night, seeing that arrow in my nightmares."

"You can't have it both ways, Asswipe," Archie told him, pushing his son away as the man tried to embrace him. "Either you were awake or you had nightmares. Speaking of which, you still sleep in the same room with Mildred? Ever thought of wearing one of those blackout eye masks in bed? You'd sleep better, I'd bet on it."

A.W. stepped back from the bed, biting his bottom lip

between his teeth, then turned to Grady. "He's kidding," he told him, trying to smile. "Dad's always kidding, aren't you, Dad? Always up for a joke."

"Yes, I've always been fond of a joke. I let you live, didn't I?" Archie grumbled, pushing himself back against the mound of pillows and winking at Dickens, who only lifted his chin another fraction.

Grady knew it was time he took over. "All right, now," he said, stepping forward, the flip pad once more in evidence. "If we're all done playing this portion of Dysfunctional Families, I have a few lightning-round questions for you, A.W. There'll be some lovely parting gifts when it's over."

A.W. glared at him balefully. "Mitzi doesn't like you, Mr. Sullivan. She doesn't like anyone who thinks he's funny."

Grady ignored that one, because there was no possible answer that meant anything. "Where were you last night, A.W., between the hours of seven and ten?"

A.W. abandoned his hostile pose and began looking around the room as if his wife might pop up from behind one of the fireside chairs holding up a cue card to prompt him. "I . . . um, that is, *we* . . . um—Dad! This is ridiculous. You can't think one of us took a shot at you, can you?"

Archie moaned, clutched his chest. "I told you, Mr. Sullivan. These are my family, my loved ones. How can you put us through this torture?"

Grady pinched the bridge of his nose, closed his eyes. "I'm so sorry, Mr. Peevers," he said, following the stupid script Archie wanted him to perform. Anything to get out of this room and do some real investigating. "But these questions are just routine. It's not that I'm looking for suspects, but only to eliminate possible attempted murderers."

Archie looked up at A.W. from beneath the fallen-front hem of his nightcap. "Oh. Well, in that case . . . answer the man, boy. Let's get this over with."

Having his father's permission, and clearly with his father longing to hear any exonerating evidence, A.W. launched into a nearly minute-by-minute recitation of his activities of the previous evening, all of those minutes spent with his lovely wife Mitzi, who could corroborate everything he said.

"I'll just bet," Grady said under his breath, then dismissed the man.

Grady skipped Mitzi, knowing she'd answer word for word as her husband had done, and called in Junior next.

Junior got right down to it. "We ate at McDonald's so there's no receipt. Daisy likes the Quarter Pounder with Cheese, and I like to watch her eat it. She puts on extra ketchup, so that it squeezes out the sides, and always licks her fingers. And french fries? You wouldn't believe it! Anyway, then we came home and played scramble until we heard the commotion in the hall."

"Scramble?" Grady repeated. "Don't you mean *Scrabble?*"

Junior winked at him. "You play your games, Sullivan, and I'll play mine. Dad? Is that it? I'm picking up my new Mercedes this morning, remember?"

"Birthday gift," Archie told Grady. "Gotta flip them a fish every now and then. Besides, he wanted one of those Ferrari things, so this is a real letdown for him. Ain't it, Junior?"

"I love anything you do for me, Dad," Junior said, then turned and walked out of the room.

Muriel was already on her way in. "Daddy!" she exclaimed, and threw herself on Archie, weeping copiously.

"Crocodile tears," Archie said, when Muriel finally let him go, stood up, wiped her eyes, and blew her nose. "Crocodile snot, too. If anyone tried to kill me, it's Muriel here."

"Daddy!" Muriel exclaimed, pressing the used tissue to her mouth as she ran out of the room.

"Do I know how to clear a room, or what? Anyone else, or are we all done here?" Archie said, looking pleased with himself.

"Oh, we're done," Grady said, shaking his head. What a pitiful waste of time. "Dickens, lock him in, I'll be back in a couple of hours."

# Ten

*Neither a borrower nor a lender be.*
                                        —Shakespeare

Pennsylvania in September could be a thing of beauty, and this day was even better than most. The greener-than-green countryside around Peevers Mansion was lush after the rain that had fallen sometime after midnight, so that the dark macadam of the winding country road still shone wetly in the sunlight that had broken through the clouds only an hour earlier.

A person could really enjoy being a passenger in a car like Grady's, because of the scenery, and because Grady was a competent driver, not a lead foot trying to take each corner at the greatest speed possible.

Annie had time to admire the huge homes that seemed so at home half-hidden behind tall trees that it was as if they had grown up along with those trees, as much a part of the land as the rocks and flowers and small streams that seemed to meander everywhere.

Then they were on a more heavily traveled roadway

leading to Route 22, known locally only as "the thru-way," although the increase in traffic over the years made many want to rename it "the parkway" during the morning and evening rush hours. Annie knew this, because she'd had to stop to ask directions the first time she'd driven to Peevers Mansion, and the thought had tickled her enough to commit it to memory.

The thruway wasn't at all crowded at the moment, however, as the rush hour was long over and it was still too early for the evening rush. There were trucks, making their way to New York for new loads, or heading out from New York to parts south and west to deliver their cargos. Annie also knew from her reading that Pennsylvania was supposed to have more interstate truck traffic than almost any state, and nearly the worst interstate highways in any state.

Not that she had to be told that one, because even Grady's luxury sedan couldn't hide all the bumps in the road as they traveled along, not speaking to one another.

They had spoken, for the first few minutes after leaving Peevers Mansion. She'd talked about the cold silence and deadly stares she'd gotten at the breakfast table, and he'd made her laugh with his rendition of "the interrogation" that had gone on in Archie's rooms.

Annie really enjoyed being in Grady's company. Because he smiled a lot. Because he was easy to talk to. Because she felt safe. And because, if she got lucky, really lucky, he might even kiss her again sometime soon.

Yes, Annie had been feeling pretty happy, or as upbeat as anyone could feel while residing in the Peevers Asylum for the Weird and Wacky. She was, in fact, so glad to be out of the place for a while, that she doubted her mood could get any better.

She'd been right. Because, just moments ago, Grady had made it worse. Much worse.

She was silent for a few moments, doing what she was pretty sure was a slow burn, then announced: "No. Absolutely, positively *no.*"

"Yes, Annie. I insist."

"You can't insist, because I refuse to be . . . to be *insisted.* And I said no. I can do that, Grady. No. No, no, no. See? I can do it all day. No, no, no, no, *no.*"

"Damn it, Annie. What's the matter with you? Or do you think I plan to take it out in trade later?"

Annie turned on the front seat of the car and glared at Grady, pretending the idea hadn't held just a teeny bit of appeal. "You wish," she said, then looked forward again, folding her arms across her stomach. "Take me back. Now."

Yes, she needed an entire new wardrobe. No, she didn't want to live the next month in the clothes she had on now, had worn yesterday. But if he thought, for even one minute, that she was going to let him buy those clothes for her? Ha!

"Then you have enough money?" Grady asked, taking his eyes off the road to look at her just as if she was ready to lie to him again.

"I have plenty of money. Enough to buy anything I want."

"I'll just bet," Grady said, shaking his head.

"Maybe you would. Me, I don't ever gamble. That's why I have enough money," Annie shot back at him, and watched as his knuckles got white as he held on to the steering wheel. Big deal, he was angry. So was she, gosh darn it.

The fact that she had a whopping $74.23 in her wallet until her job for Archie was over and he paid her the rest of the money he'd promised only made her angrier. Not that she cared. Not that she cared one bit!

She would rather walk around naked than have Grady think she needed money, would accept his charity.

Well, maybe not naked. But she'd think of something.

Archie had been generous with her, giving her enough money up front to put a hefty down payment on her new car and to outfit herself for the role of long-lost grand-daughter. She could not, would not go to him for more money. Nor would she go to Poppy. He was also too "new" in her life for her to let him believe she couldn't stand on her own two feet, without his help.

She might be seen by the world as a con artist or some other bottom-feeding scum, but she did have her princi-ples. And her pride. Besides, she concluded, pulling a face, Archie would be so happy she had to come to him that he'd probably never let her forget for a moment that she was as silly and shiftless as his children. She couldn't *stand* that!

"What if we consider it a loan?" Grady asked as he steered the car onto the exit ramp. "You already told me what Archie's paying you, so I know you're good for it."

"A loan," Annie repeated. Okay. That seemed sensible. And she was in a bind. Maybe she could swallow just a little of her pride. If nothing else, it would teach her never to be reckless with her money. She'd had so little of it in her life that she'd kind of gone nuts, throwing down cash for every purchase, then topping it off by falling in love with a twenty-pound two-hundred-dollar stuffed rabbit.

But, then, she'd never before had a pet.

"Yes, Annie, a loan," Grady said, pulling the car into a parking space near the main entrance to the mall. "That means I give you money and then you give it back. It's fairly simple, actually."

"I know what it means," Annie said, bristling as she got out, slammed the door. This guy really could get under her skin. Then she saw the sign, and smiled. "Look, there's a bank in there," she told Grady, pointing to the sign just in case he hadn't seen it. "Let's go."

He followed her. She hadn't left him much choice, she knew, but he did seem to be in an obedient mood this morning, which was nice. She walked into the bank and stepped right up to the receptionist's desk. "Hi, I have a favor to ask. Would it be possible for you to sell me a blank note?"

"Um . . . I'll get the manager, miss."

"I don't believe this." Grady had caught up to her and was now standing beside her, shaking his head. "You want to sign a note?"

"A promissory note, unsecured, of course," Annie informed him. "Ninety days, and with interest. I don't know what interest that should be, but I'm sure the manager can tell me."

"You're scary, do you know that?" Grady said as the receptionist motioned for them to follow her to the manager's desk. Fifteen minutes later—the manager had actually given her a blank unsecured note, without charge, had even helped her fill it out—Annie was in Macy's poring over the sale racks.

"Isn't it great that all the summer clothing is on sale? I should be able to go straight through September in summer clothes. No white shoes, though, because it's after Labor Day, right?" she asked Grady as he leaned against a post, still looking at her as if she might have grown a second head.

"A 1099, and now she signs a note for five hundred dollars, at a pretty nice interest, too," he said, addressing a smiling mannequin. "Do you believe this?"

Annie grinned. "Careful, Grady. I read somewhere that sometimes stores put cameras in the eyes of those mannequins, to watch for shoplifters. Right now some guy could be looking at one of the screens in front of him, seeing you talking to him. I mean, there may be a man, a big white net, and a padded room in your future."

Grady eyed the mannequin for a moment, then pushed himself away from the post. "Here, try this on," he said, pulling a sleeveless pink V-neck sweater off the rack.

Annie looked at the sweater consideringly, then shook her head. "I don't think so. See how short it is? It's one of those bare-midriff sweaters. I don't wear those."

Grady looked at the sweater. "Yeah, I can see the problem, what with that huge spare tire you're carrying around. How about a muumuu?"

"Gimme that," Annie said angrily, ripping the hanger out of his hand. "Now go away. You're making me nervous, hovering over me like this."

"Is there a problem, miss? We've been watching, you understand. Is this person bothering you?"

Annie turned to see a short, compact, fireplug of a man wearing a blazer with Security written on the pocket. He was looking at Grady as if deciding whether to climb him, grab him in a headlock, or just pull out the stun gun and take him down.

"Well . . . actually . . . ," she said, looking at Grady with an "I told you so" look and trying not to giggle.

"Annie . . . ," he gritted back at her. That little tic was working near his temple again. What fun! Then she remembered she still needed a ride home.

What the hell, she then thought, smiling, she had five hundred dollars in her purse, right? She could take a cab.

"It's all right, thank you," she said, smiling at the security guy. "Grady just hates shopping, don't you, Grady, sweetie?"

She took a step toward the security guy, her back to Grady, and spoke to him quietly, confidentially. "Honest, everything's just fine. He's my brother. It makes him *so mad* when I buy these size sixes for myself before we head for the mature woman's department to buy for him. He mostly wears Mother's things. Mother was a fairly *large* woman, you understand, but she's been gone now for a few years and Grady wanted so badly to update his wardrobe. He doesn't come in here anymore in drag because one of your salespeople noticed his Adam's apple last time, and laughed so hard Grady nearly hit her with his purse. That's why I come along now. Could you tell us if there are any sales in the women's department?"

"I'm going to kill you," Grady said a few moments later, dragging Annie by the elbow as they walked away from the security guy. "I'm going to kill you slowly and very painfully and in highly inventive ways, and there's not a jury in the world that would convict me."

"We're going the wrong way," Annie said when she could stop laughing, catch her breath. "The security guy said the women's department is back there. Oh, and I think he thought you were cute." She broke away from him and took a step back toward the junior department. "You want me to fix you up?"

"An-nnie," he growled, then stopped, smiled. Laughed. "I can't believe you did that!" he said between chuckles. "And did you see the look on that guy's face?"

"He couldn't get out of there fast enough, could he?" Annie said, slipping her arm through Grady's and marveling at how good it felt, how natural, to be walking close beside him this way. "He'll probably have nightmares for a week, imagining you in lipstick and high heels."

"That makes two of us," Grady told her, drawing to a halt. "Look, I can see we're getting nowhere fast, and there's no way in hell I'm going with you to the lingerie department, so what do you say we split up? I can meet you right here in an hour."

She tipped her head to one side. "I would have thought you'd be very much at home in the lingerie department."

"Joke's over, Annie," he said, no longer smiling.

"No, no, I'm not talking about *before*. I just meant that you didn't seem to be the type who'd feel out of place surrounded by all that silk and satin."

"Which only goes to show how little you know me," Grady said, then had them synchronize their watches so they'd be sure to meet each other in an hour.

As he walked away, Annie stared after him, considering his words. He was right. She really did know very little about him. She knew what he did for a living. She was pretty sure he did it well, because his clothes were expensive and he drove an expensive car. Maisie had told her last night that he was a real big winner with the ladies, although he never dated one for more than a few months.

And he kissed really well. She certainly knew that one.

He kissed so well that Annie had thought more than once about where those kisses might lead, and if she just might want to go along for the ride.

Which was stupid, as well as ridiculous. She had enough going on without complicating things by crawling into bed with Grady Sullivan.

She took a deep breath, let it out slowly, and went back to shopping. But it wasn't any fun anymore. She'd had a ball the first time she'd walked into a store with a bundle of cash in her pocket. She'd been having fun with Grady. But now it was just a job, something that had to be done.

Although she did smile when she finally staggered to the checkout counter under her load of new clothing, to find that Macy's was marking everything down another twenty-five percent that day. Maybe she was in for a run of good luck. That would be nice. . . .

Grady looked at his watch for the third time in two minutes, and began to wonder if he'd made a mistake. How could he have forgotten his own rule, that he and Annie were to stick to each other like glue?

What if someone had come up to her, stuck a gun in her back, and told her to leave with him without making a fuss? What if she wasn't even in the mall anymore, but instead tied up in the trunk of some Peevers car, being driven to some lonely spot and then tossed head-first into a water-filled abandoned quarry or something?

Did Mercedes have an inside handle in their trunks?

Had he developed a nonprofessional overactive imagination in the past couple of days?

It was just that she was so *helpless*. No, not helpless. That was the wrong word. Annie wasn't helpless. She was too independent, that's what she was, and with that overactive imagination he'd just accused himself of harboring. And honest. Annie was also honest, almost to a fault.

That probably bothered him more than anything. Her honesty. It just didn't jibe with what she was doing, who she was pretending to be. He really hated it when things weren't logical, when people didn't fit neatly into the slots they should fit into according to what he knew about them. Not that he knew much about Annie.

He had Maisie working the Internet for information on the Peeverses, even on the family doctor. But what about Annie? What had he done about Annie Kendall other than to kiss her in the moonlight?

Stupid! Stupid, stupid, stupid!

He looked around again, hunting for a sight of her curly black hair.

Nothing. She wasn't anywhere. She could be anywhere. He only knew she wasn't here, with him.

He felt a small shove in his back and wheeled around in a near crouch, ready to attack. "Hi," Annie said, barely visible behind a pile of beige plastic bags that looked as if she hadn't taken out the trash in weeks and now was trying to do it all in one trip. "You could help, you know, instead of standing there trying to look menacing."

He was so glad to see her, so damn glad to see her! So, naturally, he yelled at her.

"You're late!" he said, grabbing some of the bags out of her arms, leaving her still holding two huge bags in each hand.

"I'm"—she transferred the two bags in her left hand to her right and lifted her arm to look at her wristwatch—". . . five minutes late. Shame, shame on me."

"You bought all this with five hundred dollars?" he asked, feeling just a little bit lame, like some overprotective father waiting at the door for his daughter to come home from her first date. And he didn't feel anything like her father!

"I'm a great shopper," Annie told him. "Some people knit, some are good with flowers. I shop great. It's a gift. Oh, and speaking of gifts . . ." She started opening bag after bag, peering inside, finally grabbing one from him before saying, "Aha! Got it. Here you go," she said, handing him the smaller bag that had been stuffed inside the big one.

He took it with the same caution he'd use if someone handed him the front end of a rattlesnake, reached inside, and pulled out a square, flat box with a designer name on the lid. "You bought me a gift?" His eyelids narrowed. "Why?"

Annie shrugged. "A small peace offering after that little joke I played on you earlier, I suppose. Relax, it was on sale; I just had the clerk remove the price tag. Go on, open it."

It was a wallet. The most beautiful wallet he'd ever seen, unless he was overreacting, and he probably was, he admitted to himself. He turned it over in his hands, opened it, admired the many pockets for his credit cards. "It's . . . thank you, Annie."

"You're welcome. Oh, and take this, too. I forgot to put it in earlier." She held up a nickel. "I don't know why, but I'm pretty sure you should never give a wallet or purse as a gift without putting some money in it. Are you sure you like it? There was the loveliest shoulder bag that was big enough not to look out of proportion on you—kidding, just kidding!" she exclaimed as he narrowed his eyelids and growled. She made him take the nickel. "Don't spend it all in one place, okay?"

"Okay," he said, then motioned with his head toward the bag sitting beside him on the floor. It was a big plastic bag, tied shut at the handles. "I got something for you, too."

"You did?" Annie's eyes lit up as if it were Christmas morning and she'd just spied the new two-wheeler she'd asked Santa to bring her. "You didn't have to—what is it?"

Grady grinned. "Why don't you open it and see. There was this shop out in the mall. They didn't have any pink ones left, only had one left at all, as a matter of fact. I had to tell this big sob story about my little sister being sick with the chicken pox before the clerk would sell me the display one, and . . . hey! What are you doing?" He felt his heart stop, skip a beat, then start up again. "Oh, Annie, don't do that. Come on, honey, don't do that. Please."

But she was doing that. Annie Kendall was standing smack in the middle of the main aisle in Macy's, right next to a girl spraying perfume on everyone who passed

by, hugging a three-foot-high blue plush bunny rabbit to
her and crying like a baby.

Grady stood there for a few moments, feeling helpless,
then dragged girl and bunny into his arms, holding Annie
tightly, kissing the top of her head and trying to comfort
her with words that made no sense, especially to him.

What he didn't say was, "I think I might just be falling
in love with you, Annie Kendall." But he heard the words
just the same, inside his head.

# Eleven

*The meek shall inherit the earth
but not the mineral rights.*
—J. Paul Getty

She named the bunny Deuce, and Deuce rode home in the backseat, safely strapped into a shoulder harness while Annie, feeling better than she knew she had reason to be, chattered to Grady about their plans for the rest of the day.

"You'll want me to divert Dickens while you case his room, right?" she said, then laughed as he looked at her, one expressive brow riding high on his forehead.

"Case his room? Annie, that would mean I'm going to check it out so I can go back later and rob him. I'm going to *search* his room. Big difference."

"Probably not in the eyes of the law," Annie suggested, waggling her own eyebrows back at him. "Six to ten either way, I'll bet. Don't do the crime if you can't do the time."

"May I remind you that you'd be charged as an accessory? Or is this your way of wiggling out of helping me? That honesty thing again?"

"Somebody cut up my clothes, Grady. The same somebody killed Bunny One—or would that be *Uno?* Never mind, it doesn't matter. I want to find out who was in my room, and then I want to kill him. Do you think I can get away with it?"

"Not if you report the gun on your income tax as a deductible expense," Grady said as he turned onto the country road leading back to the Peevers Mansion. "Which, knowing you, you'd probably do. List it under work-related supplies, or something equally lame."

"Ha. Ha. Very unfunny, Sullivan. I'm positive I have at least some larceny in my soul."

"Don't we all," Grady said, shaking his head. "That said, how are you planning to divert Dickens?"

She snuggled more deeply into the soft leather bucket seat. "You'll see," she said, wishing she had a plan, wanting him to think she had a plan. Boy, did she wish she had a plan! "Unless you think you have a better idea?" she ventured, trying not to sound too hopeful.

"I think you should ask Archie to have Dickens give you the grand tour of the place. You could tell Archie it would make the little Peeverses nuts to see Dickens showing you around while you greedily take inventory of every room. I have a calculator in my room. You could take that with you, pretend to punch in numbers like you're doing a running total of Peevers's assets."

Annie stuck out her bottom lip, as if his answer had displeased her rather than saved her from admitting she hadn't the faintest idea about a good diversion. "No fair. You must have been reading my mind. But, since we agree, I'll run up to see Archie as soon as we get in the house."

"You do that, Sherlock," Grady said, as they pulled to a stop outside the front door of the mansion. "But give me about fifteen minutes first, to talk to Daisy if she's home."

"Daisy? Why her?"

"I have no idea," he told her as they gathered bags out of the trunk, Grady carrying most of them because Annie's arms were full of Deuce. "Maybe I'm attracted to her intellect."

"Yeah. You and Junior both," Annie said, opening the door so that Grady could precede her into the house. "The girl's *loaded* with intellect."

"Jealous?" Grady asked as he passed by her.

Annie almost said yes, which would have been ridiculous. Why would she be jealous of Daisy, or any woman Grady might consider attractive? A couple of pretty hot kisses in the moonlight did not give her proprietary rights—not that she wanted them, of course. "Just make sure you've had all your shots," she told him, then ran upstairs to put Deuce away in Maisie's room, where he'd be safe, leaving Grady to follow after her with all her shopping bags.

Grady checked his wristwatch, decided he had about ten minutes to interrogate Daisy. He'd probably only need two, but he always liked having a cushion.

He found her in the morning room, playing solitaire on the glass-topped wrought-iron table. She was frowning over the cards as if looking for another move. He'd seen less concentration on the face of a major-league pitcher in the bottom of the ninth, with three on and two out.

"Hello, Ms. Goodenough," he said, stopping a few few away from the table. "Would you mind if I joined you for a few moments? Oh, and black seven on the red eight."

She looked up at him, then down at the cards. "Oh, my goodness, you're right! Now, why didn't I see that?" She made the play, then gestured that Grady sit down, join her. "Junie is teaching me cards, you understand, and I've been practicing. We're going to Vegas next month."

Grady refused to wonder why Junior was teaching her solitaire, as he was pretty sure nobody played solitaire in Vegas. He also refused to consider the idea that starting off with something simpler, like Go Fish, might have been a better choice. "How nice," he said at last, considering it safest.

"Yeah, isn't it?" Daisy put her elbows on the table and leaned toward him, speaking very quietly. "Can you keep a secret? I think we're going to get married in one of the chapels out there." Then she sat back, frowning. "That's legal, isn't it? One of my old boyfriends, Sidney, told me you couldn't get knocked up if you did it with the woman, you know, *on top?*" She rolled her heavily made-up eyes. "Good thing I asked my friend Shirl first, let me tell you! So I'd like to be sure. Is a Vegas wedding, you know, legal in Pennsylvania?"

Grady could almost feel sorry for this girl. "Far as I know it is, as long as neither of you is already married. Are you sure Junior's last divorce is final?"

Daisy's complexion paled under her makeup. "I don't

know," she said, then clapped her hands to her cheeks. "What should I do? Shirl can't help me with that one, can she?"

It was his fault, and he knew it. He knew damn full well Daisy and Junior were nearly too dumb to live, let alone pull off a murder. He should never have bothered to come in here in the first place. So now he was stuck. "I can find out for you," he offered, trying not to grimace. It wouldn't be so bad. Maisie could probably find out on line in less than ten minutes.

Daisy reached out with both hands, grabbing Grady's forearm as she leaned toward him. "You'd do that for me? Oh, aren't you the sweetest thing! I can't imagine why Junie says A.W. says you're a dirty, pond-scum-sucking—" She sat back, smiled at him. "Sorry."

"Don't be," Grady said, standing up and pushing in his chair. "I've been called worse. Well, it's been nice talking to you, Ms. Goodenough. I'll have that answer for you soon, all right?"

Daisy also stood up, smoothing her lime green knit dress down over her twin monuments to silicone, then over her lush hips. "I just can't thank you enough, Mr. Sullivan," she said. Then, before Grady could see it coming, she launched herself against him, wrapped her arms around his neck, and planted a big wet one straight on his mouth.

He barely had time to have it register in his mind that Daisy used mint mouthwash before a hand came down on his shoulder, he was roughly wheeled around, Daisy screamed, and a fist slammed into his jaw.

"Bastard!" Junior gasped out, but he did it from the

floor, because Grady had recovered quickly, delivering a karate punch into the man's soft midsection.

Daisy dropped down beside Junior, asking him if he was all right, telling him she had only been thanking Mr. Sullivan for a favor he'd promised. She was all solicitude . . . right up until the moment Junior coughed, then heaved his lunch onto the carpet.

"Oh, *yuck!*" Daisy said, quickly standing up once more. She waved her hands in front of her, as if she could literally push away the sight and sound and even the smell of Junior Peevers at his most unattractive. "I suppose you want me to do something, Junie, baby?" she asked.

"Get . . . just get the hell out of here! Leave me alone!" Junior told her, clutching his belly, his knees drawn up to his chest. If he started calling out that he wanted his mommy, Grady wouldn't have been the least bit surprised.

"Ooooh, Junieeee!" Daisy wailed, then ran from the room on her four-inch heels, still waving her hands in front of her.

"You're an ass, *Junie,*" Grady said, rubbing his jaw, then moving it back and forth, testing to make sure nothing had been broken. It had to be a lucky punch. A sucker punch. The guy couldn't be that good with his fists. "Ms. Goodenough was just thanking me for volunteering to find out if your last divorce is final."

Junior, who had been rocking back and forth, stopped moaning and looked up at Grady, his eyes a near resemblance to the popped-out-on-stalks look of cartoon characters. "She what? She didn't! You *aren't,* are you?"

"Not anymore, because I don't have to," Grady said,

grinning. "You just gave me the answer. Still married, right? You're a real prince, Junie, baby. A real prince."

Junior struggled to his feet, glaring at Grady. "This is none of your business!"

"You're right, it's not. But I am curious. Were you going to go through with the marriage in Vegas?"

Junior's eyelids narrowed, giving him a dyspeptic look that probably was meant to be threatening. "I'll have you fired. You'll be out of here on your ear today, Sullivan!"

Grady looked at his watch and frowned. "Gee, I'm scared. And, not that it hasn't been fun, but I'm late for an appointment."

Junie was still yelling as Grady walked toward the foyer, stopping when he saw Annie and Dickens standing at the bottom of the steps. She had his calculator in one hand and a mercenary smile on her beautiful face.

"Wasn't it nice of Archie to suggest we do this, Dickens?" she was saying to the butler. "Can we start in the drawing room? I want to know everything you know about every stick of furniture, every painting on the walls. Antiques are so hot now, aren't they? I'll bet there's a small fortune in that one room. Isn't it a shame Mitzi declined to join us after we told her what we're going to do? Does she get many headaches?"

"I have no idea. Can we please just get on with this?" Dickens grumbled, his hands bunching into fists at his sides.

Grady chuckled under his breath, confident that Annie would keep Dickens occupied for either a half hour or until the butler had built up enough steam to blow the top of his head clean off.

Stopping in the empty kitchen to load crushed ice into

a small plastic sandwich bag to ease his aching jaw, Grady then slipped into the hallway leading to Dickens's rooms, already pulling his set of lockpicks from his pocket.

"And then, when I was twelve, I fell down some stairs and broke one of my top front teeth almost in half. I looked *awful*. I had to have a cap put on when I was seventeen and had saved up enough money from my after-school job. I got one of those caps with the gold back on it, too. See—" Annie said, stepping closer to Dickens, her mouth open, pointing with one finger to her perfect upper teeth.

Out of the corner of her eye, she saw Grady motion to her from the doorway of the library, then disappear once more. "Well," she said, stepping back from the clearly disgusted Dickens, "much as this has been fun, I suppose we're done now, right? Thanks so much for the tour," she called over her shoulder, already on her way to meet Grady.

"I thought you'd *never* get done," she said, catching up with him at the French doors in the morning room. "Another minute, and I was going to have to show Dickens the tap dance I performed in my first recital."

"Were you any good?" Grady asked, opening the door and motioning for her to exit ahead of him.

"I didn't go to dance classes. And I've never had a cap on any of my teeth. I was *acting*, remember. Told you I was good," Annie said, heading for the steps leading down to the grass from the patio. "But it was getting hairy. An *hour*, Grady. How could it take you an *hour* to search one room?"

"Three rooms," Grady corrected, taking hold of her elbow and almost frog-marching her toward one of the gazebos farther out on the lawn. "Plus bath. Dickens has a whole damn apartment, in which he has jammed enough stuff for a six-room house. Oh, and I spent the first five minutes opening the three locks the man has on his door, five more minutes when I was done, locking them again from the outside. That's not easy, you know. You can congratulate me at any time."

"Maybe later." Annie was biting on her knuckle. She thought she heard something in Grady's tone, something that made her ask, "Whose stuff?"

"Good question. You'll get that Junior Detective badge in the mail any day now," he answered. "Let's put it this way. There wasn't a souvenir ashtray from Atlantic City or a set of beat-up TV trays anywhere. It was all quality stuff. I found a neatly typed inventory in his desk— picked that lock, too—listing each piece and its estimated worth."

"Because . . . ?" Annie asked, sitting down on one of the benches lining the walls of the gazebo.

"Because," Grady told her, "Dickens has a little business going on, as far as I can tell. He might call those rooms his quarters, or even his apartment, but what he's really got going there is the home office of his import-export business. Two of his closets were full of nothing but folded-up packing crates. Export the real McCoy, import fakes. I've got to hand it to the guy. It's pretty brilliant. I mean, I doubt the Peeverses are antique experts, and could spot a fake."

"Wow. And he's been working here forever," Annie said, trying to take in all this information, then times it by the number she'd made up in her head. "If he sold off about twenty thousand a year, for about thirty years, that would be—"

"Chicken feed," Grady told her, pacing back and forth in the middle of the gazebo. "Chump change. A drop in the bucket." He stopped pacing and turned to look at her. "Oh, and his hobby? His painting? Guess what he paints. Come on, Annie, don't disappoint me. Guess."

Annie felt her eyes going wide, pretty sure she'd figured it out. "He *doesn't!* Does he?"

"Oh, yes, indeedy he does," Grady told her, running a hand through his hair. "Right now he's working on a Reubens, I think. And doing a pretty good job."

"Ohmigod," Annie said, getting up to do a little pacing of her own. "Why was I hoping he painted by number? You know, wide-eyed kittens, or maybe big red barns? He's really forging Archie's art, and then selling the originals?"

"There were about a dozen canvases rolled up and stuck into tubes under his bed," Grady told her. "So maybe he isn't selling off the originals, but just keeping them himself, maybe for a rainy day. We'd have no way of knowing how many of the paintings in Archie's house are real or fake, not without calling in an expert."

Annie sat down again, trying to gather her wits. "No wonder he looked so smug when I was admiring that painting on the second-floor landing. It's probably an original Dickens. Shame on him!"

She wanted to tell Archie. Leave Grady standing there

alone and run to tell Archie. He might be a mean old man, but he didn't deserve to be ripped off by his butler.

"And, besides the paintings, you're saying he's stealing other stuff?" she asked, wishing she felt less violated herself. Which was ridiculous. This had nothing to do with her, none of it. That's not why she was here, to make her own financial killing, the way Dickens had done, was obviously still doing.

"Nothing too big in size," Grady said. "Figurines, some jade pieces. Jewelry, of course. I think Mitzi would be in for a shock if she ever got her jewels appraised. I found sketches of necklaces, pins. Photographs of different pieces. He must be slowly replacing every piece of jewelry with well-made fakes. You know, I've got to hand it to the guy. He's pretty damn inventive."

Annie tried to push her mind beyond Dickens's grand larceny. "This means we can eliminate him as a suspect, doesn't it? I mean, who knows if A.W. and Mitzi will keep him on when Archie's gone, right? The best thing that could happen to Dickens is for Archie to live to be one hundred."

"My thoughts exactly," Grady told her, sitting down beside her. "But I'm still going to have Maisie check him out, although she's going to have a hell of a time doing it."

"Why?"

"Because I found his checkbook and his full name is Charles Dickens, Annie. No middle initial. Do you know how many hits she's going to get on any Internet search engine, looking up Charles Dickens?"

Annie thought about that for a while, then smiled. "Please let me be there when you tell her," she said. "I like Maisie, really I do, but if she makes one more crack like 'what's that with your eyebrows, honey? Did you do that on purpose?' Well, you know what I mean," she ended weakly.

"Maisie's a one of a kind," Grady said, taking Annie's hand and urging her to her feet. "And, speaking of one of a kind, aren't you going to ask me how my interview went with Daisy Goodenough?"

"All right, how did it go? Good enough?" Annie asked, grinning. "Sorry. Couldn't resist."

Grady took hold of her other hand, so that they stood facing each other, their fingers intertwined. "Yeah, good enough, I suppose," he answered, looking down at her. "We talked, she stuck her tongue down my throat, Junie punched me, and when I nailed him in the gut he barfed all over the rug. Just your usual, everyday, run-of-the-mill interrogation."

Annie had lost him at the tongue part. "She stuck her what where?"

"She was thanking me for a favor I'd offered to do for her."

"What did you offer to do for her? Father her children?" Annie snapped, trying to get her hands free, but Grady wasn't letting go.

"No, she wanted to know if Junior is free to marry her because they're heading for Vegas next—wait a minute. You're jealous! I don't believe this. I said it earlier, but I was only trying to get a rise out of you. But this is real, isn't it? You're *jealous.*"

"Am not."

"Are too."

"Am not—oh! Just let me go, all right?"

But he wouldn't let her go, and she didn't really want to fight him. After an only halfhearted attempt to break free, she gave up and just stood there, glaring at him. Hoping she was glaring at him, and not just looking up at him like a big, dumb puppy wanting to be petted.

"May I kiss you?" Grady asked.

Annie's toes curled inside her shoes.

"Huh?" she responded, thinking that was pretty damn articulate, considering she'd just swallowed her tongue. "You're *asking* me?"

His smile melted whatever parts of her hadn't gone to mush when he'd asked her his question. "I'm being polite here, Annie. And that's hard to do when you're horny as hell, just in case you ever wondered. Or did you think last night's kisses were enough? They weren't for me. Probably that physical attraction thing, right? I thought maybe we should investigate it some more, just to be sure that's what it is."

"All hot and bothered, huh? I'm flattered, really. Oh, you poor thing." He'd finally let go of her hands, so she lifted them both, cupping his cheeks in her palms.

"Ouch!"

Grady jumped back, holding his chin in his hand and rocking his head back and forth. "Damn. Damn, damn, damn."

"What is it?" Annie asked, concerned because he seemed to be in real pain. "Toothache?"

"Junior-ache," Grady told her. "I told you. He sucker punched me when he saw Daisy draping herself all over me."

"Oh, poor baby," Annie said, then giggled, and pretty

much ruined the moment. "Can we try again? I promise to be gentle."

"Funny," Grady said, but he took his hand away from his jaw and stepped closer, laid his hands on her shoulders. "But no face touching, okay? Just mouths."

"Yes, sir," Annie said, biting her bottom lip. "Are you sure you want to do this?" Dumb question, because if the man thought he was getting out of this gazebo *without* kissing her, he sure didn't know her all that well. Yes, she knew herself to be physically attracted to him, and vice versa. But she had also been wondering if that was all that might be between them. If there might be more, so much more. Enough to thrill her and frighten her at the same time.

So the thought of kissing Grady, being held in his arms, made her nervous, and she took refuge in a little silliness. She stood on tiptoe, her hands on his shoulders, lightly puckering up her mouth. "Anytime you're ready, Rocky." Unfortunately, with her lips puckered, it came out more as, "Anytime wou're weady, Wocky."

That did it. Grady all but swooped down on her, their mouths colliding, their lips parting, his tongue probing her without a bit of hesitation. His hands went to her waist, pulling her against him, tightly against him.

Oh yes. Physical attraction all right. In spades! And yet more, so much more. Did he feel it, too?

She felt an urge to rake her fingernails down his back, then possibly toss him to the floor of the gazebo and have her wicked way with him until he had no choice but to tell her he wanted to spend the rest of his life making love with her.

He kissed her eyes, her nose, the side of her throat.

His warm breath tickled her ear, sent shivers down her spine. This wasn't just a kiss; this was more than a kiss. Whole worlds more than a kiss. Did he feel it, too? Oh, please. He had to feel it, too.

"This is crazy," Grady mumbled beside her ear.

Okay, that's what it was. It was crazy. Mad, and crazy, and confusing, and scary—and wonderful. So she took a chance. "I can live with it if you can," she said right back at him.

He held her tightly, so that she could feel his chuckle as well as hear it.

"What?" she asked, pushing away from him a little so that she could look up into his face.

"Nothing. I was just thinking. Archie once sent Dickens with a bucket of water to toss over Junior and Daisy when he saw them making love out here."

Annie looked to her right, up at the second-floor windows, one of which was still covered with a piece of cardboard. "Oh," she said. "Were we going to make love? Because you didn't ask me that. You only asked if you could kiss me."

"One question at a time, Annie," he said, tipping up her chin with his fingers. "But, now that you mention it, I wouldn't mind at least discussing—aw, *hell!*"

Annie nearly jumped out of her skin. "Was that—no, it couldn't be . . . but was that a *shot?*"

Grady didn't answer. He just grabbed her hand and started running toward the house, stopping only for a moment when she told him she had to take off her heels if she was going to be able to keep up with him. "First the broken window, and now a gunshot. Both times while you were kissing me. Can you believe it?"

"Oh, I believe it," Grady gritted out, pulling her along with him again. "And I have to tell you something, Annie. This is all getting pretty damn *old* pretty damn fast!"

# Twelve

*The rich have many consolations.*

—Plato

Dickens stood back as Grady and Annie raced down the hallway on their way to Archie's rooms. "It's nothing, sir, miss. Just Mr. Peevers indulging in a little target practice," he told them.

Annie skidded to a halt in her stockinged feet. "A little *what?*"

Grady tugged on her hand, hard. "Keep moving. We'll find out for ourselves."

"Not if Archie's playing with guns, we won't," Annie told him, digging in her heels. "And, if he is, what are you doing out here, Dickens? Hiding so you won't have to let him shoot an apple off your head?"

"William Tell was last night," Grady reminded her angrily, but he also agreed with her, he was no longer in any mood to go crashing into Archie's rooms without first announcing himself. Maybe even waving a white flag. "Stay here," he told Annie, then cautiously approached the closed door, knocked. "Archie? It's Sullivan. Put down the weapon."

He heard movement on the other side of the door before the handle turned, the door opened, and he was looking at Dr. Milton Sandborn. "Is there a problem?" the big man asked, his grin as genial as that of a grizzly bear up on its hind legs, ready to pounce.

Grady bent his head a moment, rubbed at the back of his neck, then looked at the doctor once more. Measured him, tried to read his eyes. He got nowhere; the man wasn't exactly an open book. "I don't know. Is there?"

"Oh, come in, come in," Sandborn said, waving both Grady and Annie—who had come up beside him, slipped her hand into his—into Archie's inner sanctum. "Archie," he called out in his big voice, "put down the gun, the party poopers are here."

"I'll talk to you later," Grady said, pulling Annie along behind him as he all but stomped through the small, drapery-hung vestibule and into the main chamber.

What he saw when he got there was Archie Peevers, in his usual distasteful *déshabillé,* standing on the far side of the bed and looking toward a paper target someone—the doctor?—had taped to the wall between the windows. A Saturday night special hung from his right hand, and the idiot was grinning like . . . like an *idiot.*

"What? Not an Uzi?" Grady asked, walking over and taking the weapon from his employer, then emptying the remaining rounds, putting the bullets in his pocket. He stuffed the empty gun into his waistband. "Or how about a .44 Magnum, Dirty Harry Callahan's choice, and possibly the most powerful handgun in the world, supposedly able to blow your head clean off. You're the movie buff, Annie, do I have that right?"

"Almost word for word, I think," Annie said, and he realized she was right beside him. He'd been so busy looking at Archie, wanting to choke Archie, that he had almost forgotten about her. Almost, but not quite. There was a hole in the wall beside the target, a hole mere inches from the unbroken window. If Archie's aim had been a little worse, the bullet would have smashed the window and headed out onto the lawn, in the general direction of the gazebo . . . and Annie.

That thought shot Grady's heart into double time, and his hands clenched into fists. "What the *hell* did you think you were doing?"

Archie looked very small and very old as he crept back into his bed. "Somebody tried to kill me, sonny. I have every right to learn how to protect myself," he said, his voice slowly gaining confidence. "And where was my bodyguard last night, huh? Comes running in here way too late, and with lipstick on his shirt collar. Looks like you've got more smeared on you today. Whose body are you guarding, anyway, sonny? You can't expect me to just sit here, waiting for one of my kids to get lucky while you're playing slap and tickle with the decoy, damn it!"

There wasn't much Grady could say to that, so he turned to glare at the good doctor. "You brought in the gun, I suppose?"

Dr. Sandborn was busy searching in his huge black bag, not answering until he pulled out a vial of medicine and two syringes. "Ah, a lovely vitamin shot. Just the ticket." He looked at Grady. "Yes, it's my weapon. Bought it just this morning at a pawnshop on Hamilton Street in Allentown. You'd be amazed at how easy it is to buy weapons. There probably should be a law, or something. Here, hold this."

Grady automatically put out his hand, and the doctor placed one of the capped syringes in it. "It *is* supposed to be against the law to buy a handgun the same day you come in to buy it," he pointed out, knowing he could just as easily have been talking to Annie's Deuce, for all the attention anyone was paying him. Money was money, and money could get you a weapon, from a handgun to a bazooka, without worrying about anything as lame as mandatory waiting periods.

Dr. Sandborn looked at Annie. "You might want to turn your head a moment, little lady. Archie's ass is a lot of things, but a thing of beauty it ain't."

Annie turned her back, tugging on Grady's arm so that he had to turn with her, something he was about to do anyway. "What do you think?" she asked him, looking up at him as if he was supposed to have some answer for her.

"I think you didn't hear Archie a minute ago when he called you his decoy, that's what I think. Otherwise, you'd already be packing your bags and getting the hell out of here."

"I thought we already settled that part," Annie shot back. "I'm doing just what you said, sticking to you like glue, and except for some juvenile scare tactics, nobody's taken a shot at me, remember."

"Yet. Nobody's taken a shot at you *yet*. Give it time, the day is young."

"I won't leave him," Annie said, looking even more mulish. Cute as hell, but mulish, stubborn. He wanted to shake her, kiss her, carry her off somewhere and finish what he'd been trying to start for two damn days. "He needs me."

"He needs his head examined," Grady told her. "He needs to stop making new wills every time the moon goes into another phase. He needs to stop working his children like puppets. Pretty soon, if he keeps this up, finding the person who *isn't* trying to snuff him will be easier than adding up all the ones who've either already taken a shot at him or plan to stir some rat poison into his oatmeal. The man's *begging* for it, Annie. Surely you can see that."

"Don't call me Surely," Annie ventured, wincing as she knew her little joke had fallen very flat. "Okay, okay, so he's not very lovable. We already know that. But you're here, I'm here. Are you leaving?"

"I'm getting paid to do a job," Grady reminded her.

"So am I," she told him. "And I'm no quitter."

"No, you're not. You're a target. I just wish I could figure out why the hell you're doing this—and don't give me that line about the money, because I'm not swallowing it. There's something else, isn't there? Tell me, Annie, come on, tell me why you're—"

"You can both turn around now," Dr. Sandborn said, then took the syringe from Grady and loaded it from the vial. "What's good for the Peevers is good for the physician, I always say," he told them as he unbuckled his belt. "You game, son, or should I call Dickens in?"

"You're going to take a vitamin shot?" Annie asked.

"Yes, yes, a vitamin shot. Isn't she a cutie?" Sandborn remarked, then bellowed for Dickens, who entered the room, already pulling on a pair of surgical gloves. "Good man, Dickens. And magic with a needle. Time to turn your back again, sweetheart."

"I don't believe this," Annie whispered to Grady as, once more, they turned their backs. "Are those really vitamin shots, do you think?"

"I'm trying to forget everything that's happened since I came into this room," Grady said, his words followed closely by Sandborn's "Ouch—ah! Let the joy juice flow. Good man, good man."

"Sounds like a good idea," Annie agreed, shivering as Dickens walked past them, stripping off his gloves. "Archie and his junkie doctor. They ought to be ashamed of themselves."

"Don't hang your hopes on that," Grady said as he turned her back around, pointed to the high, wide bed. Archie was lying there under the covers, a terrifyingly wide smile on his face and a spaced-out look in his eyes. "Guess that answers your questions about what's in the syringe. My money's on Demerol."

Grady staggered forward as the doctor suddenly slapped him on the back, grabbed his shoulder, and gave him a hug. "You taking good care of Archie? He's a bastard, always has been, but he's always had reason. Not that I agreed with him about this last trick, bringing in the little sweetheart here to take the heat off him for a while. And it's not working, is it? Poor old bastard. He's really scared this time."

Grady disengaged himself from the man's grip, which

wasn't easy, for the doctor was smiling now, looking more than a little vague, and he'd been using Grady as much as a prop as anything else. "So you knew about Annie?"

Sandborn blinked, shook his head. "What?"

"Never mind," Grady said in disgust. "I had this fleeting hope I could appeal to you to exert your influence over Archie, get him to pay off Annie here and let her leave. Stupid thought. If you'll excuse us?"

He grabbed Annie's hand and dragged her from the room while she stumbled along, still looking at the good (and stoned) doctor.

"The mattress in your room unfortunately cannot be replaced until sometime tomorrow, Miss Kendall," Dickens said as they walked by. "If you were to limit your fluid intake after dinner, it might prove beneficial to your, um, *problem.*"

"My—oh, no! I don't have a *problem.* Grady—tell him I don't have a problem," Annie had to call back to Dickens, obviously mortified, because Grady was still on the move, still with one thought in mind, that of getting out of Peevers Mansion before he started babbling like the idiot he thought he was.

"You've got lots of problems," he told her as he opened the door to her room and pulled her inside. "Sit down," he then ordered as he closed and locked the door. "Sit down, shut up, and let me think, okay?"

"I'm *not* leaving, okay?" she shot straight back at him, although she did sit down in one of the pair of chairs near the window. The bed had been stripped, and only the box spring remained. "Archie isn't going to shoot me, for heaven's sake."

Grady, one hand to his head as he paced, stopped to glare at her for a moment.

"Sorry," she said, wincing. "I'll shut up now."

He grunted, feeling pretty much incapable of speech at the moment, and began pacing some more. Pacing and thinking. Thinking and pacing. He wished he had his putter. He always thought better with his putter in his hands.

He'd guarded diplomats, rock stars, a supermodel whose legs were insured for ten million bucks. He'd been shot at as a cop, had dealt with everyone from robbers to murders to a guy who'd wanted to take a swan dive off the Walt Whitman Bridge.

He was a seasoned veteran, kept a cool head, and possessed a sharp mind.

So why in hell did he feel like he was playing a none-too-bright straight man to a head case like Archie Peevers, a man who had surrounded himself with the most bizarre bunch of suspects this side of a Mel Brooks movie?

There was Dickens, who buttled for a hobby, with grand larceny and art forgery his real vocations.

There were the Peevers sons, A.W. and Junior, almost self-explanatory misfits: one of them whipped past any hope of ever finding his backbone unless he looked in his wife's closet, and the other one living on his libido and the hope Archie would croak before he ran out of women to marry.

There was Muriel. Quiet, unassuming, loyal Muriel, who called Archie "Daddy," and played the role of dutiful spinster daughter almost too well.

There was Mitzi. In another life, she'd probably been a black widow spider.

There was Daisy. Yeah, well . . .

And then there was Jefferson Banning, lawyer. Grady liked Banning, but he didn't trust him. There were too many opportunities for a lawyer to insert some of his own language into a will, and the more Archie changed that will, the better were the chances that Banning could be found out, fired from his very lucrative job.

There was also Dr. Milton Sandborn, Archie's friend and personal physician, as well as the man who probably wrote twice as many controlled-substance prescriptions for Archie as the old bastard ever received. Was that all it was? Was Sandborn using Archie in order to keep his own supply of Demerol flowing? It certainly wasn't because Sandborn *liked* Archie.

Hell, nobody liked Archie. Archie probably didn't like Archie.

"Still thinking?" Annie asked. "Because I think my foot's going to sleep, and I have to go to the bathroom. So maybe you could hurry this up a little, hmmm?"

Annie. He'd forgotten about Annie. Not as a woman, definitely not as a woman, but he had ruled her out as a suspect in this craziness.

That wasn't professional.

He stopped pacing to look at her. "Who are you, really?"

Annie's smile faded slowly, even as the light went out in her eyes. "Me? You're looking at *me* like that? You think maybe *I'm* a suspect? I'm a victim here, remember? You saw my room last night."

Grady held up his hands as if to ward off attack. "I

know, I know, but you wouldn't be the first person to make herself out a victim, just to cover her tracks."

"What tracks? Archie hired me to impersonate his long-lost granddaughter. I don't have anything to hide. Oh, okay, so nobody's supposed to know, right? But *you* know. You *know* I'm only the hired help, just like you. So how does that make me a suspect?"

"It doesn't, sorry," Grady said, but his radar was still tingling. Off base, malfunctioning, probably—but still tingling. "Maybe if you told me your real name? . . ."

"Annie *is* my real name," she said, jumping up from the bed and putting the palms of both hands against his chest as she backed him toward the door. "Now, if you don't mind, I think I'd like to brush my teeth. I have this sudden bad taste in my mouth. Good *day,* Mr. Sullivan!"

The next thing he knew, Grady was standing outside Annie's bedroom door, and Dickens was standing beside him, grinning. "Well, wasn't that unforunate? If you wish, sir, you could just bend over for me. I'd be delighted to kick you."

"You number listening at keyholes among your hobbies, Dickens?" Grady asked, his jaw tight. Then he took a shot, just to see the man flinch. "Besides painting, that is."

What had he been thinking? Dickens didn't flinch. The man probably didn't know *how* to flinch. "It is my job to protect Mr. Peevers. I was only checking to make sure you also had his best interests at heart."

"Meaning?"

The butler pulled himself up to his full height. "Meaning, sir, that you and Miss Kendall were seen—how did

Miss Katharine Hepburn and Mister Henry Fonda say it? Oh yes—you and Miss Kendall were seen *sucking face* in the gazebo. This has led me to question your priorities, and where your first loyalties lie. Sir," he ended, and Grady felt a small stab of surprise that the man didn't slap his heels together and salute.

"Oh, let's not talk about me, Dickens. Let's talk about you, all right?" Grady counted to three in his head, then pointed to the painting on the wall behind the butler. "For instance, is this one of yours, Dickens, old sport?" he asked. "You're doing pretty well with the Reubens, but I think you might not have caught the proper brush-stroke for a Turner."

Okay, so Dickens did know how to flinch. "So it was you," he said coldly. "Snooping. I should have known. None of the Peeverses can find their own backsides, let alone get into a locked room."

Grady was rather disappointed. He'd thought he'd gotten in and out without disturbing anything, without leaving any sign that he'd been there. "What did you do, Dickens? Tuck one of your hairs between the door and the frame, so you could tell if anybody had been in your room? That was sloppy on my part, not to have checked before I opened the door."

"Have you told Mr. Peevers?" Dickens asked, avoiding concurring with Grady as to how he knew, although the slight flush in his cheeks told Grady he'd probably guessed right about the hair.

Grady scratched behind his left ear, shaking his head. "Now, that's a good question. Here's my dilemma, Dickens. I was hired to find out if somebody in this house wants Archie dead. Clearly, if Archie doesn't know what you've been up to—and he couldn't, or you'd be in jail now, right?—it really isn't my job to tell him. Because, you see, with all the fun you're having robbing everyone blind, the *last* thing you'd want is to see Archie dead. Plus, there is that small fact that I broke into your rooms, which also probably doesn't fall inside the parameters of my current job description. Do you understand my dilemma?"

Dickens looked at Grady as if he'd just stuck out his forked tongue and hissed. "How much?"

Grady blinked. "How much what?"

"Money, of course. How much will it take to keep you quiet?"

Now Grady grinned. "Well, that's nice. Your first impulse was to pay me off, not kill me. And two targets in the house at one time are more than enough anyway. Still, thanks but no thanks. I'm not real big on blackmail, unless . . ."

He waited for Dickens to ask him, enjoying the man's misery.

"Unless what?" the butler finally asked, clearly hating that he had to speak, not that he was anywhere close to groveling.

"Unless," Grady went on, "you do me a little favor."

Dickens sighed. "Name it."

Rubbing his hands together, Grady motioned for the butler to follow him down the hall. "Now, here's the thing," he said, knowing he had the man's full attention. "I'll be needing the fingerprints of everyone in the house. Archie's, all the little Peeverses's, Banning's, Sandborn's, Daisy's. Oh, and Miss Kendall's, too, as long as we're doing this we might as well be thorough.

Fingerprints on glasses probably would be easiest, and you have to be careful not to mix them up, make sure you've got the right prints for the right person. Do you think you can handle that?"

The look on Dickens's face said without words, "Do ducks swim?" But that's not what he said. What he said was, "You'll want mine as well, I presume. I'll have them all for you as soon as possible. Anything else?"

Grady shook his head. "No, I think that about does it. It's a pleasure doing business with you, Dickens."

"Not really, sir," the butler said, then wheeled on his heels and headed back down the hallway just as Milton Sandborn was weaving his way toward the head of the stairs.

"Toodle-oo, sonny," the doctor called out, waggling his fingers at Grady. "Archie's sleeping like a baby and won't be any trouble for the rest of the day. Oh, and you're welcome. You're very, very welcome. In fact," he said, lurching to a halt and fumbling to open his bag, "if you want a little *boost,* I'd be most happy to oblige. No charge."

"Maybe another time," Grady told him, then looked back down the hall toward Annie's door, wondering if he could take the chance of seeing her again right then without her beaning him with some piece of forged art.

He doubted it. He'd been doing so well, but now Annie believed he didn't trust her. Women don't go to bed with men who don't trust them. And they sure don't fall in love with men who don't trust them.

He was pretty much striking out every way he turned. He decided to go see Maisie, make her life miserable with the news she had to go search the net for information on Charles Dickens.

After all, why shouldn't all the women in his life hate his guts?

# Thirteen

*Tell tale tit,*
*Your tongue shall be slit,*
*And all the dogs in our town*
*Shall have a bit.*
—Nursery Rhyme

"You're sweating, honey," Maisie said, watching from her perch on the side of the bed, her legs crossed at the knee, blowing on her still-wet nails. "Not a pretty picture, I have to tell you."

"So leave," Annie said from her position, flat on her back on the floor, the floor she'd be staying on until her heart rate dropped from its breakneck pace. She'd run in place for ten minutes, then dropped to the floor for fifty pushups. Girl pushups, granted, with her knees on the carpet, but fifty just the same. Anything to try to burn off some of her frustration at not being allowed to take a morning run on a lovely Saturday, orders of Grady Sullivan. She was hot, sweaty, and still mad as hell.

"Can't, honey," Maisie chirped. "I'm your bodyguard

while Grady's out golfing with the lawyer, remember? Besides—wow, how about that!—this is *my* room."

Annie pushed herself onto her side, propped up her head with her bent arm. "My bodyguard, sure. Just as long as defending me doesn't include maybe breaking a nail."

"Granted, there is that." Maisie, one hand still held out in front of her, looked down at Annie. "Are you going to be lying there long, honey? Because, well, I think you could do with a shower, if you know what I mean. Now go on, mush, mush, and then we can go downstairs and mingle before dinner. I'm not the sort that can stay cooped up too long. I get testy."

"As compared to your usual unfailing kindness and politeness," Annie grumbled, remembering how Maisie had told her this morning that she either had to take her shopping bags out of the secretary's room or hang up the clothing before she opened a window and tossed everything out. Maisie, it would seem, did not like clutter. Which pretty much explained why Annie was still dragging her feet about taking her purchases to her own room.

"Exactly," Maisie said, smiling. "Isn't it nice how we understand each other, honey? Oh, and I think you really should reconsider that blue dress I saw in your bags. Uh-uh, honey, not your color at all."

"You looked through my shopping bags?" Annie pushed herself to her feet, wondering when she'd given up any shred of privacy she might once have had. "Who said you could do that?"

"My room, honey," Maisie said, standing up, smoothing down her bright yellow skirt with the red rickrack around the hem. "Also, I'd hoped there might be something in them that I might want to borrow." She rolled her big, round eyes. "Color me optimistic!"

Annie gritted her teeth and opened the closet door, to pull out the blue dress she'd thought hidden inside the plastic garment bag it had come home in. Over the sound of Maisie's theatrical groan, she then gathered underwear from one of the shopping bags piled on the floor and headed for the bathroom.

Fifteen minutes later, her hair still damp, Annie was stripping off the grey-blue dress that had turned her complexion to dirty putty, slipping instead into a denim skirt and soft lime green cotton sweater.

"Not a word," she warned Maisie as she came out of the bathroom a second time, then sighed, shook her head. "Oh, all right. I give up. I didn't try it on in the store because I only had an hour to shop. How did you know it would look like that?"

Maisie preened like a satisfied cat. "What can I say? It's a gift. Some of us just know, honey. Others of us—you, for instance—don't."

Annie reminded herself that she was getting out of Maisie's room today, so instead of choking the woman, she just put down her comb, pushed at her curls, which were still being obedient thanks to her very good haircut. "I'm breaking out of here, Maisie," she said, realizing she'd been locked in this room with the secretary for the past five hours, ever since lunch. "You coming with me or not? And, please, don't think of this as an invitation."

"We have to go to your room if we're going anywhere, and you can take the bags with you, and don't forget the stuff in the closet. You can carry it all, can't you? My nails are still wet, not that I would have offered. Oh, and don't look so mad, it isn't my fault. I know I said I wanted to go downstairs and mingle, honey, but we can't, not really. Strict orders from Grady. But I have an idea. We can just stay here and look you up on the Internet while we're waiting for the boss man to get back."

Annie already had her hands full of bags, but she let them drop as she turned to look at Maisie. "Look me up on the Internet? Why?"

"Because Grady told me to do it, that's why. I just did Yahoo! so far, and got forty-eight hits with different varieties of Annie Kendall. None of them in Pennsylvania, either, not that you told us where you're from, now, did you, honey? After working on Charles Dickens for hours and hours, I thought maybe you'd take pity on me and help me out here. Are you going to help me out here, Annie?"

Annie saw something flash in Maisie's eyes, a definite glint that hadn't been there before, and had a sudden epiphany. Maisie made a lousy roommate, hogging the covers and sleeping almost sideways, leaving Annie only about two inches of mattress. She was brassy, she was sarcastic, and she was a neat freak. She played at being outrageous, maybe even was a little outrageous, but—and this is what Annie decided now—she wasn't anybody's dummy. Grady wouldn't hire a dummy.

Maisie was trying to coax her into helping her, and doing it very smoothly, too.

"Grady ordered you to check up on me?" she asked warily as Maisie hopped down from the high bed. The desk near the window was set up with laptop computer, printer, and a stack of files Annie would give her eyeteeth to read.

She'd seen the stack before, but the idea of a file containing information about her sitting on that desk had effectively narrowed her interest.

"Which one is mine?" she asked, heading toward the desk.

"Uh-uh," Maisie said, plucking a manila folder from Annie's hands before she could read more than "Archie Peevers" on a white label stuck to it. "Not unless you play nice."

"Play nice," Annie repeated, her thoughts about Maisie now confirmed. She'd play along, but only for so long. "Oh, okay, I get it. I show you mine, and you show me yours."

"Honey, I wouldn't show you mine if you begged. I'm not into that stuff," Maisie said, pulling out the antique side chair and sitting down, flipping open the laptop.

"You know what I meant," Annie grumbled, looking around until she spied a small bench in front of the dressing table. She tugged it across the floor and sat down on it, plopping her elbows on the desktop. The bench was a good four inches shorter than Maisie's chair, and definitely not built to be used with a desk, which left Annie feeling like the naughty second grader forced to sit in the little chair next to the teacher until she could behave and go back to her own seat.

"I know what *I* meant, honey," Maisie said as the laptop hummed and the *Yahoo!* web site appeared on the screen. "Now watch."

She went to the "people search" section on the server and typed in "Annie and Kendall." Moments later, much to Annie's shock, up came a listing of forty-eight names. Ann Kendalls. Annie Kendalls. Annie as a middle name, bracketed by the person's first name and "Kendall."

"Those are addresses beside each name!" Annie said, her eyes wide. "And telephone numbers! I don't believe it. And what's that—over on the end?"

"That's where I can refine the search, learn more about any of these people. But this is just amateur night, honey, just my first stop on the way to learning what you ate for breakfast last month and who you kissed in your first game of spin the bottle. My first was Lenny Bertlemann. I looked him up once, and he's doing time for car theft. But, honey, could he kiss!"

Annie dropped her head in her hands. She'd never gotten further on the Internet than the shop-at-home pages. Yes, she'd heard about the Internet's powers, the world's loss of privacy thanks to everyone's mad need for information, but she hadn't connected it to herself, until now. "I think I'm getting a migraine. And I don't *get* migraines."

"Yeah, yeah, honey," Maisie said, tapping her on the head, bringing her attention back to the screen. "So, which one are you? Come on, honey, I've baby-sat you all day, and you haven't exactly been a barrel of chuckles. You owe me."

Annie was tempted. She'd thought coming here would be informative, and maybe even a bit of a lark. That's how Poppy had played it, anyway. But she wasn't having fun, and so far her visit had been anything but informative. Someone had tried to kill Archie, her room had been broken into, and her clothing destroyed. She'd been threatened, and Bunny Uno had bit the big one. No, not a lot of chuckles in this little game.

And then there was Grady. A guy who should have meant nothing to her was meaning more to her each moment. Meaning enough to her that, yes, she would like to tell him the truth, just so she'd never again have to see question in his eyes. Those damn green, bedroom eyes.

So, yes, she was tempted to just tell the truth, let it all hang out. But she couldn't, and she knew she couldn't.

"I'm out of here," Annie said at last, standing up, pushing at the bench with her foot, aiming it in the direction of the vanity table. "I'm an American citizen, I have my rights, and I'm not going to help you. Stick *that* in your *Yahoo!* and see what you come up with!"

"Is there a problem, ladies?" Grady asked, having just opened the connecting doors between the bedrooms.

Annie stiffened, then whirled around to confront him, ask him how he *dared* to be investigating her like she was some low felon or something.

Only she didn't say a word. She couldn't. He was standing there, lounging, actually, one broad shoulder against the doorjamb. He had on loden green slacks, a predominantly white, striped golf shirt open at the neck. His forearms glinted with golden hairs over golden "golfer's tan" skin. The back of his neck and his nose were also faintly sunburned. And he had a bad case of "hat hair" that looked . . . well, that looked absolutely adorable.

She could smell the warmth of the day on him, and fresh-mown grass, and just plain *man*.

She longed to strangle him. Right after she threw him

down on the nearest available horizontal space and stripped him to his tan line.

"We were just having a little girl talk, honey," Maisie said, when Annie remained silent, staring while trying hard to pretend she wasn't staring. "Weren't we, honey?"

"Huh?" Annie said, then realized she'd just mentally forgiven Grady for wanting to investigate her, for the Great Fire of London, for any still-unsolved ax murder, even for butting into the express line at the grocery with more than twelve items, just in case he'd been guilty of any of that. She'd forgive him anything when he smiled like that, when he looked at her like that.

Which made her even madder.

"What we were *doing,* Grady," she corrected, "was looking up Annie Kendall on the Internet, so that your trusty little snoop here could try to figure out who I am. On your orders, right?"

"Guilty as charged," Grady said, pushing himself away from the doorjamb. "But why the outrage, Annie? You knew I'd have to do it sooner or later. What did you come up with, Maisie?"

"Not a lot," the secretary admitted. "Except that she won't help me, which means she's hiding something, right?"

"I am not!" Annie said, trying not to remember that her driver's license and other identification had until last night resided inside a plastic bag hung inside the toilet tank in her room. "And, for the umpteenth time, I shouldn't be a suspect. Why aren't you working with the *real* suspects?"

"Like Jefferson Banning?" Grady asked.

"Yes! Like Jefferson Banning," Annie agreed quickly. "What did you find out about him today?"

Grady started back into his own bedroom, crooking his finger to indicate that Annie should follow him, then shaking his head at Maisie, who grumbled under her breath but stayed put.

"She'll just listen at the keyhole, but I try to comfort myself that she's at least going to have to work for anything she learns," Grady said as he crossed his hands at his waist and, in one swift motion, pulled off his golf shirt.

And there were the tan lines, at the base of his neck, halfway up each nicely defined biceps. Sometimes, for the sake of one's sanity, wishes really shouldn't come true.

Annie tried not to gulp as she walked over to the window, figuring the scenery outside the window wouldn't be as dangerous as that on this side of the glass. His hair was actually mussed into bangs—bangs!—that made him look so young and sweet and adorable she could tie a blue ribbon around his neck and set him in the middle of her bed. Yes, definitely her bed.

"So what did you find out?" she asked, trying to concentrate on what was supposed to be the subject at hand.

"He's got a long, not always straight drive, is cool as ice over a twenty-foot putt, but he can't chip worth a damn," Grady said. "You'll probably want to keep your back turned for a minute."

She agreed, because she'd heard a zipper open and her imagination was already running at maximum speed. Actually *seeing* Grady without his slacks could lead to an overload. "Do you have to do that?"

"I do," Grady answered from somewhere inside his closet, his voice faintly muffled. "I wanted to shower at the club, but we were running late, and then Dickens waylaid me downstairs to warn me that it's nearly time for the dinner gong, so I have to skip the shower and dress while we talk."

"You've got hat hair," she pointed out, still concentrating on the garden below the window.

"I know," Grady said, emerging from the closet in light tan slacks and a white dress shirt, and going over to the dresser. She watched as he peered in the mirror as he pushed back his hair, getting it off his forehead. She felt so deprived. "It's a part of my boyish charm," he told her.

"Think so, huh?"

He turned, flashed her a grin that was probably illegal in three states. "Oh, definitely. Especially since I can now tell you that Jefferson Banning, Esquire, is back on our list of suspects."

Okay, so now he had her full attention. "How so?"

Grady pulled a pair of dark brown slip-on loafers over his tan socks. "Because he kicked his ball out of the rough on number six when he thought I wasn't looking, and gave me the wrong score on a par five. The fifteenth hole, as I recall it."

Annie was silent for a few moments, then said coldly, "That's it? That's your reason? Wow. Hanging's too good for him."

"Scoff if you must, Ms. Kendall," Grady said, running a finger along her jaw as he walked past her to unlock the desk drawer and pull out his pistol and shoulder holster, "but this is scientific stuff. If you cheat on the golf course, you'll cheat anywhere."

"Anywhere?" Annie watched as he shrugged into the shoulder holster. She didn't know how, but wearing the gun made Grady look even sexier. There was probably something wrong with her, some leftover awe from watching *Bonnie and Clyde* dozens of times in her youth, and she'd have to examine her reaction later. For now, she wanted to hear more from Grady.

"Anywhere," Grady repeated seriously. "And what better way to cheat than by charging Archie an arm and a leg for his little house calls, and then hiding some extra bucks for himself in Archie's will? His wills, I should say. I said it before. Old rule, Annie, the more you mess with something, the more likely it is that something gets overlooked. Like, say, a million dollar *gift* to his faithful lawyer."

Annie watched as he shrugged into a navy sport coat that pretty much finished off his *GQ* image. Thanks to great tailoring, the bulge of his holster didn't even show. "But, wouldn't Jefferson be losing all those hefty fees if Archie were dead?"

"More than made up for by being named executor. Besides, who says Archie won't decide to replace Banning one of these days. He's got to have thought of it," Grady said, shooting his cuffs. Then he stood in front of her, tying what had to be the proverbial old school tie of blue and maroon stripes.

She reached up, fixed his collar, which had a small wrinkle in it. "Now, isn't this all domestic?" he said, standing so close to her Annie experienced a slight difficulty in remembering how to breathe. "Chatting before dinner with the little woman."

"Yeah," Annie said, trying to step past him. "Just you, the investigator, and me, one of the suspects, and the gun in your shoulder holster. I'm feeling all warm and fuzzy, too."

Grady stepped to his left, blocking her way. He put his hands on her shoulders, looking down at her, his expression serious at last. "Annie? I have to investigate you, you understand that. I have to investigate everyone."

"Some investigating, playing golf with the suspects. Want to take me bowling?" she shot back at him. "Who knows, I might use a trick ball."

"Forget Banning," he said, shaking his head, his gaze still locked with hers. "Maybe I'm reaching here, granted. The guy's got a win-win situation going on, and makes money whether Archie lives or dies. Although he did kick his ball out of the rough," he ended, smiling.

"Then why did you bring it up?"

"I was stalling, trying to figure out a way to get you to smile at me again, like me again. Did it work?"

"I don't *dislike* you," Annie told him. Man, she was becoming a master of the understatement. "But it hurt, Grady. I thought we were in this together. Allies."

"I'm sorry."

"So am I," Annie said, amazed at how much she meant what she said.

They remained where they were, Grady's hands on her shoulders, Annie looking up at him, smiling slightly as she saw the new sprinkling of freckles under his eyes.

She lifted a hand, touched his jaw. "Better today?" she asked, the words coming out in a breathless whisper.

"Let's try it out and see," Grady answered, his mouth beside her ear. "Do you remember where we left off?"

"I think so," Annie said, tilting her head so that he could nibble on her neck. "Right about there . . . and maybe *there* . . ."

When his mouth claimed hers, Annie forgot any lingering hurt or anger and gave herself over to the moment. Gave herself over to Grady, who stepped forward just another little bit, placing one thigh slightly between her legs, bringing her body closer to his.

*"Hey!"* Maisie's shout was followed by a rapid pounding on the connecting door. "I'm not hearing anything! What's going on in there?"

Grady straightened, then leaned forward again, pressing his forehead against Annie's. "If we open a branch office in Timbuktu, I could transfer her there."

Annie smiled slightly, trying to regulate her breathing. "You couldn't do that to the Timbuktuians."

"I heard *that!*" Maisie called out. "Very funny, honey—*not!*"

"Come on, let's go down to dinner," Grady whispered quietly. He put a finger to his mouth to warn her not to speak, then slipped a hand down Annie's arm, took hold of her hand as they quietly walked toward the door. He was always holding her hand. She'd always thought she'd feel too confined if someone was always touching her, holding her hand, stuff like that. But now she liked it. It made her feel safe, and very close to him.

As they walked past the connecting door, Grady suddenly pounded the side of his fist on it several times before pulling it open. "You coming to dinner?"

Annie could see Maisie as she screwed up her face,

one hand clapped to her ear. "Everyone's a comedian these days. You have to put your head down on that pillow and go to sleep sometime, honey," the secretary told him as she stomped into the room on her four-inch heels, headed for the door to the hallway. "Think about it."

"Is there a key?" Annie asked, laughing at the expression on Grady's face.

"Nope," Grady said, squeezing her hand. "But I think I have a solution that will keep me from Maisie's revenge."

Annie bit her bottom lip, tried not to shiver. "Really? And what would that be? Will I like your solution?"

"Oh, brother, you two make me want to puke," Maisie said, leaning around the doorjamb and rolling her eyes at them. "Let me do this in words of one or two syllables, okay? *He* wants you to distrust Banning because Banning was giving you the goo-goo eyes the other night. And *you,* honey, you've been looking for an excuse to say yes ever since you first laid those weird eyes of yours on him. So just"—she made twirling motions with her hands—"just go do it, okay, and stop making me sick. Now come on, I think I need a drink."

# Fourteen

*Gwine to run all night!*
*Gwine to run all day!*
*I'll bet my money on de bobtail nag—*
*Somebody bet on de bay.*
                    —Stephen Collins Foster

Dickens was tall. Dickens was imposing. Dickens had an *air* about him.

Dickens, wearing white-cotton gloves and answering A.W.'s inquiry as to why he had donned these gloves with something about "a hideous skin rash caused by experimenting with a new silver polish, sir," was about as subtle as Dolly Parton's D-cups.

Grady, from his position lounging against the mantelpiece in the drawing room, dropped his head and rubbed at his forehead, trying to shield his view of the butler as the man busily went about collecting fingerprints.

He'd gotten Mitzi's without too much trouble, handing her a glass of sherry, just to grab it right back again, saying he'd seen a chip on the brim. That hadn't been so bad, but it would only work once, and even Dickens seemed to understand he couldn't use the same ploy with everyone.

Which probably explained why he had just walked behind Junior—who was otherwise engaged in slowly inching his hand up under Daisy's skirt—and dropped a dead bug into the younger Peevers's highball. No, wait. It wasn't dead. The damn thing was doing the backstroke, and probably getting higher than a kite if it swallowed any of the booze. What a way to go.

"Oh. My. Sir. A. Bug," Dickens exclaimed, rather like Little Red Riding Hood exclaiming, "What great big eyes you have, Grandma!" He dashed across the room and plucked the glass out of Junior's grip—Grady had noticed a slight hesitation, as if Dickens was giving the notion of Junior gulping down a bug a mental run-through in his mind, weighing the pros and cons. "I. Am. So. Overset."

"You're doing really well, but you might want to drop it down a notch now, okay, Dickens?" Grady muttered under his breath, strolling over to the sideboard as the butler was surreptitiously wrapping Junior's glass in a linen napkin, then placing it inside one of the drawers. "It's not like this is your only shot. We don't have to get them all in one night."

"I have an obligation, sir," Dickens responded in the belief he was whispering, which meant that anyone more than twenty feet away might have some slight difficulty in making out every word. "The sooner it is discharged, the happier I will be."

Grady looked over his shoulder, checking on the others in the room. Nobody seemed to be paying any attention.

Except for Annie, who always paid attention, blast her. "Look, Dickens," he whispered, "you've got two. It's a good start. Just save the glasses from the dinner table for the rest of them."

"No need, sir," Dickens said, leaning closer to whisper in Grady's ear. This time, thank God, the man actually did whisper. "I have Mister A.W.'s tooth glass, and the vitamin vial left here by Dr. Sandborn. I, of course, have already provided a specimen of my own prints."

"Leaving Jefferson Banning, Ms. Goodenough, Miss Peevers, and Ms. Kendall," Grady said, mentally counting on his fingers. "I can manage Ms. Kendall for you."

"Leaving me with Attorney Banning and Ms. Goodenough. Good enough—er, yes, sir, that will be fine. Everything will be delivered to your room later this evening, as I also have in my possession a set of Attorney Banning's prints. He insists upon handling the lesser figurines whenever he visits, sir, and broke one just last week. It's in my rooms, awaiting replace—er, that is . . . repair," Dickens said, then walked back toward the couches and chairs arranged in a conversation group in the middle of the room, obviously prepared to hang around behind one of the couches, doing his best vulture imitation.

Annie joined Grady at the sideboard, where he was pouring himself a small, neat scotch, as it had been a long day, and would probably get longer.

"What's up with Dickens?" Annie asked. "A rash on his hands? Why don't I believe that? And, before you try to think up a lie, I probably should tell you I saw him put that bug in Junior's drink. Please tell me you told him to do it."

Without waiting for an answer, she maneuvered herself so that her body hid what she did next. What she did next, as Grady muttered under his breath, was to slide open the drawer and see two linen napkins wrapped around two glasses. "Sonofagun," she said, closing the drawer and smiling up at him. "You're collecting fingerprints, aren't you, and you've got Dickens doing your dirty work. How'd you get him to agree?"

"He volunteered," Grady said, really not wanting to explain more than that. He'd already told her too much about Dickens, while leaving out some things, and he was beginning to get confused. "But I told him I'd get your fingerprints myself. It wasn't as if I wasn't going to tell you."

"Yeah, right," Annie said, sniffing. "And you're only taking them so you can rule me out, maybe even protect me. I understand completely. Now why don't you just eat dirt and die, okay?"

Grady grabbed her arm, holding her in place before she could bolt. "Look, Annie, be reasonable. Nobody's been in your bathroom since . . . well, since the incident. I've got it locked, remember?"

"How can I forget? I'll have to go down the hall to go to the bathroom. A person notices things like that. So what?"

"So, if I'm going to get in there with the kit I had sent up here, and lift prints, I have to have yours so I can rule you out, concentrate on prints that don't belong there. Understand now?"

She tapped a foot, almost jiggling in place for a few moments. "Okay," she said finally, "that makes sense. But then can I use my bathroom again?"

"That depends. If you want to take a bubble bath, and if you let me wash your back."

Annie grinned, then just as quickly frowned. "Are you flirting, or are you serious? Because things are starting to move a little quickly all of a sudden."

"They won't move any faster than you want," Grady promised, taking Annie by the elbow and leading her back over to where Maisie was sitting beside Muriel, patiently explaining the benefits of a good colorist.

"The cut is good, Muriel," Maisie was saying. "I like it better short, and I'm glad we got that far. But you simply have to do something with that color, honey. Grey looks fine on Bill Clinton, and it's a good look for him. But, honey," she continued, whispering, "he's a *man*. Now, think about it. Do you really want to look like Bill Clinton?"

Muriel pulled herself up in her seat, highly affronted. "We do not discuss Democrats in this house."

"Said with the conviction of the let's get rid of the capital gains tax that's causing multimillionaires to actually pay some taxes crowd," Grady said. "I know them well. Why, some of my best friends are Republicans."

"We don't discuss politics in this house," Muriel expanded, now looking up at Grady.

"We don't discuss them in my parents' house, either," he told her. "Grandpa Harford makes sweeping declarations, and Grandpa Sullivan comes from the whoever yells loudest wins the argument school of political debate. My parents sit in the middle, as referees. It's a lot of fun."

"What do you do?" Annie asked.

"Me? I'm the one who stands back, lobbing in the

occasional grenade before retiring to the sidelines to watch. It's my second favorite indoor sport. May I refresh that for you, Miss Peevers?" he asked, already reaching for Muriel's glass. After all, what the hell. He might as well help Dickens before the man got too obvious.

"I think not," Muriel responded, tight-lipped. "And I really don't see the *amusement* in politics. Running our country is serious business."

"It's a business, Miss Peevers, I'll give you that," Grady quipped. "But to change the subject, as I'm sure I should be doing, may I say how lovely you look this evening?"

"Thanks."

"Not you, Maisie," Grady said, glaring at his assistant.

"I know who you meant, honey," she said, "but since I'm the genius who took Muriel here to the beauty parlor, I'll take the credit. Besides, I also had the works, honey, as if you didn't notice, even if you haven't said anything. My hair must be at least two inches shorter. Francis, my operator, told me he couldn't remember the last time he had such great raw material to work with. That was a compliment, wasn't it, Grady?" she ended, frowning. "Damn, you know what? Now that I've said it out loud, I don't think it *was* a compliment."

Annie averted her head, coughed.

Grady quickly stepped into the breach. "You look wonderful, Maisie, as always, and I apologize if I didn't notice a great improvement on your perfection. And I'm happy you and Miss Peevers seem to be enjoying yourselves. Did I hear you say you're planning on going back another day? Wouldn't that just be gilding the lily on you two lovely ladies?"

Annie gave him a quick, hopefully unseen, kick in the ankle. Okay, so maybe he was laying it on a little thick, but it sure beat the hell out of letting Maisie get the bit between her teeth on the subject of whatever the hell goes on in beauty salons. There were some mysteries of life men really didn't want to solve.

"Why, thank you, Mr. Sullivan," Muriel said, touching her new, shorter hairdo. "And, yes, Maisie and I will be returning to the salon, on Monday, I believe. Won't we, Maisie?"

"With bells on, honey," Maisie said, grinning at Grady. "And then we'll go shopping. We'll probably be gone all day."

Monday. Okay, that was good. Maisie was being a help, even if she probably planned to get at least a manicure and one new outfit out of the deal. Grady made a mental note to search Muriel's room on Monday. Maybe he'd be lucky, and find one of those yellow-and-black paperbacks, one titled *Archery for Dummies,* or something, although he doubted it. He just couldn't get all excited about Muriel in the role of attempted murderess.

Dickens, who had left the room for a few minutes, returned to stand in the entrance and announce that dinner was now being served.

The cattle, thusly prodded, all rose and headed for the dining room, Muriel leaving her glass behind. Grady waited a few moments for the room to clear, then took out his handkerchief and wrapped Muriel's empty glass in it, handing both to Dickens as he followed everyone. "Miss Goodenough's water glass will suffice, and I'll take care of Miss Kendall."

"I'm sure you will, sir," Dickens said, stuffing the

handkerchief-wrapped glass into his cummerbund. "You might as well, along with the *body search* you're planning on . . . sir."

Grady looked at the butler through slitted eyelids, longing to pop him one in his long nose. Nope, wasn't worth the hassle. "You need to get a life, Dickens," he said instead. "Just don't make it *mine,* all right?"

"I only wish to have this obligation behind me, sir," Dickens said, his nose so high in the air Grady was pretty sure he could see the man's sinuses. "And then we are even, correct?"

"Actually, Dickens, old sport, no. I still know what you're doing. That hasn't changed. So, just because my conscience is bothering me, how about you hold a going out of the forgery and grand larceny business sale and retire, hmm?"

"I shall consider that, sir," the butler agreed, nodding. "I shall most definitely consider it. But, then, how would you know?"

Grady shook his head. "I like you, Dickens, I really do. And, frankly, that scares me."

He caught up with Annie just as she was about to sit down and held out her chair for her, then sat down beside her. "Are we having fun yet?" he asked, seeing the frown on her face.

"Heaps, and don't leave me alone with these people again or else I'm going to have to rent a pit bull," she told him. "A.W. just politely inquired if I knew the penalty for fraud in this state. He asked, because Mitzi isn't talking to me at all, which really isn't that bad, now that I think about it. But you know, all in all, I really don't like these people. Pity. I had hoped, you know."

"You were planning on liking them?" Grady asked as Dickens began serving the soup. "Do the words 'cock-eyed optimist' mean anything to you?"

"I'd like to think there's something good in everyone. I mean, look at you. You're becoming tolerable, and I didn't like you at all in the beginning." Annie picked up her spoon, taking her first taste of vichyssoise. "This soup's cold," she said, probably more loudly than she'd intended.

Daisy, seated on Grady's left, leaned across him to say, "I know, I know. Isn't it the silliest thing? Cold potato soup. My mom always used Campbell's, and she knew to heat it up first. But potato isn't my favorite. I like the one with all the little letters—in noodles, you know? I could spell my name with them. Although I always had trouble figuring out which was the *S* and which was the *Z*. For Daisy, you know? That's one *S*."

*Or two Z's, for Dizzy,* Grady thought, but didn't say anything. He just wondered if anyone else at the huge, wide table heard what either Annie or Daisy had said.

A.W. had heard it all. Grady knew that because the man snorted some soup up his nose, and Mitzi had to pat him on the back as he went into a coughing fit, which wasn't nearly as effective as the whopping *smack* Dickens gave him as he walked by, a smack that nearly sent him face forward into the vichyssoise.

"Put my foot in it, didn't I?" Annie whispered to Grady, sinking low in her chair. "I can't believe I did that. And we're not even going to talk about what Daisy said, or I'm going to embarrass myself," she ended, grinning. "Poor kid, she really doesn't have a clue, does she?"

"A.W.," Mitzi said before Grady could answer Annie, "it is not polite to notice when those of a lower order commit a faux pas. Not that either bit of trailer trash should be at the table with decent, honest people at all."

"Why, you . . . that tears it!" Annie sat up again, looked ready to pop out of her chair and launch herself across the table to wring Mitzi's scrawny neck with her own pearls.

Grady grabbed her, pulled her back down. "Now, now, Slugger. Remember, the first person to resort to physical violence in an argument is the first person to have run out of intelligent argument."

"Oh, yeah," Annie said, her head bobbing. "Oh, yeah? Well, don't look now, but I'm flat out of intelligent argument. She called me trash."

"And Daisy, too," Grady pointed out, although Daisy and Junior had already left the room, once again in a huff, and once again probably to find their way either to the nearest McDonald's or the closest Simmons Beautyrest.

"A.W.," Mitzi said now, pronounced now, "may I suggest that Junior and his . . . companion no longer be served at this table? May I, in addition, suggest Dickens just set up a trough somewhere? Surely they'd be more comfortable?"

A.W. giggled into his napkin. He did not, however, choke. He hadn't been choking for some moments. But, Grady thought, maybe Dickens thought the man needed a follow-up *smack*, because he delivered one as he passed by on his way to clear the now empty places. "Better now, sir?" Dickens then asked, winking at Annie.

Grady was right. The butler may be larcenous, but he was still a bit of all right.

"Hey!" A.W. whined. "Stop hitting me, okay? Muriel, make him stop hitting me."

"Okay, I'm outta here," Annie said, refolding her napkin and placing it on the table. "Dickens, if you don't mind, in future I'll be taking my meals in the kitchen."

"Wait!" Muriel exclaimed, looking fearful. "A.W., Mitzi—stop her. Apologize! Can't you see you're just making it all worse? If she tells Daddy what you did—"

"Oh, God, Mitzi, is she right?" A.W. asked, paling. "I thought I shouldn't have said what you told me to say, and now look what's happening."

"Relax. I won't say anything to Archie," Annie said. "I'm not a tattletale."

"Maybe not, but I am," Grady piped up, rising to help Annie out of her chair. "But I want to be accurate, Mrs. Peevers. Would that be a single-width trailer, or a double-wide?"

"See? You have to apologize, Mitzi," Muriel said, sounding more triumphant than sympathetic. "You have to say you're sorry to Miss Kendall. I don't think Daddy cares about Daisy, but being impolite to Miss Kendall could cause trouble."

Mitzi moved her head jerkily on her thin stalk of a neck, as if looking for a place to rest her gaze that wouldn't mean she had to look at anyone else in the room. She bit her bottom lip for a moment, closed her eyes, then sighed. "Very well, Muriel, if you're going to be so upset. We can't have that, now can we, as those liver spots come out so noticeably when you're hysterical.

Miss Kendall, my apologies. I'm convinced you had a very cultured upbringing . . . somewhere."

"Hey, wait a minute, honey. I've been sitting here trying to eat, be a good little guest, but now you've gone and done it," Maisie piped up, having been mercifully silent until that point. She pointed her soup spoon at Mitzi. "I grew up in a trailer camp, so you can't insult me. You know why? Because I know who I am, and I'm just as good as anyone sitting here. Probably a little better than you, A.W., because I don't need somebody's hand up my back to know when to open my mouth. And you can say what you want about Annie, because I figure she can handle herself. But now you've crossed the line. Muriel here is wearing brand-new fifty dollars a bottle makeup that I picked out for her personally. Liver spots? Give me a break, honey. A galloping case of *measles* wouldn't show through that stuff."

Grady leaned over to whisper in Annie's ear. "Are you getting all of this? I mean, who knows, I might someday want to write a book about my career in personal security. I could use this conversation in a chapter called 'What to Do When All the Suspects Are Nuts.' "

Annie shook her head. "No, not that chapter. I think it would be more like 'Personal Security, The Lighter Side.' Can we go now, or do you think Maisie's going to start a riot? I really don't like cold potato soup."

"But you're hungry?" Grady asked as Maisie and Mitzi glared daggers at each other across the table and Muriel began crying into her napkin. A.W., oblivious as ever, was done with his soup and had grabbed Mitzi's bowl. His head was so close to the table that Grady fought an impulse to suggest he just dive in.

"Starving," Annie admitted. "And I've been locked up here all day, no thanks to you. I think you owe me a dinner."

They were both quiet for a moment, trying to gauge the mood of the room, just to hear Maisie saying, "Why, of course it would be good for you, Mrs. P. And there's this moisturizer. It's to die for, honey, and would clear up that chicken neck of yours in no time. That lucky old sun hasn't been so lucky for you, right? Do you want to come with us on Monday? That okay with you, Muriel, honey?"

"I don't believe it," Grady said, shaking his head. "No, scratch that. Yes, I do. But I will tell you, sometimes that woman scares me."

"Only sometimes?" Annie asked, and the two of them, still laughing, headed out to find a place that knew soup was supposed to be served hot.

# Fifteen

*I'll risk forty dollars that he can
outjump any frog in Calaveras County.*
　　　　　　　　　　　—Mark Twain

Annie scrunched down in the seat of Grady's car and lifted up her jeans-clad legs, pressing the soles of her sneakers against the inside of the windshield.

And waited.

"What the hell are you doing?"

"Guess," she told him, moving her feet against the glass in a sort of dance. "Maybe this will help. 'My God, his mother didn't have any *teeth!*' "

"Right. And Annie Kendall has just lost her marbles," Grady said, keeping one eye on the road, the other on his once-pristine windshield. Then he held out his hand, saying, "Okay, okay. I got it. *Smokey and the Bandit,* part one—the good one. You're Sally Field, and you're practicing dance steps on my windshield. The question now is, *why?*"

Annie counted out, ". . . and tap, and tap, and heel

and toe," then lowered her legs, although she was still sitting practically on her spine in the bucket seat. "I have no idea why," she told him honestly. "It just suddenly seemed like it might be fun. Was it good for you, Mr. Sullivan, sir? It was good for me."

Grady looked at her owlishly. "I only saw you drinking bottled water before dinner. Did Dickens slip something in it?"

"I don't think so." Annie giggled. "Ah, I'm sorry, Grady. I guess I'm just trying to ease the tension a little. There *is* tension inside this car, you know, unless I'm the only one who feels it."

"Oh, I feel it," Grady agreed, turning his attention back to the road, still not sure where he'd take Annie for dinner now that they'd escaped Peevers Mansion. She'd changed out of her "lady clothes" while he'd showered, put on khaki slacks and a black knit top, and he'd been more than a little aware of the fit of her lime green sweater top ever since. Not to mention how her jeans fit her, and what they had to cling to.

Tonight was the night. He knew it. She knew it. He knew she knew it. He knew she knew he knew he knew it—ah, hell, did he really know *anything?* Did she?

She probably didn't know he was nervous as hell, more nervous than he'd been since he'd first discovered the delights to be found in backseats in his senior year in high school. If he could believe that, hang on to that, maybe he could pull it off. Right now, he doubted that highly. He felt so ineptly Harry High School right now he was surprised he hadn't broken out into zits.

"You quote movies a lot," he said after a moment, as Annie sat up once more, rebuckling her seat belt.

"Um, yes," she said, pushing her hands through those delightful dark curls and then sighing, settling back in the bucket seat. "I think I used to live to go to the movies. Great place to escape, don't you think? Into someone else's reality?"

"If you can call Hollywood's idea of reality anything close to real."

"Well, there is that," Annie said, watching the billboards as they flashed by on the thruway. "But there are more happy endings than not, so it works out. I don't go to horror movies, you understand. If I want to shriek, get sweaty palms, and have my heart rate triple, I can just look at the balance in my checkbook."

"Ah, yes, money. Filthy lucre. The folding green. Archie's giving you a pretty big payday, isn't he?"

"And I'm moneygrubbing trash," Annie shot right back at him, although she smiled, just to let him know she wasn't insulted. "But it is true, I've never seen fifty thousand in two years, let alone in one month. Archie's was pretty much the offer I just couldn't refuse."

"*The Godfather,* part one, also the best one," Grady said, nodding. "And you didn't even need a horse head in your bed."

Annie shivered. "I knew that was coming. Did you know that was coming? The minute the camera panned to the bed, I just knew that poor horse was going to be there. Well, part of him anyway. Imagine if Archie woke up to that one morning! And speaking of Archie, shouldn't we be back at the mansion, watching out for him?"

"I left Dickens in charge," Grady told her. "The bedroom door is locked, the drapes are drawn, and the two of them are playing checkers. It's a Saturday night ritual, I understand. He'll be safe enough while we're gone. Speaking of which—what are you hungry for?"

Annie sat up straight and pointed out the window. "Cotton candy!"

"Of course. Served in all the best restaurants," Grady said.

"No, no, really. Didn't you see it? That little billboard back there? There's a small fair going on tonight. At some church; I couldn't get the name. But it says to exit at MacArthur Road North and follow the signs. Come on, Grady, it'll be fun. Pull over into the right lane, okay? You don't have to pass the pickup—just slow down and pull in behind him."

"I can make it."

Annie banged her palms against the sides of her head and grimaced. "Honestly! You men. Why can't you just ease into another lane? Why do you always have to pass everyone else first? Women don't. Oh, the heck with it. Just pass the guy and get into the right lane before we miss the exit."

Grady was caught between laughter and longing to tape Annie's mouth shut. "Tell me where to go, lady, but don't tell me how to get there," he said at last, easing up on the gas pedal once he'd passed the red pickup. "Are you sure you want to do this?"

"Positive. I haven't been to a church fair in ages. I'll bet they have pork barbecue. Church fairs always have pork barbecue. And cotton candy. You've been to one, haven't you?"

"My grandpa Sullivan used to take me to Saint Mary's end-of-the-summer picnic and fair," Grady said, smiling in reminiscence. "He'd play the games, sit with all his cronies, and give me enough money to get myself sick on junk. But that was a lot of years ago. I wonder if he still goes?"

"You don't see him much anymore?"

Grady made a left turn, then followed in the direction a man holding a red flag was pointing, pulling the sports car onto a grassy field taken over by about a hundred parked cars. "I see him, but not as often. My business. My long hours." He sighed. "My loss."

"That's a shame," Annie said, when he'd come around to open her car door for her. "I never had a grandfather around when I was growing up. Or a grandmother. I had a friend once, at one of the schools I attended, whose grandmother used to have pretend tea parties with her and take her shopping on her birthday. I was *so* jealous of her."

Grady kept his voice light, just politely interested. "You and your parents moved around a lot while you were young, did you?"

Annie, who had been looking across the street at the lights on the small Ferris wheel and other rides set up on the regular church parking lot, stopped, turned to look up at Grady. "Is this a fishing expedition? Because, if it is, maybe I should go back and get my wading boots. Now, what do you want to know?"

Grady looked down at her, saw that the light in her eyes that had been there the moment she'd seen the billboard for the fair had now faded away. "Nothing. Forget it. Let's go find out what smells so good."

Annie took a deep breath, part sigh, part testing the

air. "Pork barbecue. I knew it!" She grabbed his hand, and, together, they headed across the street.

Thirty minutes, two pork barbecues and an order of homemade cheese and potato perogies split between them later, Grady watched Annie pull long, fluffy strings of bright pink cotton candy off a paper cone and shove them into her mouth. If her expression could be any indication, she was eating the food of the gods.

"That good, huh?" he asked as she licked her fingertips. One after the other, closing her lips around each tip, washing each tip with her tongue. He imagined men had suffered less undergoing Chinese water torture, or maybe staked out on an anthill, with honey poured all over them.

"Buy your own," she teased, half-turning away from him, pulling the cotton candy out of reach. Then she grabbed his hand, once more pulling him along after her. She'd been pulling him along after her one way or another ever since they met, he realized, and, sick ticket that he was, he was actually beginning to like it. "Look, Grady, the games are all over here. Win something for me. Nobody's ever won anything for me."

"Nobody?" he asked, finding that difficult to believe.

"Well, nobody but me, and I don't count. Come on, Grady, see if you can win that great big panda for me. See it? All you have to do is knock down those three wooden milk bottles with a ball. A great big softball, Grady. You can do it."

"Nobody can do it, Annie. This might be a church fair, but these games are all rigged so that nobody wins. The fair makes a lot of money, the priests all go to Confession afterward, and God lets them go back to weekly bingo games for the rest of the year. I know. Grandpa Sullivan told me."

Annie took a last bite of cotton candy, then tossed the cone in a nearby trash can. "You're just chicken," she told him, giving her fingers one last cleaning, and reminding Grady that his plans for this evening included games of quite another sort. She did a little dance, putting her hands under her arms and flapping pretend wings. "Cluck. Cluck-cluck-cluck. Chicken!"

"You'll pay for that one," Grady said as he heard laughter around him. "Now, lead me to those damn bottles."

Annie rubbed her hands together as she stood to one side, encouraging Grady as he held the first softball and glared at the trio of wooden milk bottles set on a board about fifteen feet away. "Okay, okay," she said, her voice low. "We're gonna plant our feet, balance our weight. Take a bead on those bottles, Grady. You want to hit them low, not necessarily all that hard. Placement is everything. Now, we'll both go into our windup . . . and bam! Well, that's depressing."

He'd missed. How the hell had he missed? He hadn't hit even one of the bottles, even nicked one a little. It had been a flat-out miss. But he didn't need Annie to tell him that.

Grady loved to play, golf mostly. And hated to lose. It wasn't that he wasn't a graceful loser. He was always polite, always shook his opponent's hand and smiled nicely while holding his second-place trophy. But he'd made it a habit not to take second place too often. He liked to win.

Usually, he didn't whine about losing. Tonight he felt himself making an exception.

"It's your fault. You distracted me," he said now, plunking down another two bucks and picking up another softball. "And what was with that high leg kick anyway?"

"Juan Marichal, Hall of Famer, I think," Annie told him. "He had a real high leg kick, remember? Don't you watch ESPN? I thought all men watched ESPN. I just love when they do those retrospectives on the best players."

"Really." Grady held the ball and looked at her dispassionately. "You are *not* Juan Marichal, Annie. You're barely Charlie Brown."

"And who says I couldn't knock down those bottles? Huh? Huh? *You?*"

"You gonna throw that ball, mister, or let the little lady do it?" the carny asked around the cigarette hanging from his thin lips.

"This is a private discussion, if you don't mind," Grady said, then pulled out a twenty and slammed it down on the bare wood shelf that acted as the front of the stand. "Five balls each, Annie, and this sixth one for you, just to be fair."

"Don't do me any favors," Annie growled, then spit— yes, she *spit*—on her hands before taking the softball from him. "Although I accept. You can go first."

Grady picked up one of the balls the carny had put in front of him, then stepped back a bit, believing he needed more distance in order to get the thrown ball down low enough to do any damage.

That's when the carny got into the act. "Here we go,

ladies and gentlemen!" he called out, picking up a microphone Grady hadn't seen before and bellowing into it. "The big strong man here and the little lady, in a battle of the sexes. Gather round, gather round. Lots more room here for everyone to play!" He covered the microphone with his hand, asking Grady's name.

When Grady didn't answer, Annie did it for him. "He's Grady, and I'm Annie. Tell them he gave me one of his balls, just so nobody thinks he's not playing fair."

"Ah, jeez, Annie . . . ," Grady began, wanting to dig a hole somewhere and disappear into it. But it was too late.

"Okay, ladies and gentlemen. It's Annie and Grady. And listen to this! The little lady wants you to know Grady here has already given her one of his balls. Isn't that something?"

Annie scooted over to Grady, leaning a shoulder against him and speaking to him out of the corner of her mouth. "I thought this was a church fair. He shouldn't have said it that way, and these people shouldn't be laughing."

"Ya think?" Grady whispered back, glaring down a real boulder of a man holding a hot dog in each hand and laughing so hard Grady wondered if he might injure himself. "Now, if you'll let me knock down these damn milk bottles, maybe I can walk away with at least some of my dignity intact."

"You want me to throw the contest? Take a dive? Is that it? Because I'm going to win, Grady. You can count on it. In fact, how about a little side bet?"

"That isn't what I meant. Besides, you're broke," he reminded her. "You'd be betting with borrowed money. *My* borrowed money, as a matter of fact."

She shook her head as she looked up at him, pretending amazement. "You've got a real stuck needle in that record, don't you, Grady? Okay, how about this. I win, and you let me *really* be your partner as we protect Archie? Every step of the way. No secrets. You tell me everything, let me help."

"And when I win?"

He could see her biting the inside of her cheek as she considered his question. "I'll tell you why I went to the movies," she said at last.

"Good, but not enough."

She rolled her eyes. "Okay, so I'll tell *you* everything. Answer any question you have about me. Is that good enough?"

"Deal," Grady said, sticking out his hand and shaking hers. "Now stand back, and let the master work."

The master missed, actually, but he'd gotten closer, knocking down the top bottle in the pyramid. "I'm finding the range, okay?" he said when the onlookers hooted. They only hooted louder.

Then it was Annie's turn, and she did that spit-in-her-hands thing again before rubbing the ball in her palms. As Grady stood off to one side, watching in amazement, she turned to her side, eyeing the milk bottles as she seemed to line them up with her left shoulder. Her eyelids narrowed to slits, and a look of determination came over her features that would have been comical if she hadn't been so serious about the thing.

"Come on, Annie!" a woman in the crowd yelled out. "Knock 'em down! Do it for all of us!"

"For crying out loud, now we're making a feminist

*statement?"* Grady grumbled to a young man standing near him.

"Yeah, right. Women," the young man said, then gave out a small *"ooof!"* as his girlfriend elbowed him in the ribs.

"Come on, Annie, throw the ball," Grady urged her. "Before you turn this into a free-for-all."

Annie took a deep breath, her shoulders rising, then let it out. Looked at the bottles again. Then she shook her head, just as if she were facing a batter and the catcher had offered a sign she was shaking off.

"I don't believe this," Grady said, turning away. But he had to turn around again. He had to see what she'd do next.

Annie continued to glare, deep in concentration, then smiled tightly, nodding. Obviously the catcher had now signaled for a pitch she wanted to throw. Wasn't that just peachy?

"Oh, good," Grady sniped. "Any year now, and she should throw it."

The young man opened his mouth, his girlfriend said, "Don't even think about it," and he shut his mouth again.

The boulder of a man still held his two hot dogs.

The crowd went quiet.

Annie went into her windup, a complicated maneuver that had a lot to do with raising both hands over her head as her left leg rose in a high, graceful kick.

And Grady held his breath. She was going to do it. He just knew it. She was going to knock down those damn bottles. He didn't know how he knew, or why, but he was about to be shown up by a curvy gal in a mop of curls.

Grady mentally practiced his best "second-place" smile.

Annie threw the ball, her follow-through a true work of art, and the milk bottles went down as, in typical form, "the crowd went wild."

Panda bear in tow (and ego definitely in check), Grady walked down the entire row of games of chance as Annie's banker and only a small part of her growing crowd of cheerleaders. She tossed basketballs. She threw darts at balloons. She aimed a water gun at a mechanical clown's mouth. She shot a rifle at a small red star—for that one she won a pocketknife she quickly presented to Grady as a gift.

He refused the goldfish she'd won by tossing a Ping-Pong ball into a fishbowl, but she didn't pout about it. She said she'd give it to Maisie.

Grady watched as she gave all the stuffed animals she'd won away to little children who had been watching her, keeping only the panda bear.

"Wasn't that fun?" she asked him, her eyes bright as they walked away from the stands and back to the food stands, because she had a sudden hunger for a candy apple. "But we had to make a quick run and then get out of there, before they figured it out."

"Before who figured out what?" Grady asked. He'd been in a sort of daze for the past fifteen minutes.

"That I'd worked as a carny, silly," Annie said, shaking her head at his naïveté. "Didn't you figure it out? How else do you think I knew where to hit the milk bottles? And there's this trick to getting the basketball into those undersize hoops. But if I told you either trick, I'd have to kill you, so I won't."

Grady was barely listening anymore, having zeroed in on just one thing. *"You* were a carny?"

"Only for one summer, until they caught me and sent me back," she said, then took a huge bite out of her candy apple. "It was the best summer of my life."

He didn't know her. He just flat out did *not* know this woman. He knew nothing about her. Okay, so he wanted to go to bed with her. He was fascinated with her, had been fascinated with her from that first glimpse he'd seen of her face in the photograph Archie had given him. *That* he knew. But that's all he knew.

"I don't believe this," Grady said, as she held out the apple, offering him the side she hadn't bitten into yet. "Who *are* you, Annie Kendall?"

"Uh-uh. I won, remember? Our bet? You have to show me yours, but I don't have to show you mine."

"That's before I knew you were a ringer," Grady pointed out, hoping the words didn't come out in a whine.

"No, you didn't. I agree. You just thought you were the great big caveman about to show off for the little lady. You were trying to be as *unfair* as you could be, sure you'd win. But I forgive you. It's the testosterone, you can't really help yourself." She cocked her head to one side, listening to the music he'd been hearing without thinking about for the past few minutes. "A band! And they're playing country music. Come on, Grady, let's dance."

One more time her hand slipped into his, and one more time he followed where she led. If Quinn could see him now he'd either be rolling on the ground, laughing his ass off, or already be hauling him off to the nearest shrink. This was *not* how Grady Sullivan lived. What he was doing tonight was *not* what Grady Sullivan did for fun.

Grady Sullivan played golf at the country club. Grady Sullivan dated models with long legs and wonderfully vacant heads. Grady Sullivan dined in five-star restaurants and danced in black tie to world-class orchestras.

So what in hell was he doing here? And why in hell was he smiling?

A small band shell had been set up behind a roped-off area, strung with Christmas lights, that had been reserved for dancing. Now that the sun had gone down, and there were more than a few strollers parked on the grass with sleeping babies in them, the parents had taken to the asphalt.

The area was crowded. Mothers held hands with their children, dancing with them. Daddies held sleeping tots in their arms and swayed to the music. Elderly couples held hands as they sat in folding chairs set around three sides of the dancing area, although many grey-haired couples were up and dancing themselves.

A three-year-old with bright red hair was dancing by himself, gyrating to a much faster beat he heard inside his head, whirling about smack in the middle of the crowd.

A young priest, his clerical collar slightly askew, stood at the edge of the dancers, tapping his foot and singing along with the Willie Nelson look-alike strumming his guitar and doing a damn good imitation of his hero.

"Don't you just love it?" Annie asked, her smile hurting Grady's heart. "Quick, what has forty pounds of hair and three teeth?"

"I have no idea," Grady said, laughing. "What has forty pounds of hair and three teeth?"

"The front row audience at a Willie Nelson concert!" Annie told him. "It's an old joke, and not very real, because *everybody* likes Willie Nelson. I've been a fan for years. But it is funny. Dance with me?"

He could say no. But, as he'd never been one to pull the wings off butterflies or kick roly-poly puppies, he asked the priest to hold the fishbowl, then led Annie into the crowd and took her in his arms.

After all, hadn't he been wanting Annie Kendall in his arms for a long time? He just hadn't planned on a panda joining them in the dance. But he was versatile, resourceful. He owned his own business, right? He'd cope. Considering himself brilliant, he handed the panda to the redheaded boy. After all, the kid needed a partner.

Annie smelled like candy apple and cotton candy. She probably tasted of the two confections, too, which was something he planned to find out later, when they were more alone.

He held on to her hand, pressed his other palm against the flat of her back, and tipped his head so his cheek rested on the curls that tickled at his chin.

She fit so well against him. Her sigh of contentment had to be real. Everything about her was so unaffected, so spontaneous, so very *Annie.* He knew so little about her, next to nothing. But he did know one thing. Annie Kendall, no matter who she was, no matter what her name, definitely was very, very real. Maybe too real.

Grady found himself closing his eyes as they danced, as they moved together as if they'd been dancing with each other all of their lives. Not a fan of country music, he listened to the words of the unfamiliar, rather sad song, making out words that had something to do with an angel flying too close to the ground.

And then Annie began to sing along, her voice quiet but pure, her heart in every word, "I knew someday you'd fly away . . ." She knew every word; and she wrung the emotion out of each and every one of them.

The singer went into the bridge, the beat and the melody combining in such an elemental way, making it so easy to take Annie into more complicated steps that matched mood to music.

Grady lightly pushed her away from him, holding her with one hand as she stepped back, did a small twirl, then he pulled her back against him once more, spinning them round, and round, and round before the singer began the second chorus.

She sang to him again, and he began to sing along with her when the words became more familiar. The music soared, the simple, sad passion of it beating inside Grady's chest. He let go of her hand, turning her so that they went through the steps side by side, their arms around each other's waists. Two forward, one back, another tricky forward step she followed without effort, then sweeping her into yet another turn, another twirl.

Another rush of heat as he brought her back against his chest, against the length of him. He didn't know, he didn't think. He only acted. They swayed together, moved together, two bodies responding as one . . . into the last flourish . . . into the last turn . . . into a dip where he followed her down, caught her mouth with his own.

Cotton candy and candy apples became his all-time favorite foods.

It was only when he belatedly heard the applause that he looked up, pulled Annie with him, and saw that everyone else had stopped dancing to watch them. Even the little redheaded boy was standing there, grinning, and clapping his hands.

Annie blushed. She was even more beautiful when she blushed, and smiled, and dropped into a curtsy to their "audience."

Suddenly, Grady could feel himself losing a battle he didn't know he'd been fighting. And he knew he was in real trouble when Annie bent down, kissed the redheaded boy on the cheek, then gave him the panda to keep "for your very own."

She was so good, so wonderful, so *real;* so everything he'd needed when he spent his life up to that moment not knowing what he'd wanted. She was almost too good to be true.

# Sixteen

*"I can't explain myself, I'm afraid, sir,"*
*said Alice, "Because I'm not myself, you see."*
*"I don't see," said the caterpillar.*
—Lewis Carroll

"You're not doing the two-step on my windshield," Grady said. "Does this mean you didn't have a good time?"

"Nope," she said. "It just means I've already done it, and so I don't have to do it again. I had a wonderful time tonight. You're quite the dancer yourself, you know."

"But modest with it all," Grady said, wickedly grinning at her. "I'm most proud of how modest a man I am. I tell everyone."

"Nut!" Annie felt mellow. Relaxed. And yet with an undercurrent of excitement coursing through her. She was sitting next to Grady, on her way back to Peevers Mansion, and when they got there?

Ah, when they got there . . .

"Sleepy?" Grady asked a few miles later, reaching

over to tap her on the arm, as she had her head back, her eyes closed. It was probably too dark in the car for him to see the smile on her face.

"No, not really," she said, keeping her eyes closed, still holding Maisie's goldfish in her lap. "Did you *really* have fun tonight?"

Grady put on the ticker and got over into the right lane—slowing down so that he could pull in behind the car in front of them. "I think you know I did."

"Yes, I do. It was probably when you joined in on that line dance with Father Ricky that I stopped worrying that maybe a church fair wasn't your favorite Saturday night-spot. Wasn't he cute?"

"Who?" Grady asked, turning onto the narrow, winding road that led to Peevers Mansion.

"Father Ricky, of course. We used to call priests like that Father Gorgeous. I had *such* a mad crush on Father Tom when I was in seventh grade. We all did. He coached the church league basketball team, so naturally I had to be a cheerleader. Just to be near him. Poor guy. I think we all made his life a living hell."

"Father Gorgeous, huh? So you went to parochial school?" Grady asked, keeping his eyes on the road that was marked with DEER CROSSING signs.

"Oh, no you don't. I won the bet, remember? I don't have to tell you a single thing about myself. I'm a lady of mystery, and I like it."

"A lady of mystery and pom-poms. Were you a good cheerleader?"

"I was loud," Annie said, grimacing. "Loud was about as much as they could hope for in seventh grade. But then I moved again, and retired my megaphone. I couldn't do a split, you understand. Not that I could figure out why anyone would *want* to do a split."

Grady parked the car in the drive in front of the mansion. "Did you move around a lot as a child? I get the impression you did. Whoops, sorry. No questions, right?"

Annie waited until he came around the car, to open the door for her. It was silly, she could open the door for herself, she'd been opening doors for herself all of her life, but she rather liked letting him do it for her. "Actually, I think that's pretty much no questions I don't want to answer. I'll answer that one. Yes, I moved around a lot while I was growing up."

"Because of your dad's job?"

"Sorry, that one I won't answer," Annie said, as they walked past Dickens, who had opened the front door for them. "I'll give you hints, Grady, but no clues. I'm still trying to get used to the idea that Maisie can tap her painted nails on a keyboard and find out so much about people. Hello, Dickens. How's Archie? Sleeping? Teaching himself tae kwon do now that Grady here took away his gun?"

"Mr. Peevers is asleep behind his locked door," Dickens answered stiffly. "He always sleeps soundly."

"I'll just bet he does," Grady said as he motioned for Annie to climb the steps in front of him. "What sort of knockout drops did you give him?"

"I only follow Dr. Sandborn's orders, sir," Dickens said, then turned on his heels and departed the foyer in what looked pretty much like a huff.

"Now you've gone and hurt his feelings," Annie said. "Shame on you."

"Archie's got his own branch store of the local pharmacy, and shame on *me?* How about the doctor? Take the M.D. from behind his name and he's nothing more than a pusher. Not to mention a user himself."

"He is not!" Annie responded hotly, then took a deep breath, calmed herself. "Sorry. I guess I'm not much into sweeping statements about people. You know, like con artist, and fake, and gold-digging impostor? I mean, there's a reason for everything, isn't there?"

"The word you're looking for is *excuse,* Annie, and I don't think there is one for what Dr. Sandborn is doing. Besides, we're talking about the good doctor, not you. Once this is over, when my month is up, I'm going to have a little talk with the man about the benefits to be found in retirement and maybe a condo in Florida."

"Or you'll report him?" Annie asked, still walking ahead of Grady as they walked down the hallway toward her room. She put her hand on the doorknob, then turned to face him. "Why? You know about Dickens, and you're not telling Archie on him. Why Dr. Sandborn?"

Grady put his hand on hers, forcing her to turn the knob and open the door. "Come on, Annie. There's a difference here, a big one. Sandborn is treating patients."

"No, he's not," Annie told him, walking into her room and putting the fishbowl down on the nightstand beside the bed. She should shut her big mouth, but she just couldn't. "Dickens told me. The man's retired. Archie is Dr. Sandborn's only patient."

"Really? How'd you get Dickens to tell you that?" Grady busied himself checking inside the closet and bathroom, as if he expected someone to jump out and yell, "Boo!"

"Aren't you going to peek under the bed?" Annie asked meanly. "And why you're checking out my room instead of baby-sitting Archie I still can't figure out."

"Would you feel better if I told you I trust Dickens implicitly? The man stands to lose his lucrative little business if anything happens to Archie, remember? The old guy couldn't have a more devoted bodyguard. Besides, also in case you haven't noticed, you're not the most popular person around here."

Annie lifted her chin defiantly. "They all love me," she said. "They can't help themselves. Everybody loves me."

"Nice try," Grady told her, walking back to stand in front of her, at which point she decided she was standing *way* too close to the bed. "They hate your guts, and you know it." He touched his fingers to her cheek. "Although I'm pretty fond of you."

"Really?" she said, avoiding his eyes, doing a really good impression of someone intensely interested in the weave of the carpet at their feet. "Thank you."

"You're welcome," he said, his tone low, and seductive, and she knew he was smiling even though she still refused to look at him. "Annie?"

"Hmmm?" she responded nervously, trying to fight down the sudden tension in the room. He was so close, and they were so alone together. And the bed was so big.

"We've got this problem, don't we?"

Now she did look at him. "Problem? What problem? I don't have any problems."

"Yes, Annie, you do. Because I want to make love to you, and you know I want to make love to you. So maybe it's not really a problem. Maybe it's more of a decision.

Your decision. Do I stay, Annie, or do I leave? And you'd better soon make up your mind, because if I don't leave soon I don't think I'll be able to go. Annie?"

Her breath hitched in her throat, which really upset her, because she had wanted to play this so cool, like it was just another man, just another Saturday night. But she couldn't play it cool. She didn't know how to play it cool. She didn't know how to play, period.

"Annie?" he asked again, placing his hands on her shoulders as he inched nearer. She could feel his breath on her cheek, and when she turned her head away he pressed his lips against the side of her throat.

"You don't play fair," she complained as she felt the tip of his tongue tracing her skin, sending her pulse rate into overdrive.

"Not if I can help it." He laughed quietly, moving his hands, pulling her closer, until she could feel the heat of his arousal against her thigh. She closed her eyes, tried to think, tried to remember why she thought she had to think.

His hands went lower on her back, then skimmed around her sides, sending shivers down her spine, before he cupped her breasts in his hand, began rubbing his thumbs over each nipple.

"Annie?"

She stopped breathing. The sensations racing through her body took all her concentration. All she could do was to stand there, her arms still at her sides, and *feel*.

He nuzzled her neck. His hands branded her. The pressure of his body against her thigh grew, as did the tension between her own legs.

"Annie?" he asked yet again.

*"What?"* she nearly exploded, wishing he'd just shut up and do whatever it was he was going to do, just as long as he took her with him.

Grady slid his hands to her waist, raised his head, and pushed her slightly away, so that he could look at her. "Nothing," he said. "But I was just wondering. Have you done this before?"

Okay, now she looked at him. Bug-eyed, she looked at him. "Of course I have! I'm twenty-five years old. *Of course,* I've . . . *done this* before!"

"Really?" he said, and if he didn't soon stop smiling at her that way, she was going to have to punch him.

"Yes, really. Plenty of times."

He took her hand, pulled her down beside him on the edge of the bed. "How many times, Annie?"

She pulled her hand free and popped up again, to glare at him. "Why? You want *references,* Sullivan?" She turned her back to him, stabbed a hand through her hair. "Oh, just go away, Grady, okay? Just *go away.*"

She heard the mattress springs squeak as he stood up, and soon felt his hands on her shoulders. Was powerless to fight him as he turned her around to face him.

She looked up at him, ready to brain him one if he was grinning. But he wasn't smiling. He was being serious, more serious than she'd ever seen him.

"I'm nervous, too, Annie," he said after a moment. "Because this isn't casual, is it? I sure don't feel casual about it. I feel like this might be something special. That you might be someone special."

"I know," she admitted, daring to reach up and push back the hair that had fallen onto his forehead. "But what if we're wrong? What happens then? What happens when we both leave here and get on with our lives? What happens when we're not stuck here together, constantly in each other's company? Will we still feel the same way? Will we even want to?"

"I don't have the answers to any of those questions, Annie," he told her, and she believed him. "But I'm willing to take a chance, if you are."

She pushed him away again, and began to pace. "You know this is silly, don't you? I mean, here we are. New millennium and all of that, and I'm acting like it's the eighteenth century or something. People who like each other, are attracted to each other, go to bed with each other these days. It's natural. It's what happens. I read books. I go to movies. I know this."

Grady sat down on the bed once more, crossed his arms over his chest, and watched her pace. "True enough."

"There's safe sex and all of that," Annie went on, knowing she was babbling. "I mean, that's a given, right?"

"Of course. I wouldn't dream of not protecting you, Annie, in every way."

"So, okay. So, all right. So enough talking. Let's do it." She kicked off her shoes, then grabbed the fishbowl and carried it over to the bathroom, sticking it on the floor inside. "He shouldn't see this, he's too young," she said as she came back into the room.

"He's going to be Maisie's fish, Annie," Grady reminded her, standing up to turn down the bed. "I don't even want to think about what that poor guy is going to be seeing. Six months with her, and he'll probably be able to sell his story to the tabloids."

"Good point," Annie said, watching as he pushed the button that activated the bedside radio, which had been turned to an easy-listening station. He certainly seemed to know all the right moves, now that she'd said yes. All that was missing now was black-satin sheets. She didn't think the Peevers linen closet ran to black-satin sheets. Although she could ask Daisy and Junior. They probably had them.

Oh, she was going crazy! Her mind was jumping from place to place, her stomach felt more queasy than was probably good. Wouldn't that be great? He'd touch her, and she'd throw up all over him. Talk about romantic!

"Are we being too clinical?" she asked, wishing her voice didn't suddenly have this stupid little *squeak* in it. "Because I'm feeling sort of clinical now."

Grady turned to her, slid his gaze over her, turning her limbs to water without saying a word. "Now who's asking for references?" he said, crossing the room to turn off the light, plunging the room into near darkness, with only the moonlight coming through the window allowing her to see his outline as he approached her.

It was now or never, not that he probably wouldn't figure it out soon enough.

"Once," she said suddenly, holding out both hands to keep him at arms-length. "I did it once, okay? I was twenty-two, and it seemed like time, everybody else was doing it, so I did it. So just don't expect much, all right?"

She could see the look on his face even in the dark. He was stunned. Utterly stunned. He couldn't look more stunned if she had pulled a mackerel from her back pocket and slapped him across the face with it.

But when he blinked, and then a slow smile started on

his face, and he opened his mouth, it wasn't to say any-thing she might have expected him to say. "Thank you, Annie."

"Thank—thank me? Why?"

He took her hand, led her over to the bed. "Why? Because, Annie, you don't give yourself lightly. Because I want to be the one who teaches you that once is most definitely not enough, not if it's done right. Because I want to be the one to see the wonder in your eyes, to feel your body as it realizes why it was made. Because, somewhere inside me, I feel like this just might be the first time for both of us."

She melted against him. Just melted. "Oh, you're good," she said, barely aware that he was unbuttoning her jeans. "You're really good. Tom Cruise couldn't have done it better."

She felt his chuckle before he suddenly scooped her up and laid her down on the bed, following after her as he stepped out of his shoes, his slacks.

She closed her eyes. She kept them closed as she could hear the rustle of fabric, knowing he had taken off his shirt, feeling as well as knowing as he helped her out of her sweater, slid her jeans down until she could kick them off.

He made no move to unhook her bra, strip her of her panties, and she silently thanked him for that. Loved him for that.

Instead, he used his fingertips to turn her head toward him. Kissed her eyes, her nose, the tip of her chin, the pulse beating madly at the base of her throat.

"Open your eyes, Annie," he said from above her, so

close to her, his length pressed against her side. "Just open your eyes. Look at me."

Biting her bottom lip between her teeth, she screwed up her courage and looked. The bed was awash in moonlight. She saw the expanse of his bare chest, the ripple of the muscles in his arms. She saw his wonderfully shaggy hair falling down over his sinfully handsome face. She saw the warm glitter of his eyes. She saw everything she had ever wanted, everything she had ever feared.

"I won't hurt you," Grady said, his voice low and soothing. "I would never, never hurt you."

"I know," she said, raising a hand to hold on to his arm, knowing it was true. He'd never hurt her. Not intentionally.

He kissed her then, slowly and gently at first, then more deeply, and with growing passion she found easy to return.

She was clumsy, and she knew it, but she was so very willing to learn.

There were moments. Moments she'd never forget.

Their shared laughter as she got her arm caught in her bra strap and it took the two of them to release her.

The hot stab of pleasure when his mouth first closed over her nipple.

The thrill of pleasure that radiated through her as she first dared to touch his chest, when some imp of mischief guided her hand to the waistband of his briefs as she wordlessly urged him to remove them.

The hot. The wet. The tension.

The mind-shattering pleasure as he lifted himself over her, as she opened herself to him, as she took him inside, welcomed him inside, gave herself over to his keeping.

The explosion.

The aftermath.

The words whispered in the night, the kisses that thrilled as much as the passion—maybe more.

Drifting off to sleep in Grady's arms . . . and, for the first time in her life, feeling like she had come home. . . .

# Seventeen

*My closest relation is myself.*
— Terence

September sun streamed in through the windows, a not unpleasant reminder that the night had ended. Still, Annie sighed, reluctant to start the day.

"Mornin'," Grady said from somewhere above her, and she liked the way his voice rather rumbled in his chest as she lay against him.

"Yes, I know. Close your eyes, and maybe it will go away," she said, snuggling closer.

"Well, it is Sunday. Technically, my day off. So, if you don't want to get up yet, I'll just stay here a little while longer. Oh, and by the way, it's reassuring to know you aren't nervous anymore."

"Who says?" Annie asked. "I don't remember issuing a bulletin to that effect."

Grady laughed. "You don't have to. Remember, I know where your hand is."

"It slipped," Annie said, quickly moving her hand back

up above Grady's equator. She hadn't even realized what she'd been doing, as touching Grady had become so natural to her. A night of loving could do that to a person, she'd decided, not without pleasure.

"If you let it slip again, I'll buy breakfast," Grady said, his own hand sliding down her back, tickling her lightly.

"Tempting as that sounds," Annie told him, repositioning herself so that the two of them were half-sitting against the headboard, "I think we'd better remember where we are."

Grady ruffled her curls. "I'd rather remember where we've been." When she looked at him, trying to be stern, he added, "Okay, okay. So maybe it wouldn't be a good idea if anyone saw me leaving your room."

"Good thought," Annie said, grabbing the top sheet, pulling it loose from the mattress, then hopping out of bed even as she wrapped it around herself. "Besides, if you don't soon do your fingerprint thing on my bathroom, I'm going to use it anyway. I hate skulking down the hallway."

Grady was already slipping into his briefs, having located them hanging drunkenly from the desk chair. "I'll bet you didn't have your own bathroom when you were a carny," he said easily, just as if he hadn't been waiting all night for a way to bring that particular subject back into the conversation.

"Is that your clever detective way of saying I owe you one?" Annie asked, plunking herself down in the desk chair, trying to look nonchalant as Grady pulled on his slacks, zipped them.

"Could be, or it could just be that I envy you. There

isn't a kid alive who didn't think it would be neat to run away with the circus when it left town. Is that what you did?"

Annie nodded. "But not the circus. Just a small amusement company, the sort we saw last night. They travel around, from small fair to small fair, and become part of the midway. No lions or tigers, not even a monkey. Just our wheels and darts and milk bottles."

"And B-B guns," Grady reminded her as he pulled his shirt over his head, emerging from the neck hole with his hair so sexily ruffled that Annie had to silently compliment her newly liberated sexual self for not jumping him. "And you said you'd never held a gun. See? I remember this stuff. That's because I'm a master detective. I've got a license and everything."

"A B-B gun, Grady," she repeated. "Hardly a real gun. But you're right. I can take out any target that looks like a five-pointed star. Other than that, I'm pretty much a novice."

"Aiming is aiming," Grady pointed out, bending down to kiss the tip of her nose. "Not that I'd expect you ever to aim at a person, but it's nice to know you could probably hit whatever it is you aim at. With a ball, with a dart, with a water hose. You've got a real talent, Annie."

"Planning on hiring me on?" Annie asked, beginning to feel very naked beneath her sheet now that Grady was completely dressed. She felt vulnerable. She hated feeling vulnerable.

He grinned. "Nope. I don't believe in mixing business with pleasure. Now, tell me about being a carny. Pretty please?"

Annie shrugged. "There isn't much to tell, not really.

I was sixteen, the carnies were in town, and when they left I went with them. For about three months, as we traveled through . . . through several states, I did odd jobs. Helped set up stands, broke them down again, helped in the cooking trailer, played shill a couple of times when business fell off."

"Shill?"

"Well, not quite a shill," Annie explained. "I'd just pretend to be a customer when things were slow. Win a few prizes, let the carny yell about how well I was doing. You know, make people think they could win."

"But they couldn't, because the games were fixed?"

Annie pleated the sheet as it lay in her lap. "A couple of them. Or did you think a nice, reputable, family-owned business would hire on a sixteen-year-old without asking a few pertinent questions first? So, as it happens, we got busted."

"Ah, now I understand. The carnies got busted, and you got caught as a runaway? Still, I'll bet your parents were relieved, even if you couldn't have had the best home life. Not if you ran away in the first place."

Annie bit on her knuckle, trying to decide how much she wanted to say. She had to say something. She didn't know why, but she just did. Grady made her feel honest. It was an uncomfortable sensation, as she tried very hard never to be honest about her childhood.

"Annie? Did I say something wrong?"

She shook her head, then looked up at him. "No. You couldn't know, could you? I . . . I didn't *have* parents, Grady. I had a mother, once upon a time, but she died or left or something, and I was put into foster care before I was three. And tried to get out of it ever since," she added, trying to smile at him even as she blinked furiously, to hold back sudden, stupid tears. "Running away with the carnies was about my tenth or twelfth try at getting out of the system. There were no more foster homes after that. They stuck me in a juvenile detention center laughingly called a private school, until I was eighteen. But that was okay, because at least I had books there, and I actually went to community college afterward, and then on to get my B.A."

She stood up, holding the sheet close to her. "And that's today's episode of Annie's World, the Real Story. It's also all I'm going to say, okay?"

Grady had been silent the entire time Annie had been speaking. He'd just looked at her, his eyes slowly going all soft and warm. But not with pity. She would have brained him if she'd seen pity in his eyes. What she saw there was compassion, a true sadness for the girl Annie had been, the life she'd had to endure.

"I swear I'll never ask you another question, Annie," he told her now, laying his hands on her shoulders. "But if you ever want to talk, I also promise I'll be here to listen. Okay, Slugger?"

She bit her bottom lip, nodded. "That wasn't easy," she admitted at last, smiling up at him. "I don't share well, you know? Not about my private life. I . . . I've always been pretty much of a loner, you know?"

"And your best friends were books, and television, and the movies," Grady said, stroking her hair. "You hid in the dark theater, or inside the covers of a book, and made your own realities. It's all coming together for me now. And if I ever ask you another personal question, you have my permission to clobber me."

Annie felt a real smile tickling the corners of her mouth. "That's a deal. Maisie, I get to boil in oil, though. I know she's only doing her job, but she just seems to *enjoy* it a little too much."

"I'll call her off," Grady said, his hands moving to loosen the sheet tucked in over Annie's breasts. "Next time I see her, that is. It's only eight o'clock, you know. Even us conscientious types don't report for work on Sundays before ten. Damn! Who the hell could that be, and why does he have a death wish?"

Annie had already turned her head toward the door, having heard the knock at the same time as Grady. "Okay," she said, looking back at him. "I'm not dressed, and you shouldn't be here. So which one of us hides in the closet?"

"Mr. Sullivan? If you would please be so kind as to open the door?"

"Dickens," Annie and Grady said together, both of them pretty much hissing the word through clenched teeth.

"Now I know how Jerry Seinfeld felt when he'd open the door to see Newman standing there," Annie said, then laughed. "Newman? Seinfeld's nemesis? Never mind. Old sitcom joke. I'll be in the closet, okay?"

"Hey, I watch television, you know," Grady called after her. "I've heard Seinfeld say '*New*-man.' To prove it, he went to the door, pulled it open, and ground out, *"Dick-ens."*

He could hear Annie's bubbly giggle from the closet, as she hadn't quite closed the door all the way.

"Good morning, sir," the butler said, walking into the room just as if he'd been invited, carrying with him a small silver metal attaché case that he seemed to have manfully resisted handcuffing to his wrist like some government courier. "I have those items you require."

He placed the attaché case on the bed and snapped open the locks. "Each is in its own plastic bag, labeled, of course. The Messrs. Peevers—all three of them—Miss Muriel, Miss Mitzi, Dr. Sandborn, Miss Goodenough, Attorney Banning. Prints from the other employees: the maid, cook, et cetera, et cetera. And mine. I gave you both the right and left of my own prints, as I am ambidextrous, sir, and didn't want to confuse you."

"You lifted Archie's prints? Why? I thought you said he never leaves his rooms."

Dickens looked right, then left. He pulled a small pad of paper from one pocket, a pen from another, and began scribbling. When he was done, he handed the pad to Grady even as he commented on the mild temperature expected today and the possibility luncheon would be served on the terrace.

Grady frowned at Dickens for a moment, then looked at the pad, his eyes widening as he read: *No, sir, I did not say Mr. Peevers never leaves his rooms. Mr. Peevers says he never leaves his rooms. Don't say anything, as these rooms are most probably bugged. Monitored electronically, sir.*

"You're kidding," he said, reading the message again.

"No, sir," Dickens said stiffly. "I have already read the weather report in today's newspaper, and the report states quite clearly that it will be a mild, sunny September day."

Grady pinched the bridge of his nose between thumb and index finger, trying to get his bearings. Bugged? Archie had the rooms *bugged?* Even this room? This room, where he and Annie had made love? Where Annie had told him things she believed only he could hear?

"Sir?" Dickens said, cocking his head to one side. "Are you all right? You look rather . . . disturbed."

"Oh, yeah?" Grady said, his smile tight. "You think so? Well, I gotta tell you, *Dick*-ens, old sport, you ain't seen nothing yet." He held out his hand. "Give me the key. He's still locked in, right? Give me the damn key."

Annie stepped out from the closet, Grady's tone alerting her that something was not right. "Grady? What's the matter?" she asked, now dressed in her flowered bathrobe, which covered her from neck to knee.

"I can't do that, sir," Dickens said, although he was backing up as he said it. There was just something in Grady's eyes, and the tightness of his jaw, that told him backing up was probably a good idea. Turning tail and running for his life became a viable second option. "Sir? Please don't look at me like that. I would have told you . . . eventually. The . . . the time was never right."

"Gimme," Grady said, his hand still held out, palm up, as he moved his fingers in a come-hither movement. "Archie and I are going to have a little talk, even if I have to shoot the lock out." He looked up, raised his voice. "Did you hear that, Archie? Are you listening now, or just getting this all down on tape to amuse yourself later? Doesn't matter, does it? Better get ready, old man, because here I come!"

He grabbed the key from Dickens's hand and broke into a run as he went out the door, turned right, and headed for Archie's rooms, Annie close on his heels, still asking him what was wrong.

He jammed the key in the lock, throwing the door open with enough force to have it bang against the wall and nearly hit him in the face on the recoil as he stomped into the room. "Come out, come out, wherever you are, Archie," he said as he plowed through the vestibule to see the empty bed in the middle of the larger room.

"Grady? What are you doing?" Annie asked, grabbing his arm. "Where's Archie? Grady? You're scaring me! And what's that smell?"

He stabbed a hand through his hair, then looked at Annie, took a deep breath, tried to compose himself. "It's Archie, and this whole thing smells to high heaven. He's bugged the rooms, Annie. Bugged them! And now I'm going to ring his scrawny chicken neck!"

"He—he bugged the rooms?" Annie's eyes got wide, and she clapped both hands to her mouth, speaking through them. "Oh-my-God. He bugged *my* room?" Then her eyelids narrowed and her hands balled into fists at her sides. "Where is he? I'm going to kill him!"

Annie's instant anger, mingled as it was with some genuine terror, served to calm Grady, who had to admit to himself that he had been about as angry as he'd ever been in his life. Bugging the Peevers heirs? Okay, with this crew, it was almost to be expected. Bugging Grady's rooms? The sign of a pure paranoid, checking up even on the people hired to protect him. He could live with that.

But he had bugged Annie's room. Annie, who had shared a bed with Grady last night. Annie, who had shared a painful story of her childhood with him this morning. With *him*. Not the whole fucking world!

Dickens walked up beside Grady and gave a discreet

cough as he tipped his head to the right, toward a door in the corner of the room. "The bathroom is that way. I believe I shall drive into town now, sir, for my regular Sunday morning breakfast with a few of my friends."

"You have friends?" Annie asked, then quickly put a hand to her mouth. "Oh, Dickens, I'm sorry. It's just . . . it's just—well, why didn't you *tell* me?"

"I didn't tell you," Dickens said, raising his voice. "Mr. Sullivan here *guessed*. Isn't that right, Mr. Sullivan?"

But Mr. Sullivan didn't answer. He was already all the way across the room, pulling open the door to the bathroom, as Dickens beat a hasty but still oddly dignified retreat.

Grady found Archie in the bathtub, hunched into a fetal position and mostly hidden under a blanket, only his eyes and the top of his head visible.

"How dare you! You're fired! Get out! Get out!" Archie yelled, and as the acoustics were quite good in the tiled room, he almost succeeded in sounding angry rather than frightened.

The sight of Archie, cowering, served to bring Grady down from the pinnacle of the anger he'd felt. Besides, what could he do? It wasn't as if he could punch Archie in the nose or anything. "The tapes, Archie. Where are the tapes?"

"That's for me to know and you to find out!" Archie declared, trying to stand up now that he was pretty sure Grady wouldn't knock him back down again.

Grady looked at him, even helped him out of the tub before he slipped on the porcelain. "Okay, Archie, have it your way. I'll start with your clothes closet. I imagine it's large enough to hold a whole, sophisticated system."

"No, no, not the closet!" Archie cried out, following after Grady, the tails of his nightshirt flapping around his skinny legs. "I'll tell you, I'll tell you! Just—not the closet!"

"Definitely the closet, Archie," Grady said, yanking open the door and looking inside. Then he blinked. *"Maisie?"*

"Mornin', honey," Maisie said, walking past him, into the room, patting at her hair with one hand. "Don't look at me like that. We weren't doing anything wrong. Well, nothing *too* wrong, right, Archie, honey?"

"I think I'm going to be sick," Annie said, sitting down in one of the chairs in front of the fireplace. "Maisie, how could you?"

Maisie looked from Grady to Annie, then back again. "What? You think we were . . . that I'd—oh, *please!* I gave him a pedicure, all right? Anything more than that, and the guy would have to swallow a Viagra the size of a house. Right, honey?"

Archie climbed into bed, not before Grady and Annie saw that his toenails were a rather tasteful shade of mauve, bits of cotton still stuck between each toe. "I was working up to it, I was working up to it. If these idiots could have stayed where they belong."

"Yeah, right," Maisie said, sniffing. "Look, Grady, you told me to get information. I was getting information. Boy, honey, was I getting information. Archie's got a setup in his sitting room that would've given Nixon wet dreams. State of the art, honey."

Annie was on her feet again, heading for the heavily

draped French doors that led to the sitting room. She flung them open, then looked at the equipment inside. Tape recorders. Television monitors. Earphones. A floor-to-ceiling bookcase stuffed with cassettes and VCR tapes, all neatly labeled. The labels marked "Asswipe" in red pen stood out easily.

Now Annie recognized what she'd smelled when she'd first come into the room. Nail polish. The room reeked of it, and an opened bottle of polish sat on the window-sill. Clearly Archie had just been in this room—Archie and Maisie. Painting nails and listening to every word that had been said in Annie's room.

The monitors showed her views of the drawing room, the hallway outside Archie's bedroom, the kitchen, the front drive. Not her bedroom. Thank God, not her bed-room.

Grady joined her at the huge console, picking up one pair of earphones after another, pushing buttons, rewinding tapes, listening. After he'd picked up the third set of earphones, he hit the STOP button on the machine and ejected a cassette tape.

"Yours, I believe," he said, handing the tape to Annie.

She took it, clutched it to her chest, and stomped out of the room, heading straight for Archie's bed.

"You are a mean and despicable old man, and you should be ashamed of yourself!" she told him as Archie held the covers up beneath his eyes. "How *dare* you eavesdrop on me?"

Suddenly, Archie seemed to locate his courage. Or at least his outrage. "How dare I? How *dare* I, little girl?" he shouted, sitting up in the bed. "Somebody's trying to *kill* me! Did you think I was just going to sit back and let it happen?"

Annie shook her head so hard her curls bounced. "No, I'm not buying that. You're just nosy. Mean, and nasty and nosy and . . . and a dirty old man! Shame on you!"

"Shame on me? Ha! Look who's talking about shame on me. Lucky for you I only was listening this morning. Had yourself some great roll in the hay, didn't you, girl? You and my other *employee*. I could have been murdered in my bed while the two of you were—"

"Shut up, Archie," Grady said quietly, now standing beside Annie. "Just do yourself a great big favor and shut up. Oh, yeah, and one more thing. I quit. I quit, Annie here quits, and we'll all be out of here today. You might want to go back to hiding in the bathtub until you can hire a bodyguard who can stomach you."

"But—but you can't quit!" Archie said, sliding out of the bed, mauve toenails first. "We have a contract."

"So sue me. Hopefully, posthumously," Grady said, taking Annie's arm. "Come on, Slugger. We're out of here."

"No," she said, pulling free of his grip.

"What?" Grady glared at her.

"I said, no," Annie repeated, not looking at him, but definitely feeling the heat of his glare. "I signed a contract, too, and I'm not leaving. It wouldn't be right."

"Jesus H—damn it, Annie, this isn't the time for your stupid ethics! He was *spying* on you. On *us*. Is it the money? He's not worth it. Nothing is worth it."

"Not to you, maybe," Annie said, folding her arms across her chest and turning away from him. "So go if you want to, but don't tell me what to do. I make up my own mind."

"Hah! That's my girl!" Archie said, hopping back up onto the bed, like some geriatric jack-in-the-box. "Can I pick 'em, or what? Money-hungry, sonny, the girl's money-mad. I can see it in my kids, I could see it in her. So go away, sonny. Who needs you?"

"Annie?" Grady asked, feeling his anger rising again. "Is he right? Is it the money?"

She turned to look at him. Looked straight into his eyes. "Yes, Grady. It's the money."

Archie cackled in delight, right up to the point where Grady looked at him, at which point he quickly sobered.

Then Grady looked at Annie again, opened his mouth to say something, closed it. Shook his head. "Okay." He spread his arms, closed his hands into fists. "Okay. The hell with you. I'm out of here!"

Maisie lingered as Grady made his grand exit, slamming the door behind him. "He'll be all right, honey," she said, patting Annie's shoulder. "And he's not going anywhere. I know Grady Sullivan, and he's no quitter. But first he has to go kick something."

# Eighteen

*It makes a difference whose ox is gored.*
—Martin Luther

Grady limped around the room, unable to resist giving the dresser another kick. That way his foot would hurt again, and he could curse again.

How could she? *How?* This woman, who guarded her privacy so much. This woman, who'd just found out that privacy had been caught on tape for an old man who was meaner than a snake. A man who had made his life's work browbeating his children and making everyone around him miserable. This . . . this . . . this billionaire.

Aw, shit.

"The money," he ground out, slamming his fist against his other palm. "The damned money. All right, all right, so Annie doesn't have much money. She was honest about that, the same way she was honest about why she took this job."

Honest. Nice word, but something inside him wasn't buying it. Annie told the truth, but she only told as much truth as she found necessary. Sure, he knew now that she'd been a foster child. He believed her, too. She might have watched a million movies, but nobody was that good an actor. Her story had been real, her pain had been real.

And both had been thrown out the door without a backward glance when stacked up against the fifty thousand she'd make playing Archie's long-lost granddaughter for a month.

What had he thought about her? Oh, yeah. Too good to be true. Man, he'd got that in one! When was he going to start listening to that nagging little voice in his head?

Probably not until he stopped thinking about Annie— her smile, her laugh, her wit . . . how she felt in his arms.

Grady knew what was wrong, what ate at him most. He'd seen Annie as someone he could really care about, someone he might just love, and now she'd disappointed the hell out of him.

He wanted out. He wanted far away, as fast as he could get there.

And he'd be damned if he'd leave Annie here, to make it through the rest of the month without him.

Grady picked up his cell phone, punched in some numbers. "Quinn?" he barked after two rings, as soon as he heard the receiver being picked up.

"No, Grady, it's Shelby. Quinn's in the shower. How are you? Is anything wrong? Are you bringing Annie down to meet us this afternoon? Quinn said you weren't but, well, have you changed your mind? I'd really like to meet her."

Grady took a breath, willed himself calm. "No,

Shelby, honey, we can't get away. The high price of duty, and all of that. I was just wondering if Quinn would do me a little favor, that's all."

"Oh. Well, okay, I'll have him phone you . . . oh, wait. Here he comes now." Grady could tell she'd put her hand over the mouthpiece, although he could still hear her laughing, saying, "Quinn! Stop that, you're getting me all wet. Here, talk to Grady, because now I'm going to have to go change my blouse. Honestly, darling, it isn't as if we didn't just crawl out of bed a half hour ago . . ."

"Yo, pal? What's up?" Quinn asked a moment later, as Grady was raking a hand through his hair, remembering that he and Annie had been that happy, just a half hour ago.

"I want you to do some more digging, okay?" he told his partner and friend. "Very private, just on Annie Kendall, and with the information you find delivered to me personally, either by phone or by messenger. I don't want Maisie within five miles of anything you find out. Got that?"

"I've got that," Quinn said, then added, "and you've got something, too, by the sound of your voice. What's the matter, Grady? I'm the angry one and you're the laidback one, remember? Why do I feel like we're doing some weird role reversal here? Is it Maisie or Ms. Kendall? Because somebody's sure put a bug up your—"

"Maisie is doing her usual good job, in her usual incomprehensible way," Grady cut in. "Which leaves Annie. I found out some things about her that might help in a search of her background, and I want you checking them out personally, okay?"

"Because she got to you? How did she get to you, buddy? Give me all the news that's fit to print."

Grady sat down on the edge of the bed. "Quinn, can we just leave it alone for a while, okay?"

"Wow. That bad, huh? Okay, pal, no more questions. Just give me what you've got, and I'll take it from there. But what if you don't like the answers I come up with? What then?"

"I don't like the answers *I've* come up with, Quinn," Grady told him. "And, frankly, I can't believe I could be so wrong about somebody. She's hiding something, Grady, I know it. Just check her out through the foster care system for me. She's twenty-five, but didn't enter the system until she was about three years old. Do the math, use the name Kendall, and check Pennsylvania and neighboring states. Wait—her picture was stamped Liisa of Baltimore. So check Maryland, too, while you're at it. And she spent at least two years in some sort of foster-care detention center, from sixteen to eighteen. Is that enough for a start?"

"It should be," Quinn told him. "But I'll run it as Kendall, and then run it all again with no name, just age and sex, because I haven't come up with anything on your Annie Kendall so far that matches her. What did Maisie find out?"

Grady dropped his head into his hand. "Enough to blackmail me for the rest of my natural life," he gritted out. "Never mind. Just tell me again why I'm staying on the job, so that I can look in the mirror when I shave."

"Why are you staying on the job? Oh, let me see. The money?"

"Definitely the wrong answer," Grady said, standing

up as Maisie walked into the room through the connecting doors. "Never mind. Call me tomorrow, okay?"

He flipped the phone shut and watched as Maisie walked around the room, dragging her fingertips along the dresser, inspecting those fingertips for dust. "Hiya, stud muffin, honey," she said at last, when Grady was just about ready to strangle her. "How's tricks?"

"Not funny," he told her. "Shouldn't you be packing?"

"Why? I'm not going anywhere, and neither are you. How's the foot?" she asked as he limped over to the window to glare at the scenery, which by rights should have burst into flame under the heat of his gaze.

"Not broken, yet. But if you want to bend over, I guess I can give it another shot."

"Now who's not funny, honey?" Maisie said, depositing the bottle of mauve nail polish on the dresser before sitting down on the edge of the bed. "Look, you're embarrassed. I don't know why, because from the little we heard, I'd say you did a bang-up job—"

"Maisie, you're fired."

"Right. I'll send myself a termination notice. But, in the meantime, I was the one with the earphones on, Grady, not Archie. He didn't hear a thing, honest. I was just about to sneak the tape out of there and bring it to you when you started yelling that you were coming to get Archie. Honey, if you ever want to laugh, you've got to see an old man with wet toenails and cotton stuck between his toes, trying to run around, find a place to hide. He's really scared of you, you know. Bullies are like that. They get away with whatever they can get away with, then turn tail and run when somebody finally stands up to them."

"And that concludes today's lesson in psychology from a woman who paints old men's toenails and calls it being an investigator."

"What's the big deal? I used to paint Grandpa Schmidt's toenails for him all the time. He loved it. So, I figured, maybe there's more than one way to skin a Peevers."

Grady looked at his assistant with new respect, and not a little trepidation. "If I've said it before it bears repeating. Maisie, sometimes you really scare me."

She patted her curls. "Men are always saying that to me, honey. Anyway, I did good, right? I found the taping room before you did, didn't I? And these." She ended, opening the knapsack of a purse she carried with her everywhere, dumping cassette tapes out onto the bed. "And you thought I was just another pretty face. Hah!"

Grady turned around, walked over to the bed. He couldn't help himself. He picked up the tapes, one after the other. "Muriel. Mitzi. A.W. Junior. Banning and A.W. and Junior? Now that's interesting." He dropped the others and inserted the last tape into the machine on his desk.

"I'll use my own phone to call down for coffee," Maisie said, already heading back to her own room. "You just listen, and then I'll transcribe anything you want a hard copy of, okay? Unless you still want me to pack? Leave here? Leave *her?*"

"All right, all right, you've made your point. But I swear, Maisie, if you ever repeat anything you heard on that tape this morning . . ."

"What tape, honey? What did I hear? Did I hear anything? Nope, don't think so."

"Thanks," Grady said, pushed the PLAY button, and sat down at the desk, ready to listen.

An hour later, with Maisie back in Archie's rooms, acting as nail-file-wielding bodyguard, he was standing on the first tee with Jefferson Banning, having called and asked if it was possible they could get in a round of golf that morning.

Banning was dressed in banana yellow slacks and a black top, looking very much the country-club champ of at least sartorial splendor.

Within three holes, Grady believed the guy to also be a champion cheat, or at least a man who wouldn't think twice about cheating to win.

So Grady let him win. By the time they'd made the turn at number nine, Banning was up four holes in match play, and sitting two at only thirty yards from the green on the par five tenth.

Grady had to hand it to him. The guy really could hit the hell out of the ball. He did his cheating when his long drives missed the fairway, which they'd done three times already. The guy was long as anything, but he wasn't always straight.

Grady stopped the cart beside Banning's ball, and waited until the lawyer had hopped out, chipping wedge in hand. "You know, I shouldn't say this, but I think I might play better if we had a bet going on the round," he said, shaking his head in self-disgust.

Banning squinted at him from under his golf cap. "We're already playing for five dollars a hole. That isn't a bet?"

"Not much of one, obviously, or maybe I'd be playing better. So what do you say we up the ante?"

Banning looked ahead, to where Grady's third shot had landed badly buried just under the lip of a sand trap beside the green. "Okay, if you want to lose money to me, I'm not going to argue with you. What's the bet?"

"You win and I hand over five hundred bucks a hole for each hole I'm down when it's over."

"Five hundred a hole? Did I hear that right? I'm up four holes with only nine to go, I'm sitting two with no reason I won't reach the green, and you're sitting three, in the trap. Much as I hate taking candy from babies, you're on!"

Grady waited until Banning had landed his chip ten feet from the pin, then asked, "Don't you want to know what you owe me if I win?"

"Why should I? You can't possibly win," Banning said, hopping back into the cart. Grady wondered how the guy would look with his chipping wedge wrapped around his neck. "Oh, okay, what is it? How much?"

"Everything you know about Double A Enterprises," Grady said, slamming his foot on the pedal so that Banning had to hold on as he drove the cart onto the side of the hill next to the green.

"What's the matter, counselor?" he said, as the two of them got out, Grady reaching for his sand wedge, Banning for his putter. "You're not smiling anymore."

"That information is confidential," Banning said, as Grady stepped into the sand trap.

"Really? Not from Archie, it isn't. Or didn't you know the old bastard has the place wired for sound? Fart in the morning room and he smells it coming from his state-of-the-art surveillance equipment set up in his sitting room."

Grady looked at his lie, decided where to place his feet and, with a minimum of effort, blasted the ball out of the trap, to land two feet from the cup. He wouldn't win the hole, but it would be the last one he lost or he'd know the reason why.

Actually, he did win the hole, because Banning three-putted from ten feet. It wasn't easy to putt, not when your hands were shaking and you were worried about staining your really keen banana slacks.

"Can we talk?"

Annie looked up from the book she'd been reading as she sat in one of the gazebos, because suddenly all of Peevers Mansion wasn't large enough to hold her. The book hadn't been enough to hold her interest, either, but she'd kept reading. It had been easier than thinking.

She'd sensed Grady's presence before he spoke, had actually been watching his approach out of the corner of her eye. She knew his walk, his voice, his smile. The fact that he had a flat, brownish birthmark on his left hip that had, she'd told him, reminded her of a map of Texas.

But she didn't know him, and he didn't know her. They'd slept together, made love together, and they didn't know each other. Now, most probably, they never would.

"Free country," she said, snapping out the words, and Grady, who had been standing on the first step up to the gazebo, his hand on the white-painted wood, boosted himself up the three steps and into the enclosure. Which suddenly got smaller than a bread box. "Not that I have to listen. Besides, I thought you'd quit."

Grady took off his golf cap, and Annie's heart did a small, lurching flip as he revealed his hat hair; those shaggy sandy bangs pushed forward onto his forehead, making him look like a cross between a young, earnest Robert Redford in *The Way We Were* and Matt Damon in just about anything.

"I did," Grady said, definitely catching her attention. "For about five minutes, until I figured out that I couldn't leave you here on your own. It would be like tying a raw steak around your neck, then throwing you in with the lions. So I'm staying."

"Gee, thanks. So nice to know you don't think I can take care of myself," Annie said, closing the book with a snap, then standing up and beginning to pace. She had to keep moving. If she stopped moving, she'd have to throw herself in his arms and tell him the worst moment of her life had been watching his face as she'd told him she was staying "for the money."

Grady ran a hand through his hair, but it resettled in those same cap-flattened bangs. "You know, you can be a real pain in my—" He threw back his head, sighed. "Okay, let's start over, shall we?"

"Let's not and say we did," Annie told him, knowing she sounded juvenile, but past the point of caring. She'd been to bed with this man. To *bed* with this man! And not twelve hours later, they were barely able to be civil with each other. Why couldn't life be more like the movies, with all those neat happily-ever-afters?

"Did Maisie get the rest of the tapes Archie recorded in your room?"

Annie bit her lip, nodded. "She gave them to me, yes, and told me you had her get them."

"So you know I haven't listened to them?"

"Yes. Thank you."

"And you know that Archie didn't hear what we said this morning? That only Maisie heard?"

"She told me. She also told me she's already forgotten what she heard. Right after she borrowed my new perfume, which I'm pretty sure I'll never see again."

"She has her little quirks," Grady admitted, smiling slightly. "But you can trust her."

"I know." Annie hugged herself with her arms, as if cold. "So, what now?"

Grady began rhythmically slapping his golf hat against his thigh. "So now I tell you what I found out on the golf course today. Now I tell you what Archie didn't tell us. Now I tell you why he thinks someone is out to kill him."

Annie sat down on the built-in bench directly across the gazebo. "I'm listening."

"It was all on the tapes, or at least enough of it for me to go looking for Banning to fill in the blanks."

"Jefferson? *He's* trying to kill Archie?"

"No, Banning is trying to make money no matter how it goes," Grady told her, his smile fairly close to evil. "I had Maisie do a little research, just as to Archie's will and Pennsylvania law. If Banning is executor, he gets two percent of the estate for his trouble. If he appoints himself lawyer for the estate, bam, he collects another two percent. And, if there's a trust, and I'm sure there is, and if Banning appoints himself trustee, which he can do, he stands to collect another one percent *per year,* every year. Archie says he's worth about a billion. It doesn't take a genius to do the math and see that Jefferson Banning, Esquire, stands to make himself a tidy fortune when the toilet-paper king finally excuses himself and shuffles off to that great big men's room in the sky."

Annie closed her eyes, reviewed her times table, inserted a decimal point. "Wow."

"You betchum," Grady said, glad to have at last proved his point. Besides, he didn't want Annie thinking Banning was a nice guy. Because Banning wasn't a nice guy. And neither was he, because he didn't have to point all of this out to Annie; he just wanted to.

"Now, let me tell you the other part. While Banning is acting as Archie's lawyer, he's also acting as lawyer for A.W. and Junior. Stupidly, as it turns out, they frequently hold private little meetings in the sunroom, where Archie has set up both audio and video."

Annie knitted her fingers together, sat forward eagerly. "This is getting good now, isn't it?" she asked, suddenly able to forget her nervousness at being so close to Grady after their night together, after their argument this morning. "What are they doing?"

"What they're doing, Annie, is siphoning bucks out of Daddy's company and into their own, Double A Enterprises. That's *A* for Arthur William, another *A* for Archie, Junior. Or, if you want, for Absolutely Asinine. Banning set up the corporation for them, and a whole bunch of smaller corporations under the Double A umbrella. I don't know where they got the seed money—probably that old-fashioned way, they embezzled it."

"Slow down. I think this is about to get complicated."

"Not too much. Double A has all these little companies, which really don't exist. The little companies act as the middleman in everything Archie does."

"How?"

Grady rubbed his hands together, trying to think up an easy way to explain. "Okay," he said at last. "If a train leaves Pittsburgh, traveling east, at five o'clock, and another train is going west from Philly, leaving at three o'clock—"

"That's not funny," Annie told him.

"I know, I know. I just wanted to lighten the mood a little."

"Didn't work."

"I'd noticed," Grady said, wincing. "I know—think about it this way. Double A, and all its little Double A's, are toll booths on the roads leading to Peevers Enterprises. Anything that goes into Peevers Enterprises, and everything that goes out, has to pass through the Double A toll booth."

Annie pointed at him, smiled. "And everyone pays a toll!"

"Exactly! The toll booth doesn't do anything but collect the toll. Doesn't supply raw materials or trucks. Doesn't do squat. Double A is a middleman in its purest—and most illegal—form. Prices jacked up at both ends, with Double A taking its cut. Double A even provides an accounting service for the toilet-paper king, just to keep the books neat. There is barely a penny spent by the Peevers corporation that doesn't go through Double A and come out smaller, one way or the other."

"Wow," Annie said again. "And Jefferson Banning is in on it?"

"Not to his mind, he isn't. He just set up the corporations, and takes his cut, calling it all fees. As far as the good counselor is concerned, it's all perfectly legal.

I don't think the Bar Association would call it ethical, though. However, if Archie keeps changing his will, cutting out his kids, sticking them back in, and maybe one day decides to cut Banning out as well—well, Banning's got his bases covered. He's still working for Double A."

Annie's shoulders slumped. "Poor Archie. Everybody's ripping him off. His children. Dickens. No wonder he's paranoid."

"We're not done yet," Grady told her. "For the last six months, Archie has been slowly taking back the reins, and awarding new contracts to suppliers other than those smaller dummy corporations dealing with Double A. Archie is dealing direct with many of his suppliers again. Our boys are starting to lose money they'd come to count on, they're probably pretty sure Archie knows what's up, and that could mean they're getting desperate. Archie certainly seems to think so."

Annie shook her head. "I don't get it. Why doesn't Archie just tell them he knows, and be done with it? Call the police, or the district attorney, or somebody? Report them, disown them, whatever. Get it over with. It's not like he *likes* them or anything, right?"

"Archie? Do something simple?" Now it was Grady's turn to shake his head. "He can't, Annie. If he did, it would be admitting his so-called idiot boys got the best of him, even for a little while. He'd rather take an arrow through the throat than admit that. No, he wants this quiet and private and eventually disastrous for A.W. and Junior. He wants to torture them by changing his will every week. But he also wants to stay alive until he's watched Double A go under. According to our friend Banning, that should be soon. Unless Archie dies, of course, and then Double A will be right back in business, taking the profits from both ends. Now, admit it. Aren't you proud of me? I've figured it out."

Annie looked at him, her head tipped to one side. "Don't be smug, because you haven't solved all of it. You can't prove either A.W. or Junior tried to kill Archie. And, since you can't, Archie's still in danger."

*"You* and Archie are still in danger," Grady corrected, rising, offering her his arm so that they could return to the house. "You do remember that you're the sacrificial lamb in all of this, don't you? The unexpected new heir, who could end up owning the business and heir to everything else Archie owns?"

"Everything Dickens hasn't stolen," she corrected, trying to pretend that being so close to Grady, her arm through his, their steps matching as they crossed the lawn, wasn't doing rather pleasant things to her insides.

Grady laughed. "There is that. Now, as I'm hoping we've got a truce between us, how about we unearth my handy-dandy fingerprint kit and take on that bathroom of yours. I'm in a hurry to get this solved so we can get out of here. I don't know about you, but this place is really starting to get on my nerves."

# Nineteen

*"Talking of axes," said the Duchess,*
*"chop off her head."*

—Lewis Carroll

"Poppy?" Annie stood at the public telephone in front of the minimarket on Monday morning, her hand half over the receiver as she nervously looked right and left yet again, making sure she was alone.

"Annie? Is that you? Why do I hear traffic? Where are you?"

"At a public telephone. It's Archie. He's got the place bugged," she told him, wincing, as a teenager sidled up licking a chocolate ice-cream cone, looking her up and down as if he'd like to make her his very good friend. "Can you hear me, Poppy? I've, um, I've got an audience."

"Well, tell your audience to go away, my dear."

"Public place," Annie whispered into the receiver, turning her back on the teenager. "I think he wants to use the phone."

"And how does this become your problem? Really, Annie, you should learn to care a lot less about strangers."

Annie glared at the receiver. *"Now* you tell me? Should I have done that when you found me?"

"I'll ignore that. And say it again, please. Archie has the mansion *bugged?* Did I get that right?"

"You did. Nothing goes on in that place that Archie doesn't know about. Now tell me you didn't know that. Tell me, Poppy, or I'm going to blow the whole thing by coming over there and wringing your neck."

"I didn't know. Damn, maybe he *is* paranoid. I hadn't considered that."

Annie believed him. Poppy hadn't known. He also hadn't known somebody might try to scare her away, or worse. He wouldn't have sent her in, otherwise. Would he?

"Hey, sweetie," the teenager said way too close to her ear, "how about you and me go someplace private and have some . . . *fun?"*

Annie shut her eyes, told Poppy to hang on a moment, as she had something to do. Then she turned to the teenager, who was trying hard to look like a stud but only came off looking like the before ad for pimple cream. There was a dab of chocolate ice cream on his sparsely bearded chin, another on the tip of his nose. This kid didn't need a napkin, he needed a bib. Being grounded until he was thirty-five probably wouldn't hurt, either.

She raked him up and down with her gaze, then licked her lips. "Okay, love bucket. That's fifty for against the wall, a hunnred if you want it in the car. You got condoms? I don't do nuthin' without protection, *capisce?*

Oh, and my man Vinnie's inside. He'll be out in a sec, he's just copping some chew. You give the money to him. Got that?"

"I, um . . . that is . . . ," the kid said, then swallowed so hard Annie worried his Adam's apple would shoot upward and knock him out. "Um, hey," he said, trying to smile, even as he was backing up, nearly tripping over his too-long jeans. "I gotta split, okay?"

"Yeah, do that," Annie told him, sneering, wishing she had some gum in her mouth, so she could chomp and pop it. "I think I hear your mama calling you."

She watched him go, took a deep breath, then said, "Okay, Poppy, I think we're alone now."

"I heard that, you know," Poppy told her after a moment. "I dislike pointing this out, but there are times you concern me."

"And there are times I wonder how I let you talk me into this in the first place," Annie told him, anxious to complete her call. "Now, do you want to be brought up to date or not?"

She could hear the clink of crystal and knew, although it was only ten in the morning, that Poppy was beginning his daily inroads on the liquor decanters in his den.

"I'll take your silence as a yes," she said, then quickly told him about Archie's monitoring system and what Grady had discovered because of it. "So, with Double A in the picture, Banning is thinking he wins either way, right? Or at least he did, until Grady got to him yesterday. Today he's probably come down with a whopping case of ethics. Oh, and we checked my bathroom for prints last night, and there were only mine and the maid's, so that was a dead end."

She heard the chink of ice. Poppy's drug of choice this morning must be scotch. She already knew he always took it on the rocks.

"Grady told me something else. He, er, he sort of *owed* me a little reward. He told me he'd found a scrap of material in the tree the other night, and he matched it to one of Dickens's knit shirts. The problem is that Grady won't consider Dickens a suspect because he'd be killing the golden goose. I said maybe he thinks he's got enough stuff stolen and wants out, but Grady says no thief ever thinks they've got enough. What do you think?"

"I'm supposed to think?" Poppy said. "You could have told me that before I imbibed, my dear. But I'll tell you anyway. I think Dickens is as pure as the driven slush, always have. But he wouldn't try to kill Archie. Somebody's trying to frame him. Where did Grady find the shirt?"

"In Dickens's rooms, in a mending basket," Annie said, worrying her knuckle with her teeth until she realized what she was doing. "Can you believe that? Dickens has a mending basket?" She shook her head. "Anyway, I'm with you and Grady on this one, I suppose. Dickens didn't fire that arrow."

"Thank you. It's always such a pleasure to have someone agree with me. But let's get back to this Double A Enterprises, shall we? It sounds to me like Archie is about as ripe as he's going to get. I think we move, and we move now."

"Uh-uh," Annie told him, because she'd already given that idea plenty of thought. "It's not enough. It would have been, once. More than enough. But not now. Now Archie is really in danger. Even Grady thinks so."

"But you're also in danger. Annie, we've discussed this. I want you out."

"I'd be in *more* danger if we pulled the plug now, because I could become the main target," Annie pointed out. She didn't need Poppy sticking his fingers into her plans right now. Not when he only *thought* he knew them. "Look, Poppy, I know you didn't have any of this in mind at the beginning, but it's too late to back out now, not unless I want to just disappear today, go back where I came from."

*"No! Archie owes me!"*

Annie took the receiver away from her ear for a moment, looked at it. Sometimes having her suspicions proved could really hurt. "He owes *you,* Poppy? What about me? I thought you said you wanted this for me."

"I do, I do! Annie, honey, look—"

"You still don't get it, do you? You still don't understand what I want. From Archie, from you, from all of them. Good-bye, Poppy," Annie said, slowly hanging up the phone.

She walked slowly back to her car, a definite headache forming behind her eyes.

Everyone had an agenda.

Poppy wanted some kind of revenge.

Archie wanted his children broken, destroyed.

Dickens wanted his own island, or whatever he thought he could buy with everything he'd stolen over the years.

The Peevers heirs wanted Archie's money, whether they inherited it or siphoned it off dime by dime.

And somebody wanted Archie dead.

What did Annie want? That was the question, the only question she should care about: What did Annie want?

She used to know. She used to be so *sure.*

She turned the key in the ignition and backed out onto the street, heading to the corner and the turn that would lead her back to Peevers Mansion.

She wished she could tell Grady. Everything would be so much simpler, if she could only tell Grady. But she couldn't. She'd promised Poppy she'd do it his way, play the game, wait until Poppy felt the time was right for him to step in, take over.

How Poppy hated Archie.

She hadn't realized that, but she should have. He really, really hated him. It would never occur to Poppy that he might hate himself, too, might blame himself as well.

It was funny in a way. She rather liked Poppy. She even rather liked Archie. They were both mean and nasty and selfish as all hell, but they also were both sad and somewhat pathetic. Not lovable, not by a long shot, but Annie definitely felt sorry for them. She knew what it was like to be alone, even in the middle of a bunch of people.

She also felt sort of sorry for A.W. and Junior and the rest of them. They were weak, but they probably hadn't been raised to be strong. They'd failed, because Archie had programmed them to fail.

It was all just very sad, all the way around.

Annie stepped down on the accelerator, liking the way the low-slung convertible hugged the curves on the two-lane macadam road, liking the feel of fresh air against her face. She felt free out here on the open road, free and able to be herself.

No Peevers. No Poppy. No Grady.

Her smile faded. *No Grady.* They'd spent hours together yesterday, starting with him taking her fingerprints, an oddly personal, rather thrilling, and yet definitely unnerving process.

He'd let her watch as he went about dusting for prints in her bathroom, listened to him explain that the bedroom itself was too corrupted with their prints to be of any use.

They'd examined the prints under a microscope, just to find out there were no clues there, and then he'd helped her scrub the bathroom free of the mess of fingerprint dust and the earlier mess caused by the intruder.

And then he'd kissed her on the forehead and left her there, alone.

It had been like a slap in the face, even though he'd said something about the two of them probably needing a good night's sleep before they got together today for another strategy session, another mental walk-through of everything they knew, anything they might suppose.

He'd brushed her off. It had all sounded so logical, but Annie knew he had brushed her off. And she knew why.

She had disappointed him, disappointed him terribly. "It's the money," she'd said, and from that moment on her relationship with Grady, so new, so tenuous, had taken a sharp left turn into a dead end.

He cared about her, she was pretty sure of that. But, mostly, he had stayed because he'd started the job and intended to finish it. Unlike Jefferson Banning, Grady Sullivan was an ethical man.

But there'd be no more nights together. No more giggles, or passion, or shared secrets. She'd made sure of that.

"Dumb," she said out loud, pounding her fist on the steering wheel. "Dumb, dumb, *dumb!* And when he finally finds out it will be way too late, because he'll think I didn't trust him. Why the hell did I ever start this?"

The huge black Chevrolet Suburban came over a low hill, moving fast along a quarter mile of straightaway. Annie, still caught up in her own thoughts, paid it little attention until it swerved into her lane, heading straight for her.

"Hey!" she yelled, at the same time leaning on her horn. But the Suburban kept coming. Big. Black. Windshield as black as the car, so that she couldn't see the driver.

It was *Duel* all over again, that old movie with Dennis Weaver. Only it was a Suburban, not a semi, and it was coming straight at her, not from behind.

Annie eased up on the gas, thinking maybe she could swerve into the left lane and save herself. No go. The Suburban was straddling the line, there was barely any shoulder, and the distance between them was closing fast. Too fast.

To Annie's right was a steeply rising hill where the roadway had been cut out of the local limestone. To her left was a steep, weed-choked downhill slope that ended in way too many very large trees.

She was in a deadly game of chicken, and had three seconds to react. Maybe two. "Eeny, meeny, miney, mo!" she yelled, then wrenched the wheel left, feeling the breeze as the Chevy whizzed past her.

Then the waist-high weeds were whizzing past as the

convertible sped forward, even as she had both feet jammed onto the brake. She could hear the undercarriage being ripped out by rocks and gave a frantic second's worry that the gas tank might explode.

The car fishtailed, straightened, and Annie could see an old faded red snow fence half-buried in the weeds just before the wall of trees. Would it be enough to stop her?

She let go of the steering wheel, turned off the ignition, took her feet off the brake pedal. Turned her face toward the passenger side and crossed her arms in front of her head. She tried to relax her body like it said in all the safety manuals, but that was great in theory, but impossible in practice. She was going to feel every bit of force that came along with the impact.

In amazing slow motion, the nose of the car hit the snow fence, which gave a little, held a little, and finally snapped like a rubber band in two places about twenty yards on either side of the car.

But it had been enough, had held long enough, and the car finally stopped, even as the air bag came out with a *whoosh,* cushioning her as she was flung forward, then slamming her back against the seat.

Annie sat there in the sudden silence. She just sat there, waiting for her teeth to stop rattling. Wondering if she was dead. Deciding she wasn't.

She opened her eyes, looked at the deflated air bag. If she'd been driving her old car, there would have been no air bag. And there probably would now be no Annie, a thought that had her teeth chattering again even as she tried to move and found that, yes, she could.

The left side of her neck burned where the seat belt

had grabbed and held her, but that couldn't be important now, because she could swear she smelled spilled gasoline. Her hands trembling, her fingers stiff, she struggled to undo the seat belt, grabbed her purse off the floor, and climbed out of the convertible via the backseat and over the trunk.

She looked up the hill, to see that the roadway was deserted. No big bad Chevy Suburban. That was definitely a good thing, because she felt as weak as a kitten, and could no more try to run away from a rampaging monster SUV than she could tap her heels together and wish herself to Kansas.

Still backing away from the crumpled car—her beautiful, beautiful car—Annie somehow made it to the shade of a huge oak tree and sat down, leaning against its trunk, waiting for whatever would happen next.

What happened next was one very nice passerby with a cell phone, one Pennsylvania State cop, one tow truck and, just as she thought maybe she was going to live, one very white-faced Grady Sullivan running down the hill toward her.

He looked more dangerous than the Suburban.

"What happened?" he asked her, grabbing her arms even as he inspected her visually, looking for injuries. "They said you said no to an ambulance. Why in hell would you say no to an ambulance? Do you know you're bleeding?"

Wasn't he wonderful? Wasn't he beautiful? And he cared. He really, really *cared*. She wanted to cry.

Instead, Annie lifted a hand to the side of her throat. "Not really bleeding. It just looks like it. It's really a sort of brush burn and bruise. Stan says it's going to hurt like hell, but that's about it. Stan says I was really very lucky. Stan also says I was very smart, turning off the ignition before the impact, so that no sparks from the engine could ignite the gas tank. You smell it? The tank sprang a leak. But that's the funny thing about gasoline. Sometimes the smallest spark and—*bam!* And yet, other times, you can throw a match right in a puddle of it, and the match just goes out—*pfft!* Stan said so. Cars explode a lot less in accidents than the movies would have you believe."

She was babbling, she knew she was babbling, and she'd keep babbling, because then maybe she wouldn't cry. "In fact, Stan says I did everything just right. Stan says I must think pretty quick on my feet, but I told him I'd watched *Duel*—you know, that movie with the guy who used to be Chester on *Gunsmoke?* 'Mister Dillon! Mister Dillon!' He'd chase after the sheriff, limping because his one leg wouldn't bend, yelling and yelling. You remember, don't you Grady? They still show the series on cable. Anyway, Stan says—"

"Shut up, Annie. You're in shock. You have to be in shock. Look at you—you're shivering." Then Grady looked around, rather wildly, Annie thought. That was so sweet. "And Stan? Who the hell is Stan? The tow truck driver?"

"The state cop," she told him, pointing to a six-foot-six officer who looked like a cross between Hulk Hogan and Dudley Do-right, right down to his chin strap. "I already told him everything, and he wrote it down in his little book. Do you think you could ask him if we can leave now? I want to soak in a hot tub for about three days. And maybe have some ice cream. I don't know why, but I really would like an ice-cream cone. Chocolate. Two scoops."

Grady was still holding her upper arms, still looking down at her as if he might either hug her or shake her. "I think we should go to the hospital, have you checked out. What happened? Did you lose control of the car?"

"Yeah." Annie looked down at her toes, noticing for the first time that she'd somehow lost one of her shoes. Sonofagun. And she hadn't noticed? Maybe she wasn't as all right as she thought she was. And she'd liked those shoes. They were navy, real leather, with those neat chunky heels. Damn! Now she was getting really, *really* mad. "I told him a bee got in the car and I panicked and lost control. I . . . I'm allergic to bees."

Grady looked over at the crumpled car, just then being pulled out of the weeds and back up toward the roadway. He looked at the state cop. He bent his head so that his chin rested on his chest, sighed. "Okay. If you're not going to panic, I'm not going to panic. Even if it kills me and, I have to tell you, Slugger, you're killing me here. Do you know, when I got the call, I ran out of the mansion so fast I don't even know how the hell I got here? You're driving me crazy, Annie Kendall. One hundred and fifty percent crazy. Now, if I promise to get you out of here, will you tell me what really happened?"

"I told you, Grady. A bee," she said, but she couldn't say anything after that because her panic and fear, and even her anger, all seemed to drain away at that moment, and she leaned forward into Grady's arms, exhausted. "How about that?" she said muzzily. "I think the adrenaline rush is over. Please, just get me out of here, and we can ask Dr. Sanford to make a house call. I really, really hate hospitals."

She raised her head, wincing as the skin on her neck came into contact with the collar of her cotton blouse. "Please, Grady. Just please get me out of here."

# Twenty

*When a fellow says it hain't the*
*money but the principle o' the thing,*
*it's th' money.*

—Abe Martin

Grady couldn't remember the last time he'd been so scared.

He'd been summoned to the phone by Dickens, who said a Mrs. Lattimer was calling to speak to him, and he'd picked up the phone warily, because he didn't know any Mrs. Lattimer.

Thirty seconds later, he wanted to erect a statue to Mrs. Lattimer, because she'd stopped to help Annie at the scene of the accident and had told him that Annie seemed to be all right.

Not that he was going to believe Mrs. Lattimer, or a dozen doctors, or anyone at all, not until he saw Annie for himself.

If he'd wondered how he felt about the woman, this exasperating, confounding, half the time someone who

intrigued him, the other half of the time someone who
infuriated him—well, he sure knew now.

The thought, just the thought, that something bad
might have happened to Annie had physically staggered
him on his feet. How in hell had she gotten to be so
important to him so fast?

He knocked lightly at the door to Annie's bedroom
and then opened the door. "Still asleep?" he asked when
Maisie turned to look at him.

"Out like a light, honey," Maisie said, replacing the
cap on a bottle of Passionate Plum nail polish. "I don't
know what the doctor gave her, but it sure has put a
smile on her face. Maybe I'll let her sleep through the
next dose and take it myself. You okay, honey? You still
don't look so good."

"Somebody ran her off the road, Maisie," Grady said,
although she already knew, had been present when Annie
had told Grady the whole story. "She could have been
killed."

"True, but she wasn't," Maisie pointed out. "I helped
her into her pajamas, and she's got a couple of nasty-
looking bruises across her hips, from the seat belt, and
that big brush burn on her neck, but that's it. No con-
cussion, Dr. Sandborn says, and he should know, because
he checked her over for about an hour. I thought you
said he was a quack?"

"No, I said he shares Archie's painkillers. Maybe he
was a good doctor, once. Did he say how long Annie
would be asleep?"

Maisie checked her watch. "Another couple of hours,
I suppose. Why? Are you going to let me out of here,
so I can go try on my new duds again? I'm telling you,

Grady, Muriel and Maisie were *so* grateful to me today that I just about got a new wardrobe out of the deal. And all brand names, too. I think I'm wasting myself, working for you. I should set myself up as a personal shopper."

Grady walked over to the bed, rubbed at the back of his neck as he stood looking down at Annie. Two nights ago, they'd shared this bed. The bed, and so much else.

Now here she was, out cold, definitely with a smile on her face, one arm wrapped around a big blue bunny, and she looked twelve years old. Innocent. Defenseless. Vulnerable.

God, how he wanted this over.

"Did you search Mitzi's and Muriel's rooms?" Maisie asked after a few moments. "I mean, you were going to do that while I had them out of here, right? First facials and makeup, then some power shopping. You certainly had time."

He shook his head. "No need. I never could picture either one of them climbing a tree, let alone being strong enough to load a crossbow."

Maisie stood up, walked to the other side of the bed so that she could look across it, straight at Grady. "So you're already eliminating suspects? Who else? Just so I can stop chasing myself all over the Internet, you understand."

Grady reached down, ran the back of his index finger along Annie's smooth cheek. "Dickens," he said absently. "Annie likes him."

Maisie nodded. "Ah, the Smitten Detective School of Deduction. Who else does Annie like?"

Motioning for Maisie to follow him, Grady walked out into the hall, looked around to be sure Dickens or one of the maids wasn't hovering in the hallway. "Help me out here, okay, Maisie? We've got fingerprints of all the suspects, but that's been a dead end so far. We've got motive for just about anyone. We've eliminated the ladies. Who does that leave?"

Maisie ticked off names on her newly manicured fingertips. "A.W., Junior, the attorney, Dr. Druggie. Oh, and Daisy."

"Daisy?" Grady made a face. "You're kidding, right?"

"Nope. She's young, and I've seen her working out in the exercise room in the basement. Dickens told me about it when I told him I miss going to the gym."

"You go to a gym? Maisie, someday you're going to have to give me an hour or two of your time, just so I can catch up on all that I've missed. When did you start going to a gym?"

Maisie rolled her eyes. "Honey, haven't you ever been to a gym? All that sweat-glistened flesh, all those lovely buns in those tight spandex pants. I met two of my last three boyfriends at the gym." She grinned widely and gave a little wiggle. "Bench-press me, honey!"

"Forget I asked," Grady muttered, suddenly terribly tired.

"Yeah, well, anyway, I went down to the exercise room, just to see if there was a bike, because I sort of like riding the bike, and there was Daisy, working out like she was getting ready for the Olympics or something. Running on the treadmill, weights on her hands and ankles. She was wearing one of those sports bras, but, honey, let me tell you. The sports bra hasn't been made that could keep those babies of hers in place. She keeps that up and by the time she's fifty they're going to be dragging below her *knees*. Trust me on this. I'm a woman, and women know these things."

Grady leaned against the wall, trying not to think about a jogging Daisy at fifty. "So what you're saying is we should keep Ms. Goodenough on our short list?"

Maisie shrugged. "We can't eliminate her, can we? What did you hear on the tapes? That is where you've been, right?"

Grady had spent most of the afternoon in Archie's sitting room-cum-command center, running tapes in the monitor, listening to cassettes. "Not a hell of a lot. I've disconnected the feeds to our rooms and Annie's, but left the rest in place, not that I'm holding out a lot of hope."

"I've got a hot date with Sandy tonight at eight," Maisie said as Grady just sort of lounged there, not knowing where to go, knowing he was totally useless where he stood. "Dickens already said he'd stay with Archie, and you can sit with Annie."

That got Grady's attention. "You and Dr. Sandborn? When are you opening your own agency?" he asked, impressed by her initiative.

"No, no, honey, this is pleasure, not business. I think he's cute. In an over-the-hill, probably really rich sort of way. I like my men rich."

"You like your men breathing," Grady said, pushing himself away from the wall and heading back down the hall. "Just be careful, okay? I'll relieve you at seven, so you can get ready for your *date*."

He stopped just outside Archie's rooms, with his hand on the doorknob, realizing he just did not want to go back inside and listen to any more tapes, watch one more video. He'd much rather find out which one of the little Peeverses owned a black Chevy Suburban.

He tested the handle, made sure it was locked, and retraced his steps, back to his room, then through to Maisie's, so he could use her files, work on her computer.

Maisie was a lot of things, some of them pretty strange, he was finding out, but she was one hell of an organized person. Almost compulsively so. He easily located the files on each Peevers, then scanned through credit reports, criminal records—nothing there, for anyone, except two small marijuana busts for Junior—and found the sheets with short lists of personal assets.

No Chevy Suburbans.

None for Sandy Sandborn, or Jefferson Banning, or Daisy. Dickens drove a brand-new BMW, and traded in his wheels every three years. Butlering paid some big bucks, if you knew how to do it right.

"Damn, you didn't expect it to be that easy, did you?" he asked himself, picking up the files for the estate itself.

And that's where he found it. One black Chevrolet Suburban, leased by the Peevers, driven by their gardener and all-around handyman, Joe Peters.

Grabbing the field kit, Grady made his way to the large bank of garages and found the Suburban parked inside the third door. He didn't expect to find any prints, and he didn't. None on the door, or the steering wheel, or the gearshift, even on the ignition. If O.J.'s Bronco had been wiped this clean, he'd still have his Heisman.

Grady sat in the driver's seat—it had been in the full-back position, so only Wilt Chamberlain could have driven it that way, so he knew the seat had been moved on purpose, to hide the height of the driver—and looked through the windshield. He could picture, in his mind's eye, what Annie's convertible would have looked like from this vantage point. Like a Tinker Toy, probably.

*Think,* he told himself. *Just think. They make mistakes. The bad guys always make mistakes.*

He put his hands on the wheel, and mentally reviewed everything he'd do when getting into a car, most especially a vehicle he might not have driven before.

The mirrors! He was just getting excited about the mirrors, when he realized the outside pair were controlled by remote, which left only the rearview mirror. Out came the kit again, and he held his breath as he dusted behind the mirror for prints.

Nothing. Okay, so some of the bad guys were smarter than most. He'd have to find another way to identify the driver, and youth and strength weren't factors this time. Anybody with a license could drive a car, right?

Did this mean he had to put everyone back on the list of suspects? Probably, and that really pissed him off.

He left the garages, remembering to dust the overhead door for prints and unsurprised when he didn't find any, and went back upstairs to Archie's rooms.

He heard the argument, the raised voices, before he was halfway down the hall.

Dickens was leaving the room as Grady reached for the doorknob. "You were supposed to keep this door locked. Who did you let in there?"

"Only the weak and harmless, sir," Dickens said, then lifted his chin and walked down the hall.

Grady went inside, stopping in the drape-enclosed entry foyer, and listened. Within moments, he had recognized Archie's cackling voice, then A.W.'s surprising baritone, then Junior's.

Junior's was sort of a squeak. "How can you say that, Daddy? You know we love you!"

"Hah! You'd love me six feet under," Archie responded, and Grady nodded, pretty much agreeing with the man. "Now you two listen up, and listen good. I *know.* I didn't want to tell you I know, but that damn Sullivan figured it out, and I already know Banning called you this morning to tell you I know, so there's no sense in trying to keep it secret anymore. I *know.*"

"We . . . ," A.W. said, obviously struggling to find an end for what he'd begun because Mitzi wasn't there to finish his sentence for him. "We, um, we were just trying to protect you."

"Protect me? *Protect* me? How do you figure that one, Asswipe?"

Grady stepped closer. He wanted to hear the answer to that one himself.

"If I could just get Mitzi . . . ," A.W. began, then wisely shut up. Unfortunately, not soon enough to stop Archie from winging a pillow at him, a pillow that dropped at Grady's feet as he fully entered the room.

"Getting your late-afternoon exercise, Archie?" he asked, nodding to the two sons before taking up a seat in one of the chairs in front of the fireplace. "A little yelling, a little pillow tossing. Keeps the old heart just pumping along, doesn't it?"

"Get out of here," Junior ordered, hitching his designer slacks up over the small paunch that kept pushing the waistband south of the border. "This is a private conversation."

"No, Junior, it's not," Grady said, crossing one leg over the other. "I'm the muscle, remember? Here to protect dear old Daddy from his nearest and deadliest? Now, let me guess. We're talking about Double A, aren't we?"

"You had no right—" A.W. began, then faltered. He actually looked as if he might be about to cry.

"I'm not going to argue about that with you, A.W.," Grady said, still careful to smile. He wanted to jump up, choke both men until one of them admitted to driving the Suburban. But he couldn't be sure, and he had to be sure. "Archie? Can we cut to the chase here? Do you want me to phone the police? God knows I've got their number on speed dial these past days."

"The police?" Junior went chalk white beneath his dyed black hair. "Daddy? You wouldn't do that, would you?"

"Pitiful, ain't they?" Archie asked, pulling his covers up around him, settling back against his remaining pillows. "Wetting their pants, trying to tell me they did it all for my own good. Had nothing to do with the money, but just my two loving boys trying to protect me. That's the story, sonny, the one they're trying to tell me. Double A was set up to monitor everything for me, make sure I wasn't getting ripped off by suppliers or employees. Isn't that it, boys? Isn't that why you did it?"

A.W. nodded furiously. "Exactly! You've been sick, Daddy, for a long time, but you wouldn't let us run the place. We had to do something to check up on you. We had to be able to pick the suppliers ourselves, get the best price. We . . . we were only trying to help."

It had to be the longest speech of A.W.'s life, and he

looked fairly pleased with himself as he staggered to the chair beside Grady's, and sank into it.

"Sonny?" Archie said, looking at Grady. "You buying any of this?"

Grady grinned. "Nope. How about you?"

"Not a word. So, now that the cat's out of the bag and all of that, which one of 'em do you think did it? That's why you're here, right? To tell me which one of 'em did it?"

"You already know they both did it," Grady pointed out, slightly confused.

"Yeah, I know that. But which one was the brains? I tell you, sonny, I've thought and thought about that, but I'll be damned if I can see either one of them being smart enough to set it up. So which one? Or was it Banning? Fired him this morning, by the way."

"You . . . you fired Jefferson?" A.W. asked, sitting up straight in his chair. "Does . . . does that mean you won't be changing your will anymore?"

"No, Asswipe," Archie said, singsonging the words. "It means I won't be using your little partner in crime as my lawyer anymore. Now, come on. I'm in a good mood here. Tell me who thought up this Double A thing, and I might keep him in my will. It took some smarts to think of it, and to neatly rake that ten percent off the top and siphon it into your own bank accounts. So tell me. I'd like to think there's one of you with at least half a brain."

"It was me!" A.W. and Junior said at the same time.

Grady dropped his head in his hand, laughing silently. As his favorite cartoon character was wont to say: "What maroons!" Then he stood up, walked to the middle of the room, turned to look at first one brother, then the other. "Congratulations, gentlemen. I'm willing to bet Archie has all this on tape. Just in case you ever want to have him committed, judged mentally incompetent, so you can take all his money. Right, Archie?"

"Not just tape, sonny. Smile for the camera, boys. It's over there, in that plant Muriel gave me for Christmas last year. And now get out of here, both of you. Hah! Look at 'em run! God, I love this!"

Grady waited until the door slammed, then pulled up a straight-backed chair, straddled it after setting it down beside Archie's bed. "Now what? You've been pulling all the strings so far, so you might as well tell me what comes next."

"Well," Archie said, settling himself once more, "nobody's tried to kill me in a couple of days, so I suppose that's next. How's the girl?"

"Alive," Grady said, his voice tight. "Not that I believe you care, or you wouldn't have set her up in the first place. Do you think A.W. and Junior tried to take her out?"

Archie pushed his nightcap back on his head. "Do you?"

"I don't know. As a matter of fact, I don't know much of anything anymore. So maybe you'll let me run all of this by you one more time, just so I can get my bearings?"

Archie sighed. "If you insist. But it's a hell of a thing if my own bodyguard can't figure out what's going on."

"Archie, Machiavelli would have needed a road map and a guide to figure out what's going on," Grady said, standing up, pushing the chair away so he could pace. He thought better when he paced.

"Okay, here goes," he said after a few moments. "One, you're old, maybe even dying—although I doubt it—and it really steams you that you have to leave your money behind when you croak."

"You've seen my family, sonny," Archie broke in. "Would you want to leave any of them bus fare?"

"You could have just kept quiet, then given it all away. To charity, or something."

Archie shook his head. "No good. They'd just contest the will, saying I was nuts. They might lose in the end, but half my money would be gone by then, right into the lawyers' pockets. If I hate my family, I really hate lawyers. Or did you think I had the hots for Joe College and his great big smile?"

"Did you like Banning? No, I don't think so. Okay, two. You've been playing with your will ever since you found out about Double A, about how your sons were trying to rob you, dragging Banning up here time after time, making threats to change your will."

"And Banning told them about each change," Archie put in, reaching over and picking up a glass of water. "You did know that, didn't you?"

"I suspected it. He cheats at golf, too," Grady added, just to prove his own private point. "If I may continue?"

"Oh, a monologue," Archie said. "I thought this was a discussion. My mistake, sonny. But, before I clam up, can you tell me something? Do you think Maisie likes me? Got a hot little bod, that girl!"

Grady sliced the old man a dubious look, then continued: "Somehow, I don't care how—probably thanks to Mission Control in there—you found out about Double A, the same way you found out Banning was reporting to them, I imagine. You could have fired both sons, tossed them out on their ears, even turned them over to the district attorney, and Banning to the Bar Association. But you didn't."

"Because they're my flesh and blood," Archie said, lifting a finger to his eye as if to wipe away a tear.

Grady directed a long, dispassionate stare at the man. "Right," he said after a few moments. "And you love them dearly. That, and the fact that you wouldn't want anyone to find out you'd been duped by either Asswipe or Junie, or even Joe College."

"Would you?"

"Nope, guess not. So instead of telling them you knew, or ratting them out to the police, you started taking back the reins a few months ago, then sat back and watched as they began to sweat."

"An old man takes his pleasures where he can," Archie said, smiling around his too-large dentures.

"You're all heart, Archie. But then, while you were enjoying yourself, and watching them see their scam go down the toilet—I figured you'd like that analogy—you started thinking that maybe one of them might rather see you dead than wait for the will to be read. The will you kept changing."

"Sandy suggested that part," Archie said, reaching under his covers and coming out with a large bag of M&Ms. "He said he'd kill me if he was one of my heirs. I thought about that, and decided that's what I'd do, too, so we came up with the rest of it."

Grady stopped pacing, looked at Archie. "The two of

you came up with the idea of hiring a bogus granddaughter? You and Sandy both? And he suggested that you might be in danger? Now that's interesting."

"Why? It made sense. I couldn't keep changing my will forever, and pretty soon either Banning or the boys would have figured out they could just keep a will they liked and knock me off before I could change it again. So why not give them someone else to bump off, if any of them had the guts to try." He shrugged his thin shoulders. "But, you know, until that arrow came through the window, I didn't think any of them would. I really, really didn't."

"Because it was a game," Grady said, nodding. "A rich, nasty old man playing pull the wings off the heirs. But now you're in real trouble, aren't you? Someone's taken a shot at you, and your bogus granddaughter was run off the road. Your sons know you know about Double A, they know you've got them on audio and video, and they've got to be figuring they're definitely out of the will now, if you can change it again before one of them strangles you in your bed. Man, you're screwed, aren't you?"

Grady tipped his head, smiled. "You know what, Archie? I think I'm going to take the night off. No, more than just tonight. I quit."

Archie bolted upright, choking on a fistful of M&Ms. "No . . . no!" he cried out, spitting candy everywhere. "No, wait! You can't quit on me! Damn it, Sullivan, you quit more often than an alcoholic!"

Grady kept his back to Archie so the man wouldn't see his smile. Then, slowly, he turned around. "Okay, here's the deal. You write a check to Annie, every penny you promised her, and cut her loose. I want her out of here by tomorrow morning."

"Done! I probably didn't need her anyway, right?"

"Right," Grady agreed, disgusted. "You're a real prince, Archie. A real prince. I'll pick up the check later, and we'll talk some more about suspects. Because, even if I didn't believe anyone wanted you dead before, I'm pretty sure your days are numbered now if we don't find out which one of your heirs you've finally pissed off enough."

# Twenty-one

*How cheerfully he seems to grin,*
*How neatly spreads his claws,*
*And welcomes little fishes in*
*With gently smiling jaws.*
                          —Lewis Carroll

At seven that night, Annie stood in front of the mirror over the old mahogany dresser, inspecting the way the collar lay on her navy blue blouse. No better than the last one, actually, and as she'd already tried on three, she was going to stick with this one. It didn't matter what she wore; the bandage Dr. Sandborn had taped to her neck couldn't be hidden.

She'd seen less gauze on a mummy.

She put her hands on her hips, then quickly rethought the move, as both hips were sore. Sore, and black, and blue, and even a rather lovely magenta in spots.

Still, she couldn't complain, because the seat belt had saved her. That, and the air bag. She closed her eyes, imagined once again what would have happened if she hadn't been wearing the seat belt—an image that had a lot to do with her soaring through the air like one of the Flying Wallendas until she bashed into a tree, headfirst.

"You are one lucky girl, girl," she told herself, reaching for her perfume bottle before she remembered that Maisie had "borrowed" it. Maisie also had "borrowed" her purse, her brand-new blush, and her gold chain, but who was counting? She'd gotten the woman out of the room, hadn't she?

Now all she had to do was convince Grady, when he showed up, that she was fit to go, ready to rock, hot to track down the driver of the Suburban.

She probably shouldn't wince every two seconds if she wanted to convince him. "Right, Deuce?" she asked the stuffed animal sitting in the middle of her bed. "Yeah, right. And don't think we're going to make a habit out of sharing my bed, okay? It's never good to spoil the children that way. I read that somewhere."

"What the hell do you think you're doing?"

Annie jumped, winced, then turned to watch as Grady came into the room without knocking, his expression a mix of anger and concern and drop-dead gorgeous. She smiled, put up her hands. "You can't hit me; I'm injured, remember?"

"I remember," he said, looking her up and down, his gaze lingering on the bandage at her throat. "Do you?"

"I'll take that as a rhetorical question, considering it's my body," she said, reaching over to snag one last green grape from the dinner tray Dickens had brought up earlier. Personally. He'd even stiffly inquired as to how she felt before excusing himself as she sniffed at the bloodred rose he'd stuck into a crystal bud vase. The man was just soppy over her. "Have you eaten? All they gave me was broth and fruit."

"Roast beef, red potatoes, and two helpings of Mitzi telling everyone she's been elected president of the local woman's club for the third year in a row," Grady told her absently, sitting down on the edge of the bed, patting the mattress. "What would it take to get you back in here?"

She grinned at him. "I don't know. Candy? Flowers? You down on one knee, declaring your undying devotion?"

That, she saw, got rid of the "concern" part of his facial expression. He was all anger now. "That's not what I meant, damn it," he said, standing up once more.

"I know," she told him, holding on to one of the bed-posts as she tried to slip into her shoes without jarring herself too badly. How she hated this! They couldn't even seem to joke anymore. "It was just my small attempt at levity. There goes the career in stand-up, huh? So? Are you ready?"

He shook his head. "Ready for what? You're staying right here."

"Actually, no, I'm not. Archie sent for me a little while ago. He says he's got it all figured out, and all he needs is a little help from you and me, and we'll have this whole thing wrapped up by tomorrow, Wednesday at the latest. Didn't he tell you?"

"No, he didn't tell me," Grady said, and now his face wasn't only angry-looking, it was pretty close to livid. Poor baby. "He was supposed to cut a check for you, so you'd leave. The balance of the fifty thousand you'd agreed to. That was our bargain."

Annie tipped her head to one side for a moment, looked at a spot in the far corner of the room, slowly counting to ten. Nope, wouldn't work. She could count to a million, and it still wouldn't work. She was mad. She was mad as hell.

"Your bargain? You and Archie made a *bargain.* So Archie didn't come up with the idea on his own? I should have known that the minute I saw the check when Dickens brought it to me earlier. How enterprising of you, Mr. Sullivan. *You* made the decision for *me.* Just who the hell do you think you are, anyway?"

He stepped closer, close enough for her to smell his aftershave, close enough that she could remember how it felt when he came even closer. "Annie, let's not argue. Somebody tried to kill you today."

"Maybe. I think the Suburban was trying to avoid me, there at the end. I was just supposed to be scared, not dead."

"Really? Figured that out all by yourself, did you? Well, I checked, Annie. There were no skid marks anywhere on that road. Not yours, because you were gunning it, trying to get off the road. And none from the Chevy. Whoever was driving that thing knew who'd come off worst in a head-on collision. Tell me, Annie, can you say *accordian-pleated?"*

"I don't care, I'm not leaving. Would you? If someone tried to kill you, would you leave?"

"That's not the point."

"Yes, it is. I'm hurting here, Grady. Battered, bruised, you name it. But mostly, I'm mad as hell, and I'm not going to take it anymore!"

*"Network.* Saw it," Grady said, raking a hand through

his hair. He took that last step, the one that put him close
enough to touch her, close enough to run a hand down
her cheek. Close enough to kiss. "We could fight about
this for the next hour, but it isn't going to change anything, right? You're going to drive me crazy, aren't you?
You're not going to rest until you drive me stark, staring
mad."

"Archie needs me," she said weakly, watching Grady's
mouth, almost able to taste it.

"Archie can go to hell," Grady told her, cupping her
face with both hands. "You will tell me someday, won't
you?"

Annie tried to breathe, not with much success. "Tell
you what?" she asked, her hands spread against his chest.

"The truth," he whispered, then gently touched his
mouth to hers. He kissed her gently, as if she might
break. He held her loosely, careful not to inadvertently
collide with her bruises. His lips clung, then released
slowly, so that she moved forward blindly, trying to main-
tain the contact. "The truth," he said, kissing her again
and again, lightly biting her bottom lip, slanting his
mouth first one way, then the other, ". . . the whole
truth . . . and nothing but . . . the truth. Deal?"

"You . . . you're very persuasive," Annie said on a
sigh, then damned her bruises to hell or wherever they
wanted to go as long as they didn't bother her, and pulled
Grady's head down, holding it there as she kissed him
back.

Everything else, she'd think about later. How she'd tell
him. How he'd react. For now, for just this once, she'd
concentrate on the moment, and the devil with the future,
and the past. . . .

* * *

Archie was dressed. Grady had never seen the old man dressed, but recognized the style. It wasn't that Grady was all that clothes-conscious, but it was pretty hard not to remember Nehru jackets.

"You're looking dapper this evening, Archie," he said, helping Annie into one of the wing chairs in front of the fireplace. She was being very brave, but he knew she was hurting. Which meant he was caught between admiring her and wanting to pick her up, take her back down the hall, and tuck her into bed.

Unfortunately, alone. He knew he was being selfish, but he hoped she was a quick healer.

"I also think you look very dapper," Annie said, smiling at the old man. "Are you double-dating with Maisie and Dr. Sandborn? Who's the lucky lady?"

"Anyone who can run faster than him," Grady said, sitting down in the other chair. "Okay, Archie, what's up? I thought we had a deal."

"She turned it down," Archie told him, standing still so that Dickens could wield a small whisk broom over his shoulders. "Flat. Didn't you, Annie?"

"He already knows that, Archie," Annie told him, shifting slightly in the chair. "What he really wants to know is why. Don't you, Grady?"

"Are you going to tell him?" Archie asked. "I'd sure like to hear the reason myself. Not that I'm not grateful, because my idea won't work without you."

"Mr. Peevers is feeling brilliant this evening," Dickens said, opening a drawer and replacing the whisk broom. "Indeed, he is so very pleased with himself that he is contemplating an appearance downstairs. That notion will go nowhere. It never does," Dickens ended, rolling his eyes as he retreated to the far side of the room, crossed his arms over his chest, and awaited further orders.

"Smart-ass," Archie said, glaring at the butler, before turning back to Annie and Grady, rubbing his palms together. "All right, all right, so you're wondering about my idea. Okay, here it is. Dickens—get the sack."

"Yes, sir," Dickens said, rolling his eyes yet again. He walked over to the closet, stiff-backed, and opened the door, disappearing inside for a moment before stepping back out again, a large brown-burlap sack in one hand. He carried it away from his body, as if it were nuclear waste, or alive.

"Bring it here, bring it here," Archie said, clapping his hands now. "Open it, and dump it on the floor. Hurry! Hurry!"

Grady shifted his weight, slipped a hand under his jacket, and closed that hand around the butt of his pistol. It was a reflex action, definitely, but with Archie, who could be too careful?

Dickens untied the thin rope holding the sack shut, then turned the thing upside down even as he stepped back.

Out slid a snake. A very large, ugly snake. With a bunch of rattles at the tail.

Before Annie could do more than open her mouth to scream, Grady had his weapon out, ready to fire. "Wait a minute," he said, raising the barrel toward the ceiling, slowly uncocking the pistol. "It's not moving."

"Good eye," Archie said, bending down to pick up the snake, shaking it so that the tail rattled. "It's a fake. But a good one. Well, good enough, as I doubt anyone's going to want to look inside the bag."

"Grady?"

He looked at Annie, saw that her face was white, that her breathing had become labored. "Are you all right?"

"Harrison . . . Harrison Ford," she mumbled, shivering.

Grady shook his head. *"Raiders of the Lost Ark,* right? Indiana Jones? You hate snakes? Well, why the hell didn't you just say so?" He put a hand on the back of her head, forcing her head down between her knees. "Okay. Just take some slow, deep breaths, okay?"

"O—okay," she said, holding on to his hand, squeezing it tightly. "Can't . . . can't say . . ."

"Snakes. You can't even *say* snakes. Got it. Now shut up and breathe." Grady glared at Archie. "You are one sick son of a bitch, do you know that? What the hell is this snake all about?"

Dickens held out the sack, and Archie slid the snake back inside. "The snake, sonny, is the murder weapon. Or, should I say, the *attempted* murder weapon." He looked at the mantel clock. "Ah, Sandy should be bursting in here in a few minutes, to administer the antidote and save me. But that's only secondary, you see, because it's Annie here who really saved me, throwing a chair at the snake so she could pull me to safety after that first terrible bite. Didn't you, darling granddaughter?"

Annie lifted her head and glared at him. "What?"

"Don't ask questions, little girl. Just scream, all right. I thought you'd do that right away, but you didn't. Are you up to trying it now? Sullivan can throw the chair. Or Dickens, it makes no never mind. Then, after a few moments, sonny, go open that window over there and take a shot at one of the trees, will you? That ought to bring everyone on the run."

"Grady?" Annie asked, finally able to breathe again. "What's he talking about?"

"I think," Grady answered, stroking her hair, "Archie's going to have you save him from another attempt on his life."

"But it's not a real . . . a real . . . you know."

"No, and it's not a real attempt. Not like the arrow. But I think I can see where Archie's going with it." Grady looked at Dickens, who was looking mildly disgusted. "You, too, Dickens?"

"Yes, sir. I tried to talk him out of it, but he wouldn't listen."

Annie pushed herself to her feet, took hold of Grady's forearm, gave it a shake. "Wouldn't listen to what? What's going on here?"

"Archie's going to let you save his life, and then he'll announce to everyone that he's making you his sole heir."

"No," Annie said, squeezing Grady's arm tighter. "No! That's ridiculous."

"Oh, it's more than ridiculous, Annie," Grady said, patting her hand. "It's also setting you up for the kill, and I won't allow it. For God's sake, Archie, there's already been one attempt on her life today."

"And it didn't work, did it?" Archie pointed out. "So maybe the next one is going to be on me. Or do you still think I shot that arrow at myself, huh? You want out of here, Sullivan, and you want her out of here. Fine. That's just dandy, because you've already managed to screw up most of my plan. But first you're both going to earn your money. I'm just making it easy for you. Because I'll be damned if you're going to let her get away and then leave yourself after a month, having solved nothing, if you're going to keep being as useless as you've been so far. Not now, not now that you stupidly tipped off Banning and I had to let those two idiot boys know I'm onto their scam. Not now that I know somebody really does want me dead."

"Someone, Archie? Hell, it's more like take a number, get in line. Now Banning can be added to the list. But no snake. Definitely no snake. And no telling anyone you're putting Annie in the will. Not unless you want the police here in the next hour. I've got a lot to say to them."

Archie climbed into his bed, leaned back against the pillows. "But it was such a good idea," he said, his bottom lip starting to tremble. "I thought we could flush whoever it is out into the open."

"Yeah, well, *flush* that idea right down the drain, okay? I'm getting close, Archie. Even closer, thanks to your little hobby of eavesdropping. Let Annie leave, and I promise you, I'll have this solved in a couple of days. A week at the outside. Believe me, nobody wants out of here more than I do."

Archie raised one hand, waved it languidly. "All right, all right. The check's on that desk over there, where Dickens put it after Annie refused it. Dickens, fetch."

"Yes, sir."

"No," Annie said, backing up, shaking her head. "I'm not leaving. How many times must I say it? Maybe you want me to embroider it on a pillow: *I'm not leaving.*"

Archie lifted his head, his smile hopeful. "Then you'll play along? Save me from the snake?"

"Not on your life," Annie said, her laugh hollow.

At that, before Annie could do more than look at Grady, who was scowling in that "she's driving me nuts" way again, the door burst open and Milton Sandborn charged in.

"Where is he? Where's my patient? I've got the antidote right here! Hang on, Archie—I'll save you!"

He stopped halfway into the room, looked around, then shrugged his barn-door-wide shoulders. "What? Did I miss my cue?"

"You sure did, honey," Maisie said, entering behind him, dressed all in electric blue and smelling like she'd bathed in Chanel, obviously more than ready for her big date. "*I'm* supposed to be the antidote to what ails you, remember?"

Annie sat down, hugging herself against the pain of her aching muscles as she laughed until tears rolled down her cheeks.

It was midnight, and Annie and Grady were sitting in the kitchen in the mansion, dipping Oreos into milk.

"It still just kills me to remember the look on Dr. Sandborn's face when he figured out he'd made his big entrance for nothing. I thought we'd never get that sorted out," she said, carefully opening an Oreo, then scraping off the white icing with her top teeth.

"Don't do that," Grady told her, trying not to watch.

"Do what? Eat the icing first? Why not?"

"Because you're driving me crazy, and you're too

banged up for me to do anything about it, that's why. Besides, I'm still mad as hell at you."

"Grady, we've been around the block about this a million times. I'm not leaving. First it was a job. Now I'm mad. Somebody boiled my bunny, wrecked my car. I'm not going to walk away from that."

"So it wasn't just the money, like you said it was?"

She pressed the two sides of the cookie together again, sans icing, and dunked the small chocolate sandwich into the cup of milk. "You know it wasn't."

"Not right away, I didn't," Grady admitted, reaching into the bag for another Oreo. "And, much as I understand that you're mad, I don't think that's the real reason you're staying, either. Quinn called me tonight, before Archie's little show. He had some information for me."

Annie concentrated on twisting another Oreo until it separated. "Really. What about? Me?"

"In a way. You don't exist, Annie. That's what Quinn found out, and he's one of the best at finding stuff like that out. You do not exist. No address, no credit record, no driver's license. No social security card, so don't count on collecting when you reach sixty-five. If the Peeverses let you live that long."

"Yeah, well, them's the breaks," Annie said, shrugging. "Still, I thought you said you wouldn't go digging around in my past anymore. But we've got the bottom line now, don't we? I don't exist, and you're a liar."

"So we're even," Grady said, then cursed under his breath as half his soggy Oreo slowly broke off into his cup of milk. "I never could do this right," he said, fishing in the milk with a teaspoon.

"You dunk too long. It's an art," Annie told him. "Anyway, you had your partner check me out through some foster-care systems, didn't you? Come on, you can tell me. It's the only real clue you had after Maisie struck out, right? I'm not mad. Not anymore. You were just being you, and I'm too tired to be mad at you anymore. Besides, we slept together. You probably figured you had the right to know who I am."

"I'm glad we're being so civilized," Grady told her, giving up on rescuing the Oreo and pulling a fresh one from the bag, not bothering to dunk it before taking a bite. He'd just use the milk as a chaser. "Are you sure you're not mad?"

"Positive. Are you mad?"

"That you won't tell me your real name?" He shook his head. "Not angry, Annie. Just curious. I don't like mysteries."

"Which means you're going to keep trying," she said, picking up her cup and heading for the sink. "Well, good for you. I would, too. Lots of luck."

"I'm still keeping Maisie out of it," Grady said, placing his own cup in the sink, watching as Annie ran water in both cups. "Quinn's out of it now, too. But I will find out, Annie. I'd rather you told me, but I will find out."

Annie dried her hands on a dish towel, then leaned back against the edge of the sink, looked up at him. "It's that important to you?"

*"You're* that important to me, Annie," he said honestly. He reached out, stroked her cheek. "I'm afraid for you, afraid you might be in trouble. Might have bitten off more than you can chew somewhere along the line, before answering that ad and coming here. Please, Annie,

trust me. Let me help you. I have connections, from my years on the force. I *can* help you."

Annie's eyes grew wide. "Wait a minute. You think I'm some sort of *criminal?* That's it? Is that your great conclusion so far?"

"I didn't say that," Grady told her, as she buried her head in her hands. "But you've got no paper trail. None. You need money, and have been up-front about that all along. You won't leave, even when Archie hands you the money, because maybe you want to stay out of the public eye for a while. So, yes, I think you might be in some kind of trouble. I don't like saying this, but it makes sense. Sort of."

He bent his knees slightly, so that he could be face-to-face with her. Put his hands on her shoulders. "Annie? Annie, sweetheart, are you crying?"

Slowly she dropped her hands, so that he could see her face. Hear her low, throaty giggle.

She was laughing? Damn her, she was *laughing!* Then she stood on tiptoe, kissed him on the mouth, and left him standing there in the kitchen like the world's biggest doofus.

He could really learn to hate her.

If he didn't love her so damn much.

# Twenty-two

*A large income is the best recipe
for happiness I heard of.*
—Jane Austen

"So, are we having fun yet? Because I'm not, honey," Maisie said as she waited for another Internet page to load on the computer.

Grady stood next to her, also watching and waiting. For five days they'd been surfing the net (or at least Maisie had, in between hot dates with Milton Sandborn). They'd pawed through garbage at midnight, searched every room, and stooped low enough to bribe the maids for information.

They now knew about Junior's marijuana busts *and* the fact that he had two marijuana plants growing under lamps in his bathroom. He had the maids dust and water them; money and arrogance—and redbrick stupidity—seemingly going hand in hand where Junior was concerned.

They now knew A.W. had some pretty suspicious

transactions on his platinum card, and were pretty sure it wasn't Mitzi who'd shared the tab at the Dew Drop Inn outside of Harrisburg.

They knew that Muriel was a secret drinker, which had come as a surprise until Grady thought about it for a while. Still, he'd seen the waste can in her room, and the bottles in that waste can. The gin bottles, and the giant economy size bottles of mint mouthwash.

They knew that Mitzi liked puzzles. Crossword puzzles, cryptograms, jigsaw puzzles; probably to pass the time alone in her room. They knew she owned four vibrators and had an impressive collection of soft porn in the back of her closet. Another time passer.

They already knew everything Grady thought they needed to know about Dickens. Probably more than they'd wanted to know about Dickens.

They knew that Milton Sandborn had been born right there in Bethlehem, educated in Philadelphia and Boston, and had practiced internal medicine until about twenty-five years ago, retiring early, at only forty-seven, when he'd sold his practice except for a few elderly patients who'd since died. He was still Archie's private physician, which probably meant some bucks, but not enough to keep him in the five-hundred-thousand-dollar house on Macada Road.

Sandborn was interesting.

Daisy Goodenough wasn't.

Maisie had found her easily on the Internet because Daisy, unbelievably, had her own Internet site. Even bimbos knew the power of the Internet, which was pretty scary all by itself. A Date with Daisy, she'd titled her site, and clicking on the various "Hot Dates" brought up some revealing photos of the woman that had Maisie pointing excitedly and crowing, "See? See? *Told* you they're silicone, honey! You cannot, repeat, *cannot* lie on your back and still be that perky! Or you suppose maybe she uses spray starch? I don't *think* so, honey."

The site had scored over forty thousand hits in the past year, one of them most probably Junior.

They confirmed that when Maisie hacked into the man's personal computer—Junior's secret password was, with almost disappointing predictably, his birth date—and found saved addresses for every live-sex and hot-babe site out there. Including Daisy's. Another suspicion confirmed.

They didn't bother with Jefferson Banning, as they knew who he was, knew what he was, and Grady had already found out the good lawyer had left town suddenly for a month-long vacation in Brazil; probably to check on his secret bank accounts and scope out the local golf courses in case he wanted to make the move permanent. Grady figured he'd give it a couple of weeks, then drop an anonymous note to the local Bar Association. Couldn't hurt. He really hated cheats, especially golf cheats.

While Grady and Maisie were investigating, Annie had taken over the job of baby-sitting Archie, whose paranoia had escalated to the point where he refused to be left alone. Annie stayed with him most of the day, Maisie or Grady sat with him throughout the evening, and Dickens slept on a cot in the room.

"Your turn with Archie tonight, right?" Grady said now, closing a manila folder after reading through A.W.'s platinum-card charges for the fifth time.

"Yeah, honey," Maisie said in disgust. "That's what Mom says. Annie sets the table, and I do the dishes. Jeez, talk about your lousy jobs. And if Archie doesn't stop chasing me around the room, you're going to have to tack my name on to our list of suspects."

"Not much longer now," Grady assured her, smiling.

"Gee, now where did I hear that before? I think Annie's got it, though. It's A.W. and Junior, working together. Because of that Double A thing. It's obvious."

"Maybe, but we can't prove it. We can't *prove* anything. I hate to say it, but unless Archie agrees to turning his sons in for trying to rip him off, we're going to have to wait and hope somebody takes another potshot at him while we're close enough to catch him."

"Before or after they off Archie? Because, if it was me, I could probably be happy either way." Maisie stood up, stretched like a cat. "You still don't think A.W. or Junior had enough brains to set up Double A, do you?"

"Do you? Honestly?"

"No, I suppose not. Especially Junior. Which leaves Mitzi, because you won't convince me Muriel would do anything so daring. The woman's afraid of her own shadow, and terrified of Mitzi."

Grady bent his head, rubbed at the back of his neck with both hands. "I know. A.W. is scared to death of the woman, too. Although he is running around on her."

"And you call that being *strong?*" Maisie asked, rolling her eyes. "Honey, that's the *weakest* a man can be. Cheaters are all weak, trust me on this. Otherwise, they'd get divorces and be done with it, get themselves out of a marriage as unhappy as A.W. and Mitzi's is. Only women have the strength to just walk away, not knowing where they'll go, what they'll do next. A.W. won't leave unless and until he finds a nice cozy nest to run to. Men never do, honey. Trust me on this one. You watch. One day Mitzi will just take what she can carry and get the hell out of here."

Grady looked at his assistant for long moments, believing he could actually hear the gears turning in his head. He was close. So close. He could feel it. But he wasn't there. Not yet.

"So," he said after a few moments, "what you're saying is that A.W. is sticking around because he doesn't have the guts to leave. He hates his father, but can't break away. He hates his wife, but can't break away. So he just cheats on both of them—meaning Double A and the Dew Drop Inn—and makes himself feel better. Right?"

"Right," Maisie said, reaching for her nail file. "Mitzi's staying because she's still getting something out of the marriage. Social standing. Big charge accounts. Just being Mrs. A.W. Something. But if she ever has enough, *zoom,* she'll be out of here."

*If she ever has enough.* Grady frowned. How much is enough?

The gears were still turning.

"Okay, Maisie. How about this—Mitzi's the real brains behind Double A? Her idea, she gets A.W. to go along with it, drags in Junior and tells A.W. that if anyone takes the fall it will be his baby brother. Remember, it's Junior's signature on most of the corporation papers, with A.W.'s only on a couple of the smaller ones, signing beneath Junior. A.W.'s such a dope, and a wuss, that he believes her. And then she handles the money for them, works the books. We watched her playing bridge the other night, remember? She kept all the scores in her head. She's good with numbers. Well? Could it be Mitzi?"

Maisie filed a nail, lifted the fingertip to her mouth, blew on it. "Wouldn't surprise me."

"And when she gets *enough* money," Grady went on, feeling pretty good, "she walks away. Except that somewhere along the line she figures out that ripping off Archie and ditching A.W. *isn't* enough. She wants it all. Especially when Archie started taking back the reins, cutting Double A out."

"You know, I think you're really onto something, honey," Maisie said, watching as he paced.

"Yeah, me too. So Mitzi starts thinking. Double A is there, incriminating A.W. and Junior the minute Archie blows the whistle, which he doesn't do. That, it turns out, works even better. Because now she can kill Archie, get him out of the picture, and A.W. and Junior will go down for the murder—thanks to the Double A records. Hell, Archie even has their confession on tape, just as an added bonus. It's a slam dunk that they'd both be convicted. And Mitzi gets it all."

"Mitzi and Muriel," Maisie pointed out.

"I doubt it. Oh, Muriel will get her share, but Mitzi will handle it for her, you can count on that."

"You know, honey, if you're right, Mitzi's going to have to try again, and soon. She has to, because Archie won't turn the boys in to the authorities so far, but he might change his mind. He's getting pretty antsy. Either that, or she gives it up, cuts and runs with the money she's already ripped off. Right?"

"Right, except that now that she's seen the golden

goose, she's not going to settle for just a couple of eggs. I think Mitzi's our culprit, Maisie. But we need more proof. Get out all the financial records again," Grady told her, heading for the door. He couldn't wait to get Annie alone, tell her what he'd concluded. "And, before you do, tell me if you got them on A.W. and Mitzi as joint owners, or if you also ran separate checks."

"I did them together—oh! I see what you're getting at now. That was stupid of me, wasn't it? I should have checked. You want to see if Mitzi has any accounts just in her name?"

"Her name, her maiden name. Variations of her name—M. Peevers, Mildred Peevers. You name it. Banks, stocks, mutual funds, bonds, the whole gamut. When can you have that for me?"

"It's illegal to go where I have to go, so give me a couple of hours," Maisie said, putting down the nail file and opening Mitzi's file, to check on her maiden name. "You know, you may be onto something, except you already said Mitzi couldn't climb that tree in her twinset and pearls, load an arrow in a crossbow."

"I'm on a roll here, Maisie. Don't confuse me with facts," Grady said, slipping his sports coat on over his white shirt, tie, and shoulder holster. "I'm taking Annie out to dinner, so have everything waiting for me when we get back, okay?"

"Out for dinner, huh? And then what? I'll bet I can figure out what comes next, you stud muffin, you. You know, honey, I know you want to solve this thing and get out of here. But, mostly, I think it's because you want to have all your time free to learn more about our little orphan Annie. You're nuts about her, aren't you, and she's driving you crazy. Yes? No?"

Grady closed the door on her.


"Gin! I win!"

"You *cheat,* you don't win," Annie said, spreading the cards to show that Archie had been hiding an eight behind his final discard. "Shame on you, I needed that eight."

"You need a lot of things, girlie-girl, but that's life," Archie said, gathering the cards and sticking them back in the drawer beneath the games table set up in the room. "You owe me six million dollars."

"Some people play for a penny a point, you know," Annie said, putting her elbows on the table and looking at Archie. "We'll just deduct it from the ten mil you owe me for Sorry."

"Stupid game," Archie told her, pushing back from the table and heading for his bed once more. He had been getting dressed these past few days, but he still spent most of his time in bed. He probably felt safer that way. Annie had already discovered a kitchen knife under his pillow, and after confiscating that, she'd found a baseball bat the next day, under his bed. Archie Peevers, no matter his bravado, was one scared pup these days.

"I suggested Clue, but you didn't want to play," Annie pointed out. She stood up, put her hands to either side of her spine as she tried to stretch her muscles after sitting for the past hour. She was better, a lot better, and her bruises were more yellow and green than black-and-blue, but she knew she wasn't ready for the hundred-yard dash. Maybe she'd start with some indoor sport, if Grady still wanted her. The thought didn't even make her blush, which showed her how decadent she'd become. She rather liked the feeling.

"Mr. White, in the library, with the wrench," Archie singsonged, interrupting Annie's hopeful daydream. "Who gives a flying flip? I'm one hell of a lot more interested in Mr. Unknown, in the bedroom, with the whatever. And the way it looks, no thanks to that boyfriend of yours, I'm the only one who's going to find out the mister and the method."

"That's it, Archie, keep being the optimist. And Grady's not my boyfriend."

"Yeah, yeah," Archie said, pulling the covers up over his plaid polyester slacks. "Tell it to the Marines."

Annie shook her head, both at the old man's comment and the fact that billionaire Archie couldn't have seen the inside of a clothing store since the seventies. "Archie, you're something else, do you know that? Would you like something to eat? There's some apples left in the fridge. Or orange juice? Nothing too much, because Dickens will be here soon, with your dinner."

Archie slunk down beneath the covers, so that only his face was visible. "Stay and eat with me," he pleaded, going into his old man on the verge of death act. "Please."

"Why? Maisie's going to stay with you tonight. I thought you liked Maisie."

"She hates me," Archie complained, then sighed theatrically. "And it wasn't like I wasn't going to *pay* her or anything."

"Oh, Archie," Annie said, trying not to laugh. "You *didn't!*"

"Damn straight, I didn't. Fifty bucks doesn't go where it used to. Maybe if I upped the ante?"

Maisie still hadn't returned Annie's gold necklace, and she was pretty certain she'd never see it again. She owed Maisie one, and opportunity had just knocked in the form of one randy old man. She went for it. "That could do it, you know," she told Archie, keeping her head averted. "If I were you, I'd try again. She may just be playing hard to get, holding out for another fifty."

"You think so?" Archie threw back the covers, getting to his feet once more. "I've got some cash over here, in a drawer. Annie, if I give you my choppers, will you soak them for me? Just in case I get lucky?" He turned to look at her hopefully, his fingers already in his mouth.

"Don't you dare try that with me again! Archie, I'm warning you—put those back!"

She waited until he'd gone into the bathroom, his steps dragging, and closed the door behind him. That was another thing she'd gotten him to do in the days she'd been baby-sitting him—close the bathroom door.

It was like taking care of a three-year-old with a hormonal problem.

Still, Annie knew as she picked up the book she'd been reading and settled herself in one of the wing chairs, she'd really come to like Archie Peevers. He wasn't soft, he wasn't cuddly, but he was funny. A little rude, a little crude, and more than a bit of a tyrant, a despot. But he was sharp as a tack and almost always good for a laugh. So she liked him. She really liked him.

Not that liking Archie had been part of the plan.

"Ready?"

Annie shut the book and looked up, to see Grady standing in front of her, obviously having let himself into the locked room with his new key. She checked her watch, frowning. "I didn't realize it was so late. Dickens will be here any moment, won't he?"

"Dickens, then Maisie," Grady told her, holding out a hand to help her to her feet. He was so sweet, still handling her as if she were made of glass. She'd really have to point out that she was almost all better now. "And here's Dickens now, right on time. So what do you say we blow this pop stand and find a nice restaurant? I don't know about you, but cabin fever is beginning to get to me."

"You?" Annie said, as they headed for the stairs. "At least you could go outside for a while. I've been stuck with Archie."

"And your bruises. Or had you planned on going jogging?"

"Not for a while, no," Annie told him as she peeked into the drawing room. "Where is everybody?"

"Dinner and dancing at the country club. Mitzi's getting an award for organizing the annual tennis tournament. That's why I thought we could go out. All the little Peeverses are otherwise occupied."

He helped her into the car, then got in on the driver's side, sliding a CD into the dashboard player before starting the car and heading for the main road.

"That's Willie Nelson," Annie said a few moments later, staring at the dashboard. She opened the console and picked up the CD case Grady had stuffed there. "And it's *my* Willie Nelson. See, the case is cracked. I stepped on him one day, poor old Willie." She picked up another case. "And this is my George Michael. And my Johnny Mathis. And my Barenaked Ladies. Where's my Supertramp?"

"Sorry, I'm afraid that one bit the big one in the crash. If you look in the backseat, you'll find a paper bag with one blue shoe in it, a toy from a McDonald's Happy Meal—you could explain that to me at any time, because I'd sure like to hear it—a lipstick, a comb, and one small mirror, broken. What you won't find is your registration or your insurance card. How the hell did you get past your friend Stan without them?"

"I promised to send them to him and started to cry when he told me it was against the law not to have my insurance card with me at all times," Annie said, turning in her seat to look at the bag, then facing forward once more. Why did he want to know about the Happy Meal toy? Didn't everybody collect those toys? Heck, it was a Pokemon, too, the yellow one!

"It has been almost a week, so you're a little overdue. You could give the papers to me, and I'd drop them by the barracks?" Grady suggested, his smile positively evil, the rat.

"Fat chance," Annie said, shoving Pokemon to the back of her mind because Grady was obviously being nosy again. "I know you're still looking, but I'm not going to drop bread crumbs for you. That is why you went to see my poor banged-up car, isn't it? The good Samaritan part about retrieving my CDs and stuff was just an excuse."

"You know me so well," he purred, pulling into the

parking lot of a small Italian restaurant only about three miles from the mansion and cutting the engine.

"I know you well enough to keep my license and all the rest of that stuff somewhere you'd never look for it. Besides, it's already taken care of."

"What's taken care of?"

"My license and registration. Stan's already seen them."

"State cops make house calls?"

"No. I had someone take them over to the barracks the morning after the accident."

"Someone. Would I know this someone?"

"You do."

"So, since I know, you're going to tell me?"

"You wish. And, before you start, *no,* I won't play twenty questions with you, either."

"Why won't you trust me?"

"Why won't you trust *me?* I know what I'm doing, you know. Besides, you're just mad because the car had a temporary tag and our wonderfully inefficient Penndot bureaucracy probably hasn't processed it yet in Harrisburg, even if the dealer sent in the paperwork already. But, since the car was only two days old when I got here, I'll bet that hasn't happened yet either. Or are you going to tell me you didn't try to run the tags?"

"And you learned all of this from books, movies? Right down to making sure the dealer didn't put a sticker on the back, so I could trace you that way?"

Annie grinned. "Yeah. I'm good, aren't I? But I'm probably only safe for another week, before Penndot finally processes the paperwork. Oh, do you smell that?"

she asked him, stepping from the car and inhaling deeply. "Ah, garlic. I can smell it out here. Wonderful!"

Grady bent to kiss the side of her neck, the side without the bandage. "Only if we both eat it, because I've got plans for later."

"You do? Including what?"

He whispered once more. "Let's just say that I can't wait for Penndot and plan to charm all your secrets out of you tonight. I'll start by holding you, kissing you . . . and then I'll probably just improvise. I can be *very* inventive. Now come on. We'll call a truce for now, but you can think about that improvising bit all through dinner. I won't mind," he teased, then took her hand and led her inside while she was still trying not to swallow her tongue.

Over linguine with clam sauce they talked about Grady's new theory that cast Mitzi Peevers in the role of mastermind, and Annie was with him right up until the point where she asked who shot the arrow and he said he didn't know.

"But it wasn't Mitzi, right?" Annie asked, biting into a crusty slice of garlic bread.

"Couldn't be, as both Maisie, and now you, have pointed out to me. But that doesn't mean I'm not right. It just means she had an accomplice."

"A.W.?"

Grady shook his head. "And, before you say it, I doubt it was Junior, either. Those two can barely stand being in the same room."

"Jefferson Banning?"

"Annie, I told you. I don't know. I don't even know if the Double A thing and the murder thing are connected. Let's not forget Dickens and his import-export business. There's more going on in Archie Peevers's house than even his surveillance cameras can know. Now, how's that for honesty?"

"It'll get you a merit badge in something, I suppose, but not in detecting. But I think we have another problem."

"Yeah," Grady said, reaching across the table to squeeze her hand. "But I found the key to your bedroom."

Annie felt her face going red and quickly pulled her hand away, took a sip of wine. "That's not what I meant."

"It's what I meant," Grady said, his grin warming her more than the wine.

"Can we concentrate for just a couple more minutes, please?"

"I've been *concentrating* for the last five days, Annie," Grady said, nearly growled. "If I *concentrate* much longer, I'm going to have to carry a portable cold shower with me."

"Oh," she said, very quietly. "Well, we wouldn't want that, would we? I mean, I doubt they'd even let us in restaurants."

He looked at her for a few moments, his green eyes soft, and wonderfully dreamy—or at least that's how Annie saw them. Grady probably thought he was looking dark and sexy. Men never did understand the points they could score with soft and dreamy.

"Do you want dessert?" he asked at last, although they were only halfway through the main course.

He was still looking at her. She was still looking back at him.

She put down her fork, already wound around with her next bite of linguine. It landed somewhere on the table, she wasn't sure where, and she didn't care. "I don't think I can eat another bite. You?"

He was already reaching into his pocket. "Here's the ticket for your coat. Get it, and meet me at the car. I'll pay the check."

"Okay." She thought she said the word out loud. Just in case, she nodded. Hesitating only long enough to take a big gulp of her wine, she slid out of the booth and made her way to the coat-check booth.

She'd recovered at least some of her sanity by the time Grady joined her in the parking lot. "Our problem, as I'd been saying before you looked at me with those goo-goo eyes of yours and made me forget, is that as long as you're around I don't think anyone will try to kill Archie. Or me, come to think of it. Which I never thought anyone was trying to do, as you'll recall," she said quickly, when Grady frowned. "I mean it. I think the messed-up room, the game of chicken—well, I think maybe those were both meant to keep your eyes on me, so that they could get to Archie. Except now we've got Archie under twenty-four-hour protection, so nobody is going to try to kill anybody, not until you leave. Am I making any sense here?"

"I beg your pardon. I do *not* have goo-goo eyes," Grady said after a moment.

"Gra-dy," Annie protested as he opened the door, helped her into the car, then quickly went around to climb into the driver's seat. "Will you please concentrate? This is serious."

"No," he said, leaning toward her, cupping her chin in his hand, *"this* is serious."

And then he kissed her. He kissed her, and then he touched her, and by the time he'd managed to slip the key into the ignition neither one of them was thinking very clearly at all.

# Twenty-three

*Money is a singular thing.*
*It ranks with love as man's*
*greatest source of joy. And with*
*his death as his greatest*
*source of anxiety.*
                    —John Kenneth Galbraith

Heavy breathing. Hands moving, mouths tasting, bodies straining. Two sighs that melded, became one. A slight reshuffling of bodies, and then a shared silence.

Curly-haired head resting on chest; strong, tanned arm wrapped around softness.

The indescribable mellowness of completion. The calm after the storm. Blessed peace . . .

"I've got it! We'll kill him!"

Annie opened one eye, disturbed from her very pleasant afterglow as Grady sat up, and she found herself ignominiously rolling sideways onto the mattress. "Say what?" she grumbled, opening the second eye, trying to focus. "No, let me guess. This is your version of pillow talk. Don't be insulted, but I think it's lacking . . . a certain something."

"No, no, listen a minute," Grady said, pulling her up next to him, kissing the tip of her nose. "You said nobody will make another attempt on Archie while I'm still here."

"You were *listening?* When were you listening? And with what? I didn't know men could think about sex and still listen at the same time."

"I'm the last of a dying breed. But you're right, Annie. We're just spinning our wheels here. Archie knows about Double A, and he's not blowing the whistle. Someone shot an arrow into the air, and nobody called the cops. Not to mention what happened to you. We look like wimps, with Archie calling all the shots. So all the bad guy has to do is lie low, wait for the month to be up, and then take Archie out. Unless he hires someone else. There isn't enough money in the world to keep me here, that's for sure. Anyway, in the meantime . . ."

"We're just spinning our wheels. I think I've got that part. I might even have said it first," Annie said, pushing her hair out of her eyes as she looked at Grady. God, he was gorgeous with a morning beard. Did he know that? Yeah, he probably did. "Still, and I may be overreacting here, don't you think killing Archie ourselves might be a little, well, a little *much?*"

Grady climbed out of bed, reaching for his slacks. "Okay, okay, so maybe I haven't thought it out completely yet," he said. He looked at Annie for a moment. "Pull up the sheet, please. I'm trying to concentrate here."

"Is that a compliment?"

"Probably more of a warning, because if you don't cover up I'm going to have to pounce on you again."

Annie grinned, amazed at her lack of modesty where this man was concerned.

"Annie . . . ," he said warningly.

"I'm thinking, I'm thinking," she teased, then added, "oh, all right," and pulled the sheet up over her breasts. "Happy now?"

"Actually, no, but I want to think this through."

Annie lifted an arm, indicating that she had given her permission. "Commence pacing, Mr. Sullivan. Should I be taking notes? Oh, and you didn't zip your slacks. Just thought I'd mention that, as *my* powers of concentration are sort of being diverted now."

"Damn." Grady turned his back, and Annie giggled at the sound of the zipper being closed. And then he paced. And talked. And paced some more.

"Okay, let's think about this. We kill Archie—"

"We *pretend* that Archie's been killed," Annie interrupted.

"Right. Glad you're sticking with me."

"My pleasure, plus my clothing is on the other side of the room, so I'm sort of stuck here if I don't want to set off your hair-trigger libido. Hey, your words, not mine!" she ended as he turned, glared at her. "Are we having fun yet? I'm having fun."

He kept looking at her, raked his fingers through his already mussed hair. "You know, Annie, until you came along I thought all I wanted was a willing woman. Preferably one who didn't talk much, then went away. I didn't want a smart woman. I sure didn't want a smart woman in my bed. So can you please tell me what I'm doing here?"

Annie's toes curled beneath the sheet. "I'd say it's my perfume, except Maisie's wearing it," she offered weakly. "Do I really get on your nerves? Is that what you're trying to say?"

He shook his head. "I don't know that I'm trying to say anything. No, that's not true. I'm trying not to say anything. Because we've still got issues, don't we?"

"Meaning I still won't tell you about myself?"

"Meaning you don't trust me enough to tell me about yourself."

Annie plucked at the sheet, avoiding his eyes. "Please don't think of it that way. It's not just my secret. Just solve this attempted murder stuff, okay, and then I can tell you everything."

"Promise?"

"Pinky-swear," she said, trying to smile. "Now, why would we want everyone to think someone succeeded in killing Archie?"

Again with the pacing. A person could not buy cheap carpeting if Grady Sullivan was to be a frequent guest. Annie sighed, leaned back against the pillows, and waited.

"If we say he's dead, then the person who really wanted him dead will think someone else also wanted him dead, and if anyone takes it far enough to realize that the murderer would want any of Archie's heirs dead, then everyone will be accusing everyone else, and we might finally get at the truth."

"Could you say that again?"

Grady took a deep breath, shook his head, and sat

down on the edge of the mattress. "No, and it wouldn't matter, because it won't work. Not now that I've said it out loud. Yeah, well, back to the drawing board."

Annie sat up, leaned her cheek against his back as she wrapped her arms around his waist. "There is another way, you know. Archie's way."

He turned in her arms, slowly lowered her back on the bed, followed her down. "Am I going to like this? I don't think I'm going to like this."

"Probably not," she said, rubbing a fingertip over the stubble on his chin. "But Archie will. We have Dickens announce that everyone is expected in Archie's rooms tonight after dinner, because Archie has an announcement of his own. He's going to name his heir—his *sole* heir, now that his hired investigtor-cum-bodyguard has finished his research—and that he's already changed his will accordingly, having called in a new lawyer when nobody was looking. Can't you just see it now? Archie would be in his glory. Telling everyone I'm definitely his long-lost granddaughter, and then watching while his children go berserk? I think he goes to sleep at night, dreaming about ways to make them all go berserk."

Grady pressed his forehead against hers and looked deeply into her eyes. "No. N—O, no way in hell. Not on your life, Annie, and I mean that literally."

"But you'd be there, to protect me."

"And who would protect you from me?" He rolled onto his back, taking her with him. "Don't do it, Annie. I can see it in your eyes. You're already halfway to Archie's rooms, to tell him to get the ball rolling. Don't do it."

"You have a better way? I haven't heard it so far, if you do."

Grady lightly rubbed his hands on her back. "I'd say we're having our first fight, but we've already had so many I've actually lost count. I'm close, Annie. I'm really, really close. Let me finish it." Then he smiled, lifting his head to nip at her chin. "It's either that, or you're going to be walking around here in a flak jacket and combat helmet. I don't think it's a good look for you."

Annie frowned. "Didn't do a lot for Dukakis," she said, biting her bottom lip. "Okay, tell you what. We'll make a bargain. I don't tell Archie my idea, and you back off on trying to find the real me, if you understand what I mean. You're letting Dickens play his game, and A.W. and Junior played theirs. I need you to let me play mine out as well, without interference. You're getting too close."

Grady shifted his weight slightly, sliding his hands lower, gently urging her to spread her legs. "I could get closer."

"Is that a yes?"

"Not last time I looked. Last time I looked, it was what Archie so genteelly described as his little soldier. Archie's got quite a way with words."

"His little—? Oh, that's gross!" Annie pushed herself off him, intent on leaving the bed. But she moved slowly, so Grady could catch her.

He caught her around the waist, and she squealed as he pulled her back down onto the mattress, tickling her unmercifully. She swatted at his hands, laughing, then tried to tickle him back. "Oh, stop, stop! I'm injured!"

His hands stilled, and his smile faded. "Did I hurt you? God, Annie, I forgot. Did I really hurt you?"

"Nope," she said, then grabbed on to both of his ears and pulled him down for her kiss.

Grady finally came up for air. "End of discussion?" he asked, gasping for breath.

"End of discussion," Annie promised, then ran the tip of her tongue along his shoulder blade. "You stop trying to find out what I'm going to tell you anyway when it's time, and I give you time. One more day, Grady."

He levered himself up onto his elbows. "Then I guess I'd better get out of here and get started," he said, looking as innocent as a fox on his way out of the henhouse.

"You just try it, buster," Annie said.

It was the last thing either of them said for a long time.


Maisie was still asleep when Grady stepped through the connecting door and shook his head, seeing her lying there, green-satin sleep mask over her eyes, black furry earmuffs blocking out sound. No wonder she hadn't shown up the night the arrow had come through Archie's window, or the afternoon Archie had been taking target practice.

It would take a nuclear explosion to get Maisie's attention.

That, or somebody touching her precious computer, which was Grady's intention.

He had just typed in her password, which prompted the voice of some faceless sexy male saying, "Hello, honey, you're looking gorgeous," when she sat up, slipped off the sleep mask, and said, "How do you know my password?"

Grady slowly turned on the chair, watching as his red-headed assistant slid out of bed and covered a short chartreuse nightgown with a bright yellow satin robe. "Are most of your boyfriends color-blind, I most sincerely hope?"

"Ha-ha. If you ever thought I was a morning person, honey, you'd be wrong, so no more jokes. Now, how do you know my password?"

"I'm a detective, Maisie, I know these things. Besides, you change it so often you keep the latest one taped to the bottom of the desk. You do it at work, and you're doing it here. Now, come on, splash some water on your face, brush your teeth, order up some coffee—lots of it—and let's get to work. I've got twenty-four hours to solve this thing before Annie does something I'm going to regret like hell."

"A new car?" Annie sat down with a thump, looking bug-eyed at Archie even as she clutched the keys tight in her fist. "You bought me a new car? Why?"

"Do the words 'guilty conscience' ring a bell?" Dr. Milton Sandborn asked as he eyed the level of liquid in the syringe he was holding in the air. He squirted out a small stream of the fluid, then sighed, obviously content. "That, and I told him no more vitamin shots until he replaced your car. Isn't that right, Archie?"

"Just shut up and give me the shot," Archie grumbled, already turning onto his side and hiking up his nightshirt.

Annie turned her head, not at all afraid of needles, but

willing to run a mile to get away from even the possibility of seeing Archie's skinny behind.

"You can turn around now," Sandborn said after a moment, and she did so, in time to see him breaking off the needle and tossing both ends of the syringe in the nearest trash can. "And it's simple, my dear. It was our idea you come here, so it's up to us to recompense you for losses sustained while you are in residence. Archie, does that sound high-flown enough for you?"

"You blackmailed me into it," Archie said, wincing slightly as he resettled himself against the mattress. "The girl couldn't have been so stupid as not to have insurance. She could have bought herself another car."

"True enough, but until then, she'd be stuck here, without wheels. Kind and caring person that I am, and knowing firsthand how oppressive this place is, I thought she shouldn't have to wait for the insurance check. God knows a person could go straight around the bend if unable to escape this place. Not everyone is enthralled with your company as much as you are, Archie, you understand. That said," he ended, snapping closed his black bag, "I believe I have pressing business elsewhere. A visit to my vintner, as a matter of fact."

Archie waved him away, languidly, as his muscles were relaxing at a pretty fast clip. "Oh, go, go. You're hurting my head with your highfalutin words. Amuse the hell out of yourself, I'm sure, but you're really just a big bag of wind."

"Fight nice, boys," Annie said, having at last recovered her voice. "And I do thank you, both of you. What kind of car is it? Is it out front now? Oh, and I'll sign over the insurance check when I get it. That's only fair."

Both Sandborn and Archie stared at her.

"Frightening, isn't she? All those scruples," Sandborn said at last. "It's a good thing you didn't try to palm her off as a Peevers. Nobody would ever believe it."

"About that . . . ," Annie said, standing up, smoothing down her skirt. "I've been thinking, Archie, and hiding up here isn't getting us anywhere. Grady is trying really hard, but except for that Double A thing, he hasn't been able to figure out who might want you dead."

*"Might* want me dead?" Archie leaned over and opened the drawer of the nightstand, pulling out the arrow. He waved it in the air. "What's this, you twit? My new toothpick?"

Annie held up her hands in surrender. "All right, all right. Somebody really did try to kill you. And somebody has tried, twice, to scare me away. Maybe because your heirs still think Grady is here to investigate my claim as your lost granddaughter, but more probably, now that I've considered the thing from another angle, because Grady and I are . . . well, we're sort of . . . *involved*— "

"You're sleeping with him," Archie said. "Screwing like rabbits while I'm lying here, waiting for someone to kill me. And I'm paying for it. I feel like a damn pimp!"

Dr. Sandborn was looking at Annie. She could feel his eyes on her, but she refused to return his gaze.

"All right, Archie, I think that was clear enough. But, with it looking as if I'm in danger, Grady has been concentrating more on protecting me than watching you. Which makes it easier for someone to get to you. Which also is why I think we ought to tell everyone Grady has finished his investigation, and I am your granddaughter.

I'm your granddaughter, and you're going to leave all of your fortune to me. We could do it tomorrow, right after Grady says uncle and agrees to play it your way."

Archie's eyelids were getting heavy, and he had this fairly obnoxious grin on his face, but it was clear he was still listening. "So then the killer comes after you, and we catch him in the act."

"Hopefully *before* the act," Annie corrected, still not looking at Dr. Sandborn, who had opened his black case again, this time pulling out a silver flask he then uncapped and lifted to his lips.

"What does Mr. Sullivan say about this?" Sandborn asked after taking a long drink, then wiping at his mouth with the back of his hand.

"He says he's going to solve the whole case today," Annie told him, finally looking at the man. "If he does, fine. If not, we go with my plan. Your plan," she amended, after first glancing at Archie, who was by then snoring softly. "And, in the meantime, Grady has agreed to stop trying to investigate me. He's getting close. Too close, Poppy, if we're going to do this the way you want it done. But we have to find out who's behind the attempts on Archie's life, and maybe on mine. We want the old man's full attention when we lower the boom. That is still the plan, right?"

"It is. I've had some second thoughts, but, yes, it's still the plan. Although I've made sure you have wheels, just in case you need to get out of here in a hurry. But I've waited too long for this chance, for any chance. And now you've got Archie thinking the same way again," Sandborn said, taking a single step in Annie's direction, holding out his hand to her. "I'm doing this for you, you know. It's always been for you."

"Yeah, right. Just for me," Annie said, her smile tight, her voice clipped. "I just want this over, Poppy, so I can get out of here, okay, and back to my own life."

"And Sullivan? Archie says you're . . . involved. How involved?"

Annie lifted her chin, took a quick breath. "I'll know that once we're done here, won't I, not that you have any right to know. I've kept the truth away from him because I promised you your big scene. Because, in a way, I do owe you. But he doesn't like secrets. He thinks I don't trust him."

"Do you trust him?"

"I love him, Poppy," Annie said quietly. "Anything else will be up to him."

It was after midnight. Grady had returned to Maisie's room after an evening spent watching Archie pull long grey hairs out of his chin with a tweezers and, later, listening to him snore. A true waste of six very precious hours, because even after a full day of detecting, he was no closer to an answer than he'd been that morning.

"Anything?" he asked, stripping off his jacket and tie, opening his collar button as he pulled up a chair beside the desk.

"Carpal tunnel, I'm thinking," Maisie said, not looking up. "Oh, and I finally hit pay dirt on Mitzi."

"Stocks? Bonds? Under what name?"

"Personal diary she keeps in her makeup case," Maisie said, getting up from the chair to stretch her legs. "Hey, don't look at me like that. I have to get some exercise, honey, or do you think I can sit here for twelve hours at a stretch? Besides, she bought this really fantastic lipstick the other day that would go just great with my new— okay, okay, stop glaring at me, I'll get to the point."

"You have the diary?"

Maisie put her hands on her hips, shaking her head. "No-o-o," she said, dragging out the word as if trying to get through to an uncomprehending child. "She'd miss that. I just took the lipstick. *Borrowed* the lipstick."

"Some people get ten to twenty for *borrowing* the way you do, Maisie," Grady said, then waved his hand in front of his face, as if erasing his words. "So what was in the diary?"

"Vindication, for me," she said, returning to her chair and picking up the ever present nail file. "That, and a lot of numbers. Account numbers listed under banks in the Cayman Islands, more numbers under some banks in Panama. A couple for Switzerland. And, in the back, columns of figures, along with dates. Those figures added up to a little over five mil. Oh, and there was an account at one of the local banks. Lots of money in it, all of it heading back out a couple of days later. Listed under her maiden name. So, are we done? Is Mitzi our culprit?"

Grady rubbed a hand across his eyes. He was tired, so damn tired. "One of them," he said at last. "But there's still the arrow. We have to find out who shot the arrow, who tossed Annie's room and tried to run her off the road. I don't think Mitzi's into the physical stuff."

"But if you confront her, maybe she'll tell us?"

"Maybe. If Archie lets us confront her. Five million is chicken feed compared to his billion, and maybe not enough for him to go to the police with, so that the whole world knows his sons and his daughter-in-law were ripping him off. Honest to God, Maisie, I'm not sure he'd even turn in whoever took that shot at him. He just wants to know, and then cut whoever it is out of his will, get them out of his house, his business. Justice isn't Archie's bag. Revenge, however, is right up his alley."

"Well, then, why doesn't he just throw everybody out? He's already pretty much three for three, with only Muriel still looking even vaguely honest." She wrinkled up her nose. "Man, Muriel. Talk about a waste of a billion dollars. She'll probably wait until Archie dies, then move in a couple of hundred hairball-hurling cats. And even designer clothes come in Ugly, honey, you know. Bet she corners the market."

"If we could keep our eye on the ball here, Maisie?" Grady asked, looking at the computer screen. "What are you working on now?"

Maisie sat down again. "Nothing much. Just running Daisy Goodenough through one last time. Her site's up to a little over forty-two thousand hits, by the way. Hard to believe there are people out there dumber than she is."

Grady nodded, then stilled. "Say that again."

"I said, it's hard to believe there are—"

"Okay, okay, let's go with that. Annie said something along those lines herself. Something about it being hard to believe anybody could be as dumb as Daisy."

"Except for her parents," Maisie added. "The Goodenough Bakery? That's what I have here in my notes, although I never found it on the web. Daisy just mentioned it one day, and I filed it away in my steel-trap mind.

Probably just a small-potatoes kind of mom-and-pop bakery. I mean, come on, honey. *Goodenough?* Is that what you'd want to call your bakery? Try our crullers— they're good enough!" She wrinkled her nose again, shook her head. "Not exactly a killer come-on for the customers."

"No, it isn't, is it? What would you call your bakery?"

"Are we going somewhere with this, honey, or are you at the grasping at straws stage here?"

"Maisie," Grady growled, "just give me some for instances. People don't go too far when they use an alias. And the bakery is another clue—stick with the truth as much as possible so there's less chance of tripping yourself up somewhere along the line. Her parents probably do own a bakery. Just not the Goodenough Bakery. Give me names. Think good enough, then go from there."

"My master's voice. Okay, I'm thinking, I'm thinking. Good enough. Mediocre. So-so. Ordinary. Average."

"Think *higher,* Maisie. Something better than good enough."

"Now I'm a thesaursus? All right. Excellent. Wonderful. Peachy keen. Better. Best. Spectacular—"

"Back up," Grady said, standing up, beginning to pace. "Best. Let's start with Best." He leaned down over Maisie's shoulder, watching the screen. Go to your people search, and type in Daisy Best."

Maisie turned her head, looked up at him owlishly. "Honey, you *are* desperate."

She typed in the name, sat back as the computer did its thing, then suddenly sat front, stared. Hit another button, waited, scrolled down the page, stared again. "Wow. You're going to be insufferable now, honey, aren't you?"

"This is entirely possible," Grady said, all traces of fatigue gone as all his "I'm so close" feelings of the past few days combined in something close to "Eureka!"

He leaned his hands on Maisie's shoulder, impulsively kissed the top of her head. "Ladies and germs, we have *liftoff!*"

# Twenty-four

*There are only two families in the world,
my old grandmother used to say,
the Haves and the Have-nots.*

—Cervantes

Annie had been sound asleep by the time Grady called it a night around three in the morning, but that didn't mean he wanted to sleep alone, in his own room.

It was amazing, even humbling, but for the first time in his life it was enough for Grady just to lie down beside a woman, hold her warm, sleeping body in his arms.

Keep her safe. Above anything, everything, keep her safe.

He fell asleep smiling, pleased with his success of the evening, more than a little apprehensive about some of the things he'd discovered after Maisie finally went to bed, but basically content to wait until morning to tell Annie everything.

*Everything.*

* * *

"Good morning, ladies and gentlemen," a well-rested, and quite recently and most happily satisfied Grady said as he stood just inside the door of the morning room, Annie's hand held tightly in his. "I see Dickens has delivered my messages, asking you all to be here."

A.W. wiped his mouth with his napkin, then folded it precisely, laid it back down on the table. "The note Dickens delivered had my father's name on it, not yours. I should have known he wouldn't come downstairs. He probably doesn't know the way."

Grady looked at Annie, smiled. "Hear that? He *can* finish a sentence. I think you owe me five bucks."

"Grady, be nice," Annie warned him, unable to keep her admiring gaze off Daisy Goodenough, who was trying to keep the blueberries from rolling off her stack of pancakes, and not having much success. You had to hand it to the woman, she'd turned Dumb Blonde into an art form.

Mitzi Peevers, looking a little less like a woman who'd spent fifty years worshiping the sun, her skin softer, even slightly pale, took a sip of coffee, and then addressed Grady. "Can we safely assume that you are acting as my father-in-law's messenger?"

"It's seldom safe to assume anything, Mrs. Peevers," Grady told her. "However, in this case, yes, you may safely assume that."

Daisy giggled, and nudged Junior, who was nursing a Bloody Mary, and most probably a hangover. "I heard about that, Junie. *Assume.* To *assume* makes an *ass* out of *you* and *me*. Isn't that the cutest thing?"

Annie tapped Grady on the shoulder. "I first heard that during a rerun of *The Odd Couple,* the television sitcom, that is, starring Jack Klugman and Tony Randall. Felix and Oscar. You remember?"

"I remember, Annie," Grady said, taking her hand again, squeezing it lightly. "Oscar was the neat one."

"No, not Oscar. He was the slob. Felix—"

"I know," Grady interrupted. "But, if we're done playing your private version of Who's On First, maybe we can get on with this?"

"Sorry, I'm sort of nervous," Annie told him, turning toward him to whisper the words. "They're all still watching us, aren't they?"

"All except Junior. I don't think he can focus yet this morning. I'm just taking a wild guess here, but it could be because Maisie delivered Daisy some papers yesterday, papers showing his divorce from his last wife isn't final yet."

Annie looked toward Daisy, who seemed happy enough, and then at Junior once more. "I bet it will be by next week."

"Not if we're right, and I think we are," Grady whispered back to her.

"Well? Are you just going to stand there, *whispering* like that? Not that I shouldn't expect such rude behavior from people of your ilk. Con artists and private detectives. We've had over a week of this, and it's more than enough. My father-in-law has lost his mind." Mitzi motioned for A.W. to pull back her chair for her. "I don't have time for this. I have important business in town."

"At the bank?" Grady asked, knowing his smile to be far from innocent. "Please, don't allow us to keep you.

I'm only here to tell you that Archie wants all of you—
you, too, Miss Goodenough—present and accounted for
in the drawing room at three. He'll speak to you all then."

"Daddy's going to come downstairs?" Muriel asked,
horrified. "He *never* comes downstairs."

"He's making an exception," Annie said, batting her
eyelashes. "For me. Isn't that sweet?"

"For *you?*" Mitzi came around the table, not stopping
until she was only two feet away from Annie. "Why?"

Annie wanted to say it. She wanted to say, "That's for
me to know and you to find out." But she didn't. She
just widened her eyes even more, and said, "I really don't
know. But I think it's important that we all be there.
Grady?" she asked, turning to him. "Don't you think it's
important we're all there?"

"Oh, I do, I do, Miss Kendall. And Dr. Sandborn has
voiced his concern that Archie might find the exertion,
the shock of reentry into the world, as it were, too much
for him. Which is why the good doctor will also be present," Grady said. That had been Annie's idea, and he'd
gone along with it because she'd insisted—and because
he had his own agenda where Milton Sandborn was concerned. "We're just going to be one big happy party.
Come on, Miss Kendall, let's take a ride in your new
car."

"Mitzi? What's happening? Do you think it's his will?
Can she really be some bastard grandchild? Do you think
he's going to—"

"Shut up, Asswipe," Mitzi said, glaring at Grady, and
then barreled past Annie and headed for the stairs.

"Good thing you copped her passport before we came
downstairs," Annie said, as she and Grady left the man-

sion via the foyer. "Otherwise, you wouldn't be able to have your big scene. That is how you see it, don't you? As your big scene? Gather the suspects, explain your deductions, and then turn toward the guilty party, pointing your finger at him accusingly?"

"Do you blame me?" Grady asked, leading her toward the garages. "It's every detective's dream."

"Except that you wish you had more proof, right?"

"There can never be too much proof, but I think I've got enough."

"Enough for Archie, but what about me, or the police, if Archie lets you call them in on this? You know about Daisy now, but you still can't be positive Mitzi is her accomplice. It still could be someone else, right? It would be nice to have a little more proof, just in case neither one squeals on the other one. Are you sure you checked everywhere for fingerprints? Did you check behind the rearview mirror in the Suburban?"

"Oh, boy, here we go. Annie Kendall, Junior Detective, rides again." Grady stomped off ahead of her, waving his arms to an unseen audience. "I'm brilliant. I solved the case. But is she happy? *No-o-o,* she's not happy. She's still dragging up memories of every damn last book she's ever read, every damn last movie she's ever seen, and thinking she knows more than a trained professional."

He turned to face her, and she did her best not to laugh, because he looked so flustered. Almost as flustered as he'd been that morning, when she'd finally gotten up the nerve to wake him with an extremely intimate kiss. He should be happy she read a lot of books, that's how she saw it. Especially her beloved romance novels.

"And *yes,* ma'am," he growled now, "I checked behind the rearview mirror, ma'am. I checked everywhere, ma'am. Now, give me your keys. I want to drive this thing first, just in case someone decided to cut the brake lines or something."

"And you want *me* in the passenger seat while you do this? In the *death seat*? I don't *think* so. How about the outside mirrors?"

"Annie, I'm warning you!"

"Yeah, yeah, I'm real scared. Just shaking in my boots. Come on, Grady, humor me. Did you check behind the sun visor?"

"Yes, I checked behind the—damn!"

"Aha! The Suburban was heading west, Grady, at four in the afternoon. The sun had to be a factor. But nobody remembers the sun visor. I saw it once, in a movie—or maybe I read about it. Doesn't matter, I guess." Annie rocked back and forth on her heels, feeling smug. "You want to go get the kit, or shall I? That way you can just wait out here, rehearsing how to eat crow."


Archie really pulled out all the stops, ordering Dickens to drag out the double-breasted black tuxedo he'd last worn for A.W. and Mitzi's wedding. Junior tended to wed in places like Vegas, and Reno, so Archie had never attended his younger son's nuptials.

Grady and Annie came into the bedroom as Dickens was tugging on the bright red suspenders that hopefully would keep Archie's slacks from hitting the floor. Archie had never been a big man, but now his nearly emaciated frame was just sort of floating inside his slacks, rather like those of a circus clown.

"They'd better be industrial-strength suspenders," Grady remarked, watching as Archie held on to the bed-post and Dickens pulled, ending with the waistband of the slacks closer to Archie's chin than his waistline. "And love the tie, Archie. Plaid is so *in* these days."

Annie picked up the red-and-green-plaid cummerbund and handed it to Dickens, who just looked at it helplessly. It could probably be wrapped around Archie's middle twice. "I think he looks cute. Archie, I think you look cute. Really."

"I know what I look like, girlie-girl," Archie snapped back at her. "Tomorrow Dickens is taking me shopping."

"You're going *outside?*" Grady watched as Dickens retreated to a drawer, came back with a fistful of safety pins. "Are you sure?"

"No, I'm not sure. I'm just saying it so I can watch your eyes bug out of your head. Why shouldn't I go outside?"

"Because you haven't left the house in about twenty years, or this room in ten. Or do I have that wrong?"

"Yeah, well, and I never got shot at until that damn arrow came through my window, now did I? If I can't be safe in my own house, with my high-priced bodyguard sniffing around my decoy instead of watching me, then I might as well go wherever I want."

"Oh, Archie, now I understand," Annie said, giving him a hug. "You were *afraid* to go outside. I've read about that. It's called agoraphobia. That's so sad."

"You're in trouble now, Archie," Grady told him, shaking his head. "She's *read* about that."

Archie pushed Annie away, looking flustered. "Let go of me, girl."

"Archie." Annie had tipped her head to one side, looking at him with her eyes full of sympathy. "Don't be embarrassed. A lot of people have agoraphobia. We all have phobias. Look at me. I can't even say . . . Indiana Jones."

"Yeah, she's right," Grady added, mostly because he just couldn't help himself. "Don't worry yourself over a fairly common phobia. Hell, it's the stampeding paranoia you might want to be a tad concerned about, Arch."

"That's not funny!" Annie said, whirling to face Grady, who quickly took the smile off his face. "Archie's been ill, and for a very long time. But now he's taking steps to confront his fears—aren't you, Archie? And I think that's wonderful."

"And I think you're both one great big pain in my ass," Archie said, but clearly his heart wasn't in the insult. "Now, can we get this over with? And it still stinks to high heaven that you won't tell me ahead of time. Who was it? Mitzi? My money's on Mitzi. Only one with balls. I've always said that."

"If we tell you, will you still go downstairs?" Grady asked, and Annie smiled at him, showing him that his quick insight had allowed her to forgive him for his last wisecrack.

"I might," Archie said, and Dickens rolled his eyes, holding out the too-large tuxedo jacket. "Well, I *might*. Damn it, Sullivan! Don't think I'm going to miss you when you're gone, because I won't. I've had hemorrhoids I've liked better. Some of them older than you, too."

Grady took the jacket from Dickens and helped Archie into it. "Just as long as you don't stop payment on the check," he said, then patted Archie's shoulders—well, he patted the shoulder pads. Archie's shoulders were probably in there somewhere, but not so anybody would notice.

"Can we go now?" Annie asked, already heading for the door. "Come on, Archie. It's show time."

Grady gave Archie a gentle shove. For an old, skinny man, Archie had great staying power. He didn't move. "Archie? One step at a time, okay?"

"I know, I know," Archie said, doing his best immovable-object imitation. "I've been practicing for a couple of months now. Got as far as the kitchen, once."

Dickens stepped forward. "That's true, he did. In his nightshirt. I heard the cook's screams from my rooms. The cook's screams, Archie's screams. She gave her notice the next morning. It is not one of my most cherished memories, sir."

"Nor the cook's, I imagine," Grady said, giving Archie another gentle push.

Annie walked back over to Archie, took hold of his right arm at the elbow. "Come on, we'll do this together, all right? One step at a time. It'll be easy—watch. Put one foot in front of the other, Archie, and you'll be walking out that door."

"Those are fractured song lyrics, aren't they?" Grady asked, watching as Annie gently tugged, and Archie fiercely resisted. "I know I've heard that line somewhere."

"True, but I don't remember any more than those few words," Annie told him. "Still, it's one of my favorites."

"Isn't everything . . . ," Grady muttered, taking Archie's other arm. "Okay, all together now—put one foot in front of the other . . ."

It took about twenty minutes, a lot of encouragement,

and roughly sixteen choruses of the snatch of song, but finally Archie was baby-stepping into the drawing room, to be met by his variously startled, resigned, and wary relatives.

Dickens, who had been bringing up the rear, his pocket full of safety pins, gave a mighty sigh, turned to leave the room. Grady asked him to stay. Firmly asked him to stay. He had a little surprise for Dickens, one he hadn't shared with Annie.

"Sandy? I did it," Archie said as the good doctor (depending on whom you asked) rose from his chair and walked across the room to greet him.

"So you did, Archie, so you did. That Prozac's amazing stuff. Not quite the same kick as the vitamin shots, but it seems to have done the trick. Today the drawing room, Archie, tomorrow the world. And quite possibly a visit to the nearest gentlemen's haberdashery," he added, touching the wide lapel of Archie's tuxedo, then pulling a face.

"Daddy?" Muriel was standing behind Milton Sandborn, and when he moved away she stepped forward, her arms held out tentatively, and tentatively gave Archie a quick hug. "I'm so proud of you."

"Yeah, I'm a real pisser, aren't I?" Archie said nervously, pushing her away. "Can we get on with this? A.W.'s over there looking like his shorts are already brown, and Junior's half in the bag. We wait much longer, and Mitzi will have ripped off another million and stuffed it into one of her secret numbered bank accounts. Right, Mitzi?"

Annie leaned over to whisper to Grady. "You'd better

do this quickly. I think Archie's trying to upstage your Charlie Chan act."

Mitzi, who had been leafing through a fashion magazine as if totally unconcerned with what might happen, looked up at Archie, her mouth hanging open. "I—what? Archie, what are you saying?"

Grady stepped in front of his temporary employer and signaled for Annie to lead the man to one of the many ugly red-velvet couches scattered around the room. "You could gag him, too, but that might be considered a felony—cruelty to old farts," he said, waiting for Mitzi to give A.W. a smart smack in the arm, and for A.W. to say, "What do you want me to do? And what's he talking about?"

"Yeah, Mitzi," Junior asked, belatedly coming to attention. "Numbered accounts? Where? I thought they were all Delaware corporations, because of the taxes and stuff, and the money is in banks down there. You said everyone wants to be a Delaware corporation. What's Daddy talking about?"

"Now, Junie," Daisy said, pulling him back as he tried to stand up. "I'm sure Mitzi here isn't playing the numbers. My brother, Darryl, he used to play the numbers. But he stopped, right after he broke his arm. At least he says he broke his arm. Pa said somebody probably broke it for him."

*Somebody ought to be writing this all down,* Grady thought, *because otherwise nobody will ever believe it.*

He clapped his hands, hoping for silence. When that didn't work, he put the pinky finger of each hand into his mouth and whistled loudly enough to rattle the chandeliers.

Abruptly, everyone settled in their chairs. "All right," he said, stepping into the middle of the room. "Now that I have your attention?"

"Attention for what?" Muriel asked, looking to Annie, who must have seemed the sanest person in the room.

"Am I too late, honey?" Maisie asked, dashing into the room on her four-inch heels. "My mascara clumped, and then everything just *ran* when I tried to fix it, and—can I sit here next to you, honey?" she asked Daisy. "There's plenty of room, right? You're already just about sitting in Junior's lap anyway."

"Maisie," Grady said tightly, acknowledging her presence with a small nod. "So glad you could join us."

"Oh, me, too, honey," she said, patting her bouncy curls. "I've always wanted to be in on the kill."

Muriel blanched, looked near to fainting. "The *kill?*" She had sat down next to Archie, and now turned to him questioningly. "Daddy, what's she talking about?"

"It's a surprise, Muriel," Archie said. "In fact, I have a surprise for you myself."

"You do?"

"I do. Now, just close your eyes and hold out your hands. No, no, not like that—*cup* them together. Okay, now just wait . . ."

Annie clapped both hands to her mouth as Archie quickly removed both his upper and lower plates and placed them in Muriel's hands.

Muriel frowned, then opened one eye, screamed, and the teeth went flying.

Annie shook her head. "Oh, Archie, that's mean."

Archie retrieved the teeth, replaced them. "Why? I'm

leaving them to her in my will. Thought maybe she'd want to try them out. It's all she's going to get."

"Drinks, anyone?" Grady asked in exasperation, heading for the sideboard. Agatha Christie never had to contend with a cast of characters like these, so why did he? "I know I want one."

Junior and A.W. followed him, only to be cut out of line by Milton Sandborn, who only had to refill his glass. "You'd better do whatever it is you're going to do, son," he told Grady. "I think he's finally lost it."

"And that's such a pity, isn't it? After you've spent these last years trying to hold him together. If that's what you've been doing."

"What does that mean?"

"I don't know," Grady told him honestly. "I do know that you could have seen that Archie got proper treatment for his phobia. But you didn't, did you? You just kept him juiced up with those vitamin shots, kept him alive, but vegetating, in that room up there. Now, why did you do that? And when did you finally start medicating him for the agoraphobia? Only recently, I'm betting. When you could have started treatment years ago."

Sandborn drew himself up to his best fullback stature. "You're questioning my medical expertise?"

"I could be. In fact, I have a theory I'm going to run by you all later on, and Archie's agoraphobia has just about nailed it down," Grady said. "But first things first, all right?" He left the doctor standing at the sideboard and returned to center stage, as he'd begun to think of his spot in the middle of the drawing room. Had he only been here less than two weeks? It seemed like ten years.

God, he'd be happy to see the last of this place, these people.

"Okay, folks, here's the story. Some of you know some of it, some of you think you know all of it, but you'd all be wrong, including me, if I said I had all the answers. Still, I know most of it, and that's enough for starters. First, since Archie's already brought it up—Mitzi? You talked A.W. and Junior into setting up Double A and all its little corporations. You also talked them into letting you handle the money, which was a pretty big mistake on their part, wasn't it? Oh, and I took the precaution of taking your passport and canceling your plane ticket to Rio, so you might want to tell Banning he's out of luck, too. But don't be too disappointed. Those May–December romances rarely work out."

Grady eased a hip onto the arm of the chair Annie was sitting in, and the two of them waited while the Peeverses erupted. "How do you like my opening? I'd say it's going pretty well so far."

"And good guess on the Mitzi-Jefferson connection," Annie commented, watching as Mitzi sat, stone-faced, Junior blustered, Muriel looked blank, and A.W. actually burst into tears. "Poor A.W. He's absolutely crushed."

Daisy asked Maisie if she thought she could wear white for her wedding to Junior in Vegas the next week. "It's not that I've been married before, you understand. But I'm not exactly a . . . well, you know . . . a *virgin*."

"Who is, honey?" Maisie answered, pulling a nail file from her pocket and starting in on her thumbnail. "Who the hell is?"

"That's it?" Archie complained as the din died down and Grady made no move to continue. "I came downstairs for this? I *knew* this. Well, most of it. The Banning thing kind of makes me want to puke. I didn't think Mitzi knew what sex was."

"Obviously no surveillance camera in Mitzi's bedroom," Annie said, wincing at her own daring. She really had been trying very hard to forget everything she'd seen in Mitzi's closet.

Grady grinned at her, then stood, figuring it was time to finish the first act. He already knew the second act as well, but the third was still partly a mystery to him. Suddenly, he felt like dragging his feet, because he wasn't sure he was going to like the third act.

"What else?" he asked, spreading his hands, everyone's attention definitely on him once more. "Oh yes," he said, bowing to Archie, "you want to know who tried to kill you."

"And who messed up my room and then tried to run me off the road," Annie put in quickly.

"No," Archie said, glaring at her. "*You* want to know that. I could care less. We're talking about *me* here. Go on, sonny, go on. I may be in my tux, but this ain't the Oscars, and you're not getting an award for best performance by a pain in the ass."

"You're such a warm, fuzzy person, Archie," Grady told him, smiling. "No wonder I so enjoy working for you. But all right. Be patient for a moment, as I explain. After all, I want to show you how brilliant I've been so you know your money has been well spent."

"How brilliant *we* are," Maisie supplied brightly. She jabbed Daisy in the ribs. "Listen up, honey, you're going to be *so* impressed."

Annie looked around the room. Junior's glazed eyes

were beginning to clear. Mitzi had lit another cigarette, her hands trembling. Muriel still looked as if every word that had been spoken had been said in Spanish, and she didn't understand Spanish. Dickens remained at attention in front of the closed doors. Poppy, who hadn't once met her eyes since she'd come into the room, had found a seat, but he'd brought the crystal decanter of scotch with him. A.W. was still crying.

"Archie," Grady said now, pulling Annie's attention back to him. He really was enjoying himself. And he would be, right up until she told him the truth. "Pay attention now, because we're going for the gold. One, your two sons were ripping you off, which was pretty easy, because you've been hiding out here for so long. Two, Mitzi was ripping off your two sons, which had to be even easier, having most probably cooked up the whole Double A scam with Jefferson Banning, who knew damn full well that you weren't going to leave your children, or him, a cent."

"Never signed a one of those wills. Ripped them up as soon as he'd give them to me," Archie agreed, flashing his dentures. "Why should I, when I have a perfectly good one Jefferson's daddy made out for me years ago. Named the president of the bank, my old pal Smitty, as executor. He's eighty-six, but he's honest, and his successor takes over if he croaks before I do. Drove little Jefferson crazy, it did, knowing that."

"Drove him to a lot of things," Grady agreed, wishing Archie would shut up.

"And didn't leave a cent to any of these worthless lumps, either," Archie went on, going into cackling, egg-laying mode. "Just this old pile and whatever's in it.

Everything else goes into something Jefferson's daddy called a trust. Going to build hospitals, libraries, science labs at some of the colleges around here. Anything that they can slap my name on. Doesn't matter what." He held his hands out in front of him, then spread them as if blocking out a sign in the air. "Archie Peevers Memorial Whatever. I can see it now. Smitty's going to spread me around all over the place."

The silence in the room became deafening, then broke all at once.

"Daddy? What about me?"

"Yeah, Muriel, what about poor little you?" Mitzi sniped, waving her hands in front of her. "Where will you go, what will you do?"

Annie was standing beside Grady now. "She's doing a pretty lousy Scarlett. *Gone With the Wind.*"

"Thanks, I wouldn't have known that," Grady said sarcastically, his attention on Daisy. She was disengaging herself from Junior, hopping to her feet with an alacrity that could make one think she'd just felt the wrong end of a cattle prod. "Going somewhere, Miss Best?"

Daisy hesitated for a split second, then kept walking, as if she had no idea who Grady meant.

"Uh-uh," Grady said, taking hold of her arm, holding her in place. "The lifeboat for rats deserting sinking ships doesn't leave for another few minutes. *Sit down.*" He smiled as he said it, but Daisy sat down again, between Junior and Maisie. Annie was surprised she didn't sit down right there, on the floor. She'd never heard that steely tone in Grady's voice before, and hoped she'd never have to hear it again.

"I don't understand," Archie said. "Who's Miss Best?"

"She's a lot of things, actually. She's an entrepreneur of sorts, with her own rather successful web site—we won't go into that right now. She's also Daisy Best, not Daisy Goodenough. And she's not as dumb as she pretends to be. Oh, yeah, and she won the gold medal in last year's archery contest in Ames, Iowa, women's expert division. Isn't that right, Daisy?"

"Everyone should have a hobby," Dickens said quietly, handing Grady a portable phone. "I imagine you'll be phoning the police now?"

"Thank you, but not quite yet. And, Junior? You can stop looking so surprised. We found your fingerprints on the back of the sunshade of the Suburban. You remember—the vehicle you used to try to kill Miss Kendall here?"

Junior leapt to his feet. "No! We didn't—I didn't! I mean—tell them, Daisy. We never meant to *kill* anybody!"

Daisy, her narrowed eyes now looking remarkably intelligent, crossed her arms over her chest and said, "I refuse to answer on the grounds it might incriminate me."

"She can't do that," Annie said, just about jumping up and down in her excitement as she pointed at Daisy. "She's not even under oath. Make her talk, Grady. Make her talk before she lawyers up."

Grady rubbed at his forehead. "Lawyers up? Annie, nobody has even read her her rights. Junior?" he then asked, smiling hopefully at Archie's younger son. "You want to tell me about it?"

"Yeah," Annie said, stepping in front of Grady. "It'll go easier for you if you confess, bunko. Turn state's evidence. First perp to spill his guts gets the first get-out-of-jail card. Come on, Junie. Let's cut a deal."

"Annie, *sit*," Grady said, trying not to laugh. God, she was wonderful. Nuts, but wonderful.

She also seemed to have impressed Junior by her cut-and-paste version of good cop, bad cop, because all of a sudden Junior couldn't talk fast enough.

# Twenty-five

*My face is my fortune, sir," she said.*
                                        —Nursery Rhyme

"So that's it? That's all? You're going to just let it go? Forget about it?"

Archie, now safely back in his room, even safer in his bed, looked at Grady. "Explain it to her, sonny."

Grady watched as Annie paced, her arms flapping now and then, her cheeks flushed, seemingly caught somewhere between frustration and . . . well, actually, she was pretty much just a picture of frustration. Poor baby.

"Annie, look," Grady said. "Archie doesn't want anyone to know his own kids tried to screw him."

*"Did* screw him!" Annie all but shouted. "Five million dollars is a whole lot of screwing!"

"Archie?" Grady prompted.

"Five million dollars is nothing," Archie told her. "I gave the three of them ten million apiece when they each turned twenty-five, and that never made a dent. I considered it cheap, seeing as how it kept them out of my house and off my back for a while."

Annie held up her hands, to stop Archie before he could say anything else. "Wait a minute. You *gave* them each ten million dollars? Grady," she said, turning to face him, "I thought you said Maisie's background checks showed that none of them had much money, that they were all dependent on Archie?"

"You're right, I did. Archie, you have an answer to that one?"

"Sure do." Archie held up his hands, began ticking off on his fingers. "A.W. and Mitzi tried to break away, form their own rival company, hoping to ruin me with my own money. Mitzi had this great idea that getting top clothing designers to draw up fancy toilet paper would make them rich. Stupid fools. People want soft on their asses, and cheap. Soft on their asses comes second. Hell, it's not like toilet paper is a lifetime commitment. Just use it and get rid of it. Know what my biggest seller is, boy, and always has been? The cheap stuff. And the cheap stuff makes *me* the most money. They were crawling back in three years, not just broke but in debt to their eye-balls."

"And Junior?" Annie asked, intrigued in spite of herself.

"He spread his around a little more. Up his nose, down his throat, a full three mil on a gold mine in Ghana or some damn place, another five on some big fans they were going to lower into the Atlantic Ocean off Florida, to divert the Gulf Stream so New Jersey would be warmer, if you can believe that one. His ex-wives got the rest."

"Leaving Muriel," Grady said. "She just doesn't seem the type to blow ten million dollars."

"She didn't. Her husband did."

"Her husband? We found no record of a marriage."

Dickens placed a silver tray holding a teapot and some china cups on a low table before the fireplace. "Mr. Peevers had all the records of the marriage destroyed, sir. Miss Peevers was understandably upset to learn that she had married a fortune hunter."

"I got that money back, too," Archie said, cackling. "Most of it anyway. Had the son of a bitch chased all the way to Australia before we caught up with him. Not that I ever told her. She'd just have given it to somebody else. Muriel's not the sharpest knife in the drawer, you know."

"But you love her," Annie said quietly, walking toward the bed. "That's it, isn't it? A.W.'s a spineless idiot, Junior's a waste, and Muriel is pitiful. But they're your children and you love them. That's why you won't do anything, won't turn them in to the police. You're just making them move out of the house, leave the company."

Archie sat forward, waved for Annie to step aside, so he could look at Grady. "She doesn't get it, does she? She's looking for some way to dress this up, make it pretty and sentimental and all that bullshit." He looked at Annie. "No, girlie-girl, I didn't turn them in because I can't *stand* them, because they're the most pitiful bunch of losers anyone could imagine. When I die they'll all be broke, and I couldn't be more tickled about that. I'm old, I'm mean, and I'm damn well going to die happy!"

"See, Annie," Grady said, getting out of his chair, "it's as simple as I thought it was, and explains why I was brought here in the first place. He wanted everything kept quiet. Archie just doesn't want anyone to know that his miserable, pitiful bunch of losers scammed him out of five million or, once the arrow came through the window, that one of them actually tried to kill him. Even if Daisy said they'd only wanted to scare him to death, not actually shoot him."

Annie shrugged. "She is an archery expert. When she says she hits what she aims at, I believe her. I hit what I aim at. But what if she'd missed, didn't account for wind or loft, or something, and had really hit Archie? What if I hadn't swerved at the last moment, and Junior had hit me that day on the road? They can say they were only trying to scare Archie, scare me, but that's because we're still alive. I think they should both go to jail for attempted murder."

"You know what it is, son, don't you?" Archie said, leaning back against the pillows once more. "She's just still pissed that Junior not only messed up her room, but that he tried on her lipstick while he was at it."

Annie shivered in revulsion. "I remember looking at him that night, with that lipstick smeared on his mouth, and thinking, wow, Killer Red. It just took me this long to realize I'd recognized it because it was *my* lipstick. That is *so sick!*"

"I have videos of him prancing around in Daisy's undies, if you want to see them," Archie piped up helpfully.

"Thank you, *no,*" Annie said, staggering to a chair. "All I want to do now is pack my bags, pick up my check, and get the hell out of here."

"Sorry, babe," Grady said, walking over to stand behind her, rub her shoulders. Now came the part he'd dreaded. He knew some of it, but not all of it. He needed to know all of it. "I'm afraid we still have the third act to get through. Or did you forget that you were going to tell me who you really are?"

Annie bent her head, so that he had better access to rub at her tense muscles. "Not now, Grady. Haven't you had enough for one day?"

"No, I'm afraid not. Dickens? If you'd go downstairs and bring the good doctor up, please? He's waiting in the drawing room at my request. We'll start with the two of you, and leave Annie here for last." As Dickens went to the door, obediently if reluctantly, Grady leaned down, kissed Annie's head. "I'm sorry. I already know most of it, Slugger. We'll get through this together, and as quickly as possible. But it has to be done."

She turned in the chair, looked up at him. "You *know?* How would you know?"

Grady looked over at the bed, to see that Archie was nodding off. Going downstairs had taken a lot out of the man. "Okay," Grady said, moving to sit down in the chair facing Annie's, "I'll start by apologizing. You made me promise to stop looking, and I really meant that promise. Except last night, as it got later and later, and I got more punch drunk on my success with finding Daisy—well, I sort of forgot my promise."

Annie bit on her knuckle. "Go on."

Grady stabbed his fingers through his hair, took a breath. "I was sitting at the computer, with Maisie passed out on the bed behind me, thinking how I had fooled around with Goodenough, and come up with Best. We'd already played with your name a little, Annie, but not very much. And when I accused you of using Annie Kendall as an alias, you just shot back that your name was so Annie. You never mentioned Kendall. I decided that maybe Kendall isn't your real last name, that all I really had to go on was Annie. So I started typing in some alternatives."

"How . . . how inventive of you," Annie said, unable to look at him.

"Yeah, well, like I said. It was late, I was tired, but I really felt I was on a roll. I figured, hey, if it worked once, maybe it would work again. So I typed in Annie Peevers. Nothing. Annie Dickens. *Nada.* Then I typed in Annie Sandborn. Bingo!"

Annie kept her head down, even as she reached up and wiped away tears with the backs of her hands. "You're very good, Grady. Archie was lucky to find you."

Grady reached across the small space dividing them, put his hand on Annie's knee. "I'm not that good, Annie. I still don't know why, or how, or what you and Sandborn hoped to gain. And you know what? I don't care. That's what I need to say to you before Sandborn comes up here. I love you, and I don't care about the rest of it."

"I do," Annie said quietly. "I thought I knew why I'd come here, why Poppy asked me to come here. But now I'm not so sure. I'm not sure about anything anymore."

"Not anything, Annie? How about me?"

Finally, she raised her head, her wonderful eyes awash in tears. "I'd like to believe in happy endings."

Grady took both her hands in his, squeezed them. "Then let's go for it, okay? You just sit here and let me talk to Dickens and Sandborn, then jump in when you think the time is right."

Annie nodded, biting her bottom lip. She knew she couldn't possibly talk, not without bursting into tears.

The door opened, and Dickens and Dr. Sandborn entered the room. Grady was already on his feet, going halfway to meet them, keeping himself between Annie and Sandborn. "Archie?" he called out, and the old man snorted, said, "Huh?" and slowly roused. "What now?"

"What happens now, Archie," Grady said, eager to get this first part behind him, "is that maybe you're not paranoid. Sometimes, as your family has proved, as I'm about to prove now, the whole world *is* out to get you. For starters, you might be interested to know that your devoted butler and your dedicated doctor have been systematically ripping you off for, oh, ten or twenty years. Do I have that time frame right, boys?"

An unseen hand seemed to shove a poker straight up Dicken's backside. "Sir! You *promised!*"

"Yeah, well, guess what? I lied," Grady told him. "Must be the company I've been keeping lately. Or maybe it's just something in the air around this place. Makes lying easy."

"Give it up, Charles," Sandborn said, reaching into his medical bag and taking out his silver flask. "Besides, it's not you he's after, but me. Isn't that right, Mr. Sullivan? Although I really do wish you'd not be so *smug* about it."

Annie sank lower in her chair. This was all news to her, very bad news. It had never occurred to her that Poppy could have been in cahoots with Dickens's scheme.

"Wait a minute, wait a minute," Archie said, hopping out of bed, so that everyone could see he was still dressed in his cummerbund and tuxedo slacks. "You talking about the jewels, the paintings, all that crap? Because, if you are, I already know about that. I've known about it for years."

"Sir?" Dickens squeaked, looking like a man who has just seen the governor come running down the hallway thirty seconds before the executioner was set to pull the switch. "Am I to believe you *condone* my inexcusable actions?"

"Condone them? Hell, Dickens, I applaud them! Leave money to you in my will, or let you steal what you needed after forty years of faithful service—what difference does it make? Besides, why do you think I left this house and everything in it to those damn kids of mine? But you could work a little faster, you know. That Rembrandt in the drawing room will bring in at least a million, which would keep the leeches in booze and women and fortune hunters for at least a month."

Grady rubbed at the back of his neck, trying to ward off what could end up being a real bitch of a headache. "Archie, you are so completely and thoroughly despicable that I can only admire you, twisted as that makes me feel. And you knew Sandborn here was in on it?"

"Sandy? Well, of course. I've been his only patient for close on twenty years now, and he spends like a drunken sailor, always did. Mostly because he's a drunk himself. Who better to rip off but your oldest and dearest friend? I've known for years."

"I'm outta here," Annie said, slowly rising to her feet. "I am really, *really* out of here. I can't listen to any more of this."

Sandborn reached out toward her, to take her arm, but

she put up her arms, backed away from him as if he were a hot stove. "No! Don't touch me. Don't come anywhere near me, not ever again. I should have known you were lying. You never did anything for me, or my mother. Just for yourself. Always for yourself!"

Grady put his hand on her shoulder and she instinctively turned into his arms, burying her head against his chest. "I didn't tell you because he said he wanted to be the one who picked the time. After I was here for a while, after I got to know everyone. When he thought Archie was ready. Oh, why didn't he just leave me alone? How could he believe that knowing I'm a part of *this* would be *good* for me?"

"Dickens, go down the hall and find Maisie, would you?" Grady asked, holding Annie close, letting her cry. "Hurry."

"Annie, I did do it for you," Sandborn said, daring to take a step toward her, backing away quickly when he saw the hard glint in Grady's eyes.

All three men remained quiet while Annie cried.

Maisie rushed in, Dickens still trying to explain the little he knew, and quickly took charge of Annie, holding on to her as she led her out of the room. "I've got you now, honey," she told her, looking back at Grady. "Come on, we'll go have a good cry together, and then do our nails. That'll cheer you right up. Men are such beasts, aren't they?"

Grady waited until the door had closed, then turned to look at Sandborn. "Anytime you're ready, Doctor."

"Yes, all right. Let's get this over with." Sandborn unscrewed the top of his flask, took a long swallow, shivering as the heat slammed into his throat. "Archie," he said, looking at his friend, his patient, "do you have any idea how long I've hated your guts?"

Archie hustled back to his bed, his island of safety, and pulled the covers up to his chin. "Sandy? What are you talking about? Why would you hate me? I thought we were friends."

Grady winced, then looked at his, God help him, temporary employer. "Archie, the man's been stealing from you, among other things. We'll talk about the *vitamin* shots he's been giving you—and been taking himself— and the fact that he withheld treatment for your agoraphobia for years until some other time. Still, even without that, how in *hell* can you think you two were friends?"

"Because I'm the only friend he's got," Sandborn said, plunking his huge frame down in the chair Annie had vacated, his strong legs flung out in front of him. "His kids hate him, his workers hate him. Hell, he couldn't even get a dog to love him. Could you, Archie? Remember Bonzo? Little terrier? That dog hated your guts. I've always been all you had, Archie, and then you betrayed even me, didn't you?"

The covers moved higher, so that Archie's words were near mumbles. "Sandy. What are you talking about? I never hurt you."

"Now why doesn't that sound convincing?" Grady asked, looking from one man to the other. "Dickens? Do you have any idea?"

"Yes, sir, I think I might, now," Dickens said, lifting his chin. "But, as I'll be packing, sir, I really don't have time to share that information with you. If anyone needs me, I'll be in Tahiti."

"Since Archie isn't in the mood to press charges, I

suppose you can leave. Happy beachcombing," Grady called after him, "but I'd rethink a thong if that's what you had in mind." Then he looked at Archie, who seemed near tears. "They're running like grunion in the moonlight, aren't they, Archie? One by one, out the door, until all that's left is Annie and your old pal here, Sandy. Sandy? Don't you want to get the rest of it off your chest? Tell Archie about Annie?"

"Yes, Poppy, tell Archie about Annie."

All three men looked toward the door, and at Annie, who had come back into the room, her face pale, her hands clenched in fists, her voice unsteady, but hard. Behind her, Maisie was lifting her hands and shaking her head, as if to say, "Hey, I tried to keep her away, but what can you do?"

"No," Annie continued, walking farther into the room, avoiding Grady's eyes. "Let me tell him. Let me tell him that about twenty-six years ago he seduced my mother. My then-twenty-year-old mother. Let me tell him how she ran away in disgrace when she found out she was pregnant and her married lover had already moved on to his next conquest—and that her own father had demanded she have an abortion. Let me tell him how she tried to keep me, but just couldn't seem to do it right, so she finally pinned the name Annie Kendall Sandborn to my coat, and left me outside a supermarket in Georgia. Kendall was her mother's maiden name—my grandmother's maiden name—but I didn't learn that for a lot of years. A lot of very long years."

Grady reached out to her, but she shook her head, backed away, kept pacing. "Then, Poppy—when he found me he wanted me to call him Poppy. Isn't that just . . . lovely? Anyway, Archie, Poppy found me in Philadelphia, after I'd left Georgia, traveled north, stayed in Baltimore for a while, then chased myself as far as Pennsylvania. Chased the name Sandborn as far as Pennsylvania. Because that's all I had, until Poppy showed up."

"I explained that, Annie. I—I was upset. Angry. Sheila had always been wild, unmanageable. When she told me she was pregnant, I just reacted." Sandborn shook his head, sighed. "I just reacted. I threw her out. And then I couldn't find her."

"I did," Annie told him. "I found her, five years ago, in a cemetery just outside Atlanta. She died of an overdose a year after abandoning me. I found her because I *looked*. When did *you* start looking?"

"Sullivan—*psst!* Sullivan!"

Grady walked over to the bed.

"What's she saying? Is she saying what I think she's saying?"

"If you think she's saying she's your child, then yes, she's saying what you think she's saying. Now shut up."

"But I like her, Sullivan," Archie whispered. "I mean, this one has promise."

Sandborn seemed to shrink in his chair. "So many lost years. I'd lost my wife—your grandmother—a year before Sheila ran away, and I'd already been drinking. Dipping into my medical bag when it all got too much." He looked at his granddaughter. "I was so mad, so hurt. I . . . I got lost, Annie. I got lost for a lot of years. I didn't want to find you, because you were part of *him*, a Peevers. And Sheila had disappeared. Even when I found out that she'd died, I still didn't want anything to do with you, didn't want to find you. I didn't even know if you were a boy or a girl, and I didn't care. I'll be honest about that, I was honest with you about that when we finally met. I just wanted Archie to live as long as I could make him live, and suffer every day for what he'd done."

Archie grabbed on to Grady's arm. "She came after me. Sheila came after me, I swear it. It was just a little fun. Nothing was supposed to happen. I didn't even know she was pregnant. I swear it, Sullivan, I swear it! Keep him away from me, you hear? I'm paying you, remember. You're here to protect me."

"Don't count on it, Arch," Grady said, walking over to stand beside Annie, put his arm around her shoulder. "Heard enough yet, Slugger? Because I think I know the rest. Sandborn found you—who knows how long ago, or how long it was until he decided to finally meet you. Then, finally, he told you who you were, and then told you Archie was looking for someone to imperson-ate his long-lost heir. Hell, once Sandborn found you, it was he who suggested the idea to Archie. Remember when he let that slip?"

Annie leaned into Grady for support. "I only met him three months ago, although I think he's known about me for years. He said I could come here, get to know my family without them knowing I was family. That appealed to me, because I really wasn't sure I wanted to find any more family out there. I'd found my mother, and she was dead. But getting to know my family did make sense, especially as I could walk away again if I didn't like them, and nobody would ever know."

She laughed, but the laughter was hollow. "Well, I met them, didn't I? You know, I think I was better off believing myself to be alone in the world. What a horrible, horrible bunch! They could be on posters for Dysfunctional Families."

"Be nice, Annie," Grady whispered. "You'll regret kicking them, even these two, while they're down. And, believe me, they're down. Down, and pretty well out."

She looked up at him, tried to smile. "I'm not an angel, either, Grady. I wanted the fifty thousand dollars, too. I won't deny that, won't lie to you about that. I used some to buy the car, and some clothes—because I thought I'd feel more like I fit in if I looked like I fit in. Do you understand that? But I had plans for the rest of it. I just didn't know Poppy had plans for a lot more than fifty thousand dollars." She looked over at Sandborn. "Didn't you, Poppy?"

"You *should* have it all!" Sandborn said, his face red with exertion, and maybe some small bit of shame. "You and me, we should have it all."

"I wouldn't have taken it if it had been offered," Annie said, and Grady could feel her spine stiffen. "You knew what I wanted to do with the money, how I'd planned to spend it. But you didn't care. You never cared. You just wanted your revenge, and saw me as a way to get it."

"Let me guess here, Annie," Grady said, squeezing her waist, trying to keep her close because he could feel her muscles bunching, as if she was about to run, not that he could blame her. "I know now that you work on the transplant coordinating team for the Kidney Foundation in Philadelphia. The money was going to go there, wasn't it?"

Annie nodded, unable to say anything else, and Grady thought he could actually feel his heart swelling in his chest. God, how he loved this woman.

"You want to get out of here?" he asked after a moment, as Archie hid under the covers and Sandborn sat in a chair, his head in his hands. Two old men. Two mean, unfulfilled, bitter old men who both knew they had just lost something very, very precious.

She nodded again.

"Me, too. Let's go. We'll leave the two of them here to talk this out, or kill each other, or whatever the hell they want to do. Although they'll probably kiss and make up. They're all the other one has now, aren't they?"

"I should have told you," Annie said, once they were in his room and Maisie had announced that she had packed everyone's suitcases so they could make their getaway to Philadelphia before anything else happened.

"You could have," Grady agreed, touching her cheek. "Except you and Poppy had a deal. It was his idea, and he'd control the timing of the great unveiling meant to have you named as heir and, just coincidentally, make him a very rich man when you thanked him with a hundred million or so."

"I really didn't think about that. Poppy just told me he'd been looking for me, and he thought he knew of a way to introduce me into the family without anyone knowing. I could get to know Archie, my brothers and sister. Dear God, Grady! Those three are my brothers and sister!"

"Muriel isn't so bad, honey," Maisie said, snapping

the lid on the last suitcase. "And she could use a friend." She put a hand on her hip, looked at Annie. "You've got the eyes, you know. But everything else must have come from your mother. Lucky girl. The rest of them must have waded in the shallow end of the gene pool on both ends."

"Maisie . . . ," Grady said, motioning for her to leave the room. "Why don't you go bring the car around. We'll be down in a few minutes."

"All right, but only because you promised I can still have three more weeks of vacation, paid for by D&S, in the locale of my choice. I'm thinking Paris, honey, so get ready to ante up."

"She's amazing," Annie said, getting up from her perch on the side of the bed. "If we're leaving, I have to go get my identification out of the toilet tank."

"The toilet tank? It can't be there. I looked."

Annie had her hand on the doorknob leading to Grady's bathroom. "I figured you would, which is why I moved it after the first day. Ever since then, it's been in *your* toilet tank. I knew you'd never look there."

Grady was still shaking his head as she came out of the bathroom with her driver's license, and whatever else she'd hidden right under his nose. Okay, not his nose. He wouldn't think about that.

"You wouldn't want a job with D&S, would you?" he asked her as he picked up suitcases, stuffing one under his arm and taking one in each hand. "We could open a new division. Nutty Crimes Solved by the Book or Movie. Something catchy like that."

"I'll think about it," Annie said, opening the door for

him. Archie stood on the other side of it, Sandborn behind him. "Go away," Annie said quietly.

"We came to say we're sorry," Archie told her, his demeanor so humble Grady barely recognized the man, although the dentures and the plaid bow tie were dead giveaways. "Both of us."

"I don't care."

"Annie," Grady said warningly. "It's been a long day. Don't say anything you'll regret."

"We've talked about it, Archie and me," Sandborn said, stepping forward. "We know we made mistakes. We know we're not nice people."

"Hah! You sure nailed that one, Ace."

"Annie, stop."

"Annie don't. Annie stop," she said, whirling to glare at Grady, and then looking at her father, her grandfather, once more. "Annie be good. Annie don't tell. Are you three all laboring under some misconception that I'm a saint, here? Or maybe that I'm just too dumb to know when I'm well-off? What do you want me to do, Archie? Give you a great big kiss and let you call me Daddy's little girl? In your dreams, buster! I don't like you. You're mean, and horrid, and you ruined your other children, and I thank God you didn't get the chance to ruin me."

"She's got a point, Archie," Grady said, wondering how long Annie would let the two men block the door, so that she couldn't leave. Probably just long enough to remember she had a small suitcase in her hand, at which point Archie might need Sandborn to bandage up his bony knees.

"And *you,*" Annie said, pointing at Sandborn. "You *used* me. I wish you'd never found me."

"I think you may have said something like that before," Grady pointed out. "Come on, if you're repeating yourself, it's probably time to go."

"Well?" Annie said after a moment. "Are you two going to move, or what?"

"We want another chance."

"What? I don't think I heard that right."

"Don't push, girl," Archie said, his thin cheeks reddening. "I said, we want another chance. We want you to stay, and talk to us, let us get to know you. Just tell us what you want us to do, and we'll do it." He pinched his lips together, swallowed with some difficulty. "We'll do anything. Please."

"Just for a few days," Sandborn added. "We've already sent Dickens to tell the others that they can stay. A.W. and Junior and Muriel. You'd want that, wouldn't you? To get to know your brothers and sister? Of course, Daisy is already gone, but that's no loss."

Archie reached out one thin, bony hand, touched it to Annie's cheek. "Please, child. We want you to stay."

"Do you really mean that?" Annie asked, feeling her resolve weaken, just a little. "No! I'm not going to let you two old men get to me. I'm not! You can't make up for two lifetimes of mean with one quick 'pretty please, I'm sorry, dear.' " She turned to Grady, her eyes wet with tears once more. "Grady, I'm not staying here," she told him. "I absolutely refuse to stay here with these people. I won't! I mean it! Grady? Grady, don't just stand there. Help me out here. *Say* something."

He looked at Archie and Sandborn. He looked at Annie. And then he smiled. "We'll just keep your bags in this room, Slugger, with mine."

# Epilogue

*In my very own self, I am
part of my family.*
—David Herbert Lawrence

Watching a not-nice man try to be nice is one way to spend a week, but Grady could think of other ways.

Still, he'd stayed at Peevers Mansion, because Annie had stayed, and if Annie had wanted to spend the week flagpole-sitting in Nome, he'd have done that, too. As long as he could be with her.

The first few days had been dicey, and Annie had packed her bags twice. But she'd always relented, and now she and Muriel were being more than just polite to each other. Grady had actually heard them giggling over an album of family photographs earlier that afternoon.

Mitzi was gone. Mitzi and her five million, both on their way to Rio and Jefferson Banning. Grady figured Banning would find a way to get her money, then ditch her, within six months. Three, if he was real smart. If he was even smarter, he'd never come back to the United States.

A.W. still sniffled now and again, but he seemed to be getting over his loss with remarkable strength. And he finished most of his sentences.

Junior had been drunk for five days, and nobody but Dickens had seen him. If they were lucky, nobody but Dickens would see him for another five.

As for Dickens, he'd delayed retirement, but only after cementing Archie's promise that he could copy and replace the Rembrandt before he retired his paintbrush. Archie still liked the idea that his children would discover paste jewels and good imitation art when he was gone.

You can't teach an old dog that many new tricks.

As for Sandy Sandborn, Annie's grandfather, he'd stayed only until arrangements could be made for him to register at an exclusive clinic in Arizona where, hopefully, he could beat his addiction to controlled painkillers and alcohol while working on his tan. Annie had stood over Archie while he wrote the check for a month-long stay.

Annie still liked Archie. Sometimes she hated herself for liking him, but as she told Grady, she just couldn't help herself.

Still, the two battled.

Archie wanted her to take ten million dollars, the same amount he'd given his other children.

Annie had turned him down flat. "I don't want it."

"I don't care if you want it, girlie-girl," Archie had responded. "Nobody asked you if you want it. Now, shut your trap and walk outside with me. I want to see if I can get as far as the mailbox at the end of the drive.

Twenty damn years I've had to wait for Dickens to re-member to bring me the mail."

"Must have been the pits," Annie had scoffed, taking his arm. "Waiting all that time for your girlie magazines. And I won't take the money."

"Will too," Archie had shot back, and they'd been off and running again. Grady believed Annie really enjoyed the arguments, maybe almost as much as Archie did.

Yes, watching the Peeverses playing Happy Families was quite an experience, but once Archie was tucked up in bed and the other Peeverses were doing whatever it is Peeverses do after dark, when Annie and Grady retired to their room, well, that's when he believed he could stay at the mansion indefinitely.

"I think we could probably leave by Saturday," Annie said now, lying with her head on Grady's shoulder, trac-ing a finger in a delicate pattern on his bare chest. "It's not like we're all that far away, in Philly."

"Are you sure?" Grady asked her, slightly adjusting his body so that Annie lay more fully against him. They'd made love, just as they made love every night, but he didn't think she was sleepy yet. He sure wasn't.

"I'm sure. I think I've been on my own too long to be smothered with family too much, at least not all at one time. I'd rather take it slowly. I can phone Archie, and I'll come back for the weekend, maybe next month. Besides, shouldn't you be getting back to work? I know I have to get back."

"I own half the company, Annie, remember? I can pretty much determine my own hours. Unless you think I can bill Archie for this last week?"

"You'd *bill* him to stay here with me?" Annie took hold of a single hair on his chest, gave it a quick pull.

"Ouch!"

"You're welcome," she said, allowing her hand to drift slightly south. He felt his skin tighten as his muscles rippled involuntarily.

"You're going to move in with me when we get back to Philly, aren't you?" he asked her, beginning his own expedition that followed already well-known pathways to parts of Annie Kendall Sandborn that seemed most responsive to his touch. "You wouldn't make me wait until after the wedding, would you?"

Annie pushed against his chest, straddled him. Grinned down at him. "The wedding? What wedding?"

"Our wedding, Annie," he told her, pulling her down on top of him. "Didn't I tell you? Archie already gave his permission."

He was left holding thin air as she pushed herself away from him again, and tried not to wince as she seemed to forget just where she was sitting. "You asked Archie? You're kidding! Tell me you didn't really ask Archie if you could marry me."

"Hey, you're getting ten million, Slugger. I want to make sure I stay on the guy's right side."

"I'm not taking the money," she said, looking stern, or as stern as she could look as his hands slipped up her body, captured her breasts.

"That's what I told Archie. And, since I don't want you to think I'm marrying you for your money, he's already written the check to the Kidney Foundation, giving it in your name. Now, are we going to talk all night or are you going to come here and let me love you? Because I do love you, Annie. I love you very much."

"All of it? All ten million?" Annie's eyes widened. "Gosh, Grady, I was thinking about eventually letting him talk me into accepting at least *one* million. It would have been a nice nest egg for us."

"Dare I be chauvinistic and tell you that I'll take care of my own wife, thank you very much? Except maybe I should add that I'm not exactly a pauper myself. Let Archie build his libraries, scatter a few more millions to your siblings like you got him to promise. We'll be all right on our own."

She lowered herself to him, so that her forehead rested on his. "You mean that, don't you? You could care less about Archie's money. Do you think we're both nuts?"

Grady chuckled low in his throat. "Quite possibly. Are we done talking yet? Because, if you don't stop moving that gorgeous body of yours all over me, I'm soon going to be beyond coherent thought."

"Really?" she asked, then moved against him again, touched her mouth lightly to his. "Before your eyes cross, let me tell you about something I read in a book." She kissed her way from his mouth to his ear, then whispered to him until his arms tightened around her and he had to take a deep, steadying breath.

"Someday you're going to have show me your bookshelves," he said, turning his head so that he could capture her mouth. "But not right now . . ."

Dear Reader,

What's next for Kasey Michaels? We asked her that (having some small interest ourselves), and she sent us this:

When Jack Trehan was twelve, he fell out of a tree and broke his right knee. One month later, his identical twin, Tim, ran his bike into a tree and broke his right knee.

When Jack was sixteen, he threw his first touchdown on the field, and his second later that night, with the head cheerleader. One month later, Tim caught a winning touchdown and later scored again with Mindy Frett, the head majorette, in the backseat of his Jeep.

When Jack was twenty-eight, he opened his front door one morning to grab the newspaper and found a baby on his doorstep.

That same day, Tim put a For Sale sign on his front lawn . . .

Sounded great, we told her, but what comes next? Kasey didn't know, but she was pretty sure there were two stories there; one for Jack, one for Tim. We thought so, too.

Coming up first? Jack's story: LOVE TO LOVE YOU BABY. We can't wait! Look for it in September 2001!

# ABOUT THE AUTHOR

Kasey Michaels is a *New York Times* best-selling author of more than sixty books. In addition to writing Zebra books, she also writes Warner, Silhouette and Harlequin books, and has long been known as one of the premier authors in romance. Kasey's newest mainstream contemporary romance will be published by Zebra Books in September 2001. Kasey loves to hear from her readers and you may write to her c/o Zebra Books. Please include a self-addressed stamped envelope if you wish a response.

# Complete Your Collection of

# Fern Michaels

# Put a Little Romance in Your Life With
# Rosanne Bittner